ALSO BY ALESSANDRA VU

Bargain with the Devil series
Paranormal Fantasy Romance
Bargain with the Devil - September 2024
Becoming the Devil – September 2025
Book III – September 2026

Standalone
Dark Romantasy
The Wolf and His Prey – June 2025

Bargain with the Devil

Bargain with the Devil – Book 1

Alessandra Vu

BARGAIN WITH THE DEVIL

Copyright © 2024 Alessandra Vu.

Book Cover Design: Alessandra Vu

ISBN: 979-8-9906682-1-8

Written by Alessandra Vu.

dedication:

*to anyone who's had the displeasure of dealing with a Chad –
may your revenge be swift and cruel.*

Author's Note

THE HOUSES OF JEZNIA

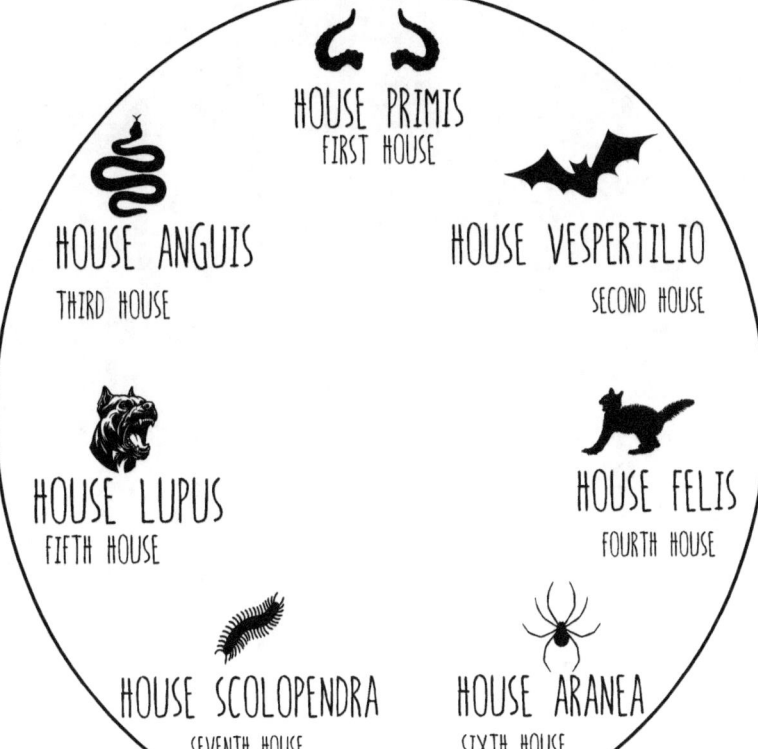

HOUSE PRIMIS
FIRST HOUSE

HOUSE ANGUIS
THIRD HOUSE

HOUSE VESPERTILIO
SECOND HOUSE

HOUSE LUPUS
FIFTH HOUSE

HOUSE FELIS
FOURTH HOUSE

HOUSE SCOLOPENDRA
SEVENTH HOUSE

HOUSE ARANEA
SIXTH HOUSE

I

"SOUNDS LIKE THERE are a lot of losers around you, Sloane," my date says before a slow smirk forms on his lips. "Lucky for you, you're sitting with an alpha."

The laugh that tumbles out of my mouth is met with a rather dead stare. *Oh no,* I instantly think. *He's serious.* My lips press together as an awkwardness settles over the table, my fingers toying with the base of my glass cup as I size him up and down for the third time that night.

He's stereotypically attractive. The kind of attractive that society has drilled into us to swoon over. Chiseled cheekbones, dark blonde hair, expressive brown eyes, a well–kept physique, and a summer tan on his otherwise pale skin. He probably has no shortage of people interested in getting to know him. And if he were to boast about a talent agent approaching him about work, I'd only be mildly surprised.

My eyes stall on the salmon–colored polo shirt he's wearing; I can almost hear him saying *masculine guys wear pink.* The color does nothing for his skin tone, but he smartly paired the shirt with dark blue jeans. The flip flops he's decided to wear tonight would have made a better impression on me if we had picked a date out in the park. But inside the restaurant, the casual shoes look a little out of place.

Gradually, my attention shifts back up to those striking brown eyes. Unironically, his name is Chad and I fear he's living up to the name.

My tongue wets my lips as I contemplate what to say and settle diplomatically on, "What does being an alpha mean to you?"

He gestures his arms as he speaks a little too emphatically and confidently. "It means protecting your woman, bringing home the money, getting shit done. I'll do all the hard work so you can stay home with the kids and look pretty."

My teeth bite down hard on my lip as I inhale sharply at his words. It shouldn't surprise me how much misogyny can appear in such short sentences, but it always does. I refrain from burying my face in my hands and instead, focus my attention on the glass of water, on the small droplets that slowly trickle down towards my hand. I don't know *why* Chad is bringing up children when I made it very clear I wanted to meet up for sex. I had objected to going on this date, but his persistence and my lack of other suitors had me caving. I can handle a measly date if it means getting laid except…

Men who think they're alpha males are *horrible* in bed. Regrettably, and embarrassingly, I have too much data to back that statement up.

I should leave, I think as my eyes slide shut. It would be the wiser choice. Men like Chad are not worth the headache. Yet, there's that trickle of irritation running down my spine as his words replay over in my head. He's *sincere* in his opinion and I consider it might be because no one's bothered to help him see the error in his beliefs. I could get up and leave, but I also could help him realize how toxic his mindset is to people who don't fit the hetero, cis male profile.

"What if I don't want you to provide for me?" I ask as I attempt to keep my tone as even as possible. He might not know how pompous he sounds. "What if I don't even want to have kids?"

His smile is frozen on his face, but I don't miss the small pulse in his temple before he answers. "You're joking, right?"

My eyebrow cocks up at his rude tone and I ask him flatly, "Does it look like I'm joking?"

Something about my question snaps him out of his stupor and he willfully digs his feet in. The expression on his face darkens as he speaks, "Ok, well, *first* of all, what's the purpose of women if you don't have kids? Secondly, every girl wants a man who can provide for them. Anyone who says otherwise is lying."

My eyebrows shoot up to my hairline as my jaw goes slack. He can't be serious. Except he *is*. This *asshole* believes the sole purpose of a woman is to bear children and be entirely dependent on a man who can up and leave her anytime he desires, leaving her to burn in a ditch somewhere.

"I don't even…" I trail off as my mind races to form a singular thought. There are too many things wrong with everything he's said. Then my words come out all at once. "A woman has every right to not have children, same as men. Life isn't about procreating, it's about *living*. If you're so concerned about the population, *you* be the stay–at–home parent.

"Also, women provide for *themselves*. We have jobs, we have our own money, we pay our own bills. What we want is a man who *adds* to our lives–"

"Bullshit," Chad replies with a roll of his eyes and a too cocky grin on his face. "Women only care about money. If we don't make enough by your standards, you won't even look our way, let alone give us a chance to prove our worth."

My fingers curl tightly around the base of my drink as my jaw works back and forth. I have now learned it's officially pointless to try and reason with him. It's no better than talking to a brick wall. But the anger and irritation running through my veins has me plowing forward against my better judgement.

"It sounds like to me you're actively seeking out women who want a wealthy man," I state. "Where there's smoke, there's fire. If you'd venture to broaden your options, you'll be pleasantly surprised by how many of us don't hold those views. We want a man who will contribute, but he doesn't have to provide. We're looking for a partnership where we're equal–"

"In what world are men and women equal?" Chad asks, arms crossing over his chest as he rolls his eyes. *Again.*

"We could be equal in this world if men weren't so threatened by a successful woman."

He laughs *loudly*, head falling back as he draws the attention of the people sitting near us. It sounds forced, as if he's trying to make me feel embarrassed by all the new attention on us. He's probably used this tactic successfully more than once, but I've never been someone to shy away from confrontation.

"You think a successful woman is funny?" I challenge him, placing my elbows on the table as I lean forward, intentionally giving off the vibe of invading his space.

His back straightens at my bold move and his eyes narrow in response. His lips quirk up slightly at the edges, like what he's about to say will be clever and smart. "When I see one, I'll let you know if I laugh or not."

He walked right into this one.

"Ouch," I breathe out. "You don't even consider your own mother successful. Poor thing wasted the best years of her life raising you and you aren't even grateful enough to consider her a successful person. If I needed any more reasons not to have kids, I'd add that to the list."

His face turns a nice shade of red before he nearly shouts, "At least she doesn't walk around dressed like a slut."

Only somewhat surprised by his words, I sit back in my seat as I inspect my outfit. A cute lace bodysuit, an oversized cardigan, skinny jeans, and a pair of nude pumps. I didn't wear a lot of jewelry because my intent for tonight was to get naked and I didn't want the hassle of one too many necklaces getting tangled with each other. The outfit is meant to entice him to take *off* my clothes. Except he's a total dick so there's no chance in hell that'll be happening.

As his statement finally settles into my head, anger trickles down my spine. *Of course* he insults my looks and slut shames me. He's too dumb to think of an actual rebuttal.

My shoulders tense as I clench my jaw, but I can't hold back the words that leave my mouth, "She probably does when she wants to get laid."

His face darkens even more and I briefly worry he's about to have an aneurysm. I've never seen someone's face turn *that* red before. It can't be good for him, but I am satisfied by how infuriated he looks. Good. He deserves it.

"My mom's classy," he snaps at me. "She knows an outfit like that makes you look easy and she's not that kind of person. She's the type you take out to a nice meal and walk around the Common and then you drive her home. She wants to fall in love first. She won't give it up easily."

"Um… it sounds like you've slept with your mother," I blurt out, unable to tame my inner thoughts or shock at what he's said. "There is absolutely nothing wrong with a mommy kink, but your interest in her sounds inappropriate."

Someone at a nearby table snorts and instinctively I glance over. Two women who look to be around my age are quietly eating their food, but the shit eating grins on their faces let me know they're invested in my conversation with Chad. The snort doesn't go unnoticed by Chad either.

Rage washes over him as his hand clenches so tightly his knuckles turn stark white. Those brown eyes I had once viewed as inviting now look at me with murderous intent. My stomach flips as I unconsciously sit a little further back in my chair. The restaurant is crowded. It's not likely he'll attack me, but the chances are never zero.

"At least she's prettier than you," he spits out. "You won't look half as good as her when you're her age."

I shouldn't provoke him. I really shouldn't, but… it's too easy.

"Just to be clear, you're *not* denying sleeping with your mom?" I ask and can't bite back the smile as the two women one table over poorly attempt to hide their laughter.

Chad moves forward, leaning all the way over the table as he grips the edges of it. A dark glare has settled on his face and unease runs through my veins.

"You think you're so funny until it's dark out and you're walking by yourself," he says in a near whisper. "You're nothing but a fucking cunt who's one bad guy away from learning a lesson."

I react on fear and instinct. My hand grips my glass cup tightly as I lift it and toss the water at Chad's face. He immediately shoves himself back from the table, wiping his eyes as he searches for a napkin.

"What the fuck?" he shouts, earning the attention of more than half the restaurant.

I stand to my feet, my legs feeling a bit like jelly as my heart beats too fast for comfort. As quickly as I can, I gather my things and toss a twenty onto the table.

"Do you think cunts play fairly?" I ask, adding fuel to the fire despite knowing better.

I don't wait for him to reply and make my way towards the exit of the restaurant.

"You *bitch!*" he shouts after me. "Get back here, I'm not done talking!"

"I'm done listening," I throw over my shoulder before hurrying to the door and slipping out.

The humid air threatens to suffocate me as an invisible layer of water coats my skin the second I exit the building. I itch to remove my cardigan to alleviate my discomfort, but instead, I keep my pace quick in case Chad comes barreling out the restaurant after me.

My hand trembles slightly as adrenaline floods my system and I dig through my purse for my phone. I can't help but glance behind me to see if Chad's following. I don't see him among the few people coming and going from the restaurant and I breathe a sigh of relief.

As much as I hate to admit it, Chad's subtle threat has left me unnerved. Woman had been killed for less than what I just did to Chad. I humiliated him and there were people to bear witness to it. My own stubborn stupidity could have gotten me killed because I couldn't keep my mouth shut.

I finally locate my phone and quickly video call Ella. Best to have a witness in case Chad's creeping around a corner somewhere. She picks up almost immediately.

"Damn, Sloane, didn't your date just start?"

Her dark brown hair is tossed up into a messy bun and she's dressed in her pajamas for the night. I spot a Ben and Jerry's pint towards the left of the screen as she sits at the kitchen island of our apartment. Her tanned skin is a little redder than usual, a tell–tale sign she spent too long out in the sun yesterday.

A calmness washes over me at the sight of my friend. She's seen me through the most embarrassing moments of my life as I figured out who I was during our college years. We were instant best friends at freshman orientation and haven't looked back since.

I quickly look both ways of the street before scampering over towards the stairwell that'll take me down to the T. Boston may be the perfect place for a woman in her mid– twenties who's eager to build her career and social life, but it's a flurry of chaos. Constant construction, unpredictable New England weather, grumpy people even *with* their cup of coffee, and tourists who never know where the hell they're going. Still, I love it, chaos and all.

"My date was a total bust. We didn't even make it to ordering our food," I answer as I descend the stairs.

There's a slight reprieve from the humidity as I make it below street level, but it's quickly diminished by the heat of an underground subway system. It's crowded, unsurprisingly. Honestly, I'm a little surprised it's not *more* crowded. After all, it's Friday night.

"That bad, huh?" Ella asks before shoving an overly large spoonful of ice cream into her mouth.

"He called himself an alpha male," I tell her as I make it to the platform.

"Ew, no," she shouts as she knocks over her phone.

"It gets worse."

"No, it can't get worse than that," she says as she places her phone back in its original spot.

"We're mid argument on his beliefs when his mom comes up in the topic. It makes sense, I promise you," I assure her when her face scrunches into confusion. "Anyway, he starts comparing me to his mom."

"*What?*"

Her mouth drops open and her eyes go wide as her spoon clatters against the counter.

"Yeah," I laugh out. "He said I dressed like a slut and that his mom was a classy woman who would never hand it out so easily."

"What the fuh…" Ella trails off as her eyebrows pinch together.

"I may or may not have told him it sounded like he slept with his mother."

Ella bursts out laughing, her hand slapping against the counter as she gasps for air. "You did not!"

"And the table next to us may or may not have been eavesdropping and laughed at him."

Her laughter escalates at the news and she tumbles out of her seat. The phone topples over and for a few seconds, I'm staring at our ceiling as Ella's laughter echoes in the apartment. Her fingers come into view as she fumbles with propping the phone up, her other hand wiping tears from her eyes.

"Sloane, you're savage."

"It didn't go over so well because he threatened me and called me a cunt."

That instantly sobers her up. "He did what?"

"I threw my water in his face if that makes you feel any better."

"Sloane, what did he say?"

"Something about walking alone at dark and being one bad guy away from learning a lesson."

"You should've done more than throw water in his face."

"What can I do? It's not like I can file a police report against him. They won't take it seriously."

Ella bites her lower lip as she digs her spoon through a particularly stubborn spot in her ice cream.

"Mm, well you met him through a dating app, right?" she asks as the piece of ice cream pops free. "Why don't you make a PSA on him?"

My eyes shift sideways as I think about her suggestion. A PSA isn't a bad idea. I've seen my fair share of them on social media, what's one more? And it would be helping a lot of women who want to avoid a guy like Chad.

"That's actually a pretty good idea," I say.

"I have them from time to time," Ella says with a self–deprecating laugh.

My eyes roll skyward as the edge of my mouth quirks up. "Shut up. You're full of good ideas."

"Like getting some wine for us to enjoy while we write up the PSA."

"Exactly. That's more than a good idea. It's a *great* one."

We share a laugh as the train finally pulls in. People quickly file out as others file in.

"Alright, I've got to go. The train's here."

"Sounds good. I'll see you when you get home."

I quickly place my phone back into my purse before entering the train. As the doors close and I scan the cabin, the lingering fear I'd been feeling finally dissipates. I've put enough distance between Chad and me. I can rest easy. My head slumps back against the wall as a heavy sigh falls from my mouth. Hopefully, my next attempt at a hookup goes a lot smoother.

"DID YOU SHOW me his profile before you went on your date?"

Ella and I are snuggled up on the couch, a bottle of wine sitting atop the coffee table as we review Chad's dating profile. Her question has me squirming in embarrassment. I did *not* show her his profile because I knew exactly what she'd say.

"No," I mumble and she slaps me on the shoulder.

"Sloane," she chastises me. "He's clearly a douchebag!"

"I know," I whine, drawing out the word as my eyebrows pinch together and I openly frown. "But admit it, he's good looking."

"Sure, if you like no flavor in your food."

A loud laugh tumbles out of me as Ella continues to swipe through his profile pictures. She's not wrong. His profile screams Grade A douchebag. He's shirtless in almost all of them. Sunglasses when he doesn't need them. Tongue out as he flips off the camera. Some random picture on a boat.

My *only* saving grace in swiping right on him was that I wasn't looking for a long–time partner. I was looking for a one–night stand. It's been five gruesome months since I last had sex. I wasn't particularly convinced he'd be any good based on the types of photos he posted, *but* I was willing to give him a chance to prove me wrong. I was in desperate need of some D and he was the first guy who matched with me who was willing to meet up.

"Look, in my defense, I *really* needed to get laid."

"Next time just use Mr. Rabbit," Ella says offhandedly.

"What do you think I've been doing all this time?" I nearly shout as I playfully shove her. "Be real with me, El, haven't you ever just needed the weight of a man pressed on top of you?"

"Too many times," she sighs out into her wine glass.

"Then stop with your judgment."

"Uh–uh, not gonna happen. You deserve to be shamed over this so hopefully next time you won't say yes to an asshole. Mr. Rabbit is *always* better than a dick with a dick."

I burst out laughing, nearly knocking over my wine glass in the process. Ella soon joins in and we're an uncontrollable mess of laughter. When it finally dies down, we're wiping tears from our eyes.

"Ok, ok. Points were made," I say before taking a sip of my wine.

Ella can't stop smiling even as her attention goes back to my phone. "We should use the same pictures he used for his profile," she suggests as she snuggles a bit deeper into my side.

We spend the next ten minutes screenshotting his pictures, properly cropping them, and setting up a secondary account in his name. We fill out his basic info the same as his real account, but when we get to his bio, I get a little more creative.

> *I'm an alpha male*
> *I protect and bring home the money*
> *You better bring home the kids even if you don't want them*
> *I've never f—ked my mom I SWEAR*
> *I threaten women who are strong, independent, and embarrass me*
> *DON'T DO THAT and you'll be safe – I mean fine*

"Put buyer beware at the top of his bio," Ella suggests.

"You, my friend, are a *genius*," I gush.

In large, bold capital letters, I type out the phrase just below Chad's name.

II

"WHERE ARE WE at with applicants for the Financial Analyst position?" my supervisor asks over our video call.

My gaze shifts to the spreadsheet on my second monitor. I know the answer off the top of my head, but I can't help but double, triple, quadruple check the answer before I reply.

"We've had three new applications since last week," I inform her, but my gaze remains on the spreadsheet.

It's a shared file, one I know my boss, Chelsea, also has pulled up. Her initials dart around the page, the subtle clicking of her mouse filtering in through my laptop's sound system. I know the information is good. I made sure to update it before the meeting. I gave myself plenty of time to double check and cross reference the information beforehand. It's accurate. It's good. I don't need to stress about it.

I direct my attention back to the video call. The fluorescent lighting in my office is anything but flattering. My eyes on the screen look sunken in and my skin looks grayer than its natural ivory. There are no windows in my office to let in any natural light. The walls are white but look more yellow than anything else. None of the furniture matches. I'm pretty sure the chestnut dresser is bedroom furniture. My desk is a dark, rich mahogany and the filing cabinets are metal. The room is tiny. I barely have enough room to fit a guest chair on the other side of my desk.

Meanwhile my manager has one of the biggest offices in the whole building but spends most of her time at home. Her home office walls are a soothing blue, her furniture matches, the room is decorated immaculately with cute little trinkets here and there. And the natural light her home office gets is envy inducing.

My fingers strum against my desk as my lips purse to the side of my face. Chelsea comes into the office about once every two weeks yet the expectation is that I'm supposed to be in the office three times a week. My blood nearly boils just thinking about it. Unfortunately for her, my resume is nearly finished with my edits. I'll be applying to jobs in no time. Fully remote jobs. I expect to have a new one within a month. *Maybe* two months if I'm picky.

"We've only had three new applicants?" Chelsea asks as her clicking continues.

She's looking for an error. I just know it. *You won't find any.*

"I boosted the post on LinkedIn last Monday," I offer without prompting. Better to be proactive in answering her usual questions. "The views are up, but people aren't applying."

She sighs heavily and her mouse clicking finally stops. Her initials appear on the outer edge of the spreadsheet and she folds her hands on top of her desk as she looks at me through the computer screen.

"What are your strategies for attracting more applicants?"

She asks me this every week and my answer always remains the same. Expectations of new hires have been forever changed since the pandemic. People want more work–life balance. They don't want to commute into an office if their job can easily be done at home. They expect higher pay or less responsibilities. No more doing the job of two people but only being paid one salary. Things are *different* but the older generation is having a hard time accepting that.

I've told Chelsea this plenty of times. I've asked she run the idea by the hiring manager, but she always give me a weird response before waving it off. Still, I have to persevere, even if I am repeating myself regularly.

"Trends are showing a sign–on bonus and being able to work fully remote will help us attract more candidates," I tell her and I don't miss the way she inhales like she's annoyed I'm bringing it up *again*. I do my best to ignore it and continue onward. "I really think there's value in asking the hiring manager if we can change it to offer remote opportunities. Obviously they'll have to come in at month end and other important times during the financial year, but I believe we'll attract more candidates if we advertise a hybrid remote job."

She taps her index finger against the back of her hand as her lips move back and forth. Normally by now, she'd be waving me off like I've wasted her time and asking me about the technician role. *This is a good sign.* A few more seconds go by before she huffs out a breath.

"I'll speak with the CEO. If he gives the go ahead, we'll tell the Finance Director the role is now a hybrid."

My jaw nearly drops open. I can't hold back my smile.

"Really?" I ask in disbelief.

"Yes. This has gone on long enough. If the finance team doesn't hire someone soon, the job will close out and we'll run the risk of losing more people from that group."

I withhold from outright clapping my hands just as the screen of my cell phone lights up, drawing my attention. I briefly catch the logo of an app across the screen. A notification from one of the dating apps I use.

It's been four days since I had my date with Chad and last night I finally gathered enough courage to try again. Ella made me promise her I wouldn't agree to any dates without her approval, but she didn't say anything about talking to men without her approval.

"Will you speak with the CEO this week?" I ask as my attention shifts back to the conversation at hand.

"I'll let you know on Friday how it goes," she says and I nod my head.

"Ok, well, that's all I have for an update. Unless you have any other questions?"

"No. I'll talk to you later, Sloane."

"Great! Talk later."

I click the end button before grabbing my cell phone off the desk. The FaceID unlocks my phone and I click on the dating app to see who reached out. My eyebrows shoot up towards my hairline as I see Chad's name at the top of my DMs. I never expected him to reach out to me.

For a brief moment, I contemplate not looking at his message, but curiosity gets the better of me.

> *u better fucking remove that profile on me, ducking bitch*

I laugh at the obvious autocorrect before staring at the message for a few moments. The app has read receipts so he'll know I've read his message. He's probably expecting some sort of reply. I could block him. There's no reason to engage with him. Especially after he threatened me four nights ago. But something about his message rubs me the wrong way. Why does he assume it was me who did it? Sure, we met up the night the profile was made, but any number of women he's dated could have made that profile. How do I know he didn't go off on another date the second I left him at the restaurant? It's best to act as though I have no idea what he's talking about.

> I don't know what profile you're talking about.

The three dots pop up and my fingers strum against the desk as I wait patiently for his reply. They come rapid fire, one after the other.

> u KNOW what im talking about bitch ill make u fucking regret this cunt TAKE IT DOWN NOW OR ELSE

Whoa there, psycho. Take it down or else? This guy seriously has a problem. Why does he think it's acceptable to continually threaten people? Thank God he has no idea where I live other than within the Boston area. I make it a point on social media to not tag any locations that are within five miles of my apartment. A girl can never be too cautious in this day and age.

If Chad got desperate enough, he could try to defame me at my place of work, but I don't believe he's smart enough to search me up on LinkedIn. Besides, even if he were to send a message to Chelsea, there's no way anyone can prove I created the fake profile. Not unless Chad confesses to saying those horrible things during our date. He's in a lose–lose situation.

> I don't know what you're talking about. Take what down? Also why are you suspecting I did something? How do you know it wasn't someone else?

The three dots pop up and I receive his final message before he blocks me.

> Your funeral, Sloane.

Normally, I'd ignore a statement like that. But there's something unsettling about how grammatically correct his response is. He took care in capitalization and punctuation. It forces the message to hold more weight. The hair along the back of my neck rises. Chad has now threatened me *three* times. Maybe I *should* be concerned.

An involuntary shiver darts down my spine as I lock my phone and place it back on my desk. He's blocked me and the dating app was the only way we communicated with each other. He can't use my phone number to try and pinpoint a location. I should be fine. He doesn't know where I live and there aren't a lot of ways he can figure it out. I'll be fine. There's nothing to be worried about.

Still... I can't shake the feeling of unease for the rest of the day.

"IT'S A SHAME you're pretty."

I'm in that weird phase between being awake and asleep. That special spot where you can still dream, but you're also acutely aware of the fact that you're awake.

My body's at peak comfort as I cuddle a pillow while the fan blows gently on my face. I may be awake but my brain has no problem taking me to a beautiful field where a handsome stranger resides. I can't make out his facial features, but maybe it's better that way. His clothes are nicely tailored to his frame and I more than appreciate how fit he is.

The clothes he wears are all black. Black button–down shirt tucked into black chino pants with a black belt. His ankles are exposed and he wears black leather dress shoes. The top three buttons of his shirt are undone, exposing a black swirling tribal tattoo on his chest.

His right hand twirls a turquoise ring, the only color he wears, on his left index finger and I find the simple act incredibly sexy.

"I detest killing the pretty ones," he states.

His voice is so incredibly deep it should be illegal. It takes me moment to realize what he's said. Does he mean he's going to kill *me?* That's not right. Isn't this supposed to be a sex dream since I haven't been laid in forever?

Begrudgingly, my eyes flutter open and the disappointment thrumming through me is palpable. He had the type of physique that would absolutely shatter my world. Why did he have to go and threaten me like that? *Stupid Chad,* I automatically blame.

My hand fumbles for my phone to check the time but something rustles in front of me and I glance at the space the sound came from. There's someone crouching in front of me. The soft glow of my phone highlights his face for a few brief moments. He has a sharp jaw, angular monolid eyes, and near black irises peppered with bits of red. He's wearing eyeliner, which enhances the unique color of his eyes, and makes him that much sexier. It's impossible to tear my eyes away from him. But his hand does just that as it lifts up to push some pitch–black hair out of his face.

Most of the hair along the sides of his scalp and towards the back have been buzzed short but he's kept the hair on the top of his head longer. It's tousled yet somehow perfectly styled. He could be a celebrity with a face and hair like that. Seriously.

A moment later, my eyes drop to the horns jutting out of his head. They look strangely authentic. Like they might belong to a goat or ram and they've been attached to a headband that he's most likely buried under his longer hair.

His tongue darts out, drawing my attention to carmine, plump lips. *Damn.* This guy really came here to kill me instead of fuck me? What kind of messed up dream is this?

But then the phone in my hand goes dark and I remember I'm *awake.*

A split second later, I violently jolt to the other side of the bed. My heart beats a mile a minute, my breaths labored and panicked. I shriek as I fall off the bed, the sheets entangling around my legs as a thud of my landing echoes within the room. Panicked, I struggle to free myself from my sheets.

My chest tightens as the seconds tick by and I worry I might pass out from my heart beating too fast. The sound of fingers snapping briefly fills the room. Barely a second later, the bedroom lights turn on. My eyes squint at the sudden onslaught of light, but I catch sight of a knitting needle that has zero business being in my room. *Thank you, Ella!*

My fingers curl around the cold needle and I finally free myself from the sheets.

"Stay back," I order, wielding the knitting needle like a knife.

I haven't found the opportunity to get to my feet and I'm forced to peer at him over the top of my bed. His expression shifts to a sweet, patronizing look; like he's dealing with a child instead of a twenty–six year old woman. Bile creeps into the back of my throat as fear overloads my senses. There's an *unknown man* standing in my bedroom and blocking my escape.

"My dear," he hums and I hate that the deepness of his voice scratches the inside of my brain in the best way. "As much as I appreciate a good stabbing, you'll do little harm."

"Like I'd take your word for it," I spit out despite the slight tremble in my hand.

The left side of his lips quirk up and his eyes squint ever–so–slightly in amusement. "You can't harm the devil. A needle like that will do you no good against me."

I glance up at his horns, at the impressive size of them. They protrude out of his scalp about two inches above his ears and follow the line of his shoulders before curling up towards the sky. They reach for the stars for about six inches before coming to a tapered tip. A very noticeably *sharp* tapered tip. Even from where I sit on the floor I can see how sharp they are. There's nothing rounded or dull about them.

Still, even despite the literal horns, there's no such thing as the devil. He may have an authentic cosplaying outfit, but at the end of the day, that's all it is: an *outfit*.

My hand holding the needle rises up in a threatening manner. His eyebrow quirks as he stares me down.

"You expect to attack me from the floor?" he asks, mildly intrigued.

Hastily, I rush to my feet. My eyes glance past him and towards the door. Ella is only a short distance away. If I can get her attention, she can call the police. Hopefully she isn't sleeping with her headphones in tonight.

"Ella," I scream as loudly as I can.

An annoyed look flashes across his face as he scowls. "No one can hear you. The room has been soundproofed."

He takes an intimidating step towards me. Just one step but it feels as though the walls are caving in. Not only that, but I finally realize how much taller he is than me. He has half a foot on me, at least. I'm not that small either. Five five, maybe fix six on a good day, but this man *towers* over me. *I'm dead*, I think as my knees go weak.

"Stay back," I demand despite my shaky voice. I scream a second time. "Ella!"

He scowls again, eyes narrowing as he winces slightly. "I would greatly appreciate it if you stopped screaming. No one is going to hear you."

He hates the screaming? *Good.*

"Fuck you," I scream just as loudly. "Like I'm going to make this easy for you!"

"You don't even know what I'm here for."

"No sane person breaks into someone else's home for good reasons."

"That's not true," he states, somewhat offended. "How do you know I'm not running away from a vicious attack?"

"You said you're the devil, right?" I ask, grateful my mind is somehow still working. "Who could be vicious enough for you that you'd be running away in fear?"

He chuckles, sinful and elegant, as a grin takes up most of his face. "You've got me there, my dear. Truth is, I've come to kill you."

I nearly drop the knitting needle in surprise as a sea of tears flood my vision. "Why?" I ask brokenly. "You don't even know me."

He clicks his tongue, head bobbing to the left. "I know more than you'd like."

I inhale a shaky breath, unable to contain the fear that's overwhelming me. I don't want to die. I'm not going to sit back and let this asshole murder me without a fight, but that doesn't mean I'm not terrified out of my mind. The knitting needle is long. If I could just jam it with enough force through his neck, I *should* be able to kill him. But the strength required to jam the needle through his neck is going to affect my accuracy. What if I swing so hard I miss and open myself up for the perfect kill shot from him?

He smirks as he takes another step towards me and I flinch, taking a step back.

"I like the fire in your eyes," he confesses. "So many become an incoherent mess of tears and snot. It's not so often I meet someone so determined to survive."

"If you appreciate it so much then don't kill me," I tell him.

"No can do," he replies. "You see, you've upset Chad and he simply couldn't let it go. Now, you must die."

"What?" I ask in utter disbelief.

Did I hear him correctly? Did he just say Chad's name? How does he even know Chad? *Maybe they're friends... Or Chad hired hitman.* That must have been what Chad meant when he said I'd regret it and that it'd be my funeral.

"How much?" I ask and he cocks an eyebrow. "How much did he pay you?"

"Oh dear, it's not like that," he replies as a sickly sweet grin spreads across his lips.

"What are you saying? That you're doing it just because he *asked?*"

"Not in the slightest," he answers. "Chad, my boy, sold his soul for your death."

The knitting needle drops from my hand. My knees buckle and I nearly fall to the floor as shock slams into me. Is this guy off his meds or something? Am I going to die because I can't reason with him?

"So, you... you genuinely think you're the devil," I say as my brain desperately tries to make sense of what I'm hearing. "And Chad, what? He also believes you're the devil and sold his imaginary soul to you for you to kill me?"

"Sure," he replies.

"What if you just... *don't* kill me and pretend you did?"

"A deal's a deal, my dear. It's nothing personal against you. It's just business."

He takes another step towards me, eyes sizing me up and down. "But I'll tell you what. I'll forgo the gruesome aspect of your death. It's a shame to dirty a masterpiece."

"Stop, just stop," I order as my hand gives him the universal stop sign. "Chad doesn't have to know about this.

Just tell him you killed me. I promise I won't tell the police you were a part of this. I'll say it was Chad who showed up to my house, threatening to kill me."

"I'm afraid it doesn't work like that. If I don't kill you then my life is forfeit."

Desperation floods me as my heartbeat thuds in my ears. My eyes shift down to my feet where the knitting needle resides. Damnit. I shouldn't have dropped it. It'll waste time picking it up, but it's my only weapon.

Without hesitating, I snatch the needle up from the floor. Just as I stand to my full height with the needle raised, he slams me into the wall. Ice cold fingers wrap tightly around my wrist that has the knitting needle. His other hand curls around my throat, his fingers colder than ice, and I gasp in shock at the sensation. He shoves a leg between mine, pushing against me to prevent my escape. A sudden gust of smoke invades my senses as he leans towards me.

"Naughty, naughty," he practically growls in delight. His head dips downwards as his face brushes against mine. "Just how I like my prey."

My blood runs cold and instinct takes over. I start thrashing against him in desperation to escape. His freezing cold fingers dig into my wrist and neck as he effortlessly holds me in place.

It's clear my struggle is useless. He's too strong. Plus, with his body trapping mine against the wall, there's little room for me to wiggle free. His grip on my throat is tight; not enough to cut off my air supply, but enough that I hesitate struggling against him.

Tears stream down my cheeks as the realization hits me. I'm going to die. My left hand slams against the wall and I realize, stupidly, it's not held down. Without thinking, my fingers curl around his horn and yank as hard as I can. His head abruptly jerks to the side. If I had any doubts about the legitimacy of his horns, they evaporate in that second. The horns are solidly attached to his head.

His speckled eyes fade to black before burning red. "You don't have the privilege of touching my horns," he growls low and throaty.

His hand cinches tight around my throat and he lifts me completely off the floor. My heart drops into my stomach as my feet start kicking in empty air. I buck against him, hit him as hard as I can with my free hand, I yank on his arm; anything to stop him from killing me. He doesn't budge.

This is really the end for me. Why? What did I do to deserve this? A disastrous date and a fake dating profile don't warrant being murdered over. I'm going to die because of a man–child. Because he couldn't handle being embarrassed by a strong, independent woman. Would he be reacting this way if I were a man? Would he sell his soul to have a *man* killed? I don't think he–

Wait, that's it!

"Stop," I rasp out as my hand starts hitting him incessantly on the shoulder. "Wait! I have something you want!"

His eyes narrow, but his hand doesn't ease up on my throat. Desperation fills me to the brim and I force out the words before he takes away my ability to speak.

"I want to sell you my soul!

III

HE SMIRKS. "It doesn't work that way, Ephirian swine."

"Why not?" I force out as best I can, glossing over an insult I only partially understand.

He huffs an irritated breath as he places me down on the floor. His hand does not leave my throat, cold fingers still tightly wrapped around my neck. But with him no longer holding me up by my throat, I can breathe and speak easier.

"My soul has to be worth more than Chad's," I state, heart hammering against my chest as I play along with his stupid game.

Sometimes the only way to win against irrationality is to join in.

His eyebrow cocks up as he stares down at me in contemplation. What I've said has intrigued him. *Good. Keep this going, Sloane.*

"Promise not to kill me and I'll sell you my soul," I say.

His head tilts towards his right shoulder, his lips pulling downward into a frown. "It's a little more complicated than that."

"Then uncomplicate it," I practically snap.

His jaw ticks and his ice–cold fingers squeeze a little too tightly around my neck; a reminder of who is really the one in power. The seconds drag on as I wait for some sort of answer from him. A heat slowly blossoms in my wrist and it takes me a few moments to realize he's let go of my hand. The one that holds the knitting needle.

My arm is yanking back before my brain has caught up. I swing my hand forward, the knitting needle poised directly above his heart. He snaps his fingers. My fist slams into his chest. My eyebrows pinch together as I stare at my empty hand. The needle was there. I saw it; I felt it. Where did it go? How did it disappear?

My eyes dart up to him and he sneers down at me. Instinct has me trying to shrink away from him but my back is already pressed against the wall. He's caged me in and I have nowhere to go to escape his wrath.

"If you're using your soul as a ploy," he starts to say before his tone darkens and he leans forward to emphasize his threat, "you better believe your death will be worse than gruesome."

"I–It's not a ploy!"

He truly believes he's the devil. If I have to sell my imaginary soul to him, so be it. I'll do whatever necessary to stay alive. And once this is all over with, I'm going to put his ass and Chad's in jail. For life.

"There is a way I can… uncomplicate it," he hums more to himself than to me. His eyes catch mine as he studies me. "You offer an interesting proposition."

My stomach flips, the bile at the back of my throat threatening to spill into my mouth. I inhale deeply, hoping to settle my stomach a little bit, when I catch another whiff of smoke. Smoke in Boston. People don't grill in my area; it's not allowed due to how unsafe it is. Same with fire pits; not enough space and too dangerous. Smelling smoke in my area only means one thing. Someone's building is on fire. With how intense the smoke is, my bet is it's *my* apartment.

My heart drops. Ella's in the next room over. What if the smoke has knocked her out? What if I'm the only way she can escape safely?

I try to shove him off me as I speak, "I need to go check on my friend and make sure she's safe. The apartment might be on fire."

He pushes me back against the wall as he leans in close. "Wrong, but I am," he nearly growls.

Confusion morphs onto my face but a second later, I'm shoving him again. "This isn't a joke! She could be in some serious trouble."

"The devil doesn't joke, Ephirian swine."

"You're not on fire," I protest as my hands shove against his chest. "Where are the flames, huh? Get out of the way so I can make sure Ella's safe!"

"The apartment isn't on fire, Sloane. I am," he practically purrs as he taps his finger against his sternum. "My soul is eternally on fire."

His devil act is surprisingly well thought through but none of that matters right now. Ella is in danger, our apartment building is on fire, and the damn fire alarms haven't gone off yet *or* they're not working. I need to wake her up and get her out of here. Is he really going to kill two people just to make sure one of us is dead?

"Wait, you can't kill her," I shout as my brain fumbles around with the logic of his game. "You weren't sent to kill her. You have to make sure she's safe."

"I assure you, she's safe. If a devil is to harm a human outside of contractual obligations, a Champion would be sent to bring that devil's severed head back to Odantha."

Even if I don't really understand what he's saying, it's clear to me there are rules he follows. Still, just because he's saying she's safe doesn't actually mean she is. Aren't devils notorious for being liars?

"You expect me to trust the word of the devil?" I ask as I embrace the rules of his game. They can work in my favor if I use them correctly.

His tongue clicks before his lips pull back in a smirk. "Clever girl." A beat passes and then he asks, "You want proof of her safety?"

"Yes!" I answer without hesitation.

"Very well," he replies as he finally pushes off me.

He snaps his fingers before walking to the door. My heart thuds loudly within my ears as my eyes dart around my room. Is there *anything* I can use against this guy?

He opens my bedroom door and turns to me, his arm extended out in my direction. I look around the room one final time before admitting defeat and following after him. My body tenses as I pass him, half anticipating he'll reach out to hold me in place, but he doesn't. I walk freely ahead of him. I attempt to make a run for it but there's an invisible force pushing back against me no matter how hard I try to run forward. Am I too panicked to do anything? What the Hell is going on?

He doesn't say anything as we reach Ella's door. I hesitate opening it, scared of what I might find behind the closed door. He opens it with little care and flicks on the bedroom light. I inhale sharply, briefly thinking I royally fucked up. Now he'll have two hostages instead of one. I shouldn't have insisted on checking on her safety. But maybe the two of us we can outpower him.

I rush over to her side, kneeling by her bed as I shake her. "Ella, wake up."

She doesn't. I shake her as hard as I can but it does nothing to rouse her from her sleep.

"Ella!"

"You've seen her, you've seen she's ok. Let us refocus on what's important. You believe your soul is worth more than Chad's."

"Ella! Wake up!"

"Sloane–"

"What did you do to her?" I ask as I whirl around on him.

I charge at him without hesitation, rage burning hot inside me.

"I merely made it so that she wouldn't wake while I'm here," he answers.

"You *drugged* her?"

He does nothing to block my hits as my fists connect with his chest. He doesn't even flinch, like my attacks are nothing but a fly buzzing around his head.

"Would you rather I kill you or do you want to weigh your soul against Chad's?"

"Stop, just stop," I breathe out heavily, hands falling to my sides as my head shakes. "You're not the devil. You're sick. Your brain is making you believe something that isn't true. You need help. I–I'll help you get help. I promise. Just don't kill me."

He chuckles but doesn't say anything. Instead, he snaps his fingers. A moment later, my body is yanked downward through the floor of my apartment. Everything goes dark as I'm dragged by my ankles through thick, suffocating sludge.

The air is thick. Pressure bears down on me on all sides. It hurts. It hurts to breathe. It hurts to move. All I can do is cling to the only thing that offers stability. The man who came to kill me.

Time drags on until finally we emerge from the muck. Our exit is violent. My body ricochets into his. He holds me steady as I stare up at him with wide, scared eyes.

The moment I inhale, my lungs are scorched by dry air. It burns and induces a coughing fit but that only makes it worse. It's as if all the water has been zapped out of the air and the vicious dryness is sucking the moisture *straight from my lungs*.

There's a faint finger snapping that can be heard over the hoarseness of my coughing. A moment later, as I inhale, a cool, soothing sensation coats my throat down into my lungs. My coughing stops. I'm able to breathe without risk of suffocating to death. The room may still be unbearably hot, but the silver lining is that I can *breathe*.

It takes me a few moments to gather my bearings before I realize we're standing in a long corridor. My apartment is nowhere to be seen. Gone are the old creaky wooden floors, white walls with photos of our adventures, and the comforting sense of home.

Instead, I stare at a floor the color of burnt maroon. The color gradually lightens as it crawls up the walls and towards the ceiling. It shifts through shades of red, shades of orange, shades of yellow until at the top of the extremely tall ceiling it's practically glowing white.

Large, black gargoyle statues line the corridor. Some are poised standing on two feet while others are on all fours and viciously snarling. The artistic style of the statues differ. Some appear cinematic; the kind of gargoyles I've seen in movies. The other gargoyle statues look grotesque and horrific in every sense.

Flames light the corridor. My eyebrows scrunch together as I peer closer at the fire. There are no torches or candles lining the walls. The fire burns freely, dancing eagerly up towards the ceiling. The flames dance and sway, curl and snap. There is nothing to contain the fire. My stomach drops.

"We need to get out of here," I rush out in terrified, quiet words. "We have to evacuate."

The hair along my arms stand to attention as my heart threatens to go into cardiac arrest. I've never had the misfortune of being inside a burning building before. Nothing could prepare me for the dark reality of it.

I glance around the hallway, desperate to find an exit. My eyes catch sight of a looming black door in the distance.

"Come on," I urge him as my fingers curl around his wrist and I give him a harsh tug.

He doesn't budge. My head snaps in his direction and he's looking at me with a mildly interested look. His eyebrow is slightly cocked as black and red speckled eyes stare down his nose at me.

"You wish to save me?" he lazily inquires. "From my own home?"

"Wha–" I don't finish the question because we don't have time. I give him another tug, but he goes nowhere. "You're going to burn to death!"

"These flames cannot harm me. I am born of Jeznia," he states evenly.

"I don't give a shit about whatever delusions you're having! We have to get out of here. *Now!*"

"Sloane," he says my name like it's a sin and my back straightens as my eyes connect with his. "We're in Hell. That is why the room is on fire."

My body freezes as my brain rushes through the events. Stranges things have happened that have no logical reason behind them. Maybe I've been drugged and I'm having the worst trip ever. Maybe I'm still sleeping. Or maybe this man standing before me really is the devil.

"I think I'm going to be sick," I murmur as I lean forward on my knees.

"If you're done panicking," he breathes out in a bored manner, "we have business to attend to."

"What business?" I ask, not lifting my head as I stare into the dark floor.

"You believe your soul is worth more than Chad's. There's only one way to find that out. We must see the Records Keeper."

"Am I… dead?" I dare to ask, head tilting back just far enough to look him in the eyes.

He stares down at me, lips pulling towards the side of his face before he says simply, "Your fate has yet to be determined. Now come."

He doesn't wait for me to gather myself. Instead, he turns away from me and heads towards the looming black door. I take a few deep inhales before following after him. There's no way I'm being left behind in a strange place.

The closer we approach the door, the better I'm able to see that it's two large doors. Shapes have been carved into them. Bats, snakes, spiders, centipedes, wolves, cats, and devils are carved into the doors while weeping, begging souls twist around them. The imagery and sheer size of the doors

unsettles my stomach. If this isn't a dream, if this is Hell…
then am I really going to sell my soul to the devil?

If I don't, he's going to kill me. I'm not ready to die. I
haven't even lived my life yet. But the harsh truth is Chad
sold his soul to have the devil kill me and if I don't do
something to stop that, I'm dead. *Dead* dead.

My train of thought is interrupted as the doors creak open,
grinding against their hinges. As a gap appears at the opening
of the doors, a ferocious gust of air is sucked into the
darkened, bleak room. Behind us, the flames along the walls
flicker wildly. My hair whips around my face and my feet
begin to slide against the floor. It feels as though we've been
sucked into a vacuum. Instinctively, I lean back against the
wind, away from the doors, to keep my balance. Shortly after,
the wind dies just as quickly as it appeared. I hastily comb my
hands through my hair as I glance at my companion.

"What was that?" I ask, unable to hide the slight tremble
in my voice.

"The seal breaking," he answers flatly and doesn't expand
on his words. "Come."

There's no hesitation as I immediately follow after him.
He's the only thing I know in this strange world and, even if
he was sent to kill me, he's the only thing that feels remotely
safe. I don't care that I'm clinging to a false notion that he's
safe. I cling to it because if I don't, I'll drop to the floor in the
fetal position and sob until I pass out.

There's a faint light in the distance as we begin our cross
of the threshold of the massive doors. The air in the new
room is stale, like no breeze has wandered through in over a
hundred years. The musty scent coats my tongue and I do my
best to ignore it as we continue forward.

As soon as we pass the threshold, the doors creak and groan as they shut without assistance. The resounding thud from them closing echoes loudly through the room. I wince as the sound bounces off my ears.

The supposed devil seems unaffected by the noise as he confidently walks towards the light. I quietly follow behind him while fighting every urge in me to grab his hand or hold his arm. He may have been sent to kill me, but it's clear he isn't bothered or afraid of this place. His stride is steady, his shoulders pulled back. He appears relaxed, like there's nothing to fear here because he owns the place.

It's a no brainer to obediently follow after him. At least with him, I'm not alone, fending for myself. If we run into danger I wholly plan on sticking to him like glue. The toughest kind of glue you can buy. He'll have to save me whether he wants to or not.

That child–like thought eases some tension out of my shoulders as I exhale loudly. My fingers flex in preparation for swiftly grabbing him if danger shows up. I won't give him any chances to ditch me.

As we walk down the darkened corridor, neither one of us speaks. Aside from the sound of our feet thudding against the ground, there's a faint fluttering noise I hear above our heads. It's sporadic. One moment, fluttering will fly past our heads from back to front. In the next moment, it'll fly overhead left to right. There appears to be no rhyme or reason to it, but the hairs on the back of my neck rise up as my heartrate quickens. Whatever it is is clearly alive.

"Do you, um, hear that?" I venture to ask as I take a few stutter steps closer to him to close the distance between us.

Best to get the metaphoric glue ready.

"I'm hearing multiple things all at once," he answers unhelpfully. "You'll have to specify what it is you're hearing."

"That fluttering," I clarify. "The one that's coming above our heads."

"That would be the bats."

"Bats," I nearly scream as I duck out of the way.

My eyes dart around the sky but it's useless. I can't see anything in the pitch black sky. Still, I can imagine bats perfectly fine. With each new fluttering whizzing past my head, I flinch and duck, fear and adrenaline pumping wildly through me. It was so much better not knowing what was above me.

"Better the bats than the spiders," he states in an even tone.

"How are spiders worse than bats?" I shriek, unable to keep my composure. "I can't stomp a bat to death as easily as a spider!"

He laughs loudly as he turns his attention briefly to me, clear amusement written all over his face. "I assure you that you cannot stomp our spiders to death. You have a better chance fighting our bats than taking on our spiders. Trust me."

The news that their spiders are more formidable than their bats is my final straw. My body comes to a screeching halt as tears burn hot in my eyes. I've hit my limit of how much I can endure. I might actually be in Hell despite how implausible that sounds. I almost died the moment I got here. The walls are on fire. *Spiders* are harder to fight than bats. It's too much. I can't take it anymore.

"I want to go home," I blurt out, my voice warbly from emotions. "Please. Please take me home."

"If I take you home right this instance, it'll be to kill you," he throws over his shoulder as he continues walking towards the faint light.

"No. I don't want to die. I didn't do anything wrong! Please just take me home," I beg from my spot where I stopped walking.

"If a devil doesn't hold up their end of the bargain, the devil *dies*," he confesses. "What makes you think I value your life more than my own?"

My mind is a jumbled mess as he walks farther and farther away from me. The fluttering above my head doesn't stop. It increases the more distance is put between us. My entire body trembles as my emotions threaten to overwhelm me.

"*Please*," I scream, eyes shut as tears stream down my face. "There has to be a loophole!"

Deals with devils are all about loopholes, aren't they? There has to be one. I can't just die like this.

"The loophole," he murmurs into my ear and my eyes snap open at how close he suddenly is, "is that I buy your soul. It's your choice, Sloane. Do we keep walking towards the light to weigh your soul or do I take you back to Ephiri to be killed?"

"Ephiri?" I venture to ask, hoping it'll bring me a miracle of some kind.

It doesn't.

"Earth," he answers smoothly. "I take you back to Earth to kill you."

He pulls back far enough to look me in the eyes. My breathing is tight and a stitch has formed in my side. My stomach churns as my eyes dart back and forth between him. How can I willingly choose death? He has to know I'll do anything to save my life. Anything. Even if that means selling my soul.

"Walk," I whisper weakly, my gaze dropping to the ground as a few more tears stream down my face. I hastily wipe them away. "We continue walking."

"Chin up, Ephirian swine," he condescendingly encourages as he lightly taps beneath my chin with his index finger. "I have a sneaking suspicion your soul *is* worth more than Chad's."

Without another word, he continues walking towards the light.

IV

I SCURRY AFTER him, not wanting to be left alone to become bat food. From what I remember, my high school biology teacher said bats don't typically attack humans, but these bats are supposedly *Hell* bats. What if they're vampire bats and they'll suck out every ounce of blood in me if given the chance? Not wanting to give them an opportunity to do so, I walk so close to the devil that my feet scuff against the back of his heels.

"As much as it pains me to say this," he speaks in that incredibly deep voice of his, "sex will not save your life."

My body reels back, mouth falling open as my brain stalls out from his random statement. Why the hell would he be thinking about sex right now? And why would he think *I* am?

"I'm *never* having sex with you," I spit out as I close the distance between us.

Even if I wish to murder him with my own two hands, he's the only thing able to protect me right now. I'll kill him when this is all over.

"Sloane," he hums my name, casting a look over his shoulder. I can't discern the expression on his face, but it feels predatory. Instinctively, I shrink back just the tiniest bit as he continues speaking, "if your soul comes back weighing more than Chad's, I'm going to make you eat those words."

I swallow thickly, unconsciously taking a larger step back from him. This asshole is big enough to overpower me. Even if I fight like hell and give it my all, he could do whatever he wanted to me and there would be nothing I could do about it. My stomach coils at the thought and I have to force back the bile threatening to spill into my mouth.

Neither one of us says anything for the remainder of our walk. Eventually, the soft light up ahead starts getting closer and the fluttering overhead begins to become more frantic. My heart pounds against my ribcage, my body flinching every time the bats get too close. I do my best to pretend they're hummingbirds. Beautiful, sweet hummingbirds in search of delicious nectar. *Not* bloodthirsty Hell bats. It helps. Sort of.

As we get closer to the light, the surrounding area comes into view. Iron spindles line the path we're walking on. Each spindle is spaced about a foot apart and comes to a pointed top in the shape of an arrowhead. My hand subconsciously reaches out, my fingertips ghosting against the tip. It's sharp. Sharp enough to pierce a body if one were to fall on the spindle. I walk as close to the center of the path as possible, not wanting to accidentally trip and kill myself in the process.

My attention shifts back towards the light and I'm drawn to the area where our path merges with another. A circular platform branches out from our pathway and within the platform is a circular counter. A large pole behind the counter extends upwards about twenty feet and a fire chandelier hangs from the top of it. That fire is the only source of light in the entire room.

I see a figure popping up and down behind the counter as we approach. I also notice three other pathways sprouting off from the circular center. Four pathways in total. If I'm looking at it correctly, the pathways make a perfect cross with the circular platform at the center of it.

We're nearly at the center now and I venture to glance over the edge of the spindles. The light from the fire illuminates the area quite well, but there's nothing there. The platform I'm standing on is a bridge. My feet pause as I dare to look over the edge, fingers wrapping around the cold spindles to keep my balance. Pitch–black darkness greets me back. We could be twenty feet up from the ground or two hundred. It's impossible to tell. A shiver runs down my spine as I shift back to the center of the path.

The fluttering has morphed into loud flapping and my eyes drift upwards towards the fire chandelier. My heart stutters at the sight. Bats the size of golden retrievers fly overhead. *The spiders are* worse? *That can't be true.* My mouth goes dry as my breath comes out in shaky exhales.

Black leather bodies connect to bone white skull heads. Smoke billows out of empty eye sockets, a trail of elegant gray swirls left in the air as the bats swoop down towards the counter. They don't appear to be attacking whoever is behind the counter; merely harassing them at best.

The fact that the bats are not attacking sends relief through me. They appear calm, at ease. So long as I don't do anything to draw their attention, I should be fine. *No sudden movements, Sloane,* I order as we approach the counter.

My companion taps his index finger against the smooth surface of the counter as soon as we reach it.

"Records Keeper, I'm in need of your services," he casually states.

"Lord Balthazar," the Records Keeper speaks in a voice that's eerily similar to fingernails grating on a chalkboard while simultaneously sounding as though it's layers upon layers of screeching.

I can't hold back the wince, my head tilting towards my shoulder. My fingers flex as I contemplate blocking my ears for when the Records Keeper speaks again, but then it turns around to face us and I nearly stumble backwards in shock.

Its head, neither human nor beast, is wrapped tightly in barbed wire. Each movement it makes, no matter how grand or small, causes the wire to cut into its skin, shredding the flesh as blood dribbles down its face. Empty eye sockets stare at us, but there's no smoke rising out of them. Instead, the fleshy bits are exposed for all to see.

Two gaping holes where the nose should be is replaced by barbed wire digging into them. Jagged skin where the lips once were now expose its teeth while a hole in its right cheek is gaping and bleeding.

A thin black shawl covers the Records Keeper's grotesquely emaciated body. Its skin is like leather stretched too tight over its bones. With each move of its limbs, they creak and grind against their joints, causing the movements to be jerky. It looks incredibly painful.

As the Records Keeper comes to stand directly in front of us with only the counter separating us from it, a god–awful smell of rotting meat and decay slams into me. The smell is my final straw.

I stumble backwards, hand covering my nose and mouth to hold back the gag. My body shakes involuntarily as the harsh reality barrels into me like a landslide. No human can look like the Records Keeper and be *alive*. Bats don't have exposed skulls for heads; they're *not* the size of a household dog. But most importantly, you can't be in your apartment in one moment and then in the next moment, be in an entirely different place. Teleportation isn't real… Unless Hell really does exist.

A sob breaks free from my mouth as I stare at the man beside me. No, not a man.

The devil.

"Don't mind her," the literal devil says, not at all bothered by my suppressed crying and trembling. "We've come here to weigh her soul against another's. Chad Dunner, 1998, United States of America."

With jerky, tight movements, the Records Keeper dips beneath the counter. A moment later, it stands to its full height with a scale in its left hand. It thuds lightly against the counter and I wipe viciously at the tears distorting my vision. The scale stands about a foot tall. It has the body of a human but the head of a hissing cat, ears flattened against its scalp and its sharp teeth baring for all to see. There is a dish in each hand.

The Records Keeper leans over, its right hand disappearing under the counter before it comes back into view. It now holds a small, white glowing orb within its hand. The orb is placed gently on the right side of the scale before the Records Keeper extends a bony, tendril hand towards me. My companion turns his attention towards me, an overexaggerated frown upon his face. There's no empathy to be found within his eyes as he stares down at me.

"Sorry. This will hurt."

I don't have time to ask him what he means. A short second later, his hand is shoved straight through my chest.

It's rough and ragged as it shreds my skin and breaks my ribs. A scream tears from my mouth as I stagger back from the sudden intrusion. Instinctively, my fingers curl around his wrist and yank in a lame attempt to remove his hand from my chest. It's a useless attempt. He's created a gaping hole inside my chest that no doctor could ever save me from. I'll bleed out in seconds the moment his hand vacates my chest.

My body sways on my feet, the ground threatening to come up and slam me in the face. His fingers twist and scrape against my insides. The pain is unimaginable. I gag but nothing comes out. Black dots blink in and out of existence within my gaze.

"Stop," I rasp out as my head lulls back against my spine.

My legs give out but he catches me with his other arm. He continues digging around my chest and I slump against him. Just as I'm on the verge of passing out, he jerks his arm once before it slides out.

With a resounding pop, he releases me from his hold and I fall to the ground. My eyes flutter as the room spins. My heart pounds within my ears. I don't know whether I gag or imagine gagging. Everything is distorted.

I barely register the red orb sitting in his hand. My head lobs forward as I glance down at my chest. There is no hole. There is no blood. I'm perfectly intact.

"How?" I ask as my fingers tentatively touch the spot where his arm disappeared into me.

He doesn't answer me. Instead, all of his attention is focused on the red orb within his hand. It's roughly the size of a tennis ball. Much larger than the ping pong sized white orb sitting on the scale. The one in his hand is a deep burgundy red, its surface as smooth as glass as it reflects the firelight from the chandelier. *Did he just pull that out of me?*

His eyebrows pinch together, lips pulling downward at the corner of his mouth as he rotates the orb within his hand. I know that look well enough. He's confused.

"Impossible," he whispers to himself, eyes glued to the orb.

A split second later, his eyes snap to me and his free hand clamps down on my head. The heat of his palm presses against my forehead and an electrifying sensation passes through us. Everything becomes muffled and blurry as the sensation zaps around my brain, down my spine to my chest cavity before zapping back up to my brain. It expels from me with force, throwing me onto my back.

My eyes blink rapidly as everything comes back into focus. I somehow manage to sit up. He looks even more confused, a scowl crossing his features as his attention is focused back on the orb.

"Records Keeper, evaluate this orb."

"Yes, Lord Balthazar," it replies as it takes the orb from his hand.

Black smoke coils around the orb before spiraling up into the Records Keeper's eye sockets. By the time the Record's Keeper is done evaluating the orb, I'm able to stand on my feet. My legs feel unsteady, but I'm not going to stay on the floor while the devil stands beside me.

"It is authenticated as Sloane Kensington, 1996, United States of America."

"Weigh it."

The Records Keeper places the red orb on the left scale. The moment it touches the dish, it slams onto the counter, nearly launching the white orb into the air. The Records Keeper removes the orbs and switches their positions. White orb on the left, red orb on the right. The same thing happens as soon as the Records Keeper removes its hands.

"Perhaps another scale," it screeches.

It procures a second scale. It is a devil with its arms extended out, a dish in each hand. The red orb is placed down first and the dishes remain balanced. But when the white orb is added, the dish with the red orb slams into the counter.

"One broken scale is a possibility, Lord Balthazar," the Records Keeper says. "Two broken scales is inconceivable."

The devil turns his gaze back to mine, eyes slowly drifting down to my feet before back up to my eyes.

"Your soul is certainly worth more than Chad's," he states nonchalantly. "Do you still wish to sell your soul to me?"

"I–if I do," I stutter, heart racing wildly as my hands go clammy, "you won't kill me, right?"

He inhales deeply, eyes ghosting back to the orb before snapping to mine. "You will have seven years, as per the contract, to fully enjoy your wish. Once those seven years are up, you come down here."

A wish. I get a wish for selling my soul. Or do I since I'm already negotiating he doesn't kill me?

"Do I get a wish? Or does not killing me count as that wish?"

He smirks, eyes glistening in the firelight as the smirk lights up his whole face. "Clever girl," he purrs.

He glances back at the red orb sitting on the scale. He stares at it for a long, hard moment, thoughts running through his mind before he stares back at me. There's some emotion swimming in his eyes, like he figured out a piece of the puzzle just by staring at the orb. It unnerves me in the worst way.

"I will not count it as your wish. So... do we have a deal?"

My throat closes up as my eyes flit around the room. My attention darts to the Records Keeper, to the white and red orbs, to the bats fluttering above our heads, to the fire chandelier and the vast void surrounding us, to the spiked spindles lining our path. This is Hell. I am in *Hell*.

If I sell him my soul, I'm guaranteed to come down here for the rest of my eternal afterlife. But I suddenly have a clarifying question: what if I'm meant to go to Heaven when I die? Would it really be so bad to let the devil kill me today? Heaven is supposed to be the best place in existence. I won't get to say goodbye to my friends and family, but I'd meet them again when they die. Maybe dying now wouldn't be so bad.

"Wait, what if.." I trail off as my eyes dart back to the devil, "what if I'm meant to go to Heaven? Do you know? Do you know if I'm meant to go to Heaven?"

He chuckles, deep and sensual, as a lopsided grin appears on his face. The kind of grin that makes him look like a child who's overly excited to tell his first joke. On the devil, it's unsettling.

"Can't tell you that. It takes all the fun out bargaining."

"But what if I'm meant to go to Heaven?" I ask as I think out loud. "That means I'd be giving that up by selling you my soul."

"Mm," he hums as his smile deepens. "That certainly is a possibility. Or," he drawls out as his eyes crinkle at the edges. "Perhaps you're coming here either way. One option is you get a wish and live for seven more years. The other option is dying and coming down here today. The not knowing where you'll end up is what makes this *fun*."

This is not even close to being fun, I think as my vision warbles and a lump forms in my throat. This is an impossible situation to be in. How do I make this choice? *Think, Sloane, think.*

If Hell thrives on good souls, if his whole purpose is to get as many deals with good souls as possible, then it means I'm meant for Heaven. But in what world are Chad and I both good souls? He views women as less than him. He probably votes to take away women's rights and women's autonomy. He literally *sold his soul* to have me *killed*. His revenge involves my literal death. How does that make him a good person?

But what if Hell thrives on bad souls? It would make sense why the devil would buy Chad's soul. It *doesn't* make sense why he'd want mine, though, or why mine would be worth more than Chad's. How am I worse than Chad? I've never once attempted to kill someone! I support equal rights, I advocate for universal healthcare and higher minimum wages, I do my best to learn about the social injustices in our country and planet. How could I be worse than Chad?

Have I just not had my villain era yet? I might not be bad now, but the rest of my life is long. Still, why would I go to Hell now if I haven't done anything worth being sentenced here? That seems unfair. Or maybe I *did* do something worth being sent to Hell and I don't remember. *Fuck. How is any of this determined?*

"Sloane, I will follow through with Chad's request if you fail to give me an answer in the next five seconds."

Gun to my head, what do I do? Gun to my head, what do I? *Gun to my head, what do I do?*

"I'll do it," I blurt out, not really sure what I'm saying.

He smirks. "What is your wish?"

Am I really selling my soul? He said I'll have seven years until my wish expires. But if I give him my wish now, the deal will be set in stone. If I have an open–ended deal, I'll have more time to figure out what the hell I've done.

"I get a wish?" I ask as I contemplate the situation I'm in.

"Only one," he states. "And no, you cannot wish for more wishes."

"Do I… do I have to give you a wish right away?" I ask. "Am I allowed to think on it? I wasn't expecting to sell my soul today. I have no idea what I'd wish for."

"You've caught me in a good mood, Sloane," he replies as he leans in as close as he can, his lips caressing my ear as he whispers, "I'll give you seven days to make your wish."

Seven days. Seven days to figure out how to outsmart the devil. Well, I found one loophole already. I can certainly find another. I can do this. Chad Dunner will lose and regret the day he ever met me.

The devil pulls away as the grin on his face drops and he stares at me like the prey that I am.

"Unfortunately for you, I still have to kill you."

V

"No!" I SCREAM, my body lunging at him before my brain has caught up. My fingers curl into his shirt as I glare up at him. "I'm selling you my soul! You said you wouldn't kill me!"

"I have to uphold my deal of Chad's bargain," he states. "I have to kill you, but as that is a conflict of interest in *our* bargain, I will only kill you on paper. That means everyone you know, everyone you love, everyone you have ever cared for will believe you're dead. A memorial will be held in your honor. You'll be buried. Or cremated, whichever your family prefers. You will cease to exist. You won't be able to speak with your friends, your family, your co-workers ever again. You have to be legally dead in order for me to fulfill Chad's wish."

It's that easy. All he has to do is *pretend* to kill me. Chad would be none the wiser and I don't have to sell my soul for it.

My hand moves quicker than either of us anticipate. The slap echoes through the empty room. My palm stings from where I've hit him. His head has turned to the side from the force of the blow. His jaw juts back and forth as his hand comes up to rub at the spot where I hit him.

He chuckles, but there's no friendliness in his tone. The reality of what I've just done has me in a chokehold. I'm going to die for real. He's going to throw our deal out the window and kill me.

"I'll give you that one for free," he states darkly as his eyes cut to mine. "The next one is going to cost you."

The black of his eyes bleeds to fiery red and my breath stalls inside my lungs as my blood turns to ice.

"I–I," I weakly stutter as I take a step back from him. "Why didn't you pretend to kill me in the first place? Why do I have to sell you my soul?"

He squares up to me, shoulders pulled taut as he glares down his nose at me. "A devil never does something for nothing. Now," he says in a low voice as his fingers curl around my wrist. "We must seal your deal."

With one hard yank, I collide into him. His other hand sinks into my hair before he pulls my head back. Before I can wonder what he's doing, his lips are atop my own.

They're hot. Like they might be seconds away from leaving a burn on my lips. My hands push against his chest, but he holds me tight until there's a strange click I *feel* inside my chest. As if an imaginary broken rib slides back into place, perfectly healed. Once the click snaps into place, he releases me.

"What was that?" I demand as I take a step back from him, hand wiping my lips as I glare up at him.

"Haven't you ever watched *Supernatural?*" he asks as a half smirk adorns his face. "A deal is sealed with a kiss."

"That's TV, it's not real life," I argue.

He reaches a hand out, fingers pushing hair behind my ear before a single finger trails down my jaw to the hand that covers my mouth. He bites his lower lip as I dumbly allow him to remove my hand.

"TV had to derive its inspiration from somewhere. Either way, Sloane, you belong to me now." He dips his head to press his cheek against mine as his whispers in a deep, husky voice, "You won't regret it. I promise."

I jerk away from him, my hands poised to shove him, but I'm suddenly back in my apartment. I've fallen off my bed, sprawled out on the floor with sheets entangled around my legs.

A dream. It was all just a dream.

"Oh thank god," I breathe out as tears cloud my vision.

It felt so real. The fear, the magic, the pain. It was the most vivid dream I've ever had. I don't think I'll ever forget the Records Keeper for the rest of my life. How disgusting it looked, how it smelled, or the sound of its voice.

An involuntary shiver wracks down my back. I can't even begin to articulate the gratitude I feel about it being nothing more than a dream. Hell isn't real. Devils aren't real. Chad didn't sell his soul to have me killed. *Thank god.*

I disentangle myself from the sheets and grab my phone off the mattress. The screen lights up and it takes me several seconds to process the time. 8:05am. I've slept through my alarm.

"I'm so dead," I say before launching to my feet.

As quickly as I can, I dress for work, apply a bit of makeup to hide the tiredness of my face, grab my work shoes, slide into my commuter shoes, grab my work bag, and disappear out the door. It's a short walk to the T station and I fluff my hair as best I can before realizing it's a lost cause and toss it up into a stylish messy bun.

Once I get to the platform and wait for the train's arrival, I dig out my phone to send Ella a text.

> You won't believe the dream I had last night. Chad sold his soul to have me killed. 😄

I barely see the *'Not Delivered'* notification beneath my text bubble as I slip my phone back into my bag. Service is always wonky around here. I'll text her when I get to work.

The commute takes longer than I remember. As soon as I reach my stop, I shove my way through the throng of bodies up to street level. I practically sprint the rest of the way to work.

My ID card won't work to let me into the building and I have to wait for someone to let me in. It's 9:17am by the time I plop down in my desk chair, a complete disheveled mess. A few seconds pass before I pull my laptop out of my bag and plug it into the dock.

It lights up and I quickly type in my password.

Invalid Account

"Invalid account?" I whisper as my eyebrows furrow together.

I double check my username. *Sloane.Kensington.* No spelling errors. Maybe it was an incorrect password. I type it again, but this time I go slowly so I know I make no mistakes.

Invalid Account

"What does that even mean?" I groan out in frustration.

This day is going horribly. I've had the worst nightmare of my life, I slept through my alarm, the commute took *forever*, the keycard didn't work, and now my laptop won't let me login. What else is going to happen?

My head falls back against the back of my chair as my eyes drift up towards the speckled dropped ceiling. IT will have to fix this and since I can't login to my computer, I can't submit an electronic ticket. I'll have to do the one thing IT hates most; drop in their office, unannounced.

Stalling to gather some courage, my mind wanders back to the dream I had. The timing of it, how I had it the same day Chad reached out to me on the dating app to take down the fake profile... did I have that nightmare because I was feeling guilty? *Maybe I* should *delete his profile.*

I pull my phone from my workbag and tap the dating app. I attempt to login to Chad's account but I keep receiving the same error.

Cannot find account.

Did Chad petition the app to delete it? That's more probable than him hacking into the account. I can't imagine he'd figure out the password. He thinks too highly of himself to figure out *Chadisdisgusting1!*. I don't understand why he didn't have the account deleted in the first place instead of wasting his time reaching out to me. Either way, it's over and I can go back to sleeping with an innocent conscience.

With a deep sigh, I rise from my chair and exit my office. IT is a short walk down the hallway. Liam's door is slightly ajar and I catch sight of him through the window. With a gentle push of the door, I plaster on the biggest, friendliest smile I have as I enter his room. I've learned to always be overly friend with IT personnel because they can make or break how quickly an issue gets fixed.

"Good morning Liam," I greet him overly pleasant as I stand about two feet from his desk. "I tried logging into my computer this morning but it keeps saying invalid account. Can you help me with that?"

Liam doesn't so much as glance my way as his fingers continue typing. *Odd.* Liam might be considered the office grouch, but he's never been rude to me before.

"Liam? Are you able to help me with my computer?"

More silence. What's his deal? My patience begins to wear thin as I speak a bit firmer.

"Look, I know I didn't submit a ticket but I can't do that when I can't even log into my computer. Could you just take a look at it?"

Liam pushes back from his desk, the wheels of his chair squeaking as he begins working on the laptop behind him. *This is going too far.* He's never *ignored* me before, no matter how grumpy he was. This is so out of character for him.

He spins around again, his eyes coasting over where I stand. Goosebumps rise along my arms as his attention shifts to his desktop. My body understands before my mind does. He types away before spinning back to the desk behind him, his eyes, again, coasting over me.

"Wait…"

Dread fills my stomach as my brain slowly pieces it together. Hesitation holds me back but when he spins a fourth time, I can't help myself. My hand shoots out in front of his face and I snap my fingers. He doesn't flinch or blink or glare at me. He behaves as though he can't see me.

You will cease to exist.

Everyone you ever cared for will believe you're dead.

My heart skips a beat as the dream floods my mind. *This can't be happening.* It was a *dream.* Devils don't exist. Chad didn't sell his soul to have me killed. Liam's just ignoring me because he decided to be asshole of the year. If I yell loud enough, he'll *have* to acknowledge me.

"Liam!"

He doesn't react. I tap his shoulder three times. Nothing. I clap my hands inches from his face. He doesn't even flinch. I hesitate only for a second and then poke him in the cheek. *Absolutely nothing.*

"LIAM!" I scream as loudly as I can.

He spins around to work on a laptop. Without thinking, my body lunges for him, fingers curling around his shirt before I tug him as hard as I can. He doesn't budge. Like he's a ten–ton statue I have no business moving.

Panic floods my system as he continues working on the laptops. I shift to lean in front of him, positioning myself directly between him and the laptop he's working on. He gives no reaction. Instead, it's as though he's looking *through* me.

Cold panic shoots down my spine as my throat cinches. He can't see me. He can't hear me. He can't feel me. Am I a ghost? *That can't be,* I think, somehow able to keep some wits about me. I bumped into people on the way here. They looked me in the eyes. It's only Liam who doesn't seem to know I'm here.

I rush out of his office and run towards the nearest cubicle. That person reacts the same way Liam did. I attempt to disturb another coworker. None of them react as if they can see or hear me. Am I dead? There's only one person who can answer that question.

I tilt my head back and yell.

"Lucifer! Satan! Whoever the hell you are! I need you! *Now!*"

"It's Lord Balthazar," his deep voice calmly states from behind.

My stomach drops. I was hoping it wouldn't work, that he wouldn't show up, that he didn't *exist*. But there he stands, in the flesh, *horns* and all.

I whirl on him, an embodiment of fear, confusion, and anger. My hand slaps him on the bicep as I glare up at him.

"Am I a ghost?" I demand. "Did you kill me?"

His lips pull down into a slight frown as he wipes the place where I smacked him like there's imaginary dirt there. "You have such moments of stupidity, it's honestly a shame."

"Forgive me for not understanding how your magical powers work," I snap at him, too angry at him to fear him. "Did. You. Kill. Me?"

"Theoretically, yes," he answers nonchalantly, but then rolls his eyes at my panicked look. "I explained this to you already."

"Then *refresh my memory*."

"You are dead to everyone who ever knew you. My magic prevents them from interacting with you in any shape or form. Honestly, you should be thanking me. You're still allowed to interact with strangers. You're not entirely alone, Sloane."

My eyes dart down to the floor, shifting back and forth between his shoes as I process what he's said. It all circles back to Chad's wish to have me killed. Balthazar said something about not fulfilling a wish means the devil dies as consequence. Which means he's made it so everyone who ever knew me will never be able to see me, talk to me, or touch me again. He's fulfilled Chad's wish without *literally* killing me. But how does my work already know I'm dead? That makes no sense.

"You killed me last night," I state and the words feel strange in my mouth but I continue on. "Work wouldn't have asked for a wellness check yet. They'd still be trying to call me, yet my login doesn't even recognize me as an employee anymore."

"It's been three days since you were discovered dead," he answers casually, like he hasn't just ruined my entire twenty–six years of life.

The news is a cold shock to my system. Three days. I've been dead for *three days*. That would be plenty of time for work to be notified of my death.

My death.

An onslaught of emotions slams into me and I'm unable to suppress them. Balthazar distorts as water clouds my vision and my lower lip trembles. I inhale a shaky breath. I'm *dead*. My parents, Ella, my friends… they all think I've died. And according to the asshole standing in front of me, it doesn't matter if I walk past them, slap them in the face, or scream into their ears until I go blue in the face, they won't see, hear, or feel *any* of it.

My eyes squeeze shut as I attempt to reel in my emotions, but it's no use. I'm utterly defeated. My hands fly up to my face, my fingertips pressing into my eyelids as if that'll somehow stop the tears from escaping, and a sob breaks through my weak defenses.

I might be *technically* alive, but I'm legally dead. That means there's nothing of my life I can salvage. I have no access to my money, my social security number, my ID, my apartment. *Oh god, my apartment.*

Ella will most likely move out. She'll help my parents clean out my room before subletting the apartment until our lease is up. Then she'll say goodbye to it forever. Goodbye to our shared memories of late nights watching movies and drinking wine, spending lazy mornings sprawled out in the sun, and random afternoons rearranging the entire apartment. She'll leave all those behind and I'll be forgotten.

Another sob tears out of me. Will it even matter if I somehow get out of my deal? Everyone thinks I'm dead. Unless the devil reverses whatever type of spell he put on them, I won't magically become undead to them even if I outsmart him.

My stomach churns at the realization. An involuntarily shake descends my body as bile rises up my throat, begging to be let free. Stubbornly, I hold it in. I won't throw up in front of him. I won't let the devil see me fall that low.

The thought of him standing there, gleefully watching me break down, births a raw anger inside me. My eyes snap open, tears streaking down my face, and I glare at him as my face morphs into the anger I feel.

"This is your fault," I state in an infuriated voice.

He smirks as he confidently holds my gaze. "You made a choice, Ephirian swine."

"No. I didn't," I reply, my voice trembling with all the rage coursing through me. "You *took* my choices from me the second you showed up to kill me. I would've done *anything* to stay alive. How is that a choice?"

He takes a menacing step towards me, but I don't shrink away. I hold my ground. The red speckles in his eyes bleed into the black as he sneers down at me.

"My existence as a devil, the work that I do... It all means there's an afterlife, Sloane. You could have taken your chances with death. If I had killed you like I planned to, you could be in Odantha – excuse me, *Heaven*, living your perfect life. Instead, you chose to remain alive. You chose to bargain with the devil. You let your fear blind you from what I was offering–"

"That's *bullshit*."

He chuckles, eyes fading to mostly black, as he takes a step back. His gaze shifts away from me as he speaks, "Think whatever you want, Sloane. *You* were the one who proposed the bargain. Not me."

Before I can say anything in retaliation, he raises his hand and presses his middle finger to his thumb in the tell–tale sign that he's going to snap his fingers and disappear from my sight.

I act without thinking.

My hand shoots out, grabbing hold of his forearm just before his fingers snap together. A second later, an invisible heavy sludge encases me, dragging me down by the ankles. My grip tightens on the devil. I don't know what will happen if I let go during transportation and I have zero desire to find out.

The pressure as we move through the sludge threatens to crush me. My entire body is consumed by pain as it feels like massive rocks press down on me from all sides. Just as I begin to wonder if this is how I'll die, the immense weight disappears.

I abruptly stumble to my hands and knees. A split second later, the heat of the floor sears my palms and kneecaps. My mouth opens to cry out, but the air is too dry. I cough and cough and cough. With each new inhale, the air singes my throat and lungs. The tears in my eyes evaporate as soon as they appear. Is *this* how I'm going to die? After all the work I put into saving my life, it'll go to waste if I die of heat and suffocation.

A faint snap echoes in the room and almost immediately, I'm able to breathe again. Yet, before I've had time to recover from my coughing fit, a hand is grabbing me by the throat and yanking me to my feet. I'm slammed into a wall as the devil shoves his face in mine. His eyes glow crimson red and his lips peel back to reveal fangs as he speaks.

"You're lucky our lives are magically connected," he growls, low and furious. "Because it would give me great satisfaction to kill you right now."

My hands claw at his too tight grip. He presses me further into the wall before he drops me with an animalistic snarl – the type of snarl that makes your skin crawl as you wait with bated breath for the predator to pounce.

He steps away from me and raises his hand to snap his fingers again.

"No," I shout as I lunge for his arm.

"You have no business in Jeznia," he declares as he dodges me.

"I have no life anymore," I yell as I keep lunging for him.

I'm aiming for any part of him. Any part I can wrap my grubby hands around and hold on tight. He's nimbler than he appears as he expertly dodges me. The one good thing coming out of our weird dance is that he's too focused on dodging me instead of snapping his fingers and making me go away.

"Where you go, *I* go," I say as I lunge for him again.

My statement must catch him off guard because he fumbles slightly and my fingers curl around his forearm. I take the opportunity for what it is and yank him close as my arms slide around his waist and I bury my face into his chest.

He's unbelievably hot. Like a furnace ready to blow. I don't care about the risks and plant my hands firmly against his back, burying myself deeper into his chest. His back muscles flex and contract beneath my fingertips, hard and sturdy.

Smoke wafts up my nose as I inhale, the lingering scents of Boston dying out amongst the intensity of the smoke. The familiar smell instantly pulls me to a fonder place. Memories of late–night fires in the middle of summer, of a roaring fire during the winter, of delicious meals and warm company threaten to overwhelm me. If I keep my eyes closed and imagine hard enough, I might forget everything that's happened.

"You go wherever I send you," he states darkly as his fingers curl around my arms and he begins to pry me free with ease.

"No," I shout as I fight against him with all my strength. "I'm your responsibility now! I have no life because of you! I have nowhere to go because of you! Take responsibility!"

"I am Lord Balthazar, heir of House Primis," he growls as his horns ignite in flames and his eyes flare dark red again.

I gasp as I stagger back, my hands dropping away from him as my mouth hangs open in surprise. In the short time we've met, I've never seen him so furious. Alarm bells ring in my mind and I find myself cowering back.

"I do *not* take orders from *Ephirian swine.*"

My spine snaps straight as a board as anger radiates down to my toes. It's not the first time he's called me that. But this time it's different. This time he says it with such disgust that it makes me see immediate red.

My fingers curl into the palms of my hands as a glare hardens on my face. Who is he to think he's better than me? Because he has a fancy title and is the devil? *Screw that.* I'm the consequences of his actions and I'm here to mess his life up.

"Now you do," I say with all the anger I have swarming inside of me. "You haven't fulfilled our bargain and until you do, I'm sticking to you."

"Then make your wish," he orders, his voice low and threatening as he curls his hand around my neck.

He squeezes tight enough for it to be scary, but I don't bat an eye. I've finally put the pieces together. He can't kill me no matter how badly he might want to. His life is bound to my wish being fulfilled and if he were to do anything to jeopardize my life in any way, shape, or form, he dies.

"No," I say as a slow, devious smile spreads across my lips. *I've got him.* "I'm not rushing into my wish the way I did with selling my soul. I'm going to take my seven days and if you so much as send me away or leave me behind without my consent, my wish will be for you to die. Do you get it now, *Lord Balthazar?* Your life is in these Ephirian swine's hands."

VI

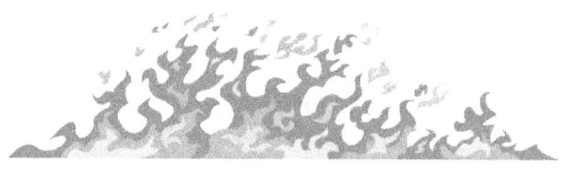

A LOUD, GUTTERAL growl expels from him as he slams me onto the floor. The wind is knocked out of my lungs as pain blossoms down my back.

His fingers are tight around my neck; I'm barely able to breathe. His face is mere inches from my own, his horns still on fire, and his eyes glow that deep red, no black to be seen, as his lips pull back into a snarl. All the rage and hatred he feels towards me is poured into that singular stare.

"When you die," he says, his voice a whisper. He enunciates each word carefully, purposefully. It's meant to instill fear and I hate that it's working. "I'll carve out a little spot to carry you with me as a special kind of torment. Be rest assured that your eternity will be worse than Hell."

My entire body trembles at the cold, calculated cruelness of his words. Maybe I should wish for his death if only it means to make my afterlife a little bit more bearable. *No, whatever you do, don't waste your wish unless absolutely necessary.* As soon as I make the wish, it'll be that much harder for me to find a loophole out of my contract. I need to drag this out for as long as I can and I've finally found the perfect way to do it. He doesn't want to die any more than I do. I can use that to my advantage.

When my seven days are up and if I still haven't figured a way out of this deal, I'll wish him dead if he won't give me more time. I'll keep forcing him to extend my time until I either have to kill him or I've successfully escaped my bargain. It might be true that I fucked around with the wrong devil, but he's playing with the wrong human.

"Sounds like you're stuck with me," I reply as I curl my fingers around his wrist. "Judging by your threat, it'll be for the rest of your eternal life too."

He snarls as he lets me go and rises to his full height while I remain sprawled out on the floor. His horns blaze brighter and hotter as his eyes glow so intensely that they lose any discernible features to them. They look like two glowing dark red lights on his face.

I rise up onto my elbows as I watch him pace the room, ripping it to shreds as he claws at the walls, smashing any decorations in his way, and overturning furniture before he's reduced to a breathing, huffing state. If he didn't look so dangerous, I'd find his behavior ridiculous. He's throwing a literal tantrum, except his tantrum is absolutely feral, and my only saving grace that's preventing me from bodily harm is our contract.

Terror pulsates with each beat of my heart as he turns his attention to me. My mouth drops open in horror as I watch his humanoid appearance *melt* off him. The skin bubbles as it slides off and plops with a wet squish that has my stomach churning. Beneath his human face is charcoal skin so tight it's tearing off his face. Cracks dart across his skin, illuminated from within by light the color of burning embers.

A dark ooze drips down his face as the fire from his horns encases the top of his head. It burns hot, wild, and tall. The glowing red of his eyes has disappeared, replaced by two empty sockets with smoke billowing out of them. His nose is gone, exposing two gaping holes, and his lips are burned off, revealing all his teeth for me to see. He has two regular front teeth and four, very sharp top canines. All in all, he is completely and utterly terrifying.

I creep back from my position on the floor as panic and worry floods me. Maybe my contract doesn't save me from bodily harm. If he were to hurt me but not kill me, would that be going against the rules?

He stalks towards me and a terrified yelp bursts out of my mouth. Overcome by my panic of what he'll do to me, I fumble around for any kind of sharp object but come up short. He kneels down, hovering over me, forcing me to flop down flat on my back as I attempt to create distance between us. He uses that opportunity to trap me on the floor by placing his hands on either side of my body.

The ooze on his face drips off him onto my chin. It smells foul, like something is rotting and dying. I involuntarily gag.

My skin begins to burn from the immense heat emitting from him. I try to break free from him, but his arms trap me in. Anytime I make contact with him, it burns. I'm unable to escape.

"If you want to fuck around with the devil," he says in a gravely, layered voice that pounds away at me from all sides.

It's a piercing, excruciating pain, similar to a sledgehammer going to town on my brain. My eyes slam shut as I wince and try to cover my ears, but I can't. Each time I raise my arms up, they get blocked by his burning limbs. I'm forced to listen in agonizing torture as he continues to speak.

"Then you better be prepared for what you get."

Everything hurts. I'm burning from being too close to him. My head feels as though it'll split open from the sound of his voice. The ooze coats me, drenching me in the smell of death.

"*Enough*," I shout as loudly as I can.

He leans forward, pressing his cheek against mine; shockingly, it doesn't burn. He whispers low into my ear, his voice back to normal, "You better think twice about who's really giving the orders here."

He pulls away and the heat and pain are instantly gone while my eyes remain closed. There's some shuffling around in the room before a snap of fingers. My eyes peer open. He's back to his humanoid appearance with his perfectly styled black hair, smooth flawless olive skin, black eyes beautifully speckled with red, and horns *not* on fire.

Notably, he's not wearing a shirt, allowing my eyes to soak in the planes of his chest, the ripples of his stomach, and the interesting tribal looking tattoo starting at the top of his neck down to his pectorals and coming to a triangular point just above his belly button. He wears two golden circlets around his biceps and he has on a pair of dark maroon parachute pants with no shoes. The outfit is enough to confuse me, stunning me out of my fear.

He snaps his fingers again. A moment later, I'm standing on my feet, causing me to stumble from the abrupt change of position. The sound of chains clinking against each other fills the room and I glance down at myself to find I'm in a completely different outfit. My mouth drops open in mortification.

A silver chain bra loosely drapes atop a lacy, black bra that barely hides my modesty. A black, high waisted skirt with slits that nearly reach up to my waist wouldn't bother me as much if I didn't feel a breeze against my bare crotch and butt. A garter belt snatched around my waist hooks into stockings that end at my mid–thigh. The outfit is finished by a pair of black stilettos.

"What the–?" is the first thing I think to say. A second later, the confusion and shock disappear only to be replaced by outrage. "No way in Hell! Change me back right now!"

"Absolutely in Hell. Wherever I go, you go," he reminds me in disdain. He looks as angry as I feel. "You either look the part or get shredded to bits."

I want to challenge him on the outfit, but I'm fairly certain he means *literally* shredded to bits. I find it hard to believe an outfit like this is going to save my life, but I suppose it can't hurt my chances. Right? Still…

I hate it. I hate every revealing inch of it. I've never been interested in exposing this much of myself to the world. No judgement to people who get enjoyment and confidence in it, that's just not me. But what am I going to do? He won't change me back and I'm not going to waste a wish on it.

"Come," he orders darkly. "I'm already late to the meeting."

"Meeting?"

He doesn't answer or bother to wait for me as he opens the door and exits the room. Irritated by his actions, but not wanting to be left alone, I scurry after him as best I can in the three–inch stilettos. I'm no stranger to heels, but I like mine with a thicker, sturdier heel. I like the stability it offers. With the current heels, I feel like I'm one wrong misstep away from breaking my ankle.

Any fear or anger I have towards him diminishes as I concentrate all my energy on walking. I manage to keep pace with him even despite my noticeably awkward walk. The key is to shift my weight onto my toes.

Once I feel more comfortable in my walk, I venture to look around at my surroundings. Even though I know we're in Hell, it's still a surprise to see the walls on fire. What's more horrifying, though, are the hands and arms reaching *out* of the flames. Singed and charred flesh dangles off the limbs. They aimlessly swipe at empty air, hopelessly trying to grab hold of something. It's a disturbing sight. My hand lays flat against my stomach as I try to become as small as possible while I walk.

Balthazar walks confidently in the center of the hallway, not at all disturbed by the hands reaching for him. I do my best to pretend they're not there, but that's impossible. My mind is running rampant. Are these human arms of souls he bargained for and they're trapped for eternity hoping for a way out? *Is this my fate?* I swallow thickly. No. I'll find a way out. No matter what.

"Uh, so you said you're late for a meeting," I say as my shoes tap against the floor. I need to occupy my mind with something else other than the possible human souls trapped within the fire. "What meeting would that be?"

He huffs out a breath of irritation before answering. "A meeting between the Houses of Jeznia. All seven Lords will be present and, since you refuse to stay where you belong, I will give you this one piece of advice. *Do not speak.* Ever. Even if they goad you into it. They'll kill you for mere sport and I'm not prepared for dealing with the consequences of that yet so it's in both our best interests if you play the perfect mute."

"If they'll kill me just for funsies, it won't matter if I speak or not," I argue.

"Trust me when I say this, your talking will encourage them to kill you. I would've killed you for that sharp tongue of yours if I could."

A scowl forms on my face as my fingers curl into tight fists. I'm half tempted to throw hands at him, but I know I'd only be digging my grave. I'm disgustingly outmatched against him. All I can rely on are my *sharp words*. Whether or not they hurt him is up for my continual discovery.

"If I didn't have to waste my only wish on it, I'd kill you too, asshole."

He chuckles deep and rich as he turns his attention to me, stopping in his place. "I'd like to see you try."

"Don't tempt me," I snap at him as I square up to him. "You might be surprised by what this *lowly* Ephirian swine can achieve."

He smirks as his hand reaches out to caress my ear. "I see I've hit a nerve. *Good.*"

Heat ignites along my ear where he's touched me and I quickly bat his hand away. A strange sensation curls low in the pit of my stomach as the heat in my ear darts down the side of my neck to my collar bone. He says nothing as he turns around and continues walking down the corridor, the exposed muscles of his torso flexing as he walks. My eyes drag down the expanse of his back to the hem of his pants. My gaze lingers on his backside, on the tightness of it even through the loose–fitting pants, and I can easily imagine how it would feel under my fingers–

What the hell? I reel back the moment I realize where my train of thought is going. How could I be thinking about him in that way? He's destroyed my life! Never mind the fact that he's the *devil*. I could never want him in that way. Suddenly, his words from the night before resurface in my mind.

If your soul comes back weighing more than Chad's, I'm going to make you eat those words.

Is he influencing me? I don't know the limitations of his powers. All I do know is he's able to grant wishes. He never said there were limitations on what we could wish for. Does that mean I could wish to have someone be madly in love with me? If yes, it's entirely plausible he could be manipulating me now for his own amusement. But if he's not doing it, could Hell be influencing me?

It'd make sense that Hell would have some sort of magical capabilities. It wouldn't surprise me if Hell could latch on to every deepest, darkest, sinful, wretched thought I ever had, amplifying it until it completely overrode my senses. As much as I hate to admit it, the devil *is* attractive. Ungodly so. Hell could exacerbate that single thought and before I know it, I'll be putty in his greedy hands. *I need to be careful down here.*

Balthazar continues down the corridor and I hurry after him, not wanting to be left unattended around the hands reaching out of the fire. Eventually, we come upon two large, iron doors very similarly designed like the ones for the Record Keeper's room. These doors, however, have golden accents on the creatures carved into the door and there are two large, golden doorknobs.

"Remember what I said. A perfect mute," he reminds me right before flicking his hand and the doors open upon his command.

I try to keep my awe at the display of his powers to a minimum. When he's not using them against me, they're incredible. I can't imagine all the wonderful ways I'd use powers like those. My life wouldn't have been in danger if I had powers to fight against the devil. I wouldn't have had to bargain to stay alive. Scratch that. My life never would have been put in danger in the first place because stupid Chad would be obliterated out of existence after he threatened me in the first place. The things I would have done to Chad if I had the devil's powers.

Balthazar walks into the room and I follow closely behind him. His entire demeanor changes as soon as those doors open. Shoulders pulled back, head held high, horns on fire as confidence oozes out of his every pore. His hands settle behind his back, fingers curling around his forearms.

All the playfulness is gone from him, replaced by the familiar energy he possessed when he threatened me with an eternal afterlife worse than Hell. My heart skips a beat, fear trickling down my back even though I know he's not directing that energy at me. *That's* how powerful his demeanor is.

I inhale deeply to calm my nerves and cast my gaze around this new room. It's perfectly circular. Stairs follow the circular design of the room, leading up to seven thrones evenly spaced from each other and positioned against the wall. There's a minor gap within the stairs to allow for an aisle from the door we're entering through. The aisle leads to the center of the room.

Each throne, made out of black stone, is carved to look like a specific creature. A bat, a spider, a snake, a wolf, a cat, a centipede, and a devil. The devil throne is empty; my assumption is that it belongs to Balthazar.

A pitch–black floor is illuminated by molten lava flowing through carved channels. There's a design in the lava channels, but it's difficult for me to make out at my height. A sky view would be better.

Lava slides down the walls, slow and steady, disappearing in a gap between the thrones and stairs. I wonder if it's someone's job to make sure the lava doesn't act erratically and harm anyone. Or maybe lava doesn't hurt them so they don't care?

The walls are a deep, crimson red while a massive fire chandelier floats about thirty feet in the air in the center of the room. No wires, chains, or rope hold it in place. It simply hovers there, I assume, by magic. Every so often, it cackles and an ember pops out, drifting languidly to the floor.

Flickering flames dance shadows across the faces of the six other devils in the room. They're similar to Balthazar in that they appear humanoid, but each devil has different shaped horns.

The devil that sits on the bat throne has horns that protrude out her forehead and curl backwards over the shape of her scalp. The devil on the snake throne has horns coming out his forehead and curling around his ears like a ram. The cat devil has thick horns coming out of his temples, about half a foot on either side, before curling downward toward the floor. The wolf devil has horns that are thin with ridges and extremely tall. The spider devil's horns are like deer antlers. The centipede devil has the smallest horns of everyone there. His horns look exactly like the horns people wear for Halloween.

My eyebrow arches upon seeing that. Does that make him more powerful than everyone here or less powerful? Do they ridicule him because of the sexy devil cosplays we have on Earth or does he have the most sway over human minds? I bite my tongue to keep from asking the question out loud.

Admittedly, it's difficult to do. I've never been in a situation where I couldn't speak unless I wanted die. I direct my attention to the rest of the room, intent on taking my mind off the burning questions.

Two steps down from every throne are two chairs: one of the left and one on the right. Some seats are empty while others are full. The devils sitting in the smaller, more modest chairs either have no horns or matching horns to the devil sitting in the throne chair. My assumption is that any devil with matching horns must be related, but who are the ones with no horns? Are they secretaries or something? Does Hell *have* secretaries?

Each devil, with or without horns, does not look terrifying or grotesque. Simply put, they look like they could be either celebrities or an average person I might see on the streets except now I know better. Just a few minutes ago, I watched as Balthazar's skin literally melted off his face to reveal what truly lay beneath. I can only imagine what these devils look like beneath their human looking skin.

They wear clothes with varying degrees of skin showing. The devil sitting at the wolf throne has her breasts on full display, wearing thin gold body jewelry and gemstones to highlight just how perky her chest is. No one appears distracted or put off by her lack of modesty.

The devil at the cat throne literally wears a loin cloth and nothing else. He sits with his legs spread wide and, if I look closely enough, I can see just the tip of him showing beneath the small piece of clothing that's supposed to be hiding his modesty. *Gross.* Others wear extravagant clothes that only expose their hands, neck, and face. I wonder why some forgo clothes while others bundle up in them. It's a strange inconsistency, but before I can ponder on it longer, Balthazar speaks.

"Greetings, my Lords," Balthazar says as he heads towards the only vacant seat in the room.

He sounds as though he couldn't care less about a single one of them. I quietly follow after him, but it's slow going. Balthazar clearly knows where every lava channel on the floor is while I'm barely staying balanced in my shoes. He doesn't offer to help me maneuver my way across the deadly room and instead, confidently walks to the stairs before ascending them. *Asshole.*

The devil at the bat throne, the one directly to the left of Balthazar's chair, openly sneers at me as her dark jade eyes size me up and down.

"What is the meaning of this?" she demands an answer as her fingers curl into her armrest.

I awkwardly hop over the last lava channel, my chain link bra clinking as I do, before I quickly dart up the stairs. I reach Balthazar just as he reaches the throne. It's large and impossibly black. It's difficult to see the corners or where it curves. In all honesty, the chair looks like an empty void.

As my eyes slowly wander up to the back of the chair, I notice the color becomes lighter. It's still black but I can see the details. The image of a devil has been painstakingly carved into the throne. It's surprisingly handsome and its horns match Balthazar's. There's no expression on the devil's face, but its eyes track me wherever I stand. *Creepy.*

"You'll have to expand upon what you're asking, Lord Carmilla," Balthazar replies as he plops down in his throne before yanking me down onto his lap.

I squeak out in surprise, my hands splaying across his sturdy chest to steady myself, and I hate every inch of myself as a light blush dusts my cheeks. Balthazar is well built and solid beneath my weight. His right finger idly trails up and down my exposed spine as his left hand rests too confidently and too high up on my inner thigh, especially considering I'm *not* wearing underwear. His right index finger plays with the hem of my stocking and the garter belt strap, but thankfully he doesn't venture any higher. If he does, I'll make sure he regrets it.

I attempt to swat his hand away as a glare settles on my face, but he effortlessly threads our fingers together.

"What is that abomination doing here?" Lord Carmilla asks as she does her best to withhold her rage.

I manage to keep my mouth shut, but it's impossible to hide the glare on my face. *I'm* the abomination? The hell is her problem? If anyone is the abomination, it's her and these devils.

Balthazar must sense my restraint because he pats my lower back as if to silently say *good job*. I ignore it.

"For the next seven years, I am to be her husband," Balthazar declares to the room and my head whips to him. I can't believe the words I've just heard. "Her family threatened to disown her if she were to remain unmarried and without children. They're extremely religious," he says, an underlying hint of mockery coating his tone.

"As part of our deal," he continues, "she's requested to go everywhere I go. Poor thing, really. She has no independence or self–will outside of her family's desires. She's merely traded me for them."

My blood boils as he speaks about me like I'm some kind of ignorant child. A glare hardens on my face. *Asshole.* His eyes meet mine and he smirks as he lifts my hand to his lips. I try to yank my hand back but he holds it tight. His lips are hot against my skin and he keeps them there in a lazy, prolonged kiss. He's clearly enjoying torturing me.

Lord Carmilla says something in response to Balthazar, but I don't hear it. I'm distracted as his voice echoes in my mind, but his mouth doesn't move.

Play the part, Sloane. You're a perfect mute.

I jolt in surprise at the sudden intrusion to my mind and attempt to yank my hand from his again. *You can speak telepathically?* I ask in surprise, my anger disappearing in an instant.

He outwardly replies to whatever Lord Carmilla has said, but keeps his entire attention locked onto me. His smirk turns mischievous as he plays with my fingers. *As a devil what can't I do?* He arrogantly asks.

His conceit brings back my anger. He acts as though he's a god, but as far as I know, gods don't play by a set of rules. Gods can bend the rules as they please, but this asshole will literally die if he doesn't fulfill his contract.

A cocky smirk spreads across my mouth as I know I've got him.

Apparently, you can't break a contract without dying in the process.

His silence tastes so sweet.

Balthazar stares at me for a long, hard moment as his jaw works back and forth. There's emotion swirling in his gaze that I can't decipher. His eyes narrow, but I don't know what that means. He doesn't look outright angry; maybe he's thinking of a snarky reply?

The devils continue talking in the room, but I'm not listening. I can tell neither is Balthazar. It's the way his eyes zero in on me with that unknown emotion that gives his lack of attention away. He's too focused on me to pay attention to anything else.

Balthazar shifts forward in his seat. My breath hitches in my throat as he leans into me. I remain still, not pulling away, too curious about what he's going to do.

His lips caress my ear as he speaks in a low, even tone, "Watch your pretty little mouth."

My stomach flips as he pulls away, his cheek grazing against my own. That smug look is back on his face, like he believes he's got me. Does he seriously think telling me to watch my *pretty* little mouth is going to shut me up? Sure, I can't deny the little tingle it gave me, but that's nothing I can't ignore or push through. Two can play this dumb game and I'm determined to win.

I lean slightly forward as I lock gazes with him and trail a finger up brazenly his sternum. "You think my mouth is pretty?" I ask as coyly as I can.

He chuckles lightly as he pinches my inner thigh. "For Ephirian swine."

Again with that insult. He probably thinks he's complimenting me since he's using the fancier term for pig. Except it's not a compliment. It's an insult and I instantly see red. My hand is around his throat before I've realized what I've done and he leers at me in such a way that I know immediately I've lost whatever game we're playing at.

"My love, as much as I enjoy your voracious sex drive," he says loudly enough for the entire room to hear, "Daddy's got to work now. Try to keep yourself entertained. If you're good, I promise to reward you."

My face immediately flushes a deep tomato red. I can tell how red I am by how hot it feels, how it spreads down my neck to my chest and flushes my ears. *I want to kill him.* He's made a mockery of me. *I want to kill him.* He treats me like I'm a child attempting to play against an adult. *I want to* kill *him.* My fingers squeeze tighter around his throat as a dark scowl appears on my face. I lean forward so our faces are an inch apart. I hold his gaze firmly as I speak with venom in my words.

"I wish..."

VII

HIS EYES FLICKER as the air electrifies around us.

Then, without warning, he snaps his fingers and we're transported out of the room. We move through that horrendous sludge–like atmosphere before it disappears. My hand remains tightly around his throat, but I'm not sitting anymore. I'm standing. The heels I wear give me some height, but he's still taller than me. He's glaring down at me as his eyes shift red.

"You finish that sentence and I'll make you regret it," he threatens.

"I doubt that if you're dead," I spit out as my fingers dig into his throat.

He steps to me, causing the lower halves of our bodies to touch. I grip his neck as hard as I can, but he appears unfazed.

"Do it," he encourages me. "Do it and find out how much I'm not bluffing."

"I wish..."

My heart pounds away inside my chest while simultaneously it feels like a category five hurricane rampages my stomach. Am I really going to wish him dead?

The air becomes electric again and I venture to guess it has to do with my intent on making a wish. I'm not imagining the electricity in the air; actual magic swarms around us. All I have to do is speak the words. *"I wish you die right here, right now."* But then my wish would be complete. I would spend the next seven years legally dead with no home, no access to money, and no way to interact with my family and friends only to end up dead in Hell. *With him.* The whole point of what I'm trying to do is find a way out of my deal, not complete it.

"I wish..." I repeat as I hold his gaze while my resolve starts to crack.

He doesn't shy away from my challenge. His eyes fade back to their black and red flecked look. The simple act distracts me. The changing colors of his eyes must be associated with his mood. I assume since they're back to normal, it must mean he's not angry anymore.

I'm proven right moments later as his face turns smug. Irritation zings down my spine as I glare at him. I want to wipe that stupid smirk off his face. I have the power to do it. I just need to speak the words and I'll never see him or his stupid smug ass face again.

"You wish what?" He asks as he juts his head in my direction.

My fingernails dig crescent shaped moons in his throat. He smiles even wider. Like he's *enjoying* this. *Come on, just do it, Sloane. Kill him.* It would be so easy. I wouldn't even have to lift a single finger.

Yet as I stand there, urging the words to leave my mouth, I realize I can't do it. Not because I don't want to, but because my end goal is more important than satisfying the need to prove him wrong about me.

With a huff of indignation, I shout, "I hate you!"

I shove him just as his boisterous laughter fills the air. A split second later, he reaches for me, pulling me flush against him. His laughter dies down but it's impossible not to see how pleased he is by the outcome. A scowl forms on my face as I glare up at him. I genuinely hate him.

"It appears we're at a standstill," he all but purrs as he grabs my waist firmly.

He holds me securely against him, a rock hard body beneath my softer one. I can't ignore the magnetic pull towards him nor the innate thought that sex with him would probably be life changing. Hate fucks are difficult to top, but I can't cloud my judgment like that. He's my enemy, the bane of my existence, the reason for why I'm trying to reclaim my soul in the first place. If I give him that part of me, it will feel too much like admitting he's won despite no romantic feelings being involved.

"Let me go," I demand as I tug against him.

"Unlikely," he replies.

I try yanking myself free, but he's too strong. "Don't test me, Balthazar. I *will* wish you dead."

"Then do it," he urges as his tone shifts to something carnal. "Do it before I'm tempted to act on my desires."

My body seizes up at his proclamation. I know exactly what he means by desires. That same wretched desire courses through me. I'm helpless against a physical response I have no control over. He may as well be emitting pheromones meant to entice me. My back goes rigid. He's the devil. He possesses magic that would allow him to do exactly that.

My fingers curl into my palms, the nails digging into my skin as I glare at him. I'm done with being controlled against my will. It's *my* choice to feel desire or not. He has no right forcing me to want him.

He must sense my sudden change because his grip on my waist tightens. His thumb grazes against my bare skin, sending tingles darting down to my nether regions.

"Stop it," I order as I push against him but he doesn't budge. I try another tactic. "Is it really that fun forcing someone against their will?"

His nose ghosts against mine but he pulls away to stare down at me with hooded black and red eyes. "I have no intention of forcing you against your will, Sloane."

"You're already doing it," I hiss as my hand presses against his chest to create more space. "You're using magic to make me feel this way."

His eyebrow cocks up as a smirk slips onto his lips. "Do tell me what it is I'm making you feel."

A shiver zings down my spine as he languidly trails a finger up my back.

My body aches in his hold. It craves the passion burning within his gaze. It's been too long since I've been touched and I go wet at the thought of letting him have his way. Something about the look in his eyes promises pleasure beyond my understanding.

I nearly give in; throw caution to the wind and consent to having sex with the devil. But I can't. I won't. My pride and dignity are worth more than mere physical pleasure. I will not engage with the enemy even as my body calls to him.

After all, it was my desire for sex that got me into this mess in the first place.

"Sloane," he whispers as he dips his head towards my ear. My name is a delicious sin upon his lips. "I will ravage you wholly until you're unable to possess even a single thought."

I swallow thickly, my knees threatening to buckle. My hands shift up to his shoulders as I grip them to help keep me steady.

"I don't consent to you using magic on me like this," I state despite my wavering voice.

Thankfully, my pride is more stubborn than anything else. I'll fight his magic tooth and nail. It won't be an easy win for him.

His lips graze my ear as he whispers huskily, "No magic. I want you free and willing."

A sharp gasp is my response as my fingers tighten around his shoulders. His hand around my waist plays with the hem of my skirt while the other hand grips me tightly around my side. His nose ghosts down my neck before his teeth clamp down on the flesh between my neck and shoulder. The tiniest bit of pain sparks to life and yet, instead of instilling panic and fear, I crave *more* of him. I'm practically dripping and throbbing for him. No one's ever treated me so possessively before. I never thought I'd want it, but here I am, nearly putty in his hands.

His lips trail up my neck to my ear. His words a delicious threat as he growls darkly, "You'll break, Sloane. I promise you that."

A tremble wracks through me, nearly causing me to throw caution to the wind, but in my small moment of hesitation, Balthazar steps back. Cold air swoops in between us, eliciting goosebumps along my bare skin. His eyes devour me – devours all there is to see, immodest bra and all.

He hooks a finger through the bottom band of my bra and gives a rough tug. I stumble into him, a slight gasp falling out of my mouth as our eyes remain locked. His lips pull back in a wicked smile, one that promises me absolute euphoria should I cave in to our mutual desires.

"I look forward to our battle," he states in a gravelly voice.

He's made the assumption he's going to win and I don't blame him one iota. This man – no, this *devil* – oozes pleasure only meant to be felt by the gods. Yet, he's willing to share it with me, a lowly Ephirian swine.

Swine. The word snaps me out of my stupor. My body cools down as anger simmers beneath the surface. Balthazar is no friend of mine. I'd be a fool to believe otherwise. I have to fight him; my soul and life are on the line.

I lean up as tall as I can, a glare settling on my face as I state in a low, threatening voice, "I'll be dead before I ever let you win."

His smirk deepens, like he's happy with my stubborn resistance. He pushes a strand of hair behind my ear. "I don't count on it."

Before I can retaliate, he snaps his fingers and disappears out of sight. For a split second, I almost call him back for leaving me alone. Wherever he goes, *I* go. But space is needed. Who knows what would happen if we spend just thirty more seconds in each other's presence? I can use this alone time to take a cold shower.

"Damnit," I groan as I remember there's no home for me to shower in.

I glance around my surroundings. The lights are off but I can tell I'm in a building. It's relatively cold too. A good sign. It means there's electricity as well as air conditioning. If I can find a light switch, I can figure out what kind of building he left me in. *Please don't be some shady business or warehouse.*

I continue to look around. Despite how dark it is outside, there's a heavy amount of light pollution filtering in. I must be in a city. Relief washes through me. Better a city than in the middle of nowhere.

It takes far too long to locate a light switch, but eventually, the lights turn on, high and bright. I squint at the assault before my eyes slowly adjust. As soon as I'm able to look around the room, my jaw drops open in utter shock.

A vague familiarity overcomes me as I scan the fully furnished luxury apartment. Slowly, I walk through it as I admire the stylish decor. As I enter the dining room, the reason for the familiarity slams into me.

Oh my god. I've seen this apartment before. It's publicly listed for sale in the Boston area. I've spent countless hours looking at this multi–million dollar condo, daydreaming of winning the lottery and owning such an excessive, beautiful place. It was my happy place to escape to while pretending to work.

Floor to ceiling windows bring in plenty of natural light during the day. It's elegant and classy as if it were staged for a magazine shoot. Artwork hangs on the walls; modern chandeliers add an element of coziness; beautiful area rugs pull the rooms together. It's a stunning apartment. One I have zero business being inside. Why did Balthazar leave me here?

Eventually, I find my way to the sizable kitchen. A moment of hesitation holds me back before I push forward to the fridge. My heels clack against the floor, echoing in the large condo. I open the fridge door and am hit with a blast of cold air. Thankfully, the refrigerator is stocked full. I grab the first glass Tupperware, pop open the lid, and approve of the contents inside.

As the contents warm in the microwave, I grab a bottle of wine from the wine rack. I don't bother with a glass. Not after the day I've had. It's a straight from the bottle kind of night.

I settle at the kitchen island when everything is ready. Just as I take the first bite of food, a cell phone magically appears, rattling against the countertop. Curiously, I grab the device. The screen lights up and the face ID recognizes me. The phone immediately unlocks and I instantly recognize the home screen. Balthazar has given me my actual phone.

My eyes linger on the many text notifications. My finger hovers above the icon but I don't have the strength to look at them yet. They're probably silly little messages; texts of videos and inside jokes. Not being able to respond to them, to send emojis, and tell them I love them is too difficult right now. Instead, I pull up social media and participate in some good old fashion doom scrolling.

My heart skips a beat when one of Ella's posts comes across my For You. It's a newer one; one I haven't seen.

She's putting Chad Dunner on blast, accusing him of my murder. Our mutual friends have liked and commented on her post. I can't help but dig a little deeper into Ella's most recent posts and see that Chad is a suspect in the investigation. Police were able to get records of our last exchange on the dating app. Ella sounds confident Chad will be prosecuted and sent to jail.

My lips pull downward as I glance through her posts. If I didn't know about the devil, I would assume Chad would be going to jail too. But it's not that simple. Chad sold his *soul* to have me killed. Having him sentenced to jail might be a lot harder than the evidence suggests.

There are several unread DMs and I finally muster up the courage to check them out. Ella sent me too many messages to count. My other friends sent multiple messages as well. Questions of *are you ok? Please respond as soon as you see this. Please let us know you're safe.*

My stomach drops as the desperate messages morph into sad goodbyes and apologies. A lump lodges itself in my throat as my vision blurs. I've lost my appetite.

Inhaling a shaky breath, I dare to check the text messages. Everyone I knew was trying to get a hold of me, desperate to know I was safe and alright only to find out I was dead. It's difficult to stomach.

My parents' last text message comes on the screen and I can't hold back the sob that tears through me, vicious and unforgiving.

> We're sorry we couldn't protect you. We love you forever.

My poor parents. I can't imagine what it's like to think their only child is dead. But I'm *not.* I'm alive. I'm unharmed. They deserve to know the truth. No matter how insane it sounds, no matter how improbable devils being real is, my parents *deserve* to know.

> I'm alive. I can't talk right now or see you. It's too dangerous. BUT I'M ALIVE.

The harsh reality sinks in when the text never leaves the box. No blue bubble with a *Not Delivered* underneath it. Nothing happens when I tap the blue arrow. My message stays exactly where I typed it. *Damn Balthazar!* My family deserves to know I'm ok, that I'm alive, and breathing well. I hate that they're grieving me. It's not fair.

All at once, sobs explode from me, heartbroken and raw, as my head drops to my arms on the counter. I went on *one* bad date and now everyone I love is suffering because of it. My parents think they failed me, that there was something they could have done to have kept me safe. Their guilt and heartache is unwarranted. They don't know devils exist; how could they have saved me from pissing off an entitled man–child who had the devil in his back pocket? It's not their fault. I need them to know it's *not their fault*.

I cry until my eyes are red and puffy, until snot dribbles down my face, until my voice is hoarse. Languidly, I push off the stool and halfheartedly wash my face with cold water. My vision loses focus as the faucet's running water sends me into a trance. Hard determination bubbles its way up to the surface, boiling and unrelenting. *Fuck* Chad. *Fuck* Balthazar. I'm going to find a way out of this contract. I'm going to bury them both. I'm going to make them regret ever crossing me.

My resolve slides into place. My pity party is *over*. Those assholes are going to pay. Even if it requires my last dying breath.

VIII

I SPEND THE NEXT hour daydreaming about all the ways Chad and Balthazar can die. My revenge will not be for the weakhearted. They need to die befitting of the pain they caused my parents.

Eventually, exhaustion comes crashing down on me. Puffy, swollen eyes feel tender to the touch and can barely stay open. A good rest is what I need. Tomorrow, I can continue planning my revenge.

I lazily clean the kitchen, dumping my half–eaten food carelessly into the sink. I'm grateful I explored the apartment earlier; it doesn't take me much time to make it the bedroom despite the vastness of the place. I'm vaguely aware the place lacks any personal touches. No photos of family and friends, no college degrees or certificates hung on the walls, no little trinkets like a car key holder. Even the bathroom lacks personal touches. No toothbrushes, toothpaste, makeup, lotions.

Sleepily, I explore the walk–in closet and any drawers I can find. Unfortunately, I come up empty handed. No clothes to be found. I'm stuck in the outfit I was forced to wear in Hell. Frustrated by my lack of clothes, the only piece I remove is the chain bra before snuggling into bed. The pillow and mattress are like clouds; I drift off to sleep before I can think a single thought.

Someone tosses something onto my face, waking me from my slumber. Confused, I shove whatever it is off as my eyes blearily open.

"Wear those," Balthazar instructs.

My groggy, sleepy state fogs my mind as I prop up onto my elbow. My eyes glance down at the clothes strew on the floor. Dark blue skinny jeans, a crisp white blouse, and nude sandal pumps.

"Why?" I croak out as I rub the sleep from my eyes.

For as long as I can remember, waking up has always been a slow process. My parents, Ella, and any friends who really know me all know to wait at least an hour before engaging in a conversation with me. Not because I'm grumpy, but because I'm a little slow to connect the dots.

Case in point. Any hatred I possess towards the devil is slow to kick in so soon after waking up. My brain is stalling on the fact that he wants me dressed. Since he officially ruined my life, I don't see why there's any need for me to leave the bed. Ever.

Balthazar smirks as his eyes rake over me. "I have no complaints with what you're currently wearing. By all means, keep the outfit on if you prefer it."

My eyes drop down and I'm starkly reminded of the indecent outfit I'm wearing. It's difficult to ignore the stiff nipple peeking through a gap in the lace bra. The A/C in the apartment is *cold* and my boob is more than happy to let everyone know.

My fingers grip the sheet as I yank it up to cover my indecency. A glare settles on my face as my eyes connect with his smug ones.

"Asshole," I hiss out as I throw one of the many pillows at him.

He laughs and the sound is like a warm bath on a cold night. Within a split second, he moves. One moment, he's several feet from the bed; the next moment he has a hand on either side of my hips as he leers over me.

"You haven't seen asshole yet," he states, but he's smiling and there's mischief dancing in his eyes. "If you keep being a good girl, you won't ever see it."

"Fuck you," I spit out. "Why would I ever be good for you?"

He trails a finger up my forearm, his dark eyes bearing holes through the sheet covering me, and it ignites a fire of want inside me. He's purposeful in dragging his ice cold finger slowly up my arm; he's *teasing* me.

His teeth catch on his lower lip as his gaze raises to look me directly in the eyes. "The reward is worth it," he promises and my body shivers against my consent.

I hate that I throb for him, for his body on top of me, for him slamming mercilessly into me, for his breathy moans to fill my ears. I can't understand it. How can I want something so intensely when my personal feelings and opinion of him are so negative?

My desire is strictly carnal. It's feral, uninhibited, so completely unlike me that it *has* to be his influence. Last night he promised no tricks but he's the literal devil. Tricks are his foreplay. He's doing something to me. He has to be. I'm not stupid enough to purposely lust after the devil.

"Stop it," I order darkly, the sheet balled tightly in my hands.

"Stop what?"

"I know what you're doing," I hiss as I lean towards him and instantly catch a whiff of the smokey scent that follows him wherever he goes. "You're tricking my body into wanting you."

He moves in a blink of an eye, his teeth catching on the flesh he bit last night. My breath hitches in my throat as pain mixes with pleasure. *Why* is this such a turn on? *Because of him. He's forcing me to feel this way.*

"You're wrong," he growls against my throbbing bite mark. "Your body is acting on its own accord."

"You lie," I whisper, but my words are firm. "You're using magic."

He drags his mouth up the column of my throat before he latches on to the junction where my neck and jaw meet. He sucks it hard for a moment before ghosting his lips against my cheeks, then down towards my lips.

"I have no use for magic when you respond so eagerly, Sloane," he murmurs against my mouth.

My body is on fire, craving his touch. All I have to do is move a mere *smidgen* and our lips would be pressed together. All bets would be off.

He's a tantalizing drug I want to inject. Five months is too long to go without the touch of another, but I have to remind myself that five months without sex is the whole reason why I met Chad in the first place. It's the reason why Balthazar showed up in my life to kill me and why I sold my soul. No matter how badly my body craves him, I *won't* give in.

My family and friends may not be able to see me, but other people can. I can go find someone else to sleep with. It doesn't have to be Balthazar.

"I hate you," I declare as I give him a hard shove.

I know if he wanted to resist it he could, but he doesn't. He allows me to push him away, even despite the small snarl of protest that falls out of his sinful mouth. Balthazar rises from the bed, a hand running through his hair as his eyes glance about the room. It looks like he's trying to compose himself, like he's just as bothered by the lust induced trance that holds me. Good. I'm glad to see him unnerved. It's the least he deserves.

His gaze eventually settles on the clothes on the floor.

"Get changed," he orders. "We have business to attend to."

"Get out of my room first."

He flashes me a smirk. "You mean my room. If you want privacy–"

"Get. The fuck. Out."

He grins even larger but offers a half bow before walking out the room. Spite has me laying back down on the bed with my phone in hand. I don't want him to be under the impression I'll jump whenever he tells me to. I'll waste some time scrolling through social media. I may not be able to like any posts due to Balthazar's magic, but I can at least enjoy the simple things in life before dealing with whatever Balthazar wants to do today.

Roughly fifteen minutes into my scrolling, I stumble upon a viral video discussing *my* murder. Hearing my name out of a complete stranger's mouth is jarring. I immediately scroll away but as the seconds tick by, morbid curiosity gets the better of me. How exactly did I die?

The creator spares no detail of what's happened so far. The story goes as follows: Saturday night I went on a date with Chad. That same night, I allegedly made a fake dating profile on him, but police haven't looked into it to confirm. That following Wednesday, Chad threatens me after I refuse to delete the fake profile. Not even eight hours later, I go missing. Twelve hours after that, they find my body in *eight* different dumpsters.

"The asshole cut me up?" I practically scream as the creator continues on breaking down my story.

They explain that my roommate quickly handed my phone over to the police for their investigation. That's how the police were able to not only discover the messages between me and Chad but also find their prime suspect. Someone leaked actual screenshots of our interaction (I suspect it was Ella since she knows my phone's passcode – you go girl!) and it doesn't look good for Chad.

"Good," I mumble to the empty bedroom.

The creator states the police haven't made any official arrets yet, but they're said to be working diligently on finding my murderer and bringing that person to justice.

A quick glance through the comment sections tells me everyone is pretty confident Chad did it. A smile spreads across my lips as I read comment after comment.

I guess Chad didn't properly think his deal through with the devil. He sold his soul to have me murdered, but he didn't think about them linking him to the case. He probably assumed a supernatural death couldn't be traced back to him.

My smile deepens. Even if they clear him of any charges, the accusations are going to follow him for the rest of his life. Bastard reaps what he sows.

I continue scrolling for a few more minutes before deciding it's time to get ready for the day. I skip washing my hair, making my shower pretty quick. While wrapped in a bath towel after the shower, I style my hair into a sleek high ponytail. The bathroom was practically empty last night, but today, it's fully stocked. Every type of makeup I might possibly need lines the counter.

My eyebrows scrunch together as I pick up and inspect a few bottles. Maybe they were here last night and I was just too tired to notice. I decide not to question it.

There's a brief moment I contemplate not putting any makeup on today but decide against it. My life may be in the shitter but that doesn't mean I have to look like it is.

I waste no time as I apply foundation, contour, highlight, blush, blue ombre eyeshadow, and fake lashes. The look is finished with a cute, subtle pink lipstick that's sealed with clear lip gloss.

Once I've completed my makeup, I dress in the simple clothes Balthazar has given me. I French tuck the white blouse and roll up the sleeves three–quarters of the way before sliding into the nude pumps. I inspect myself in the tall mirror in the bedroom, happy to see I look like my normal self, before walking out to the main area of the apartment.

Balthazar lounges on the large sectional while the news plays on a TV that drops down from the ceiling. He lounges like he owns the place, but due to my constant stalking of the condo, I'm under the impression it's up for sale.

"Do you own the apartment or are you squatting?" I ask as I glance out of the floor to ceiling windows.

It's a beautiful day. Blue skies, fluffy white clouds, bright sun filtering into the room. Honestly, I'd love to go sit outside a nice café and enjoy a slow morning.

"What do you think?" he asks lazily from his spot on the couch.

"Squatting," I answer without missing a beat.

He laughs lightly but doesn't answer my question.

"Chad Dunner is still under investigation for the murder of Sloane Kensington," the TV declares.

I whirl around at the sound of my name to see Boston news reporters discussing my case. Quietly, I approach the edge of the sectional and stop just beside Balthazar's left shoulder. He continues to watch the report, unbothered by how close I stand next to him.

"Chad's an idiot," I state as my arms cross over my chest. "They're going to put him in jail for killing me."

"Chad may be an idiot," Balthazar agrees before continuing, "but they will not sentence him to jail. Instead, your death is going to catapult him into stardom."

"What?"

"He is to be unjustly crucified by the public before they find the real killer whereupon he will create a podcast to discuss the hardships he faced during this time. He'll receive lucrative deals to appear on talk shows and own a popular YouTube channel. He was very thorough with his wish."

What in the hell? That sounds like a *list* and not one singular wish. How is Chad getting away with it?

I can't bite back the anger as I say, "I thought we were granted only one wish. Why does he get so many?"

"He only had one wish, the same as you. His stipulation for gaining wealth had to be directly linked to your death. If I didn't deliver on that, the wish would remain unfulfilled."

My mouth drops open as my brain stalls out for a moment. I'm genuinely shocked. I can't believe Chad's using *my death* to make himself rich. *That asshole!*

"I'm going to kill him," I grit out.

"*That* I can't allow," Balthazar states with no room for argument. "He will die in seven years, but only *after* his wish has been fulfilled."

"So, you're going to protect him despite everything?"

I hate how shrill my voice sounds. Especially at how it echoes through the large condo and how little it seems to bother Balthazar.

"Sloane, his soul was purchased with very clear instructions," he answers as he finally slides his gaze over to mine. There's no sympathy in those red flecked pitch black irises, no amusement or mirth, just cold, hard indifference. "If I go against them, the contract will be viewed as void and my life will be forfeited."

"This is so stupid," I shout as my hands slam into the back of the sofa. "You're the devil! You have *powers*! How are you not able to just do whatever the hell you want?"

"If devils went around purchasing souls and never upheld their end of the deal, do you honestly believe humans would keep selling their souls to devils?"

"Yes! Because nobody even believes you guys exist!"

He slowly rises from the couch as he slides his hands into his fitted chinos. He has on a tight, black henley shirt that does nothing to hide the ripples of his muscles. His hair is perfectly styled with the long hair on top pushed back with just enough gel to hold the shape, but it looks disheveled. Stylishly disheveled. The way male celebrities style their hair when they want to have some sex appeal. Balthazar's hair perfectly accentuates the black horns protruding out the side of his scalp. His whole demeanor screams pleasure inducing sex and my jaw clenches. Honestly, it's ridiculous how attractive he is.

"Sloane, that logic makes absolutely no sense," he says condescendingly. He lets his voice show how idiotic he thinks I am. "Why would humans continue to sell their souls if they don't believe in devils?"

"A moment of weakness," I answer like he's the dumbest person I know. Two can play that game. "When I'm waiting for the crosswalk to change, I beg to a god I don't even believe in. Obviously, you would catch people in a moment of rage or despair and when they're making their prayer to God, your sorry ass shows up instead."

There's a brief moment of silence before he chuckles, deep and low. The delectable sound fills me up like rich wine. His eyes crinkle around the edges as his obvious amusement unfortunately fills me with pride. *Come on, Sloane. Seriously? Who cares if the devil thinks you're funny? He wanted to* kill *you just a few nights ago.* Still, it feels like a win, no matter how small.

"That's surprisingly well thought out," he muses, interrupting my thoughts. "Your cleverness keeps amazing me, but unfortunately, you're incorrect. Most of the soul buying business is through word of mouth. Chad's college roommate sold his soul for an app he could sell for over a billion dollars. He told Chad about his deal after he became rich.

"Chad's roommate found out about selling souls during an internship at Goldman Sachs. He went golfing with a gentleman who sold his soul and told him about the process. You get the gist of it.

"If devils don't uphold their end of the bargain, no one will share the information with their nearest and dearest friends. That first year after a human sells their soul is critical. If devils flake on granting wishes, all those future customers are lost."

My fingers curl into my palms as my jaw clenches and unclenches in anger. This is so stupid. So, because Chad might recruit other potential clients, Balthazar *has* to grant his wish or his life is over? That's so dumb.

"I seriously can't believe this," I say, my arms flailing as my anger animates my body to life. "Chad's the asshole, but you have to do what he says because somebody says so? Where's your sense of empathy? Don't you ever want to help out the underdog?"

It's a shameless, desperate attempt at getting Balthazar on my side. I don't know why I bother. He's shown me zero mercy since meeting me. Why would he start now?

"Sloane, I *am* the underdog." His face pulls into a sneer so dark it sends a chill running down my spine. The image of his melting face flashes through my mind and my fear flares to life. He's no longer the playful devil he's been pretending to be. He's vicious and would kill me if only given the chance to. "You want help? *Help yourself.*"

A moment later, the sneer disappears from his face as if it was never there to begin with. He shifts away from the couch, walking around it towards me. Except *walk* doesn't truly describe the way he moves.

His gaze drifts down then up my body and my heart beats wildly in my chest as I struggle to reign in my fear. Panther flashes through my mind. He slinks towards me like I'm precious prey he can't afford to lose. A starving, desperate panther looking at me with cold, calculating eyes. And I was stupid enough to threaten his life last night.

"We have business to attend to," he states casually as he looks me in the eyes and frowns. "You should have gone with a fire theme. What are people going to think when the devil shows up with a water goddess?"

My face pinches together in confusion because I have no idea what he's talking about, but I say the first thing that comes to mind. "That opposites attract?"

"Always so clever," he states, a small grin on his face.

He reaches out and grabs hold of my hand. His touch is freezing, colder than ice. I attempt to recoil from the harsh contact, but he holds my hand firmly. Why are his hands always so cold when the rest of him is on fire? Does he have a circulation issue? Couldn't he just fix it with a bit of magic?

My thoughts are interrupted when Balthazar snaps his fingers. That brutal pressure I'm starting to get used to weighs down on me in all directions. When it feels like my head is about to pop, the pressure disappears. My hands fly up to my temples as I try to ease the lingering pain while my gaze wanders around the room.

It's a swanky office. An unnecessarily large and lamely decorated office. Too many self–serving awards and certifications adorn the wall. And weird art. As my eyes shift towards the desk, I see we aren't alone.

A man with rosy cheeks and ivory skin who looks to be in his late forties or perhaps early fifties, stands behind his desk with his hand gripping the back of his plush leather chair. His brown hair has been gelled and combed, he wears a three piece suit that stretches over his noticeable belly, and he's about the same height that I am. There's nothing outwardly special about him, but his office says it all. Wealthy. Successful. Asshole.

"Mr. Johnathon Thomson, what a pleasure to make your acquaintance," Balthazar greets him in a liquid voice.

Balthazar approaches the desk before elegantly sitting himself down in one of the guest chairs. He lets his arms very loudly plop down on the armrests. I stand awkwardly in my spot because I haven't the slightest clue what the hell is going on. Should I sit down next to Balthazar? Continue to stand here awkwardly? My indecision draws Johnathon's attention.

"Who is she?" he asks and his voice is tight.

It's then that I notice a little bit of sweat dribble down the side of his face and how clipped his breathing is. He's clearly anxious, and to be fair, so would I be if the devil just popped in at my office.

"Never mind her," Balthazar says from his seated position. His back is facing me, making it impossible to see what type of expression he wears on his face. "What I want to talk about is *you*. It is my understanding that good old Jeremy informed you about who I am. Let's not waste my time and get down to business. What is it that you want?"

Johnathon's eyes remain glued to me. I can't help myself as my hand bends at the wrist to give a short sort of wave. A tiny smile, full of awkwardness, graces my lips. Hopefully that'll ease some of his worries. It's a bit annoying to have him staring so hard at me.

He swallows rather loudly as his eyes dart to Balthazar, then back to me.

"Is she like you?" he asks. "I don't see any horns on her."

"I said never mind her," Balthazar repeats in a threatening tone.

Balthazar lifts his arm in the air and aggressively swings it like he's trying to swat a bug away. Nothing happens, but Johnathon's eyes go wide before he looks around the room. His tongue darts out as he licks his lips before his eyes settle on Balthazar.

"S–so you really are the devil," he says more to himself than anyone else.

"Indeed I am. Let us discuss business."

"Of–of course."

Johnathon quickly pulls out his chair and lands in it with a loud thud. The wheels roll against what sounds like plastic as he scoots himself into his desk and plants his palms down on the surface.

"I'm going bankrupt," Johnathon dives right in. "The business isn't doing well. My wife and kids don't know, but we're days away from having our home seized. We'll have to pull the kids out of school and put them through the public system. We'll lose all our friends and connections. We'll become social pariahs."

"There are worse things than that," I state in clear annoyance. "Like having someone wish you dead."

Balthazar huffs out a quiet chuckle, but otherwise says nothing. Johnathon doesn't react at all, like I'm not even there.

"Lauren will stick by me at first, but if I don't fix this quickly, she'll serve me divorce papers within six months. She expects to have a particular lifestyle and if I can't provide that, she'll find it elsewhere. She's very beautiful. Any man would be lucky to have her."

"Sure, but it'll cost that lucky man a million dollars a year," I say with a roll of my eyes.

Balthazar clears his throat to hide his laugh and he shifts in his seat. Again, Johnathon reacts as though I'm not there.

"Jeremy said you grant wishes so I–"

"I grant one wish in exchange for your soul," Balthazar interrupts him, his voice deadly serious. "No 'I said this but I meant that' exchanges. No 'you didn't give me what I wished for' refunds. No ten day free trial. You tell me your wish, I grant it the way I hear it, and I take your soul for safe keeping. Seven years to the date, you'll simply stop living. Do we have a deal?"

Johnathon breathes very heavily as he swallows again. More sweat dribbles down the side of his face as his fingers curl and uncurl against the desk.

"W—will it hurt?"

"You have to be more specific than that, Johnathon. There are a number of things that will hurt."

"When you collect my soul will it hurt?"

"Oh Johnathon," Balthazar says his name in a sickeningly sweet tone. The kind of tone that lets people know they're clearly being played with, but they have no way of protecting themselves against it. "All good things in life hurt, don't they? It hurts you every time you have to pay off Lauren's enormous credit card bills. It hurts you every time you submit payment for your children's private education even though you're convinced they're dumb as bricks. It hurts you to kiss Tom's ass and make him happy every week even though he's a royal dick. But the larger picture? That life you lead? It makes it all worth it, doesn't it?"

"Y—yeah," he stutters, but he doesn't look like he believes what he says.

In actuality, he looks like a deer caught in the headlights. Eyes wide, dripping in sweat, anxious and afraid. He's desperately clutching onto a vision, a dream, that's doing him more harm than good. It might be better for him in the long run to go bankrupt. It'll weed out the poison. Sure, it'll suck when Lauren leaves him, but maybe he'll find someone who actually loves him instead of his money.

"It's not worth it," I tell him, but Johnathon doesn't even glance my way.

Balthazar leans forward, resting his elbows on his thighs as his fingers link together. His face remains out of my view as he stares straight at Johnathon. The man gulps loudly.

"Think of all the lives you've destroyed," Balthazar says. "Did any of them ever recover? You framed a man for embezzlement. He still has five more years left on his prison sentence. What about the woman you fired after having your way with her? Do you know where she is now? I do. She's working at a call center that allows her to work from home and she limits her interactions with men as much as possible. Do you want to end up like them?"

My mouth drops open as I gape at the man sitting at the desk. He did what now? Rage explodes from me like a volcano as words pour out of me, hot and vile.

"You bastard," I yell as I advance towards him. "You piece of shit!"

Johnathon doesn't even flinch as I scream. Nor does he look my way when I round his desk. I reach out for him to gain his attention except my hand goes right through the chair when I try to yank him back from the desk.

"H—how do you know about that," Johnathon asks as I try grabbing him again.

My hand goes through him like he's air. I look over at Balthazar for an explanation but he's not paying attention to me. He's smirking a vicious smile, eyes gleaming as he stares at Johnathon.

"I'm the devil. What *don't* I know?"

IX

"I–I'LL DO IT," Johnathon stutters.

Balthazar's smirk deepens as he stands up from the chair. "That's the right choice, Johnathon. Now, tell me what your wish is."

"Twenty–one million dollars," he answers. "I want twenty–one million dollars."

"Not more?" Balthazar asks.

"Why would you ask him that?" I snap angrily at Balthazar. "He doesn't deserve the amount he's asked for! Don't give him *more!*"

Balthazar's gaze flickers over to me briefly, but otherwise he doesn't react.

"No, not more," Johnathan answers. "I only net three million a year. I'm not sure how I would explain more."

A slow smirk spreads across Balthazar's mouth as he stares at the man seated before him. "Very well. Twenty–one million dollars in exchange for your soul. That's the deal. Do you agree, Johnathon?"

"Yes, I agree."

Balthazar disappears in a blink of an eye only to reappear kissing Johnathon on the lips. The man's eyes go wide before he's pushing himself back from the desk, but by then, Balthazar has already moved. He's to the left of Johnathon and when Johnathon's chair comes to a stop, Balthazar shoves his hand right into Johnathon's chest.

A yell of complete and utter pain pierces the air. Empathetically, I wince. I know what that feels like. Originally, I thought I wouldn't wish that kind of pain on anyone, but after what I've heard Johnathon's done, I don't feel like it's enough. Balthazar catches my gaze as he rummages through Johnathon's chest.

"Funny, your soul is more slippery than usual."

Balthazar's lips pull into a handsome grin, one that's surprisingly not malicious or sarcastic. It's sincere and it's easy to see he's having fun. The smile reaches his eyes, crinkling around the edges. He's genuinely enjoying himself.

Johnathon wretches from the pain. A bout of sympathy blooms in my chest as I look down at Johnathon. His skin has gone ghostly pale. It's difficult not to feel sympathy when being confronted so directly by his torture. I remind myself he framed an innocent man and sexually assaulted a woman. He deserves this, but that doesn't mean it's easy to watch.

"Almost got it," Balthazar says, before yanking his arm out of Johnathon's chest.

A small, ping pong sized orb is pinched between his index finger and thumb. It shimmers in the office light as Balthazar holds it up. I note it's another white orb and not red like mine.

Balthazar studies it for a short moment before letting it drop into his palm, fingers encasing around it, and he gives his hand a quick shake. When he opens his hand, the orb is gone.

Johnathon's loud panting fills the room as his hand clutches his chest. Balthazar snaps his finger and smiles down at Johnathon. He looks like a cat staring at its prey, eager to play and torture it before it eats.

"Our deal has been fulfilled. Twenty–one million dollars has been deposited into your account ending in 1387. Seven years to the date, you will simply drop dead. Enjoy the rest of your life, Johnathon."

"Wait," he heaves out from his chair as he stares at Balthazar. "You deposited twenty–one million dollars into my account?"

"Yes, per our agreement."

"No! No, it was supposed to be twenty–one million dollars over a seven year period," Johnathon shouts as he somehow finds the strength to get to his feet. "Take it out! Do you know how much I'll be taxed on that? How am I going to explain to Lauren and the government where I got that much money? I only need three million a year!"

Balthazar glances at me and wiggles his eyebrows as he smirks. *He deposited the lump sum on purpose.* A light laugh tumbles out of my mouth as I hold his gaze. Balthazar's grin deepens before dropping from his face as his dual colored eyes connect with Johnathon's.

"I'm afraid those terms were not specified. You wished for twenty–one million dollars. It now sits in your bank account. Your wish has been fulfilled. Enjoy the remaining years of your life."

"No! You can't do this! I sold you my soul! You have to fix this!"

Balthazar walks around Johnathon's chair and gently takes my hand. His cold fingers thread through mine and he spares Johnathon one last look. No words are exchanged between the two of them as Balthazar calmly lifts his hand and snaps his fingers. This time, the transition isn't so dense. The pressure bears down on me and still hurts more than I'd like, but my head doesn't feel like it'll split open.

When we resurface, we're sitting at a two person table, in the sun, on an outside patio. My eyes dart around the area and the hairs along my arms rise up. The buildings, the cars, the décor… it's very European. The tables surrounding us are full and lively. It takes me a moment to make out the words being spoken and I realize they're not speaking English. They're speaking French. *Does that mean we're not in the States anymore?*

"Where are we?" I ask as my heart begins to thunder against my chest.

I'm not scared or excited. Perhaps a little worried? If he leaves me here, I'm royally screwed. I never contemplated the idea that he could cross continents. I suppose if I really thought on it, I assumed he was limited to the Americas.

My eyes flicker up to the sky. The sun blazes hot and bright, giving off midday vibes. It was barely nine in the morning when we met Johnathon. That much time couldn't have passed. If we really are in France, it's in my best interest not to tick Balthazar off. I have no passport, no form of identification, and the US Government thinks I'm *dead*. I'd have no way of getting back to America, so if he leaves me stranded here, I'm screwed.

"Paris," he answers lackadaisically.

Paris. He brought me to Paris. We're drinking coffee and eating pastries in *Paris*. I'll be truly screwed if he up and leaves, but strangely enough, I can't focus on that anymore. The reality is much more intoxicating than I anticipated.

I'm in Paris; a city I've always wanted to travel to but never had the chance in my twenty–six years. I have half a mind to thank him for my experience, but considering all that he's done to me, bringing me here is the least he could do.

My fingers curl around the handle of the ceramic mug as I inspect the pastries sitting in the three tier display on our table. Everything looks delicious. I'm vaguely aware of Balthazar as he sips his drink while idly watching our surroundings. People walk by our café's little patio. Judging by how many have their phones out to document their experience, I'd wager we're in a more touristy area.

I sip my drink and nearly moan at the rich flavors of my latte. If only there was a shop this good near my apartment. I'd be in heaven if I got to enjoy drinks like this every morning.

I grimace at the useless thought. What apartment? What heaven? I died, sold my soul, and am destined to go to Hell.

"Penny for your thoughts," Balthazar breaks the silence.

I glare at him over the lip of my mug. "My thoughts are worth more than a penny, *Lord* Balthazar."

I drawl his title, attempting to make it sound like an insult. I want to make him feel like a child *pretending* to be a Lord. The very least it'll do is show him how little I care for his reputation.

Instead of glaring, his smiles large and wide, his lips parting to expose the sharp canines of his upper teeth.

"You vex me, Ephirian swine," he admits as his nose scrunches despite his smile.

That stupid insult. I do my best to ignore it and concentrate on the fact that he's smiling after admitting I annoy him.

Quietly, I set my mug down on the table and tap my fingers against it. I shouldn't ask, I *really* shouldn't, but I'm too curious for my own good.

"Then why do you look so happy about it?"

"Because when you vex me, Sloane," he states calmly, but there's a twinkle in his eyes, "I want to devour you."

"Screw you," I reply as I sit as far back in my chair as humanly possible, angry at the heat filling my cheeks.

I don't create much distance between us from sitting back in my chair, but the act itself satisfies me. He probably doesn't mean a word he says. He's probably just saying stuff like that to get a reaction out of me.

Bitter resentment lingers on my tongue as I realize how easily he moves me across the board. I practically play into it too, but how can I not? He treats my life and situation so cavalier. Like I didn't unfairly die and lose everything I've ever loved. It's impossible not to react when he behaves the way he does.

"I know you're more sharp–witted than that," he replies before taking another sip of his drink. "Where's that fiery spirit we got to see with Mr. Jonathon Thomson?"

"He deserved to go bankrupt," I say as I cross my arms over my chest and glare at him. "Why did you grant him the wish?"

"Granting a wish is part of the bargain."

"Then why not pass on the deal?"

"Souls are currency, Sloane, and only a fool would willingly be poor."

"His soul can't be worth that much," I protest. "Not based off of what I know of him. You should've just let him go bankrupt. Instead, you helped him."

"Did I?"

My face twists into an expression that shows my exasperation. "Are you being serious right now? You gave him *twenty–one million dollars*. Obviously, he'll have a bit of trouble explaining where it came from and the taxes will be a pain but still. You basically threw him a rope tethered to a tree so he could climb out of his grave."

My arms remain crossed over my chest as my gaze shifts away from Balthazar to our surroundings. I must look like a child pouting after being told I can't have dessert before dinner, but I'm too angry to care. Balthazar doesn't care about the crimes Johnathon committed. He willingly helped Johnathon instead of helping the people who Johnathon screwed over. I'd ask him where his morality was, but it's pointless. Balthazar's a devil born in Hell. There's no such thing as morality to him, which makes everything suck that much more when someone with powers has the ability to help people in need but chooses *not* to.

"Mm, perhaps I did," Balthazar replies calmly, not at all sounding bothered by what I've said. "But I'm fairly certain the man he stole the money from will not be pleased about the turn of events. I suspect Johnathon won't make it past the end of this year."

"What are you talking about?" I ask, turning my attention back to him as I try to understand what he's saying, but none of it makes any sense.

Balthazar sips his drink as he watches a few people walk by us. He's taking his time, purposely choosing not to answer me immediately. Maybe it's a show of power or a reminder of how much I don't understand. Whatever it is, it's irritating the hell out of me. Is he going to make me repeat myself?

Finally, he speaks.

"Johnathon failed to specify where the money should come from. I had a little fun and took it from a very dangerous man who is currently vacationing in Dubai. His team will most likely notify him of the missing money in the next few hours. After that, I don't imagine Johnathon will live much longer. It's never a good idea to steal from a bad man."

"Doesn't that go against your agreement?" I ask, venom dripping from my voice.

He found a loophole in his deal with Johnathon so easily, but he couldn't do that with Chad's deal? Make it make sense. My anger has me practically leaping across the table to throttle him, but I settle for gripping my mug a little too tightly.

"I've been *begging* you to find some sort of loophole out of Chad's wish and all you've done is gone on and on about how important it is to fulfill a wish. Yet with Johnathon's wish you found a loophole right off the bat."

His eyes slide slowly over to mine. Balthazar regards me quietly for several prolonged seconds. The intensity of his gaze has me to fidgeting in my seat. His stare is stifling, as though it has the ability to remove all the oxygen around us.

"The less details there are to a wish, the less filling it requires," he states slowly. Like he's trying to explain a complex math problem to a child. I bite my tongue to hold back any frustrated words that might leave my mouth.

"Johnathon wished for twenty–one million dollars," he continues. "He didn't specify how he was to receive it or where it would come from or how much of it would be tax deductible. He merely wished for the money. I did my job and fulfilled it as he stated it.

"Chad Dunner, however, had a more detailed wish. He thought long and hard about it before he summoned me. I was handed a one page, single spaced, Times New Roman, eleven font document. He worded it quite perfectly, making everything on that page dwindle down to one singular wish. I wager when he combines his brute determination and his fancy education at Harvard, he is rather unstoppable.

"The irritating fact is if I do not follow Chad's wish to the T, it will remain unfulfilled and my life will be forfeited. For your own conscious, Miss Kensington, you should know Chad knew about the existence of devils long before you threw your drink in his face. You were merely the catalyst to him pulling the trigger."

My jaw works back and forth as I process what he's said. He's basically telling me that if a wish is worded correctly, a person can back the devil up into a tight spot. A wish that seems to be multiple wishes packed into one can be worded perfectly enough that it technically is only *one* wish. Who knew Chad was so smart?

Based on how Balthazar granted Johnathon's wish, I assume he prefers screwing people out of their wishes. It makes sense. He is the devil after all. And from what I've seen, he's not that much different from how devils are portrayed in the media.

What's confusing, though, is *why* he's telling me this. I haven't made my wish yet. He's giving me information that would put him at a disadvantage. Why? If I word my wish correctly, I could kill him *and* still get something more out of the deal. So why is Balthazar giving me this information when it gives me more leverage against him?

A knowing grin appears on his face as his finger trails around the lip of his mug. "Your wheels are turning, Miss Kensington. It appears I've given you much to think about."

There has to be some larger scheme that Balthazar's playing at. He's made it pretty clear how much he values his life, so he wouldn't willingly hand over information that might make it easier to kill him. Or maybe he knew I'd take the information with a heavy dose of suspicion and anticipates I'll waste more time trying to figure out his motive than figuring out how to properly word my wish. *I can't trust him*, I think sourly as I strum my fingers angrily against the tabletop.

His lips peel back into a larger smile, exposing those sharp canine teeth. "I imagine we'll have great fun together."

I frown at his words. It's impossible to think the devil's definition of fun and mine could ever intersect.

X

"EXPLAIN THE HOUSES to me," I demand after we've sat in a prolonged silence.

I've finished my latte and nibble on one of the many pastries residing at our table. I'm not surprised that the pastry is divine. Not too sweet or heavy and it melts in my mouth.

"You don't want to explore the city?" Balthazar asks, a teasing smirk on his face as he gazes out towards the bustling town where excitement *oozes* off the people.

I hesitate to answer because honestly, yes, I would love to explore Paris. I haven't had many opportunities to travel outside of the States. The only times I've left the country were to visit the neighboring ones during Spring Break. Canada and Mexico.

Europe seemed like a faraway dream for me. One that I'd achieve in my forties or fifties after I *maybe* settled down. I could never have anticipated how easily I'd get to Europe, that a simple snap of the devil's fingers could transport me anywhere on Earth.

Now that I'm here the itch to walk around the city, to take in the sights and smell of the place, is annoyingly incessant. I almost scratch that itch except I recognize Balthazar is using Paris as a ploy to not answer my demand.

"No, I don't," I regretfully sigh out as I sink further into the chair. Time to get comfortable. "I'd rather you give me information on the Houses."

"There's nothing to tell," Balthazar says in a bored tone as he snaps his fingers, eyes still lingering out towards the public and not on me.

My gaze darts down to the ceramic mug in front of me. My latte has been magically refilled. What a nifty little trick.

"That's a bullshit answer and you know it," I state right before biting into my third pastry.

He laughs loudly as his eyes slide over to mine. The smile is wide, boisterous, and a touch sincere. He's enjoying himself, enjoying my frustration, and I hate him for it. This isn't funny. Nothing about my situation or me is funny, but he can't seem to stop laughing around me.

"Tell me about the Houses," I demand again as my fingers curl tightly around my mug.

"Why do you want to know?"

I could lie, but it seems pointless too. Who cares if he knows the truth? It won't change anything.

"It might help me find a way out of this ordeal."

"You mean your bargain with me?"

"Yes."

His lips pull back in a wicked grin and he leans forward, placing his arms on the table. "I assure you it won't. Me and you? We're stuck together for all eternity."

"That might be true," I say, a slight frown marring my face. He's trying to throw me off my game, but I won't let him. "*I'll* decide what is or is not useful information to me. So... spill."

Balthazar's gaze softens the slightest bit before he leans back in his chair and heaves out a deep breath. Like he's saying with unspoken words that I'm no fun. *Good. I'm not here to be your entertainment.*

"It's all rather simple," he says, his deep voice sounding dull and listless. "House Primis was the first House formed, hence the name."

At the blatant look of confusion on my face, Balthazar rolls his eyes, but explains anyway.

"It's Latin for *first*. All the Houses have Latin names. I'd find it cliché if it weren't for the fact that Jeznians came before humans and their wretched Latin based faith."

I wrack my brain for the term Jeznians. He hasn't used that one specifically, but he's referred to Hell as Jeznia. He must mean the inhabitants of Hell came before humans. *Interesting.* Before I can ask him to expand on that, he rattles off the names of the seven Houses.

"House Vespertilio, the second House to be formed, is the House of Bats. House Anguis is the House of Snakes. House Felis is the House of Cats. House Lupus is the House of Wolves. House Aranea is the House of Spiders. The seventh House formed, House Scolopendra, is the House of Centipedes."

That's why devils, bats, snakes, cats, wolves, spiders, and centipedes are carved everywhere. It also makes it a lot easier to figure out who belongs to which House since their thrones have their representative carved on the back of them.

"Why is House Primis called House First but the others are named after creatures?"

"Honestly, I haven't the slightest clue nor do I care."

I frown as I glare at him. He's being difficult on purpose. He's already given me more information than he probably thinks I deserve. Still, it's not enough. I only have the names of the Houses and their mascot. That does absolutely nothing for me.

Balthazar smirks as he pops a grape into his mouth. "See? I told you it would be of no help to you."

"The seven Houses rule Hell together, but is there a hierarchy?" I ask as I ignore his statement. "House Primis came first, so does it have the most power?"

"It does, but not because it came first," he answers distantly as his eyes shift back towards the bustling tourists.

He doesn't expand on his answer and my irritation is about through the roof. He's testing all of my patience. I imagine he's doing it on purpose and is waiting for me to lose my composure. Which, to be honest, I'm pretty close to doing. I don't like being toyed with on a good day, never mind the fact that I'm dead to everyone who cares about me, I have no support system anymore, and it's all because of him. It's a miracle I'm not throwing the table over and throttling him.

My eyes slide shut as I inhale deeply. All those gentle parenting videos I've randomly seen recommend deep breathing to regulate emotions. I pray this works as I inhale deeply a second time for good measure.

"Why does House Primis have the most power?" My tone is clipped but I've managed to not lose my cool.

"Because it does," is all he says as his gaze continues watching the tourists.

"That isn't an answer," I shout and I'm half tempted to chuck a pastry at him. "Why are you being so unhelpful?"

"I've been plenty helpful, Sloane," he replies, voice low and steady. He keeps his eyes on the people walking past us and it makes his words sound even harsher as he speaks. "I've allowed you to sell your soul instead of killing you. I've entertained you by bringing you everywhere I go instead of putting you in your place. I've told you the names of the Houses when you have no right to know them."

His gaze slides back to mine and those black eyes are as cold as space. Warning bells go off inside my head at the cold, detached look within his gaze. I brace for whatever he's about to say.

"Simply because things are not going the way you want them to does not mean I've been unhelpful. You're rather spoiled and entitled, aren't you?"

My mind goes blank. He's made very valid points, much to my chagrin. I want to cry out, to remind him that he *ruined* my life by granting Chad's wish, but it's pointless. Balthazar isn't human. He's a goddamn *devil*. That means I can't appeal to his empathetic side. He doesn't have one. I've been forgetting that because of his humanoid appearance and I've been getting irritated at him for being incredibly difficult. Except, from *his* point of view, he's been rather lenient; more so than I deserve.

My teeth gnaw on my thumb nail as my mind rolls over information after information. I need to come at this from a different angle. One less *entitled* and *spoiled*. My jaw clenches and unclenches on my thumb nail as I stare at Balthazar, but not really *at* him. My gaze is focused on the middle of his tie as I think of a different way to get him to open up. What would provoke him? Not anger. Anger is bad. He'll melt off his human appearance again and probably maim me. Amusement seems to be the best bet, but I'm not sure how to do that on purpose.

I think back on everything I've been told and all that I've seen since meeting Balthazar. Suddenly, an idea pops into my head. If I ask questions at random, questions that have no rhyme or reason to them, maybe he'll be provoked into answering them to figure out where my train of thought is going.

"The Lord with the small horns, the horns that humans use for Halloween costumes and cosplays, is his House the second most powerful or the weakest?"

Balthazar regards me curiously for a few moments before asking a question of his own, "What's your logic for why his House would be the second most powerful?"

So not *the second most powerful House.*

"There's power in thoughts and intents, right?" I readily offer my answer. The more intrigued he is, the better it'll go for me, even if I already suspect the answer. "The general public associates his horns with *the* devil, not just a devil. His horns are everywhere on Earth. Stickers, costumes, logos. I thought maybe it gave him power of influence over humans or something. My first thought when I saw him was: is he the most powerful devil in the room or the most ridiculed?"

"You have such a peculiar, yet intelligent mind, Sloane."

"When you say it like that, it doesn't sound like a compliment," I gripe and this time I do toss a small pastry crumb his way in direction.

He chuckles as he wipes the crumb off his lap. "Lord Ruulin, unfortunately for him, is the weakest devil among the Lords. Therefore, House Scolopendra is the weakest House."

"Interesting that you still honor him with the title Lord."

"Mm," he hums. "A Lord is a Lord by no easy feat."

"But you introduced yourself as *heir* to House Primis," I state as I recall his angry introduction when he said he wouldn't take orders from *Ephirian swine.* "That means you were born into the role. How is that difficult? Isn't that just nepotism?"

He stares at me for a long time with no emotion on his face. I squirm in my seat at the intensity of his stare, but he continues to have no reaction. A solid minute passes before he finally speaks.

"That answer is for another time," is all he says.

My eyebrows furrow together in confusion. What does that mean? *Stop it. Don't push him on it. Refocus. You're talking about Houses.*

"Which House is the weakest House again?"

"House Scolopendra."

"... What is that in English again?"

"Centipedes," he answers before taking a sip of his drink.

"You said centipedes was also the last House formed, right?"

"Mhm."

"The bat house was formed second, right?"

"Mhm."

The bat house sat to Balthazar's left. It's hard to forget when the Lord stared at me with such open and clear disdain. I'm pretty sure she wanted me dead and the only reason why she didn't act on it is because a technicality allowed me there.

The centipede house isn't anywhere near Balthazar's throne. It's across the room. The only reason why I remember that is because the Lord's horns are just that memorable. I can't, however, remember the House to Balthazar's right.

"What's the third House that was formed?"

"Anguis." At my blank look, he offers with an eye roll, "Snakes."

That's right! Snakes sat to his right. So, by that logic, the second and third most powerful Houses are on either side of House Primis and the weakest Houses are farthest away. I don't know whether this new information will help me or if all I've done is just learn more about Hell.

I highly doubt I'll be able to ally myself with one of the Houses unless I have something in return to offer them. But what could that be? These are *Lords of Hell.* Things like money and fame probably mean nothing to them. That's the kind of stuff humans care about. What the hell do devils care about?

"That's enough conversation for now," Balthazar interrupts my thoughts right before taking a large sip of his drink. "We have business to attend to."

My eyebrows pinch together in confusion as I tilt my head sideways. "Business?"

A sinful smirk spreads across his plump lips. "Souls to purchase and lives to ruin."

XI

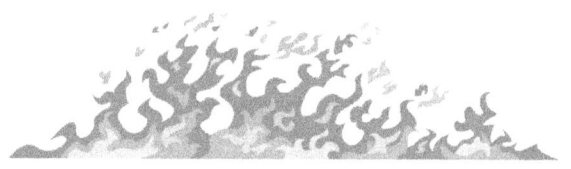

W E SPEND THE next three days meeting with men of varying ages and races who are desperate to either keep their wealth or have their lives propelled into wealth. Honestly, by the fifth man we've met, I can't help but roll my eyes and shake my head. It gets old real fast, yet Balthazar approaches each one as if he's hit a gold mine.

After the tenth deal I witness being made, I buckle down and study. I observe my enemy, looking for any weaknesses he might have. In my time of analyzing Balthazar, I notice his approach changes depending on the situation. If a man is losing his wealth and wishes to hold onto it, Balthazar approaches the man condescendingly, like he's dealing with a child. If his actions could speak, they would say *you're the idiot who lost your wealth, now* beg *me to let you keep it.*

When he's dealing with a man who's never had wealth but desperately wants it, Balthazar's voice loses its patronizing tone. Instead, it takes on a sultrier timbre. Even the way he moves is more seductive. My guess is it's because he's trying to persuade the man into giving up his soul for something he's never had. After all, it's much easier to fight for things that are in danger of being taken away than it is to give up something invaluable for an idea. Balthazar has to convince these men their wishes are worth it, that the outcome is worth losing their eternal souls over.

As I watch him throughout the three days, I conclude what Balthazar does is art. He approaches each new deal like a blank canvas. The words he uses are his paintbrush and the way he moves his body is the paint. He seamlessly puts them together to construct a beautiful piece of art that's too tempting *not* to purchase. By the end of Balthazar's presentation, none of the men hesitate to put their souls up for auction, if only to get a sweet glimpse of the painting Balthazar has constructed. I hate to admit it, but what he does *is* impressive. He must be Hell's number one soul snatcher.

I also realize how unique Chad's wish is. If the majority of Balthazar's days are like this, it's a rare experience for him to kill someone. Perhaps that's why he feels so compelled to grant Chad's wish to its fullest. No matter how eager he appears when talking to these men, Balthazar *has* to be bored with the same wishes day in and day out. Receiving Chad's wish must have felt like hitting the jackpot. It's a goddamn miracle I managed to prevent Balthazar from killing me.

"Check your account ending in 9245. You'll see the money has been deposited," Balthazar states as he finishes the ninth deal today.

Finally, I think as I push off the desk I'm leaning on only to gasp in shock at a surprise visitor. Every hair on my body stands up in alarm as I stare at the newcomer. I scan her up and down in a lame attempt at trying to figure out if she's friend or foe. Honestly, it's difficult to tell on appearances alone.

She's about my height, give or take an inch, with waist length box braids and gold jewelry clipped in the hair. She has soft, sepia brown skin with warm undertones, a diamond shaped face, sharp amber eyes, high cheekbones, and a rounded jaw. Her lips are painted black, there's a light dusting of rose blush on her cheeks, and black eyeshadow enhances her entrancing golden eyes.

She's dressed in form fitting black clothes that look like Under Armor. She wears black shoes with Velcro instead of laces. The rubber soles of the shoes oddly wrap around the heels and toes. Her hands are behind her back as she stands with a perfect posture.

All in all, even I can tell she's dressed for stealth, not combat, but her clothes don't fool me. She has the lean body of a gymnast but the stare of a killer. I shiver as we lock gazes. She's a lethal combination and we might be screwed if she's foe.

"Lord Balthazar," she speaks in a low, quiet voice because her mere presence speaks volumes enough. She extends her hand towards him and a folder blurs into view. "I've intercepted a deal."

Oh, thank God, I think to myself, grateful she's an ally. I would hate to get caught up between him and her. Though I have to wonder... if he dies, does that mean I die too?

Balthazar says nothing as he leaves the man, I believe his name is Oliver, trembling and spent on the floor after his soul extraction. I pay Oliver little attention as I watch Balthazar pluck the black folder from her hand. He flips it open, eyes scanning the paperwork. From where I stand, I can't see over his shoulder and have zero idea what the contents of the folder say. So, I turn my attention to the unnamed woman because she's more interesting than a sobbing, moaning Oliver.

Her amber, calculating gaze is already on me and a chill darts down my spine. There's no emotion on her face or in her eyes. Only cold detachment. She stares at me as if I'm a fly, but I can't tell whether I'm a fly minding my own business on the wall or I'm buzzing around her face, pestering her until she swats me into oblivion. All I know is I need to tread carefully around her.

While Balthazar may find my threats worthy of killing me over, he also doesn't shy away from letting me know he finds me entertaining. I highly doubt this woman would find anything I do even remotely amusing. She'd kill me first, then ask questions later.

I clutch my hands together in front of my waist as I pinch my lips together. I'll do my very best not to piss her off.

"Umbra, take Sloane back while I handle this. Then pay a visit to Ofello. It appears he's not upholding his end of our bargain."

She bows her head as her hands rest by her side. "Of course, Lord Balthazar."

He turns his attention to Oliver and offers him a sickening sweet smile. "Thank you for your business. I wish you all the best."

With a snap of his fingers, he disappears from the room. Oliver pushes himself to his feet, his chest heaving up and down as he looks between me and Umbra.

"M–my wish?" he asks.

"Granted," I say confidently as I nod my head at the cell phone on his desk. Based on how the past couple of days have gone, I know Balthazar would never leave a wish unfulfilled before leaving a room. "Check your accounts."

He lunges for his phone and signs in to multiple accounts before a whoosh of relief exhales from him. He slumps into his chair, clutching his phone to his chest, as his eyes slide shut and he begins to weep.

"Thank God. Oh, thank God."

"No, not God," I interject as a frown mars my face.

Why do we always give credit to God when a god is nowhere to be found? I suppose God might exist since Heaven and Hell exist, but it's very clear to me who actively participates in human lives and it *isn't* God. Credit should be given where it's deserved.

"God had nothing to do with this. You should be thanking the devil."

I don't hear his response because the cold fingers of Umbra wrap around my wrist before a black cloud envelops us. Fear immediately grips me as we're completely encased in black. It feels as cold as death.

Air whips wildly around us. I can't tell which way is up, down, right or left. It feels like we're tumbling through an infinite abyss. Something picks at my feet, climbing its way up my legs and I scream as I fight it off. It's slimy and cold but thankfully falls off with a rough kick. Umbra's cold fingers continue to grip my wrist, but I can't see her. I can't see anything, not even my other hand that I hold right in front of my face.

All too suddenly, the black cloud disappears and we're back in the apartment in Boston. It's a bit disorienting. My hand reaches out, grabbing hold of the back of the couch as the room sways. My heart hammers inside my chest but thankfully my breathing is mostly calm. I shift my attention over to Umbra as she stares at me with that unreadable, apathetic gaze.

The silence drags on. Awkward as it might be, it's even more terrifying when she looks at me like that. I open my mouth to thank her for bringing me back to the condo, but she speaks before I do.

"Do not underestimate Lord Balthazar," she says in a voice devoid of any emotion. "Devils often think they can get the better of him because he shows mercy. They think his heart makes him weak. The other Houses expect him to fail because of it, but they do not understand his heart is his driving force. They fail to remember that the heart never forgets. What they see as a weakness is Lord Balthazar's greatest strength."

I swallow thickly as I hold her gaze. I recognize the threat for what it is. *Don't think you, foolish girl, can toy or trick Lord Balthazar.* She's got me all wrong. It's not my intent to trick him. I only care about finding a way out of this stupid deal.

Still… her warning leaves me on edge.

"Why are you telling me this?" I ask. It goes against logic to reveal trade secrets, doesn't it? Why is she eagerly handing out this information?

Her gaze drops to the floor for a moment as she takes one tiny, miniscule step towards me. All the hairs on my body rise up as terror fills me to the brim. She instills more fear in me than I've felt these past few days hanging out with Balthazar. I need to be on guard around her.

"If you put our objective at risk because you think you can pull one over Lord Balthazar," she states as her eyes slowly rise up to mine. "I would advise you to think again."

Fuck. If I had any doubts she was threatening me, those doubts are out the window. She's made it loud and clear that if I attempt to screw over Balthazar, she'll return the favor tenfold.

For the first time since I've met him, I think I might have bitten off more than I can chew. Still, I can't give up just because I'm afraid or overwhelmed. This is my eternal life on the line. I'm not giving it up without a fight. I'll find a way out of this deal before it kills me. I have to.

"Duly noted," I tell her because in all actuality, I don't want to provoke her.

It's silent for almost ten seconds, yet Umbra doesn't make any indications that she'll be leaving any time soon. I could remain silent, as that's the easiest way not to get on her nerves, but the reason for her abrupt appearance nags at me.

I clear my throat as I ask as casually as I can, "The deal you intercepted for Balthazar... is it an important one?"

"All deals are important."

"Right."

A second, heavy silence falls between us. The urge to ask more questions threatens to overwhelm me, but I don't imagine I'll get anywhere with Umbra. She appears to have said all that she wants to and won't reveal any other information.

After the silence becomes too much to bear, I push off the couch and walk into the kitchen, more than unnerved when Umbra follows suit. I do my best to quell the fear that flashes down my spine as she stops at the kitchen island and rests her hands atop the marble while I open the fridge.

"Is there something I might help you with?" I ask and try my best to sound uncaring.

I don't want her to know how much she scares me. While Balthazar could easily kill me, I know he won't because if he does, he dies. Sure, he could cause me bodily harm, but most of the time he treats me with amusement.

Umbra is different... I have nothing to hold over her head. If she wants to kill me, she can. I don't know if her killing me would also kill Balthazar. He seemed unworried about Johnathon being murdered within the year despite his contract saying he gets seven years to enjoy his wish. Maybe if someone else unrelated to the contract kills the human, it won't kill the devil. It's a loophole I hadn't considered. Balthazar could have sent Umbra here with the intent to kill me because he's grown bored of having me around.

The thought turns my blood cold.

"The Lords say you wished Lord Balthazar to be your husband," she says in that dead tone, ripping me out of my thoughts.

"Mhm," I hum, too afraid my voice will betray my fear.

I pull out a glass container from the fridge and pop it into the microwave.

"You had your pick of humans to be your husband, yet you wished the devil to fill that role."

She says nothing else and since there isn't an actual question in there, I keep quiet. It's difficult to do when the need to answer her unasked question screams at me, but I bite my tongue. I now know better after watching Balthazar make deal after deal after deal.

I've watched him countlessly withhold information from men as he explained the terms of their agreement. He never asks any clarifying questions either. He repeats back exactly what he hears word for word. He never infers or expands upon any assumptions he has. He never answers questions that aren't asked of him. He only gives out what's required. So, if Umbra won't prod me with an actual question, I won't give her an answer.

The microwave dings three times to alert me it's done. I pop open the door and steam rushes out along with a delicious, aromatic smell. I carefully grab the container from the microwave and set it on top of the white marble counter.

"Why?" Umbra asks.

I open my mouth to answer and then close it. *There I go assuming,* I think and I'm proud I caught myself before answering her question. Why could mean any number of things. She could be asking why the Lords think that. She could be asking why I wished for a husband. She could be asking why I am here. I shouldn't assume I know what she's asking.

I stall for time as I try to calm my racing heart. I don't want to sound haughty or arrogant when I speak with her, but I also don't want to sound weak and afraid. But I *am* weak and afraid. Knowing me, I'll overcompensate by sounding arrogant and haughty. I'm doomed.

I turn around and pull open three drawers before I find the silverware. Umbra says nothing as she waits for me to respond. Is she mad? Or does she not care? My hand trembles as I grab a pair of chopsticks. Without making eye contact, I turn back around to face her and stir my food around.

"Why what?" I finally ask.

A soft, little chuckle escapes her and my eyes dart up. She's not smiling. In actuality, she looks angrier than Hell. An unamused laugh? That's never a good sign. I glance back at my food and do my best to breathe normally. I can't, however, hide the trembling of my hands.

"Why did you wish for Lord Balthazar to be your husband?" she clarifies.

My eyebrows furrow together as I try to remember what he said to the Houses. Something about coming from a severely religious family and my parents wanting me to get married. I wished to get married to shut them up. So that's what I tell Umbra, but she immediately starts shaking her head.

"I know why you wished for a husband, but why did you wish it to be Lord Balthazar?" she asks.

"Because he was there?" I don't sound convincing at all. "I was scared and he's handsome – it's honestly annoying how handsome he is. So, I asked him if he'd do it and he said yes. Said it'd be fun."

She stares at me in silence with that cold, hard, indifferent, yet beautiful face. I begin eating my food as my eyes wander her body once more. She's very fit. Alarmingly so. Her clothes do nothing to downplay her strength. She looks like the type of person who could easily fight twenty men at once. If she ever wanted to attack me, I'd be dead in a heartbeat.

Umbra doesn't say anything in response to my mediocre answer. I momentarily forget myself as I ask, "Do you have powers like Balthazar? Are your muscles because of magic or self–discipline?"

"Only devils have powers," she answers and my eyebrows pinch together in contemplation.

"So... you're *not* a devil?"

She doesn't answer but she holds my gaze. The noodles held in my chopsticks slide out of my grip and plop onto my plate. She glances down at them, then back at me with severe judgment. Embarrassed, I clear my throat and try to keep on topic despite my reddening face.

"*Are* you a devil?" I ask more directly.

After a prolonged silence, she finally answers. "No."

That means she doesn't have powers. Which means she must spend an insane amount of time training to make herself look like that and honestly, that makes me even more scared of her. Using magic to make yourself buff is easy. Spending hours honing your skills and training to the point that your body looks like hers is absolutely terrifying. She knows her body better than most people ever will. She knows how to push herself past her limits and when exactly those limits will hit. I do *not* want to get on her bad side. Ever.

"Um, do you want something to eat?" I ask, deciding it'd be in my best interest to offer some form of hospitality. "Perhaps something to drink?"

Her eyes narrow as she leans forward on the kitchen island and it takes literally all of my willpower not to recoil away from her. I hold my ground, hoping she can't sense how afraid I am. She can probably kill me before I even see it coming.

I desperately try to steady my breathing and pray she doesn't have heightened hearing because my heart is beating a mile a minute.

"Lord Balthazar would rather ally with Zyvn than shackle himself to a human. No matter how entertaining it might be."

I don't know who or what the heck Zyvn is, but that's not important right now. Umbra is angry about this matrimony and I haven't the slightest clue why. But the *why* isn't important right now. My safety is in jeopardy.

My heart leaps to my throat as my stomach churns. I've lost my appetite as my survival instincts kick into high gear. I've got to placate the predator before she rips my head off.

"Maybe..." I wish my voice sounded firmer but it'll have to do, "Maybe my soul was worth the inconvenience."

"No. It isn't."

"My soul *is* different, though. Do you know much about souls?" I ask as the image of my burgundy, tennis ball sized soul flits through my mind. Every single soul I've watched Balthazar extract has been white and the size of a ping pong ball. Why is mine different? "Are men and women souls different? Like, do they look different from each other?"

For the first time since I've met her, true emotion captures her face. Her eyebrows furrow together as little wrinkles on her face form from the muscles bunching together. She looks genuinely confused.

"I see now why he's agreed to your wish," she mutters to herself. She quickly moves on from the topic, not allowing me an opportunity to ask her what she means. "Do not keep Lord Balthazar up here for more than a few hours. If he dies in your presence, know I will hunt you down and flay you alive for what you've taken from me."

"I'm not going to kill him," I nearly shriek and it shocks me to learn I'm speaking the truth. Wouldn't I kill him if it meant getting out of my deal?

Umbra scoffs as she openly rolls her eyes at me like I'm the dumbest person to exist in Hell *and* on Earth. Great. "If I had concerns about you killing him, you'd already be dead. The cold is what will kill him if he spends too much time up here."

"What?"

She might as well be talking in tongues because I have *no* idea what she's talking about. I wish I could sound more intelligent if only to have her think about me in a better light. But no. I sound like an idiot.

"The cold," she bites out, somewhat irritated. "It starts in the fingers and toes before creeping its way towards the heart."

Is that why Balthazar's fingers are always so cold compared to the rest of him?

"After the fall of Hapshein, the Creator didn't want Jeznians to roam freely in Ephiri. Hence, the cold. It sets in as soon as we leave Jeznia. The only way to stop it is to return home. We have forty–eight hours before it kills us."

My mind is racing as I soak in all the information she's willingly telling me. I've got to store this information away for later. It might prove useful later on.

She takes the opportunity while I think to walk around the kitchen island and square up to me. I shrink away but the distance I've created is useless. Her presence is suffocating.

"If you keep him up here longer than twenty–four hours," she states in a calm, quiet tone, "I'll rip out your spleen."

I think I'm gonna be sick, I think as my eyes dart back and forth between hers. My stomach is clenched so tight I'm grateful I didn't eat much of my lunch. She's standing less than three feet from me, but it feels like she's breathing down my neck. Lucky for me, I have no desire to keep Balthazar around for longer than necessary.

I open my mouth to tell her that, but someone else beats me to the punch.

"Umbra, you're still here."

XII

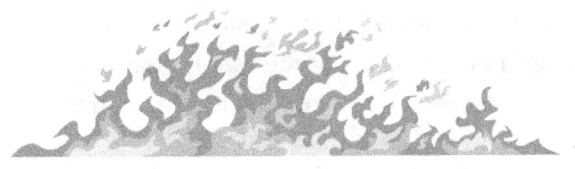

Bотн оur Attention turns to the entryway of the living room where Balthazar stands. He's pushed the long sleeves of his form fitting shirt up towards his elbows as his arms cross his chest and he casually leans against the door frame. The tips of his horns are engulfed in calm flames. He has an unreadable expression on his face while his dual colored eyes are solely focused on Umbra.

"My apologies, Lord Balthazar–"

"I–I asked her to stay," I cut in.

If I cover for her, maybe she'll be less inclined to kill me. Or, judging by how angry she looks, I might have just convinced her to slice me in half. Shit.

"I was hoping to learn more about Hell, but she's not very forthcoming," I continue on because once I commit to something, I *commit.*

Balthazar chuckles as he pushes off the door frame and walks into the kitchen. "No, she's not. That is precisely why I employ her."

His crimson freckled gaze slides over to me and he offers a devilish smile. "Next time you have questions about Jeznia–Hell, direct them to me. I'm more than happy to answer."

Well then, since he willingly offered, I'm going to take him up on it.

"She said only devils have powers," I say. "Why is that?"

"Oh ho, I'm surprised she said as much," Balthazar says as his gaze slides back over to Umbra.

She remains completely stoic, but I don't miss the way her fingers curl into her hands or the way Balthazar doesn't smile despite how amused his voice sounds. Shit. I should keep my mouth shut moving forward.

"What else did she say?" Balthazar asks as he turns his attention back to me.

"Nothing else. Well," before I can even consider stopping myself, the words pour out of me like I'm a faucet and some unknown force has turned the dial all the way on. "She said she isn't a devil, which means her body looks the way it does because she spends hours working out and training... which means she's scarier than a devil who uses magic to make himself buff because that means she's dedicated to making herself into a physical weapon instead of taking the easy way out by using magic to do it."

A light blush tinges my cheeks at the end of my rambling. Balthazar snorts lightly in amusement as his fist comes up to press against the smile on his lips. Umbra, on the other hand, looks like I've puked all over her and she wants to beat me to death for it.

"Careful, Sloane, you're shaking in your boots."

"Should I *not* be afraid of her?" I retaliate, my voice showing the mild irritation I feel at his teasing.

"No, you should not. Umbra is ordered not to harm you under *any* circumstances. If she fails to adhere to my orders, she knows the punishment she'll be subjected to. Trust me when I say this: harming you is not worth it for her."

My eyes dart over to Umbra but she isn't looking at me. Was her threat empty or is she ready to go against Balthazar's orders to protect him? I'd put my money on the second option.

"Your silence is very telling, Sloane," Balthazar mutters darkly.

Shit. My look to Umbra gave me away, didn't it? I go stiff as a board at the realization. I might as well have shouted from the rooftops that Umbra threatened me. She's going to kill me even if it means going against Balthazar. Why would she want her boss to be married to such an idiot? I've got to think of a way to get out of this mess. Any way to save my skin.

"I was just thinking… isn't there a possibility she would go against what you ordered?" I ask. As an afterthought, I say, "Hell isn't known for its loyalty."

"Umbra would have to carve out her own heart if she ever wanted to go against my order," Balthazar states darkly before turning his full attention to her.

"I remember giving you explicit instructions to speak with Ofello, not linger with my wife," he says as he stands to his full height. It makes their height difference that much more stark. "You ought to thank Sloane for lying on your behalf. The next time you disobey me, it'll cost you a limb."

"Yes, Lord Balthazar," she says with a nod of her head before turning her attention to me. "Thank you," she says with zero emotion.

They're mere words to her and have absolutely no meaning behind them. Without waiting for a response, she disappears in a cloud of black smoke.

"You didn't have to do that," I say as my fingers grab the chopsticks resting in the container. "Is it so bad that she looks out for you?"

His face looks aghast as he turns his attention to me. I've clearly offended him by what I've said. My lips press together as I drop my attention to the food. He obviously has no idea how she vouches for him or threatens others on his behalf. Looks like I still need to work on not divulging more information than need be.

"You believe me in need of being looked out for?" he asks before adding, "And by a Shadow Seer, no less?"

"First of all," I say as I look up at him, "you say that like I have a clue what a Shadow Seer is."

When I pointedly *don't* continue the rest of my list, Balthazar rolls his eyes so obnoxiously that I feel like I'm talking to a fifteen year old boy.

"Every House has House Aides," he says through clenched teeth. "Shadow Seers are bound to House Primis. As their name alludes, they're very good at hiding within the shadows. We use them to spy on the other Houses or other inhabitants who are a threat to our power. Despite Umbra's appearance, they're trained in distant combat and poison, not hand to hand."

My eyes dart to the uneaten food on the kitchen island. I won't be finishing that. Better to be safe than sorry. She may not have put something in there to kill me, but there could definitely be poison in there to warn me to stay in line.

I glance back at Balthazar when my mind hitches on the word *bound*. He also said she'd carve out her own heart before betraying him. Does that mean…?

"Is she a slave?"

"What would possess you to ask such a question?" he asks. He's slowly losing any and all patience he has for me.

"You said she's bound to you and would kill herself before betraying you."

"Slaves are a liability," he answers with a dismissive wave of his hand. "They'll eventually revolt and you'll have a civil war at your doorstep. Shadow Seers are not born but made. She requested to become a Shadow Seer and was granted the request after passing her trials."

"Is that true of all House Aides? Being made after passing a trial?" I ask. Maybe I can use that as a Hail Mary if I can't find a way out of my contract.

"As far as I know. The Houses are rather elusive with how they conduct their business, but that is not the matter of our discussion right now. Do you truly believe me in need of help from a Shadow Seer?" He asks it the way a fifteen year old would; all entitled and offended.

It's my turn to roll my eyes.

"Doesn't everybody?" I ask. I'd find his superiority complex irritating if I didn't expect it from a devil. "Do you really think yourself so invincible that no one is capable of taking you down? You should be more mindful of how you treat Umbra unless you want to be stabbed to death like Caesar."

He openly scoffs as he turns away from me. Yet, all too suddenly he whirls around. Anger has a hold over his entire body. His arms and legs are tense, his mouth puckers towards the side of his face, his eyes narrow, and his eyebrows dip down as he scowls. He can't drop the subject, too enraged by the idea that someone thinks he might require outsider help to stay alive.

"You're lucky I'm unable to kill you right now for uttering such ridiculous words."

His words make me bold when he probably intended that they make me demure. He *can't* kill me so what do I have to be afraid of?

"You're such an idiot," I spit out. "You don't deserve the loyalty Umbra is offering you. All she wanted to do was make sure I knew who I was messing around with, that I didn't forget my place beside you, and what do you do in return? Threaten to take a *limb*. You deserve to be stabbed in the back and I hope she uses a twelve inch dagger to do it."

He moves fast as he grabs me by the throat and slams me into the refrigerator. Pain blossoms on the back of my head from the violent motion, but this time, there's less fear thrumming through me. Sure, it's still scary that he's gripping me around the throat, but. He. Can't. Kill. Me. No matter how desperately he wants to. His life is tied to mine.

"You better watch how you speak to me," he growls low and threateningly.

"Or what?" I ask challengingly as I let my rage burn, scorching away any fear I might feel.

"Just because I can't kill you, doesn't mean I can't harm you."

"If you hurt me, Balthazar, I *will* kill you. And now I know to specify my wish so that I'll get more than just your death out of it. You basically handed me a loaded gun. Don't tempt me into pulling the trigger."

He snarls loud and angry and it sounds every bit the panther I imagine him to be. It shoots fear straight into my heart and the only thing that prevents me from shaking in my bones is knowing that I have him trapped. He can roar and growl and hiss all he wants, but that's *all* he can do.

However, what I don't expect him to do is lean himself into me, pressing the entire weight of his body on top of me as his cold grip on my throat loosens, but he doesn't let go.

He dips his head forward, lips ghosting against my ear as a low, guttural growl emits from him. Shivers dart down my spine and my hands reach up to grab his shirt. They grip the fabric tightly, but don't move. My mind battles my body — push him away or pull him closer.

"I will break you, Sloane," he murmurs so deeply an involuntary shiver wracks my body. What do people say? Fear and lust walk a tightrope? They've got me pegged.

His teeth pull at my earlobe as he presses further into me. The coldness of the fridge contrasts perfectly against the unnatural heat of his body. That smokey scent fills my senses and I glance up at the ceiling of the apartment as my fingers hold onto his shirt so tight I imagine they're stark white.

I study the smooth pattern of the ceiling and try to disassociate from what's happening, from how badly my body suddenly *wants* him. He is the literal devil and here I am *craving* him.

The weight leaning into me is so intoxicating that I can't help but imagine how it'd feel to have him pounding mercilessly into me. How passionate and feral it'd be. My body yearns for it despite how much my mind protests. Balthazar is raw, untamed power and if he were to unleash it on me, there would be no going back.

Something suddenly snaps inside me. This is a power struggle happening between us and I keep relenting to him for no reason. He isn't the only one with the power here and I won't let him forget it. He thinks he can break me? He was the one who said he'd ravage me wholly, not the other way around. If anyone is going to break first, I'll make sure it's *him*.

My hand darts up to the back of his scalp as my fingers lace through his silky thick hair. I hesitate only for the briefest of seconds before yanking his head back as hard as I can. He hisses as his lips pull back in a snarl but I don't recoil. Even as he stares down at me with his head tilted backwards, his eyes ablaze, his lips pulled back, and a threat lingering within his mouth, I don't draw back. I put every ounce of anger and dominance I can into my voice. It's low and menacing, as I breathe out the words slowly, purposefully, and without hesitation.

"Not unless I break you first, Balthazar."

His eyes flash deep red and his head tugs against my firm hold. His hair remains clutched within my fingers and, as his top lip twitches in that snarl, the image of me holding a wild predator by the neck flashes through my mind. I'd never stand a chance. The predator could rip itself out of my hold within a heartbeat if it wanted to.

That's when it hits me.

Balthazar is *allowing* me to grip him like this. Instead of being angry by that fact or irritated at how weak and helpless I am compared to him, the realization makes me *drunk*. This powerful devil who can make wishes come true at the snap of his fingers has handed me the reins and is bowing down in submission. *Who is going to break who?* I wonder as a pleased smirk darts across my face.

"Tread carefully," I murmur sensually as I pull his head back even farther. A quiet growl sounding almost like a purr escapes his mouth. "My finger's already on the trigger."

Without another word, I release him and shove him away. He takes a step back and I use that opportunity to quickly walk around him, exiting the kitchen. I beeline it to the bedroom.

The door closes loudly behind me and, even though locking it is futile when Balthazar can transport himself into the room, I lock the door anyway. My heart hammers inside my chest, my body vibrating as that drunken feeling of true power courses through me.

I loved every second of that. There's no denying it. The image of him with his head pulled back, his eyes hooded, and the snarl on his lips replays over and over inside my mind. That was *hot*. He was completely at my mercy. *By choice*.

I can't think straight. My hands shake with adrenaline and I hate how desperately my body is begging me to go back there and finish what we started. He's the devil who accepted a deal to kill me. *That was before he knew you*, I pathetically think and a million alarm bells go off inside my head.

He's the exact definition of a bad boy except he's lacking any and all of the good qualities. He plays with people's lives because he can. He would dismember his employee because she disobeyed him. I would be dead if I hadn't had anything of value to offer him. He's all wrong without a single ounce of good in him.

Yet my body is on fire.

I need to cool down. Desperately, I rush to the bathroom, turn the shower on, and rip my clothes off. The water is barely lukewarm when I step under it. The shock to my system is exactly what I need. The water washes over me, head to toe, but when my eyes close, all I see is him.

My imagination runs rampant of what it'd be like to undress him piece by piece. How much fire there would be within those pitch black eyes of his. I'd make him watch me undress as I withheld permission for him to touch me. He'd fight against himself, his muscles twitching with every minuscule attempt at reaching for me. I'd take my time removing each of my garments, taking joy in tormenting him. And if he was a good boy who listened well, I'd give him a little reward.

"Oh, dear god," I groan as I turn the faucet all the way to cold and shrivel up when the cold water hits me.

It does the job, flushing the rampant lust out of my system. Now I understand what he meant when he said being good would be worth it. Except I want to be dishing out the reward, not receiving it.

No!

I do *not* want any kind of giving or receiving rewards. *Absolutely not.*

A heavy sigh blows out my mouth as I concentrate on the cold water, on the path it takes as it descends down my body. After a few moments, all thoughts of Balthazar are gone. Unfortunately with a clear mind, I realize I've destroyed the fake lashes I glued on earlier today.

Mildly irritated at myself, I pluck them off before tossing them haphazardly onto the sink counter. The next ten minutes are spent washing the full makeup off and rinsing myself down. I finish the shower with a hair wash and hot water to warm myself back up.

Once out of the shower, I take advantage of all the skin care products lined up along the countertop. It's really upped my skincare routine and I've noticed a subtle glow to my face these past few days. Honestly, a little extra self–care is the least I deserve after being "killed" by the devil.

After another twenty minutes spent in the bathroom, I come out in an oversized t–shirt and underwear. Thankfully, Balthazar is nowhere to be found. I'm not sure I'd be able to handle any more of him today.

I grab my phone and check the time. It's only 6:15pm, but after spending all day listening to selfish, greedy, desperate men beg and plead with Balthazar for money, I have zero desire to go out and interact with the world. Instead, I want to snuggle up in the plush king sized bed and watch some *Pride and Prejudice*. It's the perfect movie to end the long day with.

Sometime later when I've reached the scene where Elizabeth walks around the room with Caroline Bingley my phone lights up. My eyes flit down, briefly seeing a text message across the screen. Strange. Why would I be receiving a text? Balthazar made it impossible for me to interact with anyone from my old life so does that mean *he's* texting me?

I'm tempted to ignore it but a second alert goes off. My eyes roll at the idea of Balthazar texting me, but I grab my phone anyway and unlock the screen. My heart instantly drops. It's a text message from my mom. Three little dots as she continues to type a new message hide the previous messages she's sent and I'm suddenly overwhelmed at the idea that my mother is texting her dead daughter.

Tears flood my vision as a wave of nausea slams into me. I can't imagine what she must be going through right now. Here I am playing will–we–or–won't–we? with Balthazar, the literal person responsible for me being dead, while my mom's *grieving*. How messed up is that?

Another text comes through and I battle about whether I should read it or not. She could be saying anything and everything; things she would never dream of saying to me if I were still alive.

Maybe I was a disappointment to her in some way and now she's finally talking about it with me. Or maybe she's telling me she'll bring me back from the dead just to kill me all over again for allowing myself to be murdered. We loved each other fiercely, but as I got older, we said it less and less. Now that I'm dead, we'll never get to say it again.

The phone drops from my hand as I curl up into the fetal position and ball my eyes out. I keep on crying until I fall asleep.

XIII

"TIME TO WAKE up, Sloane, there's no rest for the wicked."

I groan into my pillow as I yank the comforter over my head. "The wicked rest plenty."

Grogginess coats my tone, leaving no firmness to it, but I mean every word I speak.

"The truly wicked do not," Balthazar murmurs just above my head. "Come now, we've got much to do."

Begrudgingly, I toss the comforter off and gaze at Balthazar. The first thing I notice are his eyes heavily lined in black eyeliner. Next is the fact that he's sans shirt, leaving his large chest tattoo out in the open on full display. Golden circlets adorn his biceps and he wears a pair of dark maroon, nearly black harem pants.

In my groggy state, my eyes linger on the curves of his muscles, how they ripple down his torso, and I'm reminded again of a lean predator. Balthazar isn't the largest man I've seen, but he's built like a weapon. It's an enticing thought to think a weapon such as him would willingly submit to a weak human like me. Wouldn't that mean *I'm* the one in power and not him?

"My eyes are up here, Sloane," Balthazar teases and, judging by how sugary sweet his voice is, he's enjoying every second of my gazing.

"Do you use magic to look like that?" I ask as I prop myself up in bed. The question does what it's meant to; it deflates his ego. His shit–eating grin disappears from his face while I bite back my smirk as I continue talking, "Umbra isn't a devil, so she has to work very hard to look the way she does. Honestly, it's impressive. What about you? Do you take the easy way out?"

He stares at me for a few moments, his eyes flitting back and forth between my eyes before he answers.

"I used to use magic when I was younger. I didn't understand the discipline it required or the determination it took. I used to make fun of creatures who had no magic. I believed their lives to be pathetic because they had to waste time on something I could do with a snap of my fingers."

There is something strangely authentic about his voice as he speaks and it hooks me in. He could be feeding me lies for all I know, but my gut tells me he's speaking the truth. If he said he never used magic to make himself stronger or more attractive, I'd question the validity of his statement. But this… it sounds too genuine to be a lie.

The casualness of our conversation lifts an imaginary weight off my shoulders. The exhaustion from mentally scheming multiple days in a row and needing to have a snarky comment always at the ready is overwhelming; it's refreshing that we're having a gentle and calm chat for once.

"So, why'd you stop?" I ask curiously.

"I realized magic only gets you so far. It's no fun threatening someone's life when you can't physically rip their arms off. Using magic to do that is rather... lame."

My mouth immediately drops open. Gentle conversation my ass.

"I'm sorry, you can *rip someone's arm off?*"

"Mm, I intend to do so today," he says offhandedly before smirking wickedly. "Go get ready. You won't want to miss it."

He disappears from the room before I have a chance to formulate a response. Shock washes over me as I remain seated in bed, my mouth still hung open as my mind plays over his words. He can physically remove someone's arm from their body just by giving it a yank?

The thought equally terrifies and amazes me. I can't comprehend the amount of strength that would take. It's mind boggling. It's horrifying.

Yet it's also *amazing*.

To have that kind of strength would mean I'd never feel physically threatened ever again. I'd feel comfortable walking down darkened alleys in the middle of the night. I'd never have to be on alert as a man walked behind me. I could keep my head high, *knowing* if he dared to attack me, I could just rip off his arm. The security and safety I'd feel as a woman walking out in public would be intoxicating.

Some dark part of me wants that kind of power and to use it.

A few more seconds pass as I think about ripping arms off assholes before I finally slink out of bed and throw my hair up into a bun. After a quick shower, I study my makeup supplies on the counter. Considering that Balthazar's outfit means we're going to Hell, I guess I'll go with a fire theme so I won't piss anyone off.

Drawing the flames takes considerable time. Between the shape and using three colors, red, orange, and yellow, I'm sure I've wasted at least forty five minutes getting them just right. I glue on the fanciest eyelashes I can find and take advantage of the glitter highlighter before tousling my hair. Once my hair and makeup are complete, I walk out into the bedroom where a black outfit sits on the bed, courtesy of Balthazar.

It's a lace thong bodysuit and a high waisted black mesh skirt. I quickly change into the outfit before examining how it looks. The bodysuit fits like a glove and the see through mesh skirt ends at my ankles. I openly frown at my ass being on full display. I like the bodysuit and I like the mesh skirt, but I don't like them paired together. I wouldn't feel comfortable going out in public with my butt out for everyone to see.

Except we're not going just anywhere. We're going to Hell where the inhabitants would call my outfit *modest*. The thought strangely eases me, knowing I won't draw too much attention to myself dressed as I am.

Holding onto that thought, I slip on the black designer brand name heels Balthazar left me.

I glance at the mirror again and, with my new perspective of the outfit being Hell appropriate, I'm amazed by what I see. A badass stares back at me. I look like I go around breaking hearts for *enjoyment*. Guys like Chad would slut shame me and call me ugly because I'd be something they could never have but desperately want.

My lips pull back into a smirk.

This is the kind of energy I want to exude from now on. I'm dead to anyone who loves me. I might as well reinvent myself into someone I'd be too scared to show them. Besides, it'll only be temporary. Once I figure out how to get out of this deal, I can embrace the old me when I return home.

"You look absolutely ravishing," Balthazar's voice interrupts my thoughts.

I turn to him, the smirk turning a little more coy as I walk confidently towards him.

"Don't I?"

He chuckles as he wraps an arm around my waist, pulling me flush against his body and stares down at me with open hunger. My heart flips at his candid appreciation. I've never denied my attraction towards him, but I've always hated that magnetic pull.

Today, though, I don't hate it so much. It's hard to hate it when I have that sinful image of him submitting to me last night. The beautiful arch of his throat, those heated hooded eyes, the slight tug against my hand as he defiantly fought my grip–

"We'll be meeting with the Lords again," he says, pulling me out of my thoughts. "Remember to be my pretty little mute."

My eyes roll skyward as the smile falls off my face and I reply in a dead tone, "Seen, not heard. Got it."

He chuckles again as he squeezes my hip and then snaps his fingers. The pressure of traveling is something I'll never get used to. Each and every time it presses down on me from all sides as if squishing my body between the floor and a ten ton boulder. Who could ever get used to a feeling such as that?

For a brief moment, I think about how much better it is to travel with Umbra instead of Balthazar, but then my head feels like it's splitting open from the pressure. A painful moan is ripped from me right before we arrive in Hell.

Balthazar snaps his fingers before I have an opportunity to breathe in. There's no insanely dry air to make me cough or heave. No excruciating heat that burns my flesh. He adapted me to Hell as soon as we arrived.

"How are you feeling?" he asks and the question catches me off guard.

He's never once asked about my well–being before. It's strange that he's doing it now. My eyes dart back and forth in his gaze, hoping to find some trick or hidden answer in there. Is he being considerate because of last night? It can't be that simple. Can it?

"Fine. I'm fine," I manage to answer as our eyes stay glued to each other.

"Do you require a moment before we head to the hall?"

"Um... no... why are you–" I stop myself short before I finish the question.

"Why am I?"

"You're being... weird," I venture to say and he openly laughs.

"Am I?"

"You're being nice," I point out.

He arches up an eyebrow while he smiles. "Do you want me to stop?"

"Kind of."

Balthazar chuckles at my answer as a frown pulls at my lips. His arm remains comfortably wrapped around my waist as we continue to gaze at each other. He dips his head forward so our foreheads are almost touching each other.

"If you prefer it, I can go back to treating you like Ephirian swine."

He's teasing me. His black and red eyes are dancing in delight at how uncomfortable he's making me feel. *Bastard.* Two can play this game.

I close the distance between us, pressing my forehead into his as our noses touch and I square up against him.

"I may be Ephirian swine, but you live *beneath* me."

His eyes flash red and a low growl escapes his mouth. My breath hitches in my throat as his fingers grip me painfully tight around the hip. Tight enough to bruise. He slides his head down to my ear, his breath hot, and it elicits goosebumps down my body.

"You never fail to disappoint," he whispers sensually and a tingle zings through me. All too suddenly, he's pulling away. "Come, we should go."

He says nothing else as he releases his hold from me and walks out of the room we're in. It takes me a few seconds to recover before I'm scurrying after him.

We walk down the same hallway as before. Or at least it's identical. The decaying arms reach out for us from the flaming walls, their hands grasping at empty air. I walk the exact path Balthazar takes and desperately try to keep my attention away from the walls. I'm afraid if I look directly at them, I'll stumble right into them and won't be able to break free.

The hands continually swipe and miss their target until the fire fades away, making them disappear with it. Several feet later, we reach the grand doors leading into the throne room. The sheer size of the doors is daunting and the ease in which Balthazar opens them with his magic still amazes me. I can't suppress the little prickle of envy that blooms within my chest. I want powers like that.

Only when the doors are fully open does Balthazar hook his arm around my waist and usher us into the room. He's the last to arrive just like last time. The murmurs of the Lords die down as he walks across the room towards his empty throne.

Remember, do not speak, he reminds me telepathically.

I won't.

His fingers squeeze my waist in silent reply as my heels clack against the floor. I once again have to take particular care so I don't step into one of the lava channels and burn off my foot. Balthazar walks as though the floor is one solid slab of stone, his foot never once getting close to any channel. He's clearly memorized the layout. *Bastard,* I think. He smirks but says nothing.

"What is she doing here?" the devil beneath the wolf throne demands to know.

House Lupus, Balthazar reminds me. *The fifth House. Lord Priscilla.*

I stumble in my steps, but Balthazar quickly corrects me. I gape at him in open shock. He's *willingly* supplying information without being prompted first? This seriously can't be because of last night. There's absolutely no way, but that's the only thing that's changed in our relationship. What is he playing at?

Better for you to memorize the Lords' faces instead of my own, Balthazar teases and a slight blush dusts my face.

I quickly turn my gaze away from him and at Lord Priscilla of House Lupus. She's plump with a rounded face and sharp, near black eyes. Her alabaster skin is marred by a scar along her neck and her hair is an odd shade of blonde. It's wrapped around her head in plaited braids and her antelope–like horns have two tiny flames at the tip of them.

She wears a see through black robe that does nothing to hide her modesty. The hem is lined in red and black gemstones. Her feet are bare and, admittedly, I find her outfit a little underwhelming. She's basically wearing a decked out bathrobe to a meeting with the Lords of Hell. Then again, two other devils are completely naked. Was this meeting last minute or something?

Balthazar clicks his tongue as a serpentine smile spreads across his lips. "Lord Priscilla, I'm sorry to hear your memory has escaped you. Perhaps we should think about replacing your seat."

Her face darkens into a shade of red as her hands curl into fists. She straightens up in her seat as a glower grabs hold of her face.

"That's not a bad suggestion," the devil sitting at the cat throne says.

Lord Idris of House Felis, the sixth House.

Priscilla immediately turns to him, her fangs bared as she raises her left hand.

"You so much as make a move, Lord Idris, and I will spear you where you stand."

He chuckles, the sound warm and rich, as he wiggles his eyebrows in amusement. Lord Idris has smooth tawny brown skin, short black hair, and a dad bod physique. He doesn't wear a shirt but instead is draped in layered, golden necklaces. Some of them are bejeweled while others are plain chains.

He wears a cream colored skirt that reminds me of a kilt. His legs are completely spread apart but the cloth of his skirt drapes over his knees and keeps his goods hidden from view. I don't imagine he's wearing any type of underwear under that skirt and I'm grateful for the length of his garment.

His horns extend out of his temples before curling down towards the floor. Golden circlets with dangling chains adorn his nearly black horns while his face is adorned in a full face of makeup. Dark smokey eyes, shimmering eyeshadow, and luscious lashes. I'm grateful to see I'm not the only one who takes makeup seriously.

Down two steps and to the left of Lord Idris's throne sits another devil. Due to the proximity between the two, my assumption is the devil is associated with Idris's house.

I glance around the room, doing my best to memorize everything I see. Each House has two seats located on the fifth step–slash–landing. There is a seat on either side of the throne, creating a triangular shape.

Not a single House has all three seats filled. Only two Houses have both additional seats empty. There's no congruency on how the additional seats are being filled. Some Houses have the right one occupied; other Houses have the left one filled. Does it mean something or is it a matter of personal taste?

Balthazar and I steadily walk up the stairs before he discards me in the chair on his right side. The decision to have me in the right seat instead of the left feels premeditated, like the left seat was *not* an option for me to sit in. What is the significance of me in the right versus left seat?

Doing my best to play the part of a *pretty little mute*, I fluff my mesh skirt as I cross my leg over my knee. I spare a quick look around the room and regret it. These devils look ready to murder me. As much as I hate to do it, I need to embrace the role of Balthazar's pathetic wife. Better that than accidentally provoke a devil into killing me.

The Lord who sits at the bat throne on Balthazar's left surprisingly pays me no attention. If I remember correctly, her name is Lord Carmilla. She originally protested my presence but apparently doesn't this time around.

However, the devil sitting in one of Carmilla's chairs does. She openly stares down her nose at me with fair, pinkish skin, dark red lips, green vibrant eyes, and the hatred of an entire world. She's dressed similarly to me, but a touch classier. She wears extravagant jewelry and her make up isn't as done up as mine.

Her long, dark auburn hair is styled in a fancy braid that's pulled over her left shoulder. Her horns protrude out her forehead and curve back over her scalp in the same exact way as Carmilla's. Both they're horns are so incredibly black and shiny that they reflect the light spilling from the fire chandelier hovering in the middle of the room.

Clear disdain washes off her as she turns her attention towards the other devils. When she speaks, her voice is dripping with utter disgust.

"It's absolutely absurd Lord Balthazar is still entertaining this Ephirian trash–"

"Ivy, you shoot too high. My wife is Ephirian swine," Balthazar clarifies, his voice full of mirth.

Odd that swine is lower than trash, but I store that information away in case I ever need to insult someone from Hell.

Prick, I think as loudly as I can so Balthazar can hear it. There's a faint chuckle behind me and it should annoy me that he finds my insult amusing, but it doesn't. Instead, our insults are gradually shifting from outright hatred to dark humored affection. It should alarm me that I'm slowly becoming attached to the devil who owns my soul, but I'm too grateful for the lightheartedness after such enduringly difficult days.

Ivy lips turn downward in disgust as she glares at me like I'm spoiled meat she's accidentally stepped on while walking through her pristine neighborhood.

"She has no right to be here," Ivy states before she glances over at Carmilla. "Am I wrong, Mother?"

Ivy is the spitting image of her mother, but admittedly, they look more like sisters than mother and daughter. Ivy appears to be in her mid–twenties while Carmilla doesn't look a day over thirty. It's freaky to think they could look so close in age as mother and daughter but I guess that's how immortality works.

Carmilla is dressed in a glittery black gown that hugs her upper torso and flushes out past her waist. Her hair, a shade lighter than Ivy's, drapes down her back and shoulders in soft, beachy curls. Her eyes have a hint of blue swirling within the depths of green and are exponentially colder than Ivy's.

Carmilla clasps her hands together in her lap as her elbows rest on the throne's armrest. "There are no laws that forbid her presence."

"Mother–"

"As Balthazar's wife she has every right to attend these meetings," she cuts Ivy off. Carmilla keeps her head high as she addresses the other Lords. "After the Ephirian's wish is complete, I suggest we amend the law, preventing something like this from ever happening again."

The devil at the snake throne, the one directly to our right, laughs loudly. "No, I should think not, Lord Carmilla. It's far too entertaining having an Ephirian in our presence."

"Majority vote rules, Lord Meik," Carmilla states coldly.

"Aye, it does. I wonder just how many would rule in your favor," he hums as mischief dances in his gray eyes.

"My Lords, I'm rather bored with the topic at hand," Balthazar cuts in. "Either get to the point of this meeting, or my wife and I will leave for some marital bonding."

He says it so matter of fact as if he's discussing the color of the sky, yet I can't help the heat spreading through my cheeks. Bonding could mean a number of things, but we all know he's alluding to sex. I've never been in a room full of people where someone talked so openly about having sex *with me*. It's humiliating and the only saving grace is that no one appears to care. Well, no one but Ivy. She's clearly repulsed he would even touch me, let alone have sex with me. The urge to taunt her flare's to life within me.

Careful there, Sloane. She'll remove your head for looking too long.

I swallow thickly as I quickly turn my eyes away from her. *Duly noted,* I reply.

"Where is Finthorn?" Balthazar asks the Lords.

A moment later, a devil magically appears in the center of the room. He's dressed in a three piece tailored suit with tan skin that reminds me of Greece, short black hair, and deer–like horns that are similar to the devil sitting in the spider throne, though his are much smaller in comparison. Like he's a fawn barely growing his horns out as opposed to a full grown deer.

The air shifts behind me as it drops a couple of degrees. I risk a glance at Balthazar. His entire demeanor has changed in the presence of Finthorn. There is no kindness, amusement, or even mischief to be found. He looks every part the unforgiving heir to the most powerful House in Hell… no, Jeznia.

"Tell me why you're here," Balthazar demands, his voice low, cold, and menacing.

It sends a shiver of fear wracking through my body as goosebumps dart down my arms. He's only directed that kind of hatred towards me once and I nearly shit myself as his face melted off to reveal his real appearance. I never want to be on the receiving end of that kind of anger ever again.

"My Lord, I must admit I'm a little confused about why–"

"Wrong answer," Balthazar growls as he snaps his finger.

Finthorn's leg audibly cracks and he grunts as he shifts his weight to his other leg. Amazed horror fills me. It looks like Balthazar snapped his femur in half. I've heard that's one of the most painful breaks a person could have. Yet, Finthorn stands there breathing heavily through the pain and doesn't cry or scream. Just shifts his weight onto his other leg as a grimace darts across his face.

"Is it so wrong that I want more business?" Finthorn asks through his pain.

There's a harsh glare on his face as he pushes all the hatred he feels into his dark gaze at Balthazar.

"Why do you get the west and east coasts all to yourself while the rest of us are left with the slim pickings of the middle? The highest populations in the U.S. are on the coasts and we're just supposed to let you have them all because you're a Lord?"

The fire in the chandelier above us flickers as cold air whooshes through the room.

"Yes," Balthazar answers in that layered voice and my entire body shifts to attention.

The only time I've heard that voice felt like someone was pounding away at my brain. His voice hasn't reached that level yet; it lacks the gravel and bite to it, but I imagine he's nearly there.

"You're free to challenge me for those souls, but to *steal* them from me is an egregious miscalculation."

The fullness of his voice bellows out and I wince as it bears down from behind me. Thankfully, his voice lacks the physical effects it had the last time I heard it. That would mean he has control over who feels the full wrath of his voice. It's an equally terrifying and amazing thought.

"The only reason you are alive is because of Lord Taron. Should you steal from me again, my retaliation will be worse than death."

"This is bullshit," Finthorn loudly snaps as he whirls around to where the demon on the spider throne sits. "You must think so, Lord Taron! A Lord shouldn't even *be* a Contract Liaison, yet you all let him prance around stealing our merits!"

"On that we agree," Taron responds as his eyes shift to Balthazar. "No Lord in our entire history has sullied their reputation in such a way. Contract Liaisons are for the desperate. Merits are for the weak and poor. You hail from the most prominent House in all of Jeznia. You disgrace us with this folly."

The air shifts around Balthazar as the fire above billows and sways. The temperature in the room plunges briefly as another gust of cold wind blows through. Every time someone says something Balthazar dislikes, he physically makes the room uncomfortably cold.

So far none of the other devils have done anything remotely similar. Is it because they can't, because they fear him, or because they find the action to do so pointless? Knowing what they think of him and how they react to him could be useful information for me. It's important I study them as best I can. I might discover something important.

"Need I remind you I come from the desperate and poor," Balthazar's voice booms in that layered, grating voice, like fingernails scratching down chalkboards. I can't help that my shoulder and ear meet together in an attempt to block out the noise. "Do you think I care for *one second* what you think of my reputation?"

He stands up from his seat and walks down to the landing I sit on. Intense heat emits from him. His horns are on fire and his black eyes glow a deep red as he glares at Taron.

His fingers rhythmically curl and uncurl as he stops at the very edge of the landing, his back taut as the exposed muscles ripple down his back. His anger is practically a physical being in the room, suffocating us in its fury.

I shy away from him, pressing my back firmly into my seat, but I can't take my eyes off him. His mere presence demands every bit of my attention. *This* is the devil I've been threatening to kill. But it's also the same devil who *submitted* to me last night. *Holy shit,* I think.

"If you think it so prudent I step down from my position as Contract Liaison, *come and take it from me.*"

The flames on his horns burn bright and hot as the fire connects at the crown of his head before descending down his spine in a clean yet wild line. The fire extends out the bottom of his back and into a tail, large and thick, as it sways the way a cat's tail does when it's irritated and moments from lashing out.

My heart beats ferociously in my chest at his outward display of rage before I find the courage to look around the room. None of the Lords move in their seats, but their eyes flit around to each other like they're silently asking how they'll deal with the problem that is Balthazar. Their faces are frozen, their jaws clenched, and their hands grip the armrests of their thrones. In that moment, I become aware of the truth. These devils *fear* him. Every. Single. One.

The realization should provoke terror in me, terror at the fact that I've been spending so much of my time with one of the most feared devils of Hell, but instead, a strange flood of satisfaction captivates me. I've held my own against Balthazar. I've dared to challenge him and refused to back down. I've pushed him into a corner and watched him roar and hiss and snarl, but not once strike me down.

These devils fear him, but *I'm* the one that has him on a *leash. Holy shit*, I think again as a wicked smile spreads across my lips. Such a delirious, delicious revelation to stumble upon during a meeting with the Lords.

"M–my Lord, I did not mean to offend you," Finthorn stutters as he drops to his knees, quickly changing his tune now that Balthazar is clearly upset. "You know how the system works; how important merits are to us low born. You no longer have use for merits. You are the High King's son. Jeznia is yours for the taking. Please, my Lord, I beg of you, free up the east and west coasts to us lowborns."

Balthazar says nothing as he descends the remaining five steps to the floor. He stops about three feet before Finthorn. With the attitude of someone royally pissed off, he extends his arms outwards, his palms turned towards the ceiling as he slowly spins around the room.

"What would you have me do?" he asks in the voice I'm most familiar with. Deep, low, and seductive. "Do you think I am worthy of High King Zagon Primis, the greatest devil to exist?"

He continues his slow turn about the room, pausing briefly to look each devil in the eye as he faces them. None of them answer him.

"Do you think it is my birthright to inherit Jeznia simply because Zagon Primis has taken it by force?" He cups his left hand around his ear as he continues to slowly turn. Seconds pass by, but not a single devil speaks. "Your silence is very telling, my Lords. Wouldn't you agree, Finthorn?"

"Please, Lord Balthazar," Finthorn begs as he bends forward so his forehead touches the floor. I've never seen someone beg for their life before. I should be mortified by how fascinated I find it, but mortification is nowhere to be found. "I meant no offense–"

"You *stole* from me," Balthazar snarls in that grotesque voice as he bends down at the waist, his arms pulled back and poised to strike as Finthorn refuses to look up from the floor.

"*Please.*"

Balthazar stands to his full height as he turns his attention to Taron. "I will respect your position here, Lord Taron. Finthorn isn't merely a member of House Aranea, but he is of your blood. How would you prefer I proceed?"

Taron remains stiff in his seat as he stares at Balthazar. I imagine to show mercy here is to admit weakness. If Taron asks Balthazar to spare Finthorn's life, there's potential each and every one of these devils will use Finthorn against Taron. But it's clear from his hesitation he doesn't want to sentence Finthorn to death. It's a tricky, delicate situation to be put in.

I lean forward in my chair as my left arm crosses over my waist and my right elbow rests atop my knee. I watch curiously from my seat as my finger taps my chin in contemplation. How will Taron proceed?

"If you kill him, Lord Balthazar, I expect you to pick up his territory," Priscilla of House Lupus says. *Interesting.* She's publicly allying herself with Taron. I wonder what she expects to get out of it. "Are you prepared for that additional workload?"

Balthazar chuckles deeply, but it lacks authentic amusement. He turns his attention to her as she sits to Taron's left.

"I am not," he replies. "Admittedly, my wife requires much of my time. I wouldn't be able to pick up his territory even if I desired to."

"Then we're done here–" Taron starts to say, but abruptly stops.

Balthazar moves too fast for me to catch it. All I see is the aftermath. He grips Finthorn's shoulder with his left hand while his right arm is extended out in a clean, straight line. In that hand he holds Finthorn's left arm. The *entire* left arm.

Blood drips out of the amputated arm while blood gushes out from Finthorn's body. The pain is enough to make Finthorn scream and it's a scream full of utter agony. Finthorn reaches around to clutch the gaping, bleeding wound as Balthazar releases him and lets the arm thump to the ground, listlessly.

Finthorn's yells of pain echo throughout the circular throne room before the pain becomes too much to bear and he loses consciousness. My hand covers my mouth as I stare down at the mess and my stomach churns at all the blood, at the limb barely a foot from Finthorn's body.

It's gory. It's disgusting. It's terrifying.

Everything happened too quickly for me to see. I didn't blink. I was watching Balthazar carefully, but I *still missed it.* He ripped that devil's arm off in a blink of an eye and as easily as tearing a piece of paper in two.

The realization that this brutal yet nonchalant violent act could very easily be directed at me pummels into me. I don't have the slightest clue why Balthazar lets me get away with threatening him and this moment right here has me questioning my resolve.

Do I really stand a chance against him? Can I really find a way out of my bargain? I'm but a mere ant compared to him. He could crush me between his fingers if he so desired. At the moment, he finds me entertaining. He submits to me and lets me win. What happens when he loses interest?

Balthazar says nothing as he turns towards his throne and walks steadily up the stairs. He glances at me with cold, unforgiving black–red eyes as he walks by me and a shiver involuntarily wracks down my body. He's a true apex predator. A panther would never stand a chance against him. No one could... yet, I've been dumbly threatening his life.

Balthazar snaps his fingers before he sits in his chair. "Lord Taron, if you let him die on your watch, you're responsible for his territory."

Taron goes red in the face but doesn't retaliate. He stays quiet as he glares at the fearsome devil sitting behind me. I remain frozen in my chair. My eyes can't tear away from Finthorn. I watch as his chest slowly rises and falls. He's not dead yet and no more blood seems to be exiting his wound. Is that why Balthazar snapped his fingers? Even if the bleeding has stopped, Taron needs to act now if he wishes to prevent Finthorn from dying.

Balthazar shifts in his chair behind me, but I refuse to look back. Instead, I shrink into my chair, hoping not to anger the beast that fooled me into thinking I stood a chance against it.

"Let it be known, my Lords, if *any* of your relatives steal from me again, I won't be going after only them," he declares. He pauses for dramatic effect before asking, "Have I made myself clear?"

It is so incredibly quiet that we could hear a pin needle drop. One by one, each devil nods their head before vanishing out of the room. Taron is the last to leave and when he does, Finthorn is gone with him, arm included.

XIV

WHEN WE'RE THE last ones in the throne room,
Balthazar transports us back to the condo in Boston. Thrown
off by such an abrupt change in location, I fall to my hands
and knees. It's difficult to land standing when you're sitting
pre–transport.

Balthazar grips me firmly by the bicep as he yanks me to
my feet, his fingers already ice cold. My heart skips a beat as
fear darts down my spine. He could easily remove *any* limb
from my body. I instinctively yank my arm from his grasp
and he arches an eyebrow at me as he stares down at me.

"Problem with how I handled the situation?" he inquires.

There's something strangely distant in the way he asks
me. Like he's preparing for my answer to be the opposite of
what he wants to hear.

"No," I answer.

Despite everything, despite the blood, despite the
realization of how dangerous Balthazar truly is to me, I
honestly mean it. Who am I to judge how he handled the

situation? The other Lords didn't seem surprised or disturbed. They seemed *pissed*. Pissed that he has the power to do *what* he wants *when* he wants and there's *no one* that can stop him. If they're not bothered by the punishment he gave, then I have to believe what Balthazar did is normal.

Besides, I'm not under any illusions that Hell– no, Jeznia is a fair or just place. It's supposed to be where the worst of the worst end up. Ripping someone's arm off for stealing seems a bit mild if I really think about it.

"There's no need to lie, Sloane," Balthazar sighs out as he takes a step back from me.

My eyebrows furrow as I stare at the empty space he creates between us. His actions are coming off... considerate of me being scared of him. Why is he doing that? Is this another trick?

"I'm not bothered by it," I double down as my eyes snap up to his. "Honestly, I expect Hel–Jeznia to be run that way, but I won't lie... it's difficult to watch."

He clicks his tongue as his eyebrow arches up and his eyes narrow slightly, emphasizing the angular shape of them. He boldly looks me up and down.

After his visual assessment, he crosses his arms over his bare chest, causing the muscles to bugle. He lifts his eyes back to mine, the arch of his eyebrow more severe as he speaks.

"Then what is the issue?"

I have no idea what he's insinuating. I'm not lying when I say I don't have a problem with how he handled the situation. Other than that, I don't know why he thinks I have a problem.

"What makes you think there's an issue?" I ask as I place my hands on my hips.

"You're... stiff."

I stare at him for a few moments before forcing myself to shake out my body. It's awkward and unnecessary, but it's the only thing I can think to do. He chuckles lightly, the small smile on his face actually reaching his eyes.

"Cute, but you're still stiff."

"I mean can you blame me?" I ask in a huff as my hands fly up in the air. "I didn't even see you move, but then all of a sudden his arm was ripped off his body!"

My voice is a bit high and a little too shrill. It gives away exactly how I feel about what just happened.

"You tore that guy's arm off like it was paper. You could do that to *me!* How am I supposed to react if not like this?"

He steps towards me, the playfulness gone from his face as his cold gaze bears down on me. "Then stop threatening to wish me dead and start playing nice."

Instinct begs me to stand down, but my stupid personality won't let me. *Don't let the predator smell fear* is the stupidest advice ever, yet apparently, I live by it. It's why I threw the drink in Chad's face and why I've threatened the devil on more than one occasion.

I don't step up in challenge to Balthazar, but I don't cower away either. My shoulders hold strong and my head remains high as I meet his unforgiving gaze. Even as fear overloads my senses, I find a way to use my voice. It wavers, giving away exactly how afraid I am, but I don't stutter. I speak the words clearly and refuse to break eye contact.

"My wish is the only leverage I have against you."

He works his jaw back and forth and the glare softens on his face. His icy demeanor gradually evaporates as he studies me. Cold fingers ghost against my arm before retreating back to his side, like *he's* the one afraid to touch me.

"You're too brilliant to harm," he whispers so quietly I almost miss it.

My heart flutters at the obvious compliment. The devil, who is powerful enough to make the other Lords afraid, thinks I'm *too brilliant* to hurt. It does something weird to me as my fear disappears and is replaced by something else. Something I'm curious to explore, but equally desire to smash into itty bitty little pieces.

Balthazar quickly turns to exit the room but pauses to throw over his shoulder. "Get changed. We're going out for food."

WE TAKE A 5 minute walk from the condo to a nearby café. The café patio is full when we arrive but Balthazar tells two people at a corner table by the shade to leave with the snap of his fingers and – big surprise there – they do. Then, one of the employees quickly clears the table for us before pulling out the chairs. I'm fairly certain that's *not* a part of their job. Embarrassed they've been forced to do something like that against their will, I offer a quiet *thank you* as I sit down.

"A chai latte for her and a hazelnut latte with oat milk for me," Balthazar tells the employee.

"Of course. I'll get that to you right away."

A quietness falls over us as we sit in our chairs. The new feeling brewing inside of me unsettles me as I sit across from

Balthazar. Every time I think about the meeting – about how cruel and powerful he had been – fear nips at me, but something else swats it away. Something carnal and foolish.

He had been so *vicious*. I saw the aftermath of an arm amputated from a body with no anesthesia or medical prep work. It was savage, unnecessarily barbaric, and yet, watching the entire room shift as everyone went on edge... I can't keep from replaying it over and over in my head. How would it feel to command a room the way Balthazar does? I won't ever know.

The silence drags on as we wait for our beverages to be delivered. We don't spare each other our attention, preoccupied by our own thoughts. My mind wanders to anything and everything as the time drags on.

Randomly, Balthazar's order pops into my head and my eyebrows pinch together at the oddness of it. A hazelnut latte with oat milk. Not exactly the kind of drink I'd expect the devil to order. Black coffee would suit him better. Hazelnut latte is too sweet and... oat milk? He drinks oat milk?

"What is it?" Balthazar asks as his eyes scan the street beside us.

A brownstone that's been converted into store fronts at the ground level with apartments on the upper levels resides across the street from us. Small trees evenly spaced from one another line the sidewalk. Cars continually drive past our view, keeping the street minimally busy. Pedestrians quickly pass by our line of sight as they hurry off to whatever destination they're heading towards. All in all, a very normal Boston midmorning.

"There's a lot for me to process right now," I confess. My eyes linger on his face for a moment before turning to observe the sidewalk. I decide to start the conversation light and ask, "The devil drinks oat milk?"

"What would you have me drink? Blood milk?"

My eyes snap to him as a glare forms on my face. He's smirking before I even meet his gaze. My stomach tightens at that stupid sexy smirk. He's too handsome for his own good and I hate that I'm not immune to it.

"I didn't peg you as someone with a food allergy or someone who cared about the environment or animals," I state, unable to hide the irritation in my voice.

"Animals are wonderful creatures," he says languidly. "It's a pity humans showed up."

On that we agree.

The barista–turned–waiter arrives with our drinks and quickly jots down our food order. It's not long before we're left alone again. I glance around the patio, at the triangular shape of it, and the greenery used to make the mostly concrete patio inviting. It's not the homiest outdoor patio I've been in, but they've done a decent job at making it welcoming.

My eyes drift back out to the sidewalk and the many pedestrians as my mind circles back to the deal I've made with Balthazar. Even though it seems impossible to break free from it, I'm still convinced there's a way out. I've watched Balthazar take advantage of every loophole he can find when he makes deals. There's no way there *isn't* a loophole in our deal.

However, the biggest issue of our deal is Balthazar's life being anchored to the deals he makes. That seems like it'd be bad for business. Why would devils willingly get in the business of buying souls when the stakes of leaving a wish unfulfilled are so high?

"Balthazar." He idly sips his latte as his eyes slowly shift to mine. "I know you've already answered this but seriously, why is there a rule that you'll die if a wish is left incomplete?"

He silently regards me for a few moments before setting his drink down. He's relaxed in his chair, currently dressed in a casual but fitted outfit. The clothes fits him like a glove and his aesthetic gives off the A–list–celebrity–causally–dresses–down–gets–caught–having–coffee–with–unnamed–woman vibe.

I, on the other hand, don't look nearly as bewitching. The lace thong bodysuit and mesh skirt have been exchanged for a plain summer dress and comfortable sandals. I didn't bother removing my makeup but now my flame eyeshadow no longer matches my outfit. A mildly irritating fact but I wanted to feel comfortable in my outfit since we spend most of our days dolled up to barter for souls. I took every opportunity to embrace comfort over aesthetic as did Balthazar, but the lucky bastard looks like a Greek statue no matter what.

As I wait for Balthazar to answer me, my attention wanes as I start to notice the many stares we're receiving. Well, not *we*. Balthazar. I don't blame them. Balthazar's appearance is unearthly. Literally. His beauty is impossible not to draw the eye. There's something about him that draws people in and I haven't figured out if it's his magic or just him.

He inhales deeply, drawing my attention, but just as soon as our eyes connects, he looks away, tapping his finger lightly on the table before he speaks.

"A long time ago, I believe under High King Drokna's rule, devils used to take advantage of humans. They would purchase human souls and give nothing in return despite saying they would. Much like today, when devils took human souls, they'd leave the humans in Ephiri – Earth until their contract ran out.

"As I stated previously, the business of buying souls is through word of mouth. Humans rightfully complained about being deceived and lied to; it ruined Jeznia's reputation. Fewer and fewer humans were interested in selling their souls when there was little incentive to do it.

"When Odantha, Heaven if you will, found out about what the devils were doing, there was a brief war. Odanthians invaded Jeznia to remove the souls who had been wronged. It was a short, but brutal war from what I've learned. Too much of Jeznia's population had been decimated.

"When Jeznia finally surrendered, it was Odantha who brought forth the stipulation that the devils' lives be linked to the deals so that devils would be forced to complete wishes."

It falls quiet for a few moments as I think over his words. If there is a loophole (which there totally is), it's not going to be easy to find. I don't know what Odanthians are, but they defeated the devils of Jeznia. It's probably difficult to defy the rule they put in place. Maybe I could get them to help me. If I plead my case to them, maybe they'll force Balthazar to give up the contract.

"How does one… come into contact with an Odanthian?"

Balthazar offers me a stare like he knows exactly what I'm planning.

"Odanthians can only be bothered to show up when something's gone wrong," he says with a bite to his tone. "You ever wonder why it was only me who showed up at your apartment and not a Champion?"

"Balthazar, seriously, you've got to stop assuming I know what you're talking about when you throw out your terminology," I say in exasperation as my eyes roll. "You *know* I have no idea what a Champion is."

He chuckles more than he should and I'd toss a pastry at him if I had one in reach. "Champions are Odanthians specifically trained to fight Jeznians. You might call them angels, but I believe *real* angels would care more about humans than Odanthians do."

All the friendliness disappears from Balthazar's face and a breeze too cold for this warm day blows through. Goosebumps dart down my arms from the sudden chill. He's angry but I don't know why.

"Odantha doesn't care I came to kill you because I was honoring a contract I bought fair and square. They won't help you, Sloane. They don't care about you."

He spits out the words like he's been personally betrayed by them. I want to ask him more about it, but he might vanish out of thin air to avoid answering the question and then I'd be stuck with the bill when I don't have money or magic to pay for it.

Silence graces us once more and my eyes drop to his fingers strumming against the table. It takes a solid ten seconds of staring at his hand before I remember Umbra's words and yank out my phone to check the time.

"You need to make sure to go back to Jeznia by 11am tomorrow," I inform him.

"I beg your pardon?" he asks somewhat shell shocked by my demand.

"Umbra told me about the cold, how it sets in as soon as you leave Jeznia," I tell him as I slip the phone back into my purse. "I know technically you've got forty–eight hours before it kills you, but you should get back within twenty–four just to be safe."

He works his jaw as his fingers caress the side of his mug. "I see Umbra told you more than just her not being a devil."

"Stop acting like a child," I snap at him. "It's unbefitting of a Lord of Jeznia."

He laughs. Laughs so loud his head tilts back and he exposes the column of his throat. *Damn,* I think, *he's absolutely stunning.*

"Miss Sloane Kensington," he hums my name sensually as his mirthful dual–colored eyes lock onto me. "You never cease to amaze me."

A blush blossoms on my cheeks as I shyly push hair behind my ear.

"What is the cold?" I ask as I change topics. I am *not* ready to dive into what he just said.

"A failsafe the Creator designed to keep the balance. Before you ask; yes, the Creator is what you think it is. Your version of whatever god you believe in, but not the all–knowing kind. Just the kind that knows how to create something and disappear without a trace. A bit of an asshole if you ask me," he says somewhat dramatically.

"The cold sets in as soon as a Jeznian leaves Jeznia," he continues. "It'll act fast, killing a Jeznian within forty–eight hours if they stay in Ephiri. If a Jeznian dares to venture to Odantha, it'll kill them in twenty–four hours. It essentially freezes Jeznians to death from the inside out.

"The heat is the Odanthians version of the cold. They heat up the farther they are from Odantha."

"So, they burn to death from the inside out."

"Yes," he answers before taking a sip of his drink. "If you ever shake hands with a person whose hand is abnormally hot or cold, like it'll burn your hand or freeze it, now you know why."

His statement suddenly has me questioning every single encounter I've ever made. It causes him to grin and, in that tranquil moment of silence between us, the barista delivers our food. He asks us if we need anything else and we politely dismiss him. The food looks delicious and I'm more than happy to dig in.

"I find myself in an agreeable mood today," Balthazar randomly states as he eyes me while I chew my food.

My face scrunches together in confusion as I try to decipher what he's just said. *Does that mean he's giving me permission to keep asking questions?* I'd love to keep pestering him if he'll let me.

"I feel the same way," I reply instead of asking a question. As an afterthought, I add teasingly, "It's nice to not want to kill you for a change."

He laughs boisterously again, sharp and deep, causing me to happily join in with him.

"I'm glad to hear that, Sloane," he replies as his laughter dies down but the smile doesn't disappear.

He's so incredibly handsome and things are going so well right now that it's hard to believe there was a time when I genuinely hated him.

"Perhaps there's something else you'd like to inquire about," he offers and he's trying to sound indifferent but he sounds equally as invested in answering my questions as I am in asking them.

It's strange. Maybe he's never had someone genuinely curious about his origins before. *Probably not*, I think as all the previous deals I've witnessed flash through my mind. Not a single person wanted to know about the place they were destined to live for eternity. I was the only one who asked Balthazar if he knew where I was meant to go before I sold him my soul. He didn't answer, of course, but no one else has asked him that. Do they all just assume they're going to Jeznia?

That small difference between me and them reminds me how similar his deals are. I'd hate my job if I had to do the same thing day in and day out.

"Do you like being a... what did they call it? Contract something."

"Contract Liaison," he answers effortlessly.

"Do you like that job?"

He exhales quietly, his eyes going faint. "Did you forget? This job is beneath me."

"Ok, first of all, fuck those guys. If you like your job then they can rot in Hell– no, wait, they can freeze to death in Odantha."

Balthazar chuckles, eyes alight with mirth as a softened grin adorns his face.

"Secondly, fuck those guys," I repeat as a large smile plasters its way onto my face and Balthazar allows himself to chuckle a little more loudly. "They suck."

"They'd yank your spine through your mouth for speaking those words," he states, his voice full of amusement and playfulness.

"So long as you don't tell on me we won't have any problems," I reply as my eyes fall to my food and I take a few bites. "Capeesh?"

"Yes," he hums out, clearly enjoying himself. After a beat, he says, "I don't hate being a Contract Liaison. It's certainly better than where I came from."

Need I remind you I come from the desperate and poor immediately rings through my head. My eyes snap up to

Balthazar and the words fly out of my mouth before I realize the seriousness of my question.

"Were you not always a part of your House?"

A split second later, it dawns on me what I've asked and I immediately blush as I hold up my hands in surrender.

"Sorry, that was rude to ask. You don't have to answer that." Trying to keep things playful, I rush out the words in a joking tone, "Please don't hurt me."

He scoffs, thankfully in amusement as the right side of his face pulls up in a half smirk. "I'm tempted to. Believe me."

"Sorry," I say again, though a small smile has formed on my lips. Yesterday, I genuinely would have been afraid for my safety, but today things are different. Balthazar's... softer. "What you said made me think about this morning's meeting and I blurted out the words without thinking. I didn't mean to be rude."

He inhales deeply as he leans his head into his hand, elbow resting atop the chair's armrest, while his eyes remain focused solely on me. He stares at me like he can see into the soul I no longer own.

"Thinking about the comment that I come from the desperate and poor?"

"Yeah," I answer honestly. His tone sounds inviting so I don't withhold the words that flow from my mouth. "Your dad's the High King; I'm guessing that means he's in charge, that he rules over Jeznia. If you come from the desperate and poor, wouldn't that mean you didn't grow up in his House? Are you a bastard or something?"

He smiles, the edges of his eyes crinkling. "You think we'd care if someone's born out of wedlock?"

"Well, no. But then why...?"

"Jeznia is a cutthroat world," he answers plainly. "Its occupants murder, steal, rape, and plunder as much as they want to, so long as they're able to stay on top. There are two rules Jeznians live by: never attack someone stronger than you and know when to keep your head down. The first part is easy for a lot of Jeznians. The second part... not so much.

"Every century, Zagon Primis sires nearly two dozen offspring. He rounds them up when they're about three years old, brings them home, and then promptly declares if they are to associate with House Primis, they must deliver results. What that means is to fend for yourself to prove how strong you are. After all, Zagon Primis is looking for a second in command, someone who can hold their own and be equally as powerful as him.

"Each and every one of his offspring ends up dead before two decades pass. There's a lot of weight in the Primis name, but it's not enough to protect you from someone who's stronger than you. Historically, his children have acted brazenly, provoking those older, stronger, and wiser than them. It's never long before they all end up dead."

He pauses to sip his drink and I wait with bated breath for him to continue. His life is horrifyingly fascinating. It's exactly the kind of life I'd expect from Hell yet hearing him recount his past deeply enthralls me. I want to hear more if only to learn about who Balthazar the devil is.

"In my case," he continues, "my mother didn't want to grant Zagon the satisfaction of taking me away. When he came looking for me, she hid me. Told him she miscarried in the last trimester. It's not uncommon for that to happen so he didn't investigate. He had twenty three other prospects to tend to.

"My mother was smart but weak. She lacked the merits to improve her life and instead put all her devotion into me. As soon as I mastered the illusion of making myself appear older, she forced me into the Contract Liaison role. She was not a devil herself and couldn't teach me how to use magic, but she analyzed how it worked to give me suggestions on how to improve. She wasn't perfect," he says this with a softness I didn't know he possessed, "but she was my mother."

His gaze becomes unfocused as his thoughts wander. I wonder what type of mother she was. I can't imagine she was very loving. Definitely not someone who would scoop him up in her arms when he was upset or crying. But there's a certain tenderness on his face that speaks volumes. That tenderness must be exactly what Umbra was talking about when she said Balthazar has a heart that shouldn't be there.

"I was ten when I got my first job," he continues speaking, drawing my attention back to the conversation at hand. "Five years ago, a week after I turned thirty, Zagon finally discovered my existence–"

"I'm sorry, you're *thirty five?*" I ask incredulously as I interrupt him.

His eyebrows furrow together as he answers, "Yes."

"Thirty five, not three hundred?"

"Correct," he replies as a small dose of amusement takes over his expression.

"You're thirty five years old. Only *nine* years older than me. *You're* thirty five years old and the other Lords are how old?"

"I believe the youngest is around..." he pauses to think before saying, "five hundred years old."

My mouth drops open in shock. I can't believe the information I'm hearing. He's *only* thirty five years old.

"What is so surprising?" he asks as the amusement on his face is replaced by mild irritation.

His jaw ticks as his eyebrow arches up and his eyes flash all red for a moment.

"It's just that you're... you're a *baby* in comparison to the other Lords."

His jaw juts out as his eyes narrow in obvious anger. "A baby," he nearly growls.

"Yes! You're only thirty five years old! They're five hundred or older! You're a baby to them!"

People are starting to look at us now that I'm practically yelling. I can't find it in me to care. I'm too hung up on how young he is. Shouldn't he be at least a century older? Why is he so young? And why are they so afraid of him when he's practically a baby?

"I ask this as respectfully as I can. Like genuinely, I don't mean *any* offense," I tell him as I hold my hands up in surrender. "But why are the other Lords so afraid of you? They're older. They should have more experience and power than you. You've barely started out compared to them. Make it make sense."

He clicks his tongue as he stares at me with an indifferent expression. I don't think I've offended him, but it's hard to tell. He doesn't immediately answer my question and instead sits there for a solid minute before he finally answers.

"The simple answer is they've grown complacent," he states. "They rely on their reputations and their House Aides to scare people into obeying them. That's not to say they're weak. They're still very powerful. More powerful than most Jeznians. However, what takes them considerable strength and effort to accomplish is like breathing to me. My work forces me to use my magic every day; I spend hours using it, honing it, developing it–"

"Wouldn't that mean other Contract Liaisons are more powerful than the Lords? They use magic every day like you."

"I have Primis magic, the other Contract Liaisons do not."

"So… magic is hereditary?"

"Yes. It's why Ivy is inclined to become my wife, mistress, sex partner… anything that will get me to sire a child with her."

Ivy… Ivy…which one was she again? That's right! Ivy's the daughter of Lord Carmilla of House Vespertilio. The second House that was formed. One of the most powerful Houses in Jeznia, only second to House Primis. I take a brief moment to praise myself for remembering that all on my own before I ask him my question.

"If you had a kid with her, would that child become the most powerful Jeznian?"

"Quite possibly."

"Then why don't you do it?"

He tilts his head sideways as his eyebrow arches up curiously. "Are you sanctioning this? I suppose if my wife allows it, I'll do it."

"We're not married, asshole," I quip as I roll my eyes and he offers me a wink and a grin. "Seriously, though, why don't you do it?"

"Because she's not a part of House Primis," he answers plainly.

"Why is that important?"

"Whoever births the child *owns* the child. I could try to take it by force as Zagon does, but he purposely chooses those too weak to win against him. His magic is powerful enough that he doesn't require an equal partner in passing down magic. Since he doesn't need a strong partner, he can steal his children without any resistance. I would have to fight Ivy and her entire House–"

"Wouldn't your dad help? This kid could become even more powerful than him!"

"If I were a worthy second–in–command, I'm sure he would. As it stands, I haven't proven my worth yet. A *possibility* that the child could be powerful is not enough to go to war against a House."

"Ok sure, I guess that makes sense. But your dad's magic must be on the same level as a god. So, wouldn't that make you a demi–god? Couldn't you fight the House by yourself?"

He smiles wide. "You give me far too much credit, Sloane. I may be powerful, I may frighten the Lords, but I am not powerful enough to take on an entire House on my own. Half the reason why the Lords fear me is due to my association with Zagon Primis. No one ever thought one of his children would survive as long as I have. They're afraid of upsetting him."

"Right. You said his kids die before they're...?"

"Before me, I believe there was one who made it to twenty years old."

"I know you answered this already but when did Zagon find you?"

"Five years ago."

Right. When he was thirty years old. A solid decade older than the previous successor.

"He must've shit bricks learning how old you were."

Balthazar chuckles and I love how it lights up his face. His delight is obvious as it crinkles the edges of his eyes and his laugh reverberates through his chest.

"Perhaps he did. To find me alive and well when the rest of his children were dead... Zagon was furious that my existence had been kept from him. As punishment, he impaled my mother at the entrance of our village."

Gone is the amusement from him. His voice turns monotonous. There isn't even a hint of anger in his tone, but he curls his fingers into a tight fist. That's the only tell that shows he's angry about his mother's murder. I want to reach out to touch him, to comfort him, but I miss the opportunity as he continues to talk.

"However, that was the first and only time Zagon Primis ever paid attention to me. I may be the only child of his who has lived the longest, but where my strength currently stands, I'm not worth his time. According to him, I still have a long way to go before I'm worthy of standing by his side."

"Do you want that?" I ask and he blinks at me like I've suddenly grown a second head. I repeat my question because he honestly looks a little confused by it. "Do you want to stand by his side?"

"It isn't my decision to make."

"Alright, I get that. You're a Primis and he's the ruler of Jeznia. Daddy decides your future and all, but still... Do you want to stand by his side?"

"No," he answers. I expect him to say he wants nothing to do with Zagon but instead he says, "I'd rather stand in front."

"So do it," I instantly reply and his eyes flash almost white. "It'll take time and you'll definitely need to train or something, but it's not impossible. He's not infallible. Is he invincible? 'Cause that would make it a lot harder to achieve."

Balthazar's head tilts back as a deep, loud laugh expels out of him. It's different from the other ones he's had today. This one is rich and heavy, washing over the entire patio in a seductive timbre. I immediately notice a shift in everyone as their eyes are drawn to Balthazar while he laughs. He looks so free, open, and inviting. A perfect lure for unsuspecting prey.

"All Jeznians can be killed," he answers as his laughter settles down, but his voice is thick with amusement. "Zagon Primis included."

"What if I..." I trail off as I contemplate my words. I honestly don't think I'd waste my wish on killing Balthazar's father, but I am curious if it's possible. "Could I wish him dead?"

Balthazar stares at me for a long time. A warm, gentle summer breeze blows through the patio as idle chatter floats around us. He sits in his chair posed for relaxation as the wind caresses his thick hair, daring to toss a few strands free. Our gazes stay locked onto each other and I can't stop the thought, *He's so handsome.* Too handsome. Out–of–my–league handsome.

The expression on his face is hard and unrelenting. His sharp jaw clenches as his eyes narrow in deep consideration. The silence drags on to the point where I think he won't answer me. Maybe I should say something, anything, to move on from the heavy silence. But then he finally answers.

"My magic would have to be more powerful than his in order to achieve that. Currently, wishing Zagon Primis dead would only get the both of us killed."

But it is possible, I think. So long as there's someone more powerful than him.

"That's enough conversation for today," he says as he pushes back from the table. "We have lives to ruin."

XV

"DO WE HAVE a deal?"

Balthazar is staring into the face of a sixty–something year old man who has been diagnosed with stage IV pancreatic cancer and isn't ready to die yet. He doesn't look incredibly sick so I imagine he's only just begun treatment. That is if he started it at all.

Guilt eats away at me as I listen to this man beg. It's the first person I've met who hasn't wished for money. His desperation is a stark difference to the other men who begged for money. This man has more to lose than any of them did.

I glance away from him to distract my mind and take in the appearance of his home. It isn't anything extravagant. A typical middle class household in the suburbs. Pictures of his family are scattered throughout. We're seated in the living room where the walls are painted a neutral beige and *Live, laugh, love* decor runs rampant, courtesy of his wife I presume.

Tears stream down his face as he clutches his chest. His gaze keeps shifting to me like he's looking for reassurance and I try to avoid his eyes as best I can. My lips pull into a frown as my arms tightly hold my stomach. It never crossed my mind that a situation like this could occur. I always imagined people who summoned the devil would wish for fame and fortune or force someone to fall in love with them. I never contemplated someone selling their soul to *stay* alive. It's heartbreaking.

"You should really think about what you're doing," I warn because I can't hold it back. Seeing him weep about his impending death strikes a chord in me. He reminds me of how desperate I had been to not die; that the desperation to live caused me not to think about *the after* of selling my soul. "Think about the consequences of what you're asking."

The man's lower lip trembles as he stares at me before a sob escapes his mouth. Balthazar snaps his fingers while throwing me a dirty look.

"What you're doing is attempting to save your life," Balthazar states as he directs his attention back to the man. "You'll have seven long years to prepare for your death, to get your little duckies in a row, and make sure the people you care about in life are cared for. Is that not worth our deal?"

The man glances at me again and I attempt to open my mouth but can't. So *that's* what Balthazar's little finger snap did. Hot rage boils through me. *Asshole.*

The man glances away from me just as I grab a pillow off the couch I'm sitting on. I chuck it as hard as I can at Balthazar sitting in the only solo chair in the entire living room and it hits him in the face.

He whips his head around, his face pulled into a menacing glare, but I glare right back at him as I angrily point at my mouth. His glare is immediately replaced by an approving smirk. Piece of shit is *happy* I can't talk.

Balthazar raises his hand up like he's going to snap his fingers and then very purposefully misses snapping them together. I strut over to him and hit him on the shoulder as hard as I can. He laughs before curling his arm around my waist and pulling me down into his lap.

"Forgive my wife," he says as he looks at the man, "sometimes she gets a little too invested in our play sessions and forgets where we are."

My eyes go wide while I try as hard as I can to open my mouth to object to what he's said but my lips physically cannot open. So I do the only thing I can think of and slap him on the forehead. Normally, I'd aim for the cheek but I can't get a good swing in while sitting in his lap. The force of how hard I hit him leaves a quickly fading pink mark on his olive skin.

The entire room shifts as the temperature drops a couple of degrees. If I weren't so angry at him for making me mute, I'd be about ready to pee my pants in fear. He's genuinely pissed I hit him.

Balthazar slowly turns his attention back towards me, the amusement gone from his eyes, but I hold my ground. No matter how worried I might be about how he'll retaliate, *I* have the real power. I point my finger at my mouth again and glare at him in defiance. He works his jaw back and forth as he holds me tight against him.

"We'll be back in a moment, Derick," Balthazar says, but keeps his eyes on me.

We transport out of the room before appearing in the middle of the sidewalk. People walk around us as if we hadn't just manifested out of thin air. It's a little disorienting.

A moment later, Balthazar snaps his fingers and my mouth immediately opens.

"You do that again, Balthazar, and I swear–"

"That you'll kill me," he interjects in a bored tone as he still holds me against his firm body.

"No, I'll stab you. In the dick. And I'll make it hurt. *Do not ever* take away my ability to speak. Do you understand me?"

He stares down at me with an unreadable expression on his face and his temples rapidly pulse as he clenches and unclenches his jaw. As the silence drags on, worry ebbs its way down my spine. Did I go too far threatening to stab him in the dick? Is he contemplating all the ways he could hurt me without doing too much damage?

No, he wouldn't. He said I was too brilliant to harm. I guess now is the moment where I find out just how much he means what he said. If he doesn't retaliate against me, then I'll know with certainty that he won't hurt me no matter what I do. I find myself oddly nervous to find out the truth. What'll it mean to me if he does nothing?

Balthazar shifts forward, muddling my thoughts, and my breath hitches in my throat. He dips his head down, pressing his smooth cheek against mine. That intoxicating, smokey smell invades my senses, enveloping me completely. I refuse to pull away. Pulling away shows fear. I boldly meet him head on, turning my face towards his. My heart hammers against my ribcage as I wait with bated breath. Will he retaliate?

"Threaten me again, Sloane," he whispers against my ear, his cold fingers tightly gripping my waist.

I wait for the rest of his warning, but it doesn't come. He's... telling me to threaten him? Why would he–

Suddenly, the image of us in the kitchen, my hand gripping his hair as I hold his head back, flashes through my mind. He willingly gave me dominance when he didn't have to. He let me threaten him and did nothing about it. Absolutely nothing. In all actuality, it seemed like he enjoyed it a little too much. Now, here we are in a very similar situation.

That addictive sense of power slams into me as his words repeat in my head. *Threaten me again*. He *wants* to submit and the realization is enough to dampen my underwear. He wants to submit *to me*.

A sensual chuckle escapes my mouth as something dark and sinister in me grabs hold of my control. I haven't the slightest clue what I'm doing, but it's second nature to me as my hand slowly slides up his chest, up his neck, to his soft and silky hair. My fingers grip tightly on the thick strands and I yank his head back the same way I did in the kitchen.

I'm still angry at him for making me mute without my consent and I use that as fuel as I glare up into his greedy red speckled eyes. There's defiance there as he glowers at me; we both know he could get out of my hold if he really wanted to *but he won't*. He'll stay put.

"I'll stab you in the dick if you *ever* take away my ability to speak again," I repeat in a low, husky voice. I shift forward so that my chest presses against him. "Do. You. Understand?"

"Yes," he breathes out without hesitation and my entire body ignites in desire.

"Good boy," instinctively comes out of my mouth, similar to the way I'd compliment a misbehaving dog when it finally listens to me.

His eyes flash white as his other hand comes to grip my hip possessively. He pulls me tight against him and his head tugs against my hold as he tries to bend his head forward towards me. My grip remains tight on his hair and he doesn't force his way out of it, instead complying to stay where I keep him in place.

"Shouldn't I get a reward?" he asks, the timbre of his voice so deep and sensual it sends tingles down my spine.

Fuck.

Fuck.

I want to feast on him right here on the sidewalk. Ravage him and punish him for daring to use his magic on me without my consent.

My hand releases his hair and his head drops forward at the sudden loss of tension. His hands come up to grab my face, but I swat them away as I force myself to take a step back from him. He takes that step with me, instinctively following after me, but I shake my head no. My right palm lies flat against his chest and I firmly push him back.

"You don't get a reward for acknowledging a command," I tell him and a low growl rumbles in his chest.

I feel it vibrate against my hand and it almost smashes through my will power to resist him.

"Show me you know how to listen," I say as I lift my hand off his chest, "and I'll give you a reward."

"A reward of my choosing."

I smirk as I reply, "No. Something we mutually agree on."

He glares dark and angry as he takes a step towards me. I take a step back as I raise my finger and wag it at him.

"Uh–uh. You don't get to do something to me without my consent. It'll be a reward we mutually agree on. Now... tell me you understand."

He's clenching his jaw again as his hands curl into tight fists. He hates this. He hates how much he *loves* this. My smirk turns sly as I hold his gaze.

"Don't keep me waiting, Lord Balthazar. *Tell me* you understand."

He huffs an angry breath of air, but he finally loosens his jaw. "A mutually agreed upon reward."

My grin widens as an euphoric high rampages through me, making my knees go weak. My heart feels like it's about to leap from my chest. Lord Balthazar, heir to High King Zagon Primis, the devil who strikes fear into the six other Houses, is *complying to me*. I don't think there's anything else in this world that will ever make me feel as powerful as I do right now.

He watches me closely, waiting for some sort of reply to his acknowledgement. I step to him, placing my palms against his chest as I lean up towards his face.

"A show of good faith," I whisper before kissing him.

It's quick, not lasting more than a second before I pull away. He trails after me to deepen the kiss, but I push against him and he abruptly stops. Before either one of us can say or do anything else, Umbra appears to the left of me. She's dressed in the same outfit from before and only briefly glances at me before settling her golden eyes on Balthazar.

"Lord Balthazar, Derick is contemplating rescinding his proposition."

He groans as he runs a hand through his hair.

The action is so simple, yet enticing as he effortlessly avoids the horns on his head. His sexiness is incredibly distracting. It takes me a moment to remember who Derick is. Stage IV pancreatic cancer.

"I don't think you should take the deal," I say as Derick's sobs echo through my head. "It doesn't seem right taking his soul for eternity just so he can live an extra seven years."

Balthazar arches up an eyebrow as he stares down at me with what looks like slight irritation. "I know I've mentioned this before, Sloane, but I'll repeat it again. Our business is through word of mouth."

"I'm aware," I say, not quite following what he's trying to say.

"That means Derick is friends with people who willingly sold their souls. You spent all day with me the past several days. What are the kinds of people we interacted with?"

Ooooh. Now I get it. It's in our nature to sympathize with someone who's sick and dying. Most people, me included, fear dying. That's why I made the bargain with Balthazar in the first place.

However, I made the deal with Balthazar because he showed up in my life unannounced and unprompted. What Balthazar's saying is that Derick *summoned* him. That means Derick knows exactly how the system works. The only way Derick would know that is by being friends with people who have already made deals. People like Johnathon. Assholes who assault and frame people.

Balthazar grabs my chin as he tilts my head up towards him. "Don't let your human heart cloud what's in front of you."

"Lord Balthazar," Umbra cuts in. "If you don't show up now, he won't make the deal."

Balthazar's eyes dart back and forth between mine before he suddenly vanishes from sight. I look at Umbra and I'm not the least bit surprised she's already looking at me. We stare at each other in silence. She's completely still. Like a statue bolted to the ground. I can't get a read on her and it makes me uneasy.

I know that as long as she's loyal to Balthazar, she won't harm me, but there are other ways to get around that. She could ally herself with Taron and use him to get to me. Or any other House since none of them like me and want me dead. She technically wouldn't be betraying Balthazar if she was doing it *for* him.

I should try to get to know her. If she hates me a little less than she currently does, hopefully she'll feel less inclined to work with another House.

"Balthazar said you had to complete a trial to become his Shadow Seer. Was the trial difficult?" I ask curiously.

She doesn't answer. Perhaps another question?

"How long have you known Balthazar?"

Dead silence. What's a question she'd *want* to answer?

"Do you... have a favorite way to kill someone?" I ask a little unsurely. I honestly have no clue if she'd want to answer that.

"Dagger to the top of the spine, severing all central nerve connections to the brain."

My face pulls into a weird mix of morbid regret and mild fascination. "That... sounds very painful."

"Not when your nerves are severed. You become paralyzed so you won't be able to fight back. Your organs shut down in the process, causing you to suffocate to death. It's quick, but more importantly, quiet."

I slowly nod my head as I try to maintain a facial expression of indifference. "That, uh, that method suits you and your line of work."

A very tiny smirk darts across her face before it disappears completely. *Yes! Point for Sloane.* Dealing with devils and demons is pretty similar to dealing with humans. Just stroke their ego and everything will go smoothly.

"The deal is secured," Balthazar says as he suddenly reappears. "What of Ofello?"

"An honest mistake that he assures won't happen again."

"Honest?"

"Confirmed."

"Very well. What did he lose?"

"Left ear, hearing included."

"Clever," Balthazar replies with an amused smile. "Keep an eye on him and Finthorn for the next few days. I suspect when Finthorn's feeling better, he'll make a move."

"Of course, Lord Balthazar."

They exchange no other words before she vanishes in a cloud of black smoke. Balthazar turns his attention to me and extends his hand as a mischievous grin spreads across his lips.

"Shall we?"

For the first time since I've met him, I don't hesitate to take his hand.

XVI

THE NEXT DAY is long and tedious. We hop from person to person only to hear every single one of them beg. The constant begging bores me, causing my mind to drift to the day I met Balthazar.

Honestly, to my chagrin, my situation isn't much different than theirs. I begged and pleaded for my life the same way they beg and plead for what their greedy little heart desires. It's a little demoralizing to watch. I could argue the reasoning behind my begging was pure and good but, to someone like Balthazar, it's all the same. A pathetic human weeping and begging for something useless.

It's a strange thought to think life is useless but, as I've learned, there *is* an eternal afterlife. Part of me regrets making the deal. I should've taken my chances and let Balthazar kill me. Except the more I think about it, the more I believe I was destined for Jeznia from the start. My soul is different from all the other souls I've seen. It's the size of a tennis ball and red.

Red.

A theme of Jeznia. All the other souls I've seen are the size of a ping pong ball and white. Does that mean those souls are destined for Heaven and I'm the sorry sucker who was always going to Jeznia no matter what? It doesn't make sense, though. I'm *better* than these assholes. Why would they get to go to Heaven and not me?

"Something on your mind?" Balthazar asks as we depart from yet another man's office.

We're somewhere in the middle of South Carolina. The man's work office we left was decorated heavily in right wing propaganda. I would've outwardly objected to granting a wish to such a terrible person if I wasn't already confident Balthazar was going to screw him over. The man wanted to sell his soul so the Democrats would lose every possible election for the foreseeable future. That way the "damn liberals would stop ruining the country."

Balthazar smiled and smoothly talked his way into garnering a deal. Except when they hashed out the details, all the man said was that he wanted the Dems to lose. He didn't specify for which elections, for which states, or for how long. South Carolina is already a red state. The Democrats won't be surprised if they lose their mid–term elections come this November and it won't really upset the balance of the overall country.

"Why is my soul red?" I ask.

"You're not going to chastise me for the deal I just made?" he inquires as he arches an eyebrow while we walk through the business parking lot.

The air is hot and humid and all I really want is to be back at the condo, but I've learned if Balthazar hasn't snapped his fingers yet, there's a reason for it.

A soft gust blows through, caressing the skirt of my A–line floral maxi dress. The breeze is a short reprieve from the sticky humid air.

"If I was the one in charge of that deal," I say, not at all interested in the topic but knowing Balthazar won't move on until he hears an answer, "I'd grant the wish by having the Republicans win South Carolina's November mid–term elections by a landslide. Wish fulfilled."

Balthazar smirks proudly. "She's learning."

I ignore his comment.

"Why is my soul red?" I ask again.

"I don't have an answer for that."

"Yes, you do."

"I don't know why the soul I pulled from you is red," he states.

That's a weird way to answer the question. I'd wager he's withholding information. He's being *very* specific about the words he chooses to use. He only does that when he's making a deal. That means there's something he knows I want to know but isn't divulging it. *She's learning indeed*, I think to myself as I contemplate the best way to prod this puzzle.

"The other human souls..." I begin to ask. "Are they destined for Heaven–er, Odantha?"

"You believe the men we've interacted with are going to Odantha?" he asks, truly aghast I would think such a thing.

"No but... are all souls white?"

"No, souls are not always white."

"Then why haven't we seen a soul that was another color? I know we haven't talked to the entire population on Earth, but statistically we should've seen at least *one* different colored soul."

"We've only made deals with humans," he states.

"Yeah and?" I ask in clear frustration.

It takes me about five feet of walking before I process exactly what he's said. *We've only made deals with humans.* Humans aren't the only creatures in existence. There are other highly intelligent creatures. Balthazar is one of them. Is he saying he has a soul?

I glance at him out of the corner of my eyes. I never considered it, but I suppose he could have a soul. If souls are glowing orbs someone with magic could come along and pluck right out of you. I nibble my lower lip as I form the question in my head before speaking. When I think I've formed a fail–safe question, I ask it.

"Have you ever seen or heard or learned of a human soul that *wasn't* white?"

"I have not," he answers.

What does that mean? *I'm* human, but my soul isn't white. It's red. I ask Balthazar my next question.

"Have you seen other red souls?"

"Yes."

I knew he wouldn't give an answer without being asked, but it's annoying as hell.

"Who do they belong to?"

If I sound a little irritated, it's entirely his fault.

"Jeznians."

My eyebrows pinch together as confusion overwhelms me. *Jeznian? As in Hell? That doesn't make any sense.* "I'm not Jeznian."

"No, you are not. I checked."

"Then why would I have a red soul?"

A sly smile spreads across his lips as he turns his eyes to me. "It is a curious thing, indeed, why the orb was red."

I frown as I stop walking. This is fun for him. It's fun because he has a puzzle he wants to solve and there are no clear answers. Unless he's just toying with me.

"You seriously have no idea?" I ask.

"Haven't the faintest," he replies, full of curiosity and enjoyment as he keeps walking. "That's what makes it all so intriguing, wouldn't you agree?"

No, I wouldn't, I think glumly. This is fun for him but this is my soul we're talking about. I'm human but not. Did I ever stand a chance of going to Odantha or was I always destined to go to Jeznia from the moment I was born?

We're nearly at the end of the parking lot where there's a small, man–made pond swarmed by geese. There are five benches sporadically placed around the pond and it's clear from Balthazar's trajectory that he's aiming for one of them.

Sweat coats my body as I begrudgingly follow after him. I'd rather *not* sit outside in this weather. I hate the humidity. It tires me out, weighs me down, completely changes my attitude. Even New England humidity can be too much for me to handle. I honestly have no idea how people in high humidity areas do it.

"If my soul is Jeznian," I thoughtfully start to ask, trailing a few feet behind Balthazar, "does that mean I was always destined to go to Jeznia?"

"Does it matter?" He inquires as he elegantly sits himself down on the bench.

I guess since I already sold my soul it doesn't. The geese immediately flock to Balthazar as if he's one of their own. Like he's been gone for weeks and they've missed him. They barely pay me any attention as I plop down beside him, my skirt billowing causing the slit to open and expose my leg up to my mid–thigh. Balthazar has magically procured some feed to give the geese and languidly tosses out the seeds as he relaxes against the bench.

"Do you know prior to making a deal if a human is meant to go to Odantha or Jeznia?" I venture to ask.

"I do."

"Was I meant to go to Jeznia?"

"What do you hope to achieve by hearing the answer?"

"Why can't you just answer the damn question?" I snap at him as anger begins to build deep in my chest. The kind of anger that makes me see red, has me lash out, and I won't recognize the aftermath.

"If the answer is no, is that going to help you?" he dodges answering my question by asking one of his own. "If the answer is yes, will that change how you feel about making the deal? No good is going to be achieved by learning where you were meant to go before the deal was ever made."

"That's not your choice to make," I angrily state. "Was I or was I not meant to go to Jeznia?"

He's quiet for about thirty seconds as he keeps his attention on the geese, flicking his wrist to toss some feed their way. He's stalling. I know he is. Why won't he answer the question?

My mouth opens to demand he answer me, but he finally speaks.

"With a red soul like that living inside you, Sloane," he says, never once meeting my gaze, "you were always destined for Jeznia."

Some part inside of me breaks, shattering into a million pieces to be gone forever. *You were always meant for Jeznia.* Why? I lived a good life. I cared about people's rights. I wasn't filled with hate or bigotry. I wasn't making back door deals with the devil for an absurd amount of money or rigging elections. I donated and protested for important causes that actually *helped* people. Why would a person like me be on a one way trip to Jeznia?

"Well?" Balthazar asks as he tosses some more food the geese's way. "Do you feel better about your situation now that you know the answer?"

"Fuck you," I spit out, crossing my arms over my chest as I glare at the geese eating their food. I'm absolutely *seething*. "Why would you buy a soul destined for Jeznia? That makes no sense. The soul is already going there. How is that good for business?"

"Devils purchase souls so they can torture them in their afterlives," he answers in a detached tone. "Devils live for a very long time. It gets rather boring without the occasional human soul to have a little fun with."

My heart sinks upon hearing the words. That means I've sold my soul to be eternally tortured. I knew Jeznia wasn't rainbows and sunshine, but it's also different from what I expected. I never anticipated there'd be seven Lords and a High King that ruled the world. Or that actual jobs such as the Contract Liaison existed. Or that the citizens would be vying for merits to improve their lives.

Upon learning all that new information, some secret part of me hoped that by selling my soul to Balthazar, I would be integrated into their society. No matter how twisted Jeznia is, it *can't* be worse than being tortured for eternity.

"What would've happened to me if I hadn't sold you my soul?" I ask.

I anticipate him to not answer, to ask me what good will it be in knowing, but he withholds nothing from me as he tosses more feed to the geese towards the back of the group.

"You'd wander the Wastelands, destined to be eternally lost."

That sounds exceptionally better than being tortured forever. "Do you torture the souls in the Wastelands?"

"No. That's why devils are so eager to purchase living souls prior to death. They can only torture those who live within the walls of Jeznia. The souls out in the Wastelands are out of their reach."

"How come?"

He blows out a heavy breath before answering. "Anyone who ventures out to the Wastelands becomes lost, regardless of where you hail from. There's old, deep magic there that even Zagon could not stand up against."

I sigh in defeat as my head plops against the back of the bench and I stare up at the blue sky. It's so overwhelmingly hopeless that all I feel in this moment is apathetic indifference.

"I'm to be tortured for the rest of eternity when I could have been wandering the Wastelands," I breathe out as a white, fluffy cloud drifts by, briefly blocking out the sun. "Maybe I could have found a way out with my special, one of a kind soul. And before you tell me it's never happened and is impossible, we don't actually know that since I don't have a human soul. I could do it. I could escape the Wastelands."

"It's a shame we'll never find out," he says without an ounce of sympathy in his voice.

"You're an ass," I snap but it lacks the usual bite.

"I'm *the* ass."

His statement immediately demolishes any self–pity I might be harboring. I snort as I try to keep a smile off my face. He's being serious. It would be rude to laugh at him.

But I can't keep my mouth shut even though I probably should.

"Keep telling yourself that. It's not the compliment you think it is, Mr. Fancy Smancy Lord of Jeznia," I quip before pressing my lips together to hold back another laugh. "Who the hell calls themselves *the* ass? That just sounds stupid."

"Shall I show you how much of an ass I can be?"

His voice is cold, devoid of the friendliness I've become accustomed to. The air shifts around us, the hot South Carolinian air dropping several degrees. Enough to make goosebumps dart down my arms. It honestly feels amazing, but I know what the temperature drop means.

The geese squawk and flee, sensing immediate danger to their lives.

I chance a glance at him out of the corner of my eye. His gaze is glued to the pond a few feet from us and the hair along my arms raises up in alarm.

Judging by the look on his face, I've pissed off the beast. My body knows there's danger and is reacting to the perceived threat, but I now know better. Balthazar *won't* hurt me. He's had multiple chances to follow through with his threats but he never does. He growls, he snarls, he hisses and thrashes, but he never does anything. He's the big, bad beast that rips arms off devils who steal from him, but allows this weak, bratty human to walk all over him.

The urge to roll my eyes at him scratches beneath the surface, but wouldn't it be so much better to indulge him? How will he react? A morbid curiosity builds inside me, wondering how far I can push him before he lashes out. I've insulted him, I've threatened to wish him dead, I've smacked him upside the forehead... is there nothing that I *can't* do?

As nonchalantly as I can, I sit up in my seat, lifting my head off the back of the bench. Balthazar's as still as a statue, eyes burning holes into the pond. I honestly don't know why what I've said has him so pissed off. Is it because I embarrassed him? He can be so confusing at times. One moment, he's as happy as a clam, the next moment, he's as easily offended as a child. I don't get it.

My fingers curl and uncurl in my palms as I try to calm my racing heart. I can't deny the fact that he's angry or the possibility that he might actually lash out at me. It makes me a little anxious. History dictates he won't, but everyone has a limit. I might finally hit his today.

Inhaling a somewhat excited, shaky breath, I say as steadily as I can, "Alright then. Give me your worst."

His head snaps to me, eyes wide and feral as his horns ignite. Heat washes over me and I noticeably flinch. He doesn't miss the flinch and he sneers at me the same way he did at Finthorn. Looks like I got too cocky in our relationship. I forgot my place and he's finally had enough.

I swallow thickly as apprehension befalls my face. Will he actually do something? Or maybe this act *is* his retaliation. Maybe he's dishing out mental terrorism as punishment and we'll laugh about it in a day or two. If that's what he's doing, he's doing a damn good job at it. My mind is *reeling* with the *Will he or won't he?* But it wouldn't surprise me if in a second or two he breaks out into a shit–eating grin and shouts his version of "Gotcha!"

Balthazar suddenly moves, pausing all my thoughts, and I instinctively hold my breath. He slowly rises from the bench and turns towards me. I don't mean to, but I scoot into the corner of the bench to get farther away from him. The metal armrest pokes into my left side as my right side rests against the wooden, slated back. I lift my right foot up onto the seat to help push me back while the skirt of my dress pools around my groin.

Balthazar moves like a panther stalking its prey; slow, steady, and with great purpose. He holds my gaze as the flames on his horns flicker and sway in the wind. I press as hard as I can against the bench as he looms over me.

Ok, I might have bitten off more than I can chew.

He leans forward to grip the back of the bench while his other hand grips the metal armrest. He places a knee in between my legs before sliding it forward against my crotch. It's hot. Hotter than a human body ever could be. With his knee pressed against me and his arms caged around me, he's successfully trapped me on the bench as he glares viciously down at me.

I finally release the breath I'd been holding, unable to hold it any longer. My chest heaves up and down as fear rears its ugly head. I try to tamper it down with logic. Balthazar won't hurt me. He's never hurt me. He's proclaimed I'm too brilliant to hurt. Trust that he won't do anything. Still, staring into the face of the enraged beast obliterates any logic I might have. I might have seriously overestimated my safety with him.

The seconds tick by but Balthazar doesn't move an inch once he's trapped me. He merely glares at me, horns ablaze. The waiting is killing me. *Either do something or get over whatever you're mad about.*

"Do it," I encourage despite my quiet, soft voice.

Better to rip the band aid off in one go than pull it off painfully slow. My heart rams against my ribcage but I hold on to the confidence that Balthazar *won't* hurt me. He won't because he's been having too much fun with me these past few days. He's confided in me about his origins, about wanting to step ahead of his father. He won't hurt me. He's just playing psychological warfare against me. I'll prove to him I can compete against him and we'll see who pulls back first.

I lean forward towards him, propping myself up on my elbow as I grab hold of all the courage I have.

"Show me the asshole that Lord Balthazar can be. Show me the Lord that rips the arms off of devils who steal from him."

His eyes flash white for a quick second. A moment later, his knee presses firmly into me and he slowly begins to rub it up and down my crotch. My eyes widen in shock and I try to scoot away from him, but there's literally no space to move with how he's trapped me on the bench.

"What are you doing?" I hiss out as my eyes dart around the public area we're in. Thankfully, it's empty.

"Showing you how much of an ass I can be," he says in that low, addicting voice.

He slides his knee up and circles it around my clit with such precision that if it were not happening to me right now, I'd find it difficult to believe it'd be possible to do. A slow, tantalizing pleasure begins to build within me. My hips rock against him as his knee moves down, my body seeking more of that delicious feeling. I hate myself for it, for how eagerly I seek him out. I try my best to keep myself immobile, but my body does what it wants no matter how hard I fight it.

"Stop fucking around," I order but it doesn't sound as angry as I want it to.

My body is embracing this wonderful, delicious feeling, almost as if to remind me how long it's been since someone's last touched me. Still, I can't do this with him. The teasing, the back and forth, is as far as I want it to go. Afterall, Balthazar wanted to kill me only days ago. How could I so eagerly jump into his arms before the week has even ended?

"Show me what you really mean," I demand.

Balthazar says nothing as his knee goes up, around, and down in that unhurried, rhythmic pace. His eyes never look away from my face as he watches for any and all kinds of reactions.

My fingers grip the fabric of my dress as I squeeze my thighs against him during a sinfully good rub. I'm on fire, ramping up to be metaphorically devoured even though I swear I don't want it. Lust does strange things to judgment. I need to hold on to reason as hard as I can. *Come on, focus, Sloane. You don't want this.*

"Stop it," I order him again and I'm grateful for how hard my voice sounds. "Either do what you threatened to do or go fuck with someone else."

My hips rock against his knee despite my words, my breath hitching in the back of my throat. The pleasure is steadily building and I'm desperate for it. It's been five long months since I've done this with another person and it's so much better being teased by someone else than by myself. *Jesus Christ, Sloane. Have some decency! Some pride!*

"I'm only interested in fucking with you," he states, using that low, sexy voice, the one that makes me shiver.

He doesn't miss it – the way my body trembles as he speaks. He drinks it all in. There's a subtle quirk to his lips as if he's pleased with himself for what's happening to me. I hate it, hate being putty in his hands like this.

"I'm not playing with you, Balthazar. Either do what you threatened to do or go fuck with someone else."

"No, I want to fuck with you," he repeats as his greedy liquid black eyes make their way back to my gaze.

"Too bad. I'm not playing with you," I say and I thank God there's actual bite to my words as I glare at him.

I'm hanging on by a thread, but I won't give in. I told him I wouldn't sleep with him all those days ago, so I won't. *I won't.*

I plant my palm on his chest and give a push as I say, "Get out of my space."

He does the exact opposite as he dips his head forward, keeping a solid six inches of distance between our faces. He confidently holds my gaze as his eyes darken with desire. There's no anger to be found in his expression. I involuntarily shiver as his lust calls to me.

As if we're in slow motion, his eyes briefly drop to my lips before glancing back up. He parts his mouth to speak, his voice so low it sends a vibration throughout my body.

"I want to fuck you."

That wasn't a slip of the tongue.

Not by a long shot. Balthazar meant *exactly* what he said and it sets my entire body ablaze. That familiar heat pools in my groin, wetting my underwear as he continues to hover over me, his eyes hooded and challenging. I clamp my mouth shut, knowing if I dare to open it, I'll accept. I'll sleep with the devil who not only *owns* my soul but showed up in my life to *kill* me. I'll sleep with him because it'll be the best sex I've ever had and ever will have. No one will be able to compare to him, to his raw, unmatched, carnal power. And apparently, that's more than enough for me to say *To hell with it! Let's do this!*

"I want to fuck you, Sloane Kensington," he repeats in that low, sinful voice. "You said I can't do anything to you without your consent. So… give me permission to fuck you."

Fuuuuuck.

He's submitting again.

Fuck, fuck, fuckity fuck.

Someone who can take whatever he wants whenever he wants is submitting to *me*. He could use his magic to compel me to want this so badly I beg him for it. He could take it by force if I say no. But he does neither. He *submits* and he *asks* for things he could very easily take. It drives me insane with lust.

He slips his head forward, his cheek ghosting against mine as his lips caress my ear while he speaks.

"Are you going to answer me?" he asks in a deep, husky voice. "Will you let me fuck you good and hard?"

A whimper, an actual godforsaken whimper, escapes my mouth as I press as hard as I can against the bench. He moves his thigh, sliding up, circling it around my clit, then back down my crotch. He must feel the wetness of my underwear. I'm soaked through at this point. I should feel embarrassed, but I'm too consumed by the need to be fucked *good* and *hard* to care.

My fingers grip my dress tighter as if that will somehow help me. I want to throw myself at him, to stop dancing around our desire, to just have mind blowing sex after my five month dry spell. So, what's stopping me again?

"Sloane."

"What?" I ask, the word full of lust and barely there restraint.

"Let me fuck you."

"Um."

My head is reeling as I try to come up with any reason for why I shouldn't get in bed with the devil. I'm sure there's a million and one reasons, but not a single one comes to mind. All my brain is telling me is to do it, to get railed so hard I can't walk straight for a week.

"Let. Me. Fuck. You," he growls into my ear and I shiver against him.

"The magic..." I start to say as I grasp at any kind of reason. "Give me the magic word."

I'm not even sure he knows what I'm asking for. He's not human; he hasn't grown up on Earth. He might not have heard the phrase before. As I debate whether to say '*forget it*', that one delicious word leaves his sinful mouth.

"*Please.*"

A hard shiver wracks through my body as my chest arches up to him. The desire to dominate him overpowers me, overshadowing my need to be absolutely wrecked by him. I act without hesitation. My hands pull his face back far enough to slam our lips together.

"Good boy," I murmur against his lips, wholly settling into my role like it's a part of me, and he growls into my mouth as his hands grip me roughly, painfully. "Say it again. Beg for what you want, Lord Balthazar."

He rips his mouth away from mine and leaves searing hot kisses down the column of my throat. His teeth graze against my skin before he bites the muscle connected to my shoulder hard enough that his sharp canines pierce my skin. I hiss in pain, my fingers grabbing him by the hair and yanking him back. His pupils are so dilated that I can't see any red in them as blood smears his lips. It's a glorious sight and my crotch twitches for his cock.

"Please, Sloane," he murmurs, eyes bleary. "Let me fuck you."

Another tremble wracks through me at the power I command. A strong wind blows through the parking lot, causing ripples along the pond's surface as Balthazar stares at me like a drug addict begging for heroin. I've got him eating out of the palm of my hand. I could give in, let him screw me the way he's begging to, but we've only just begun. He *wants* to submit, to be ordered around as though he's not one of the most powerful beings in all of Jeznia. Who am I to deny him that?

My fingers grip his hair harder as I hook my right leg around his knee on the bench. "Tell me how badly you want it."

His upper lip pulls back in a snarl as a low growl reverberates through his chest. He's fighting his urge to submit and it's probably getting him off even more. My other hand reaches up and my thumb wipes at the smeared blood on his lips. *My* blood. I never knew how sexy it could look outside of me.

"I'm waiting," I coo as my eyes focus on my thumb rubbing his plump bottom lip.

"I can't stop thinking about it," he confesses and I slip my index finger inside his mouth.

It's hot and wet and a light gasp escapes me as his tongue flicks against my finger. My mind runs rampant with ideas of what else that tongue could be doing as I withdraw my finger from his mouth.

"I've been wanting to fuck you ever since you highjacked your way to Jeznia with me. You defy all survival instincts of your species, readily challenging me whenever I threaten you. No one has ever provoked me the way you do, not after what they've seen I'm capable of. Yet you do. It drives me mad with lust. I can't stop thinking about fucking you. I can't stop masturbating to the thought of my cock inside your warm, tight pussy."

I immediately sit up straighter in my seat upon hearing those words. "You do?"

He buries his head into my shoulder as he groans out, "All the fucking time."

"Show me," I order breathlessly as intense pleasure washes over me.

I want to see it. I want to see the kinds of faces he makes as he thinks about fucking me. How does he touch himself thinking it's me wrapped around his cock? What kinds of noises does he make? I want it all burned into my memory so I'll never forget.

Another groan passes through his mouth as his fingers grip me tight enough that they'll leave bruises.

"Sloane," he growls. "Let me fuck you."

"No," I manage to say despite how my crotch aches with need to be filled to the brim with a thick, hot cock, *his* cock. "Not until you show me how you touch yourself when thinking about me."

"Sloane–"

"That's an *order*, Lord Balthazar," I state firmly with no room for argument.

He pauses only for a moment before peeling himself away from me and standing to his feet. My heart is in my throat as impatience has me nearly ripping his pants off. I want to free him from his restraints, to see his cock fully erect and dripping with desire. Desire for *me*. My fingers twitch to grab at him but by some grace of God, I remain still. *Patience,* I remind myself.

Balthazar stares down at me, but I don't meet his gaze. I watch his hands. I watch as they roam over the thick bulge in his pants, heading north to the button of his pants. My tongue darts out, licking my lips as I watch him unbutton the pants before grabbing the zipper. He pauses and I wait for him to continue, but he doesn't. My eyes snap up to his, my lips parting to order him to continue except he's not staring at me anymore. He's staring off in the distance before a scowl grabs hold of his face.

"*Fuck*," he growls, all the anger and hatred he possesses drowning in that one word.

XVII

"WHAT?" I ASK in slight alarm as he swears angrily
again.

He doesn't answer me. Instead, he snaps his fingers and
his outfit is changed in an instant. He wears a fitted, three-
piece, pinstripe Armani suit with his hair slicked back. A
pentacle dangles between his horns, connected by a thin
golden chain. Pitch black fingernails and rings of varying
sizes adorn his hands. Smokey black eyeliner and glowing
soft red eyes stare at me. Warning bells go off inside my
head. I've never seen him dressed like this.

"Balthazar, what's going on?" I ask as I stand up from the
bench and quickly fix my dress.

"A deal."

Angered shock courses through me. "Are you *kidding* me
right now?" I shriek, my own lust rampant and raging at
being interrupted.

He stopped because of a *deal?* Is this some sort of twisted
foreplay?

"I never joke about these matters," he states.

"You stopped us from having sex because of a *deal?*"

"Yes."

My mouth drops open because I honestly have no idea what to do with this information.

"This is bullshit," I spit out.

I had finally consented, finally threw caution to the wind, and decided to indulge my carnal desire. Yet the moment I do, Balthazar slams the door in my face. He probably intended to do that from the start. Especially after I talked a big game about never having sex with him. This is probably him showing me who's really the boss.

Feeling the bitter sting of rejection and embarrassment, I blurt out, "See if I ever agree to have sex with you again. Today was a fluke. It *won't* happen again. You lost your chance."

He glares harshly at me but says nothing as he snaps his fingers. My maxi dress is replaced by an all white Dolce & Gabbana suit. My hair is slicked back into a middle part low ponytail and, although I can't see my reflection, I imagine my makeup looks very similar to his.

"Balthazar–"

"Time is of the essence," he states before grabbing my hand and snapping his fingers again.

We transport out of the parking lot in South Carolina and show up in the corner of a private hospital room with a single bed. There's a woman propped up in the hospital bed with an IV and other tubes hooked up to her. Her fair freckled skin looks a bit flushed and she's covered in a light sheen of sweat. The pink headband she wears is damp from said sweat. Her dyed blonde hair is pulled back into a high ponytail to keep out of her oval shaped face.

She looks sickly, her body a little too thin for her height, but she doesn't look like she's knocking on death's door. The room smells of chemicals and bleach. It's such a stark difference from the lust induced moment mere seconds ago that it feels like whiplash.

Balthazar doesn't spare me a glance as he walks over to the woman's bed. She can't be much older than Balthazar. She's clutching something in her hands and all I see are bits of white against her pinkish skin. She watches him approach with fierce determination burning bright in her brown eyes.

"I knew you'd come," she says in a heavy southern accent, her voice physically weak, but her words strong and assured. She sounds confident and unafraid.

"You summoned me," he states.

"Yes. Yes, I did," she agrees and she glances at me still standing in the corner of the room. "Devil in trainin'?"

"Maybe one day," he says without any emotion. "Tell me why you've summoned me."

This is an entirely new version of Balthazar that I haven't seen before. He's almost tender despite removing all emotion in his words. He stands tall with his hands holding his forearms behind his back. There's no cockiness in his mannerisms or stature. No condescending tone when he speaks to her. There's a strange air of familiarity that swirls around them. I want to ask how they know each other, but it'd feel like intruding upon a very intimate moment.

"I wanna sell you my soul," she says.

He tilts his head to the side and I finally find the courage to approach her bed. Neither one of them spares me a glance as my shoes clack against the linoleum floor.

"Why do you want to do that?" he asks in a quiet voice as I come to stand beside him.

There are tears in her eyes, some streaking down the sides of her face, and her lower lip trembles.

"They caught the illness too late. I've got kids. Three of 'em. I don't have any family other than these kids. They'll go straight to state. I can't leave 'em behind. My babies didn't do anythin' wrong." A sob breaks through her facade and she uses the tissue in her hand to wipe her nose. "I'll sell you my soul, but you've gotta take care of my babies. Promise me."

A lump forms in my throat as I stare at this grieving, dying woman. It's hard not to feel for her. Her kids are probably wonderful people and I can't imagine ever losing my mother. But she summoned Balthazar and as he said, this business is word of mouth. That means she knows people who have sold their souls. No matter how kind she seems or how sad her backstory is, she's not a good person. I can't let myself feel sorry for her. She doesn't deserve it.

I force back my tears as best I can and wait for Balthazar to explain the terms of the agreement.

"That I cannot do," he says.

My head whips around as my mouth drops open in shock. What did he just say?

"You've gotta," she begs him as more tears slide down her face. "I've seen you take deals for less than that. If you don't wanna take care of 'em, set up money in their names."

"It doesn't matter the wish you make," he says quietly, calmly, and with no ounce of remorse. "I will not purchase your soul."

Five seconds pass before an ear piercing sob rips out her. Her hands smother her face as she cries into her palms.

"Why?" she demands to know, her voice muffled by her hands. "I've seen you take souls worth nothin'."

"You have it backwards. *Your* soul is worth nothing."

What would make a soul worth nothing? The only difference between her and the other people Balthazar has made deals with is the fact that she's a woman. Is he seriously discriminating against her because she's a *woman?* I knew the devil wasn't a good entity, but I never thought the devil would be sexist. The thought makes my blood boil.

"Please. Please, you've gotta take care of my babies."

She's sobbing uncontrollably and I can't handle it. It's clear how much she *loves* her children. In the face of death, she's thinking about *their* future. Not her own fate. She's worried she'll leave them impoverished and suffering instead of worrying where she'll end up in the afterlife once she's sold her soul. She's not begging him for more time. She's not even considering herself in the equation. She's only thinking about her kids. That's enough to speak to my humanity even if she's a bad person.

I reach out and tug on the sleeve of his suit. "Balthazar, take the deal," I urge him.

"I will not."

"But her kids—'"

"Will not be the first children to lose their parent," he coldly cuts me off, refusing to look me in the eyes. "They'll figure it out. Her soul is worth nothing. There is no deal worth making."

I can't figure it out, can't figure *him* out. Why give up the chance at having sex he claims he thinks about all the goddamn time for a deal he *knew* he'd turn down? Make it make sense.

If her soul is worth nothing to him, if a deal is impossible, why not ignore her summons? Why show up and destroy her morale, take away all of her hope, and tell her how worthless she is? The only logic behind it is it gives him a high; it reinforces how much better he is than her. He's probably getting off on it right now and the thought churns my stomach.

"You're a sick bastard," I say as disgust fills me to the brim.

"You should expect that from a devil," he replies but his attention is on the woman.

"No. You're worse than that. I wish I never–"

Snap.

HONK! HONK!

"–met you."

The abrupt change in location has me stumbling to my hands and knees. I barely miss landing a chewed up piece of gum as I fall onto the sidewalk. People walk past me, completely ignoring me, as if seeing someone magically appear and fall down on the sidewalk is an everyday occurrence to them.

More car horns assault my ears and the ocean–city smell of Boston fills the air. I rise up onto my feet and go to wipe my hands on my pants but stop. This is a *white* Dolce & Gabbana suit. Somehow I've managed not to dirty my knees when I fell. It'd be a shame to dirty them by wiping my hands on them.

Instead, I rub my palms together as I look around. I don't recognize where I am, but it's distinctly Boston. Old New England styled buildings mixed in with modern ones, crowded streets, people yelling at each other with thick accents. Boston through and through.

"Sloane?"

It takes me a second to realize someone has called my name.

"Sloane, is that you?"

I turn around and come face to face with Chad. He's a good five feet from me and dressed relatively nicely. Slim, fitted jeans, baby blue polo shirt, hair done up, and... is that makeup?

He looks completely shell–shocked, which I guess I would be too if the person I wished dead was standing five feet from me. Wait a minute. He shouldn't be able to see me. Balthazar said everyone from my old life *can't* see me. Chad should be included in that.

"Can you see me?" I ask as I wave my hand in excitement at him.

Someone I know might actually be able to see me! Does that mean other people from my life can see me too? I should visit Mom and Dad, let them know I'm not dead or hurt! Then go see Ella. Why the hell did I ever take Balthazar at his word?

"Of course I can see you, you're standing right in front of me," Chad snaps, his face shifting into a scowl.

Hot white anger slams into me at his open hostility. All the excitement at being seen has disappeared as I glare at him. *How could I have forgotten he's a royal dick?*

"Whoa ok, first of all, lose the tone," I order haughtily. "Second of all, do you have any idea how hellish my life has become? You wished me *dead*, Chad. I've got no money, no place to live, no way to get a job. I don't exist anymore."

"Except you do. *I'm staring right at you.* The fuck is this shit?" he asks as his arms gesture wildly at his sides. "You're supposed to be six feet under! Your parents *buried* you. You're telling me you weren't in that coffin?"

"Does it look like I was in the coffin?" I ask as my anger morphs into deeply rooted rage. I cross the distance between us and smack him as hard as I can on the chest. "How dare you? How *dare* you? You didn't like being exposed as a misogynistic asshole so you *murdered me?*"

"I told you to take the profile down, but you didn't listen," he yells back as he shoves me away from him.

"So?! That doesn't mean you sell your soul to have me killed!"

"What are you so pissed about?! You're not even dead!"

By now we're starting to cause a scene from all our yelling and the people who walk by us are giving us looks as they pass.

"I *am* dead! My entire life was ripped away from me! I can't see or talk or touch my friends and family ever again. I can't even message them! Balthazar's magic prevents me from doing so because of *your* wish," I say as I jab my finger into his chest.

"Fucking touch me one more time, Sloane, fucking do it," he eggs me on as he glares down at me.

He's got a good three inches on me and normally I wouldn't be so easily intimidated by a man that close to my height, but the look in his eyes has me worried. It's eerily similar to the look Balthazar gets when he's thinking about murdering me. Except that's all Balthazar can do without killing himself in the process. Chad has no restraints since I'm already dead in our world. Would there even be an investigation or would Balthazar make it as though it never happened?

My entire body suddenly goes cold as pieces of the puzzle slide into place. Was this Balthazar's plan all along? To have Chad kill me? No. It can't be. If Chad kills me, Balthazar dies... doesn't he? Except when Balthazar extracted my soul, it was a *Jeznian* soul. What if my soul is still inside me?

What if a deal was never actually made? What if these past few days were leading up to this exact moment?

"Shit," I breathe out as I suddenly go lightheaded. My hand comes up to loosely cover my mouth. "I'm going to be sick."

"Gross," Chad shouts as he shoves me, *hard*.

I trip over my heel and fall flat on my ass, my palms scraping against the sidewalk. They sting a little and when I glance at them, a very thin layer of blood coats my palms. With everything that I'm currently processing, I don't move. I just sit where Chad shoved me, my mind racing a mile a minute.

He kneels down beside me, his presence menacing and dangerous. Chad leans towards me and it draws my attention up to his murderous face.

"I'm going to kill you, Sloane," he states in a slow, firm voice. He leans all the way forward to whisper in my ear. "And I'm going to get away with it too."

His words snap me back to the situation at hand. I act, I don't think. I grab him by the throat and *squeeze*. My anger has turned poisonous and it shrouds my judgment. There's only one thing running through my mind right now. It's killed or be killed.

My lips pull back to bare my teeth and the words sound otherworldly as I speak.

"Not if I kill you first."

My fingers squeeze tighter and his eyes widen as he realizes I mean business. We begin to brawl on the sidewalk and that's when people finally decide to intervene. Arms grab around my waist and under my armpits as people attempt to pull me away from Chad.

"You're done, Sloane," Chad roars as three men pull him off me. "Y'hear me! *Done!*"

I laugh maniacally, my feet kicking at empty air as I try to hit him. Sadly, he's just out of my reach.

"Come and get me, Chad. I'm right here," I goad him as I'm held in place.

I fight against the arms holding me back, my desire to maim, mangle, and kill Chad overwhelming me. He ruined my life. I'm not going to let him get away with it. I'm the one who can get away with murder. *I don't exist.* Chad's face has been plastered all over the news since my murder has gone national and he made himself the number one suspect. He has more to lose than I do. I'm going to take it all from him.

"It's ok, it's ok," someone says confidently from the crowd. "You can let them go. Sibling quarrel. They've cooled off now."

The people don't let us go, probably worried that if they do, we'll go right back to fighting. Chad and I stare each other down, his face hardened in hatred while I smile like a deranged psychopath at him. However, as soon as the smell hits, both our faces change into disgust. Rotten meat that smells like it's been left out in the sun for too long slams into me. I glance around to look for the source and my blood goes cold as I find it.

"Jesus Christ," I breathe out.

Chad notices the source of the smell seconds after me and panics.

"Oh shit! Let me go! Let me go," he practically shrieks.

We stare at a creature the shape of a human, but that's where the similarities end. Skin dangles off at random places and is various shades of rotten yellow, green, brown, and purple. Like the body isn't sure what stage of decomposition it's in. Part of its lips are gone as if they've rotted away and fell off, exposing stained yellow teeth.

There are no eyes in its sockets and the sockets are charred black. It has no discernible features. No hair, no eyes, discolored skin, and it is so incredibly emaciated it shouldn't even be alive. The strangest part, though, are the clothes. This putrid smelling thing is wearing a *designer suit*.

As soon as the men let go of Chad, he bolts. High tails it out of there as fast as he can. The people who are holding me finally let go, but instead of running, I stay put. I've seen similar things like this during my visits to Jeznia. I'm confident I can handle whatever it is.

I glance around the circle of people and notice no one else seems alarmed that there's a literal monster amongst the group. Can they not see it? That can't be right. I see people make eye contact with it, nod their heads at it as a thank you for interjecting. But none of them are alarmed by what they see when they should be. It they don't see what I'm seeing... what do they see instead?

The creature takes a step towards me and that rotting smell intensifies. I immediately recoil as I gag.

"Oh, sorry," it says and has a distinctively male voice. "I forget those that are like me can see the real me and smell the rot."

I stare at him in utter confusion and horror. "People like you?"

He smiles, the little parts of his lips that he still has cracking and seeping black ooze down his mouth and chin. It's absolutely disgusting and I force back another gag.

"Yes, like me," he says. "Other people who have sold their souls."

XVIII

THE THING STANDING in front of me is *human?* It looks like a creature straight out of a Stephen King novel.

"Y–you sold your soul?" I ask as my hand rises up to pinch my nose and I breathe through my mouth.

The rotting scent coats my tongue as I inhale and this time, I can't suppress the gag. If he's offended, he doesn't say anything. I take a sidestep from him, hoping the wind will blow his disgusting odor away from me.

My eyes dart up and down his body as if I'll somehow figure everything out by simply looking at him, but I come up empty handed.

"Yes. I sold it about five and a half years ago."

"Why do you look like that?"

"Because I have no soul," he answers cheerily, like he's the weatherman telling me the sun will finally be out after a week's worth of rain.

"But why do you..." I can't figure out how else to ask it other than *why do you look like that?*

"Without a soul, the body begins to decay," he answers my unfinished question.

I'm horrified but also morbidly curious. Horrified that if I don't find a solution to my problem, I'll look like him in five years. But more so morbidly curious to know more about his situation and if there's anything I can learn from him that will be useful.

"Does it... hurt?" I ask as I stare at a piece of flesh dangling off his neck.

Black ooze drips out of it and stains the collar of his suit. I grimace at the sight.

"Like a bitch," he answers in that same cheerful voice. "You get used to the smell, but the skin falling off hurts every time."

There's a few seconds of silence as we stare at one another. His smile is gone and, with no eyes in his sockets and a disfigured face, it's hard to tell what kind of expression he's making. However, he makes no attempts to leave, which is kind of nice. I have a million questions running through my head. He's been nice enough. Hopefully he'll continue to answer them.

"How do you know the reason why you're decaying is because of your missing soul?"

He shrugs his shoulders as he slides his hands into the pockets of his pants. "You figure it out by asking around. At first, you don't realize what's happening to you. You think it's stress or some horrible disease. The first to go is clumps of hair or if you're unlucky, some teeth.

"You go to the doctors, but they literally can't see what you're talking about. They write you off as overstressed, overworked, overtired and prescribe some time off to help the hallucinations stop. But when the first chunk of skin comes off you, *that's* when you reach out to the buddy who set you up with the devil.

"You realize the same shit is happening to him. And the guy he reached out to is even worse off than him. And the guy that guy reached out to tells him it's all happening because the body decays without a soul and it'll keep decaying until you drop dead on the seven year anniversary of selling your soul. Bing, bang, boom."

For some reason, hearing him explain it like that hits me hard. That will be me. I'll start decaying and lose my hair and teeth. I'll start losing pieces of skin and smell like rotten meat.

No. It won't be me, I think harshly. For one, Balthazar didn't actually make a deal with me and two, if he did, I'll find a way out of it. I'm not going to let myself succumb to a decaying body and an eternity of torture. I won't.

"You must have just made your deal," he says completely unprompted. "You still look normal."

"Thanks... I guess."

"That guy you were fighting with, did he sell his soul too?"

"Asshole sold his soul to have me killed."

He makes an over exaggerated and highly amused *oh.*

"He must be pissed to see you alive and kicking."

"Yup," I breathe out heavily as I look down the sidewalk.

Chad's long gone. Apparently he's too chicken shit to talk to the monster. Jeznia will eat him alive when he dies. *Good. It's the least he deserves.*

"But the devil has to kill you, doesn't it?" the man asks. "Or else it'll die too."

"Oh, he's killed me in every sense of the word except physically. I guess my family has already had my funeral. At least, according to Chad."

It's a weird statement to make. It *should* fill me with hurt, anger, and injustice. My parents shouldn't have had to bury their daughter. That's not how life is supposed to go. But instead of feeling those emotions, I feel weirdly detached. Like I can't process my own funeral having come and gone on top of Balthazar's betrayal.

"It's a shame you missed it," he chirps cheerily. "I've always wanted to attend my own funeral."

I laugh lightly. Millions of other people probably want the same thing. I'm glad I missed mine. I wouldn't have been able to stomach the pain and misery of my parents and friends.

"Are you afraid of dying when the time comes?" I ask him as I look into the charred holes where his eyes should be.

"No."

"But you're going to be tortured for eternity. That doesn't scare you?"

He laughs, loud and hearty, which catches me completely off guard. "Sweetheart, I've been tortured every day of my life. There's not much else they can do to me."

"There's always something worse that can be done."

That removes the smile from his face and he rubs his chin. A piece of flesh drops to the sidewalk. I can't help the look of disgust that crosses my face, but I do my best to get rid of it as fast as I can.

"I suppose you're right. But there's no sense in worrying about it now, is there? I'll deal with it when the time comes." He claps his hands together before looking up and down the sidewalk. "Would you like to get out of here? I can answer any other questions you might have. At least to the best of my capabilities."

I hesitate to answer. It's an odd proposition, but the way he suggests it alludes to the fact that he knows more than he probably should. I'm curious how that came about. Maybe I can find out how to get out of my bargain with Balthazar, but it's unlikely. If this man is still decaying to death, he doesn't know how to get out of his own deal. How would he know how to get out of mine?

Still, his ease in which he approaches his impending doom makes it seem like he knows something about Jeznia he shouldn't. Maybe going with him will be a total waste of time, but there's a chance I might hit the jackpot.

I glance around the area, but I see no signs of Balthazar or Umbra. It's strange he hasn't finished up the deal yet, but then again, he probably expects me to be dead. Which honestly, it sucks– no, it's perfectly fine he's left me for dead. I don't want to be around a sexist asshole.

I don't know why it surprises me to find out Balthazar's sexist. I should've paid more attention to the fact that he's only made deals with men. All I concentrated on was that those assholes would be spending eternity in Jeznia. I should've paid better attention to the gender of Balthazar's deals, but I was too bored out of my mind to care.

Feeling ashamed and regretful, I turn my attention back to the unnamed man. I offer out my hand with a small smile.

"I'm Sloane."

His slimy hand grips mine and it takes every ounce of willpower I have to not yank my hand back. I force myself not to think about how wet and squishy it is and pray the handshake will be over soon.

"Hello, Sloane. I'm Matt. Would you like to grab some lunch?"

I open my mouth to agree, but then realize I have no money. "I don't have money."

"I don't mind paying."

"Are you sure?"

He huffs a laugh. "It's not a problem."

This time I smile wide and large as my hand slips away from his. "I would love to accompany you to lunch. Thank you for your generosity."

ROUGHLY TWENTY MINUTES later, we're seated in a dive bar on Pearl Street. It's surprisingly busy and when we arrive, I get the impression Matt's a regular. He cheerily greets the staff as we walk to a table towards the back. He must be a decent patron because everyone enthusiastically greets him back.

The waitress doesn't waste any time bringing over a specialty beverage for him. My eyebrow arches as I stare at the already prepared drink. He must come every day around the same time for them to know what drink to make and when to have it ready for him.

It's barely noon but I decide it's late enough in the day for an alcoholic drink. I order a hard cider from the tap and the waitress excuses herself to get it. My attention wanders around the place. I like the down to earth vibes of the Irish bar. Most people are engrossed in their conversations, too busy to pay us any mind. It shouldn't be a problem to continue our conversation here even with so many people.

"What do you think of the place?" Matt asks as he sips his beverage.

I do my best to subtly hold my finger beneath my nose, acting as though I'm resting my chin in my hand, but really I'm trying my best to not inhale his smell. He's been kind enough that I don't want to offend him or be rude.

"It's nice," I reply. "You seem like a regular."

He chuckles. "I am. It's my favorite place in all of Boston."

I don't really know what to say in response to that but thankfully the waitress comes back with my cider. Matt orders his usual and I order a cheeseburger with fries.

"So," he says as he claps his hands together. They squish upon impact and I can't withhold the disgusted look that darts across my face. "What kind of questions might you have for me?"

I stall for a moment to collect my thoughts. Languidly, I bring the hard cider to my mouth, reveling in the tart carbonation.

"Tell me what you know," I say as the glass gently taps against the tabletop.

He stares at me with a semi frozen expression on his face. "What do you mean?"

"You gave me the impression you knew quite a bit," I answer as I lazily spin my glass.

I've learned quite a bit watching Balthazar these past few days. I won't give Matt the upper hand. He sold his soul. That says *a lot* about his character. Instead of giving him an opportunity to manipulate information out of me, I'll force him on the defensive.

"Instead of wasting my time asking you questions you might not know the answer to," I say as I wipe away a condensation droplet on the glass, "I figured it'll be easier for you to just tell me what you know. As you so correctly assumed, I'm new to all this. I sold my soul less than a month ago."

It's best to give as little information as possible. I won't shy away from the truth, but I won't divulge the whole truth either. Balthazar expertly walks the tightrope as if he was born to do it. He's shown me how purposeful you can be in giving and asking for information. Even though he's betrayed me, I am grateful for this small lesson he's bestowed me.

Matt exhales loudly as he leans back in his seat. "Well, I mean, what's there to know? You summon the devil to sell your soul for a wish. Except, the devil is an asshole and finds ways to grant your wish, but not in the way you want it. When you point out how he went on and on about having to honor your deal because if he didn't he'd end up dead, he aptly points out he *has* fulfilled the wish. It's your fault for not specifying the details.

"So then you come to terms with your new situation and how pieces of your body fall off without warning. Thankfully, the magic the devil uses conceals what you really look like to everyone else so you can continue to live your life. The only people who see what you really look like are the devil and others who sold their souls.

"Eventually, your seven years are up and you drop dead wherever you are. I've seen it happen once. This dude was literal bones, walking down Newbury Street when out of nowhere, he face plants into the cement. It was like he had a stroke. One second he was fine, the next, poof. Dead"

Matt doesn't know shit, I think irritably. At least I get a free lunch out of this wasted trip. As if on cue, the waitress comes out with our food, asks if we need anything else, and leaves once we excuse her. The food smells heavenly and I hunch over my plate so the smell of the fresh hamburger and fries overpowers the decay leaking from Matt.

"Do you know of anyone who's ever gotten out of their deal?" I ask as I chew on a fry.

"Would I look like this if I had?"

"Fair point," I grumble as I eat more fries. "So, what'd you wish for?"

He's chewing his food but immediately stops when I ask him the question. He stares at me for what feels like ten full minutes before he finally chews the rest of the food and swallows.

"Something stupid and foolish. What about you?"

I regard him for a moment. It's interesting he won't share what he sold his soul for. He's been, from what I can tell, rather transparent about everything else. Why would he feel the need to keep his wish a secret? It's disconcerting and raises the hair on the back of my neck. I follow his lead as I rub the salt from the fries off my fingertips.

"Not something worth eternal damnation," I answer.

He snorts. "Ain't that the truth."

We eat in silence for a little bit but I decide since he's treating me to a meal, I might as well pass the time participating in small talk with him. I ask him about his work (he works in Finance), if he has any family (surprise, surprise, he does not), what he likes to do for fun, and other unimportant topics.

Matt happily answers all my questions, too pleased to share his life story with a complete stranger. He either doesn't talk to many people that often or he loves hearing his own voice. I'd venture a guess it's the latter.

About forty–five minutes later, he places two one hundred dollar bills on the table as he stands, clearly not wanting change, and I now understand why the staff here likes him so much. I follow his lead as I get up from my chair and realize my nose must have shut down because Matt doesn't smell so horrible anymore.

"Well," I awkwardly begin, not quite sure how to say goodbye, "thanks for the meal–"

"Before you head out, I'd like to show you something towards the back," he says. "If you don't have anywhere you need to be?"

My mouth shifts to the side of my face. I'd really like to get going, but it's not like I have anywhere to be. Balthazar's left me for dead and I'm dead to the rest of the world. I don't have any money for a taxi or to take the subway. Unless Balthazar comes to retrieve me, which he won't, I'll have to figure out my next steps. As much as I'd like to say goodbye to Matt, he did treat me to lunch. I suppose I could spend a little more time with him.

"Sure. Lead the way," I answer.

He smiles and I hold back a wince as a small piece of his lip falls off. Wordlessly, he leads me to the back of the bar and through a door, slipping off his suit jacket in the process. The doorway leads us outside to a narrow street. A building lines the other side of the street while trash cans sit on the curb.

Matt holds the door open for me to step through. I walk out towards the edge of the sidewalk. As I turn back to face him, things quickly take a turn for the worse.

Matt lunges for me, his actions fast, but there's enough time for me to react. My arms shoot up to block him despite me having zero skills at fighting. I've never been in a fight in my entire life. Minus the little scuffle I just had with Chad. However, this situation is significantly worse than with Chad because Matt is *slippery*. Like his body hasn't been decaying out in the open skies but submerged in the deepest depths of the ocean. He is basically waterlogged and he knows it.

In the short time we walked down the hallway of the bar to the outdoors, he discarded his suit jacket and rolled up the sleeves of his shirt. All harmless acts that I thought nothing about, but now... Now, I regret not seeing the actions for what they were. His intent to make it as difficult as possible to fight against him.

Despite being at a disadvantage, I refuse to roll over and make it easy for him. My heart pounds loudly in my ears as adrenaline rushes through my veins. Fear makes my movements sporadic. I kick, punch, and flail like a wild beast trying to get free. Matt keeps me close to him, grabbing my clothes any time I try to shove him away.

My best plan of action is to get distance and run. He's so desperate to hold on to me that he doesn't attempt to do whatever it is he set out to do. Rape me? Kill me? Both? Either way, we're locked in a struggle. Eventually, one of us will tire out and I'm determined to make sure it won't be me.

"You sure know how to cause a fuss," Matt grunts as my foot connects with his stomach.

I spin on my other foot, preparing to run, but he clamps down hard on my jacket. I attempt to shimmy myself out of it when a thin piece of fabric is wrapped tightly around my neck. He releases my jacket and tightens the cloth around my neck. My eyes go wide as I realize he's trying to strangle me to death.

Desperation floods my mind as fear imbeds itself into my bones. My hands reach up as I attempt to pull the cloth from my neck. It's no use. He's got it too tight. I attempt to inhale, try as hard as I can, but all I manage is a wisp of air. *I'm going to die,* I think as my vision blurs with unshed tears. If I can't break free soon, I'll suffocate to death.

I try to get my fingers in between the cloth and my neck but it's too tight. I can't create any space to slip a finger in. As time ticks by and I slowly lose the ability to breathe, I thrash around in a desperate attempt to free myself. He pulls harder on the cloth around my neck as he steps onto the middle of my back, creating more tension and tightening the noose around my throat. Even as black dots blink in and out of my vision, I continue to fight.

My arms reach behind me but it's an awkward angle. I can reach him, I can *touch* him, but I can't grab him. He's the perfect distance away.

"I wished for immortality," Matt pants out, his breaths loud and heavy.

It feels as though my pulse is inside my ears. My vision warps as he squeezes tighter on his hold.

"But you know the devil. There's always a catch to whatever wish he grants."

Matt's breathing has calmed down a bit now that I've lost most of my ability to fight against him. My hands drop to the cold pavement beneath me. My consciousness is starting to wane.

"I can have immortality, but only if I can find it," he states. "It took me awhile to figure it out. I have to kill people like you so I can steal your remaining years on earth. Lucky me, you have seven whole years to give me. I bet that guy you were fighting with has seven more."

I can't fight the slide of my eyes as they shut. *Nothing*. It was all for nothing. My desperate attempt to stay alive, selling my soul, befriending Balthazar... it was all for nothing. My consciousness fades as the world goes black.

XIX

I WAKE WITH A raging headache. A groan slips out my mouth as my hand drags up to rub my face. Such a simple act exhausts me. My body is weak and heavy. I want nothing more than to fall back asleep.

"Lord Balthazar, you have impeccable timing," someone says behind me. "You've arrived just in time to watch me gain another seven years."

Someone rolls me onto my back and I blearily blink my eyes open. Wherever I am, I'm tucked away in an alley and cast in shadows. A small victory as I imagine being out in the sun would make my headache worse.

I try to wrack my brain for what's happening, but everything's murky. All I know for certain is that my neck throbs in tandem with my headache. I attempt to open my mouth to ask whoever is talking if they know what's going on, but my tongue feels glued to the roof of my mouth.

Suffocation can cause memory loss, a deep voice echoes inside my head. Before I can ask the voice any questions, a finger snap echoes down the alley. As if encased in magic, I'm as good as new. No headache. No heavy, weak body. No lost memories.

I instantly remember Matt strangling me. My eyes come into focus as I look at the somewhat immortal man towering over me while Balthazar stands stoically behind him. Is he here to save me? Or is he surprised to see me still alive?

My eyes connect with his. They burn a deep red. The temperature around us drops so drastically, both Matt and I visibly shiver. Balthazar's *pissed*. I guess he isn't happy to learn Chad left the job unfinished.

Balthazar's horns ignite as the skin of his face bubbles and splits open. Flames dart down his horns, setting the top of his head completely on fire. The freezing air is rapidly replaced by incredibly dry heat.

Balthazar's eyes burn up as smoke billows out of the empty sockets. Skin slides off him, dropping to the ground with a sickening squish. Black ooze drips down his face as he stares at me. His charcoal skin is cracked and splitting, light the shade of glowing embers shining through the cracks.

The sudden change in Balthazar's appearance draws Matt's attention.

"My Lord?" Matt cautiously asks.

"*You dare to steal from me?*" Balthazar bellows, his voice layered and grating.

Matt immediately drops to his hands and knees, bowing low to the ground. "No, my Lord, I would never dream of it!"

"*Lies.*"

A leather spiked whip suddenly appears in Balthazar's hand and he snaps it at Matt. It connects, tearing his shirt. The spikes drag along his back, splaying black blood in their wake, and Matt screams in agony.

"I'm not lying," Matt cries out but keeps his face pressed against the pavement.

I cringe as I scoot away from him, not wanting the blood to spray on me. The white Dolce & Gabbana suit is stained and dirty, but I'd rather avoid getting gross rotten blood on my face and hair.

"I haven't stolen anything from you, I swear!"

Another crack of the whip, another painful cry filling the air, and more black blood spilling onto the pavement. Some flesh is ripped off in the process. I wince and hold back a gag. It's brutal. I'm not sure I'll be able to watch the whole thing but it's nothing short of what Matt deserves after he tried killing me.

"My Lord! Please, *please* tell me what I've stolen! I'll return it!"

"*Her.*"

Matt's head snaps up. He looks briefly at Balthazar before turning his attention to me.

"Her?" he asks, completely confused, but then realizes what Balthazar means. "*Oh.*"

Another snap of the whip.

"I didn't know," Matt shouts as he crawls forward to Balthazar's feet.

At this point, Balthazar's human appearance has completely melted off him. He stands before us entirely naked in his charcoal colored skin as cracks dart across the surface like lightning. Light the color of fire peers through the cracks. The tribal looking tattoo along his chest glows in that same color. Fire flows down his head, wrapping around his shoulders before swaying down his arms. Flames lick down his waist and thighs. He looks exactly like what nightmares are made of. If any of that murderous intent was directed at me, I'd be terrified beyond comprehension.

"I didn't know," Matt repeats as he grabs onto Balthazar's feet. "I would never dare steal from you, Lord Balthazar. I thought she was just another human who sold her soul. I didn't – I didn't know she belonged to you."

"I don't belong to him," I state and Balthazar offers a menacing growl. I flick him off in response before finishing my statement. "He only cares about his own life."

Matt lifts himself up just enough so he can peer at me while still bowing down at Balthazar.

"Chad, the guy who wants me dead? His wish hasn't been fully granted yet," I inform him. At this point, I don't even care that I'll end up dead as long as it means I take Balthazar down with me. "You kill me... you kill this asshole in the process."

Matt moves fast, somehow procuring a dagger. He reaches for me, but he's not faster than Balthazar. In a split second, Balthazar's entire hand has gone through Matt's back. Balthazar lifts the arm he's skewered Matt with and bends it at the elbow so he can look Matt in the face. He says nothing as Matt begins to burn from the hole that shouldn't be there.

"Please, I'm sorry! Please don't kill me! I'm not ready to die!"

Balthazar leans in so close that they practically touch face to face. *You should have thought of that before trying to kill my wife.*

Matt is unable to form any more words as the fire consumes all of him. Agonized screams pour out of him as he tries to break free until finally he stops moving all together. He goes limp on Balthazar's arm and we watch as he burns to a crisp before Balthazar discards him haphazardly onto the pavement.

For a few moments, neither one of us does or says anything. We just stare at Matt's burnt and smoking body. But then I get to my feet and start to walk away.

"Where do you think you're going?" Balthazar asks in his normal voice; the deep one that always sparks a little tingle in me. Not this time.

His question loosens what little control I have. I whirl around, suddenly overwhelmed by all my emotions. I almost died. *Twice.* And Balthazar, someone who I had stupidly thought I could trust, set me up. He sent me straight to Chad to be killed. I miraculously got out of that situation only to wind up in Matt's greedy hands where I almost legitimately *died.* All because of Chad and his stupid wish.

Hot tears burn my eyes as they trail down my face.

"I hate you," I scream right before lunging at him.

Smoke swirls around Balthazar as his human appearance slips into place. He does nothing to stop me from hitting him. I slap him hard across the face before shoving him. He takes two steps back from the push. I angrily pound my fists against his chest. He remains still, not once lifting his hands to stop my assault.

"I hate you," I scream again, my voice cracking as I continue to cry. "If you're going to kill me, just do it! Stop playing these games! Just kill me!"

"I don't want to kill you, Sloane," he says evenly, eyes hooded as he stares down at me.

"Who cares what you want?" I snap through hot tears and I glare up at him. "I'd rather you do it than Chad!"

Balthazar's eyebrows pinch together as his hands firmly settle on my waist. When he speaks, his voice is surprisingly gentle. "That wasn't Chad, Sloane. That was a man named Matthew Johnson."

"I know," I haughtily reply as I wipe my face clean on my suit sleeve. "Matt was the whole reason Chad ran away. Matt's appearance scared the shit out of Chad and he went running."

"*What?*"

I'm so enraged by his fake surprise that I grab him by the horn and yank him down so we're eye to eye.

"You have the *audacity* to pretend you didn't snap your little fingers and drop me right into Chad's lap?" I ask, my voice quiet yet wavering as I try to contain my fury. "I know everything Balthazar, so stop pretending."

He doesn't attempt to break free from my grip and stares me head on. The red speckles in his irises have disappeared, his eyes pitch black as his face morphs into how I feel. Pure fury unleashed.

"Tell me what it is you think I've done, Sloane," he orders, voice low and barely contained.

My eyes dart back and forth between his angered ones before I unload everything, fingers tightly curled around his horn.

"I know, I fucking *know*. You never made a deal with me. That's why when you took my soul, it was red. Because it wasn't mine. It's some Jeznian who pissed you off and you killed them for it. Your whole plan was to keep me close and then let Chad finish the job. That's the catch, right? If Chad wants me dead, he has to kill me himself. You've been playing me this whole time and I was too stupid to see it."

"Quite the opposite, Sloane. I haven't played you. I've sat back and watched your own cleverness piece things together."

My heart falls out of my chest upon hearing those words. My fingers release his horn as I take a trembling step back, overcome by the shock that washes over me. Why am I shocked? I already *knew* he concocted all this. So why does it hurt? Why are there tears blotting my vision as if he's broken my heart?

He shifts forward, arms snaking around my waist and I'm too shell–shocked to push him away. Balthazar dips his head, his cheek pressing into mine as he gently holds me to him.

"But you're wrong, Sloane," he whispers, his hot breath caressing my ear. "I fulfilled Chad's wish and I have no intention of letting his putrid hands near you. You're *mine*."

Angered that he'd claim such a bold statement, my hands come up to his chest and grip the fabric of his shirt. I push against him but hold tight to his clothes. My body literally fights my mind. *Push him away! Pull him closer!* I nearly died because of him. Do I want him to comfort me or to walk away from me? I honestly have no idea.

My lower lip trembles as the events of today replay over in my mind. How Chad and I grappled on the sidewalk. How I managed to get away from him only to end up in Matt's crosshairs. Our fight had been violent, difficult, and terrifying. Matt truly meant to kill me. The only time I had ever known fear like that was when I first met Balthazar. Except this time I had no witty solution to get myself out of it. Matt would have killed me if Balthazar hadn't shown up.

Balthazar's hands cup my cheeks, his cold fingers brushing away the tears as he remains bent down so we're eye to eye.

"You thought you would die," he states.

I nod my head as the red speckling returns to his black eyes and the anger disappears from his face.

"You thought it was my doing."

I nod my head again as I sniffle.

"Sloane, if I want you dead, I promise you that I will do it myself."

The statement immediately comforts me and I can't suppress the laugh that escapes my mouth. It's absurd a statement like that would make me feel safe. He's talking about *killing* me and I'm *relieved* to hear him say he'll do it himself.

"I hate you," I laugh out and he smiles that devilishly handsome smile.

"I know you do. I wouldn't have it any other way," he says as he tenderly wipes away the last of my tears.

He holds my gaze firmly, confidently, and unwaveringly. My eyes flit down as a light blush dusts my cheeks. Balthazar's looking at me like I'm the most important person in his entire world. Which is crazy. Why would he feel that way about a bratty human like me?

He dips his head, forcing me to look him in the eyes again, and I quickly avert my gaze up past his head. My eyes land on his horn. The horn I grabbed and yanked. The one I have zero privilege to touch according to our first meeting. I should apologize for that. Right?

"Um... sorry."

He scoffs as he stands to his full height. "For what?"

"For touching your horn."

I chance a glance at him. He's arching an eyebrow as he peers down his nose at me. There's an unreadable expression on his face and it fills me with unease. The one time I touched his horn it made him so upset that he intended to brutally murder me for it.

Right now he doesn't seem mad enough to kill me. But maybe he's thinking about it, which as long as it stays that way, it won't be a problem. *Ugh, I shouldn't have brought it up in the first place. You can be so stupid, Sloane.* He might have forgotten I touched his horn without his permission. Why did I have to go and remind him?

After a prolonged pause, Balthazar turns away from me, his hands sliding into his pant pockets as he throws over his shoulder, "That's not something you need ever apologize for."

H<small>E DOESN'T GIVE</small> me any opportunity to ask him what
he means because he snaps his fingers and we're back at the
condo. Before I can open my mouth to ask him to clarify,
Umbra suddenly appears in a cloud of black shadows.

Balthazar glances at her before inquiring, "Has she been
removed from the list?"

"Yes, Lord Balthazar."

"Has The Magistrate been notified?"

"Yes, they've assigned a Guard to her for the time being."

"Did they?" Balthazar hums. "Interesting choice; not the
route I would've taken."

"What are you guys talking about?" I ask as I follow
Balthazar into the living room.

He doesn't answer as he quietly walks over to the study
area and jots something down on a piece of paper. When he's
done, he extends the paper to Umbra. She readily accepts it,
tucking it away inside her outfit.

"Take that to Ofello. If he asks any questions, remind him of the terms of our agreement."

"Of course, Lord Balthazar."

"Are you seriously going to ignore me?" I ask, irritation laced in my voice as I stand in the center of the room.

Umbra says nothing as she disappears in black smoke. Balthazar's black–red eyes connect with mine and he runs a hand through his hair. Is he stalling? That's unusual, even for him.

"What is The Magistrate and a Guard?" I pointedly ask, my arms crossing over my chest as all my weight shifts to my right foot.

"The Magistrate consists of three Wardens that investigate which souls should be protected and offered entry into Odantha," he answers with a sigh. "They're rather boring and rigid, but I can't deny their competency. I've informed them about my decision regarding Sarah. They've chosen to assign a Guard to her."

"And a Guard is?" I ask, my chest tightening as I wait for him to answer.

"Guards monitor the entrance of Odantha, ensuring those who don't belong there stay out. They also guide souls to their correct place in Odantha."

"What are you saying?" I ask as my heart thumps against my chest. "You're not talking about the woman we met in the hospital, are you?"

There's a pit forming in the bottom of my stomach as I process what he's said about a Guard's job. Is he saying he told Odantha her soul is worthless and they assigned her a Guard to make sure she doesn't try to break into Heaven? *He can't be serious.*

"I am," he answers simply.

My anger explodes within me like a nuclear bomb.

"Are you kidding me?" I shriek and it's a damn shame there's nothing within my vicinity to throw at him.

"What appears to be the problem?" he asks curiously as his head tilts to the side and his eyebrow arches up.

My mouth opens but nothing comes out. There's too much to say. *Everything* is wrong about this situation.

"All she wanted was for you to look after her kids," comes out first. The rest is unleashed without a single ounce of regret. "Why did you bother showing up if you knew her soul was worthless to you? To hold it over her and show off your superiority?

"You're such a sexist piece of shit. I shouldn't be surprised, but I am. I can't believe I deluded myself into thinking you weren't half bad. But it was right there, slapping me in the face and I refused to see it."

The curiosity has disappeared from Balthazar's face as he stands stoic and tall. His hands slide into the pockets of his pants as he rhythmically clenches and unclenches his jaw. He says nothing. He simply waits for me to unload everything. I do without mercy and without hesitation.

"You have zero issues taking the souls of men who make sure misogyny stays intact. Yet when it comes to a woman, suddenly her soul is *worthless*? How is that possible? She summoned you the same way all those assholes did, but it's only her soul that's worthless. That's bullshit."

"You're upset I refused to buy her soul?" He asks neutrally, his voice devoid of any emotions that might give away what he's really thinking.

"Yes! You go on and on about how your job of making deals with humans is through word of mouth, that the people who summon you are bad people worthy of spending eternity in Jeznia. So sure, she might be a bad person, but she wanted to protect her kids. She's the first person I've seen who gave two shits about someone else other than their own greed. The only difference I can determine between her and everyone else is that she's a woman. Which honestly makes it a damn miracle you bought *my* soul.

"You accepted the deal with the conservative asshole who wanted all Democrats to lose. He's basically admitting that he wants to keep minorities oppressed and you agreed to it. You accepted that deal! But this woman who wanted to keep her children safe, comfortable, and out of poverty has a worthless soul decided by *you*. Is it not as much fun for you to grant the wishes of women? Tell me, are our souls worthless because we're less selfish than most men?"

His eyes flare deep red as they narrow. "It's a bit rich hearing you talk to me about selfishness."

His voice is cold and detached, yet his body vibrates in rage. Steam rises off him and I realize he's doing everything in his power to prevent his appearance from burning off him. Somehow, him showing restraint makes his anger towards me feel *personal*. Like all those other times when he allowed his real self to show was just an act to terrorize me. But this? This is him genuinely holding himself back to not cause me harm.

I subconsciously take a step away from him as he glowers.

"In the short amount of time we've known each other, you have only been selfish," he states in that monotonous tone of voice. "You've demanded I take you places no human has the right to be. You've demanded I supply you with information no human has the right to know. You've only thought about your own self–preservation the same way these greedy men have. Though your preservation is *righteous* and *moral.* According to whose standards?

"You're so high up on your moral pedestal that you don't even realize how you're *using* Sarah to make yourself feel better. You're patting yourself on the back for protecting her from the big bad wolf, yet you're too blind to see your savior complex is there solely to make you feel good about yourself."

My mouth drops open in complete shock. A defense is at the tip of the tongue, ready to prove how wrong he is. Except I can't force the words out. I'm too stunned, too horrified by what he's accused me of. No one has ever accused me of being selfish before. It stalls my mind as I process everything he's said.

"Sarah doesn't need you to save her from whatever prejudices you've deemed I have. She's plenty capable of speaking for herself. You're horribly misguided."

"Fuck you," flies out of my mouth as my anger barrels into me, knocking the shock out of my system.

He smirks, the action viscous with no warmth or teasing to it.

"It's about time you've had a taste of your own medicine, Sloane. Or are you one of those people who can dish it but not take it?"

"Fuck you," I say again and I'm mildly ashamed at my repetitiveness. Thankfully, more words fly out of my mouth, my brain finally jumping into high gear as it sees the flaws in his argument. "Then explain it to me! Explain to me why you favor men over women because from where I'm standing, you *are* a sexist pig. The one woman who summoned you miraculously has a worthless soul. That's not a coincidence, Balthazar."

"Do you honestly believe *any* Jeznian would care about a human's genitals or their gender?" he asks, his voice exasperated with anger. "You're *all* Ephirian swine to us. The color of your skin, the sex between your legs, your sexuality, your health, or lack of it – *none* of that matters to us. The truth is that you're *all* worthless in my eyes."

Balthazar inhales deeply and the steam coming off him gradually disappears. His hands remain inside his pockets and he works his jaw back and forth. He might be waiting for some kind of rebuttal from me, but when it's clear I have none, he continues to speak.

"I didn't create the system of oppression in your world, but admittedly, it makes my job as Contract Liaison easier at finding the trash. I like making deals with trash; they never see their future coming even when you spell it out for them. Seeing the look on their faces when they're face to face with their eternity is like drinking a fine wine outside, cozied up by the campfire.

"Sarah's soul isn't worthless to me because of her sex; *you* decided that all on your own because of your world view. Perhaps your own internalized misogyny decided that her sex was the only possible reason for why she's worthless. You never once considered there might be another option. I'd laugh at your hypocrisy if it didn't piss me off so much."

He turns his gaze away from me as he runs a hand angrily through his hair. He acts like he can't even handle the sight of me. Anger pulsates down to my core. Despite everything he's said, he hasn't explained how he's *not* exhibiting sexism in denying Sarah's deal. He's also not taking accountability for his own faults and is instead only finding fault in me.

My mouth departs to say that, but he shifts his gaze back to me and the words die on my lips. The anger I see in his eyes strikes me straight through the heart. In that moment, I finally see what his anger really is. *Hurt.* I've hurt him. Badly.

"When I make a deal, all I care about is the *stain* on the human soul," he says in a firm, but quiet tone. "The darker the stain, the better. Eviler people are more fun to torture."

He takes a moment to collect his thoughts before he continues on.

"I saw Sarah's soul the moment I arrived in that room. Stains are impossible to miss. They're dark inky blotches on an otherwise pristine white soul."

He unblinkingly holds my gaze, his face devoid of the anger he held moments before. When he speaks, his voice is soft, tender, and warm.

"Sarah's soul was so white it was practically transparent. The walls of Jeznia are no place for her."

My eyes blur upon hearing how gentle he sounds. This – *this* is the heart Umbra was telling me about. The heart that others think is a weakness but it's not. He *cares*. God, he cares so much. Everything about Sarah's deal had been different from the start. The way he dressed, the way he spoke to her, the way he handled her request... he practically doted on Sarah during his visit. An odd thought considering *how* the doting came across at surface level, but knowing how he behaves regularly when he makes deals, I can't unsee it now.

"She is destined to spend eternity in the Fields of Prosperity in Odantha," he says in that same quiet, gentle voice. "Would you have me rob her of that peaceful afterlife, Sloane?"

My tears break free and slide down my face as complete and utter shame burns me from the inside out. I'm frozen in my spot, speechless. I finally understand what he's saying. He told Sarah her soul was worthless so she wouldn't try bargaining with another devil. This would guarantee her afterlife in Odantha.

Shit. Everything he said about me was right. I projected my own prejudices, my own world views onto him. I didn't stop to think about other options. I thought of the worst reason for why he rejected her deal and exploded on him.

Even worse is my weaponization of Sarah against Balthazar. Like she's some trophy for me to hold and praise myself for protecting her. He's completely right in calling me selfish and calling out my savior complex. I'm not protecting her; I'm making myself feel good about me. *Look at me standing up for the woman! Look at how good I am!* It's disgusting.

I *am* selfish. I *do* have a savior complex. Acknowledging that makes me realize how I've been hiding behind my allyship. How I used my support of people of color, of LGBTQIA+, of wanting access to health care for all as a *measurement* for how *good* I am as a person. When in reality supporting *basic* human rights doesn't make me a good person at all. It just makes me a person.

I can't believe the *devil* of all people had to educate me on how terrible of a human I am. It fills me with horror, shame, and regret. I can barely swallow as I stand motionless in my spot.

"I'm so sorry, Balthazar," I whisper and his face contorts into angered anguish.

He waves his hand dismissively, turning his face away from me to hide his expression. I take a step towards him and when he doesn't react or keep his distance, I take two more.

"Balthazar, I'm sorry."

"I don't need your apology," he states in a clipped tone as he focuses his attention on the floor. "Apologies are useless in Jeznia."

"That may be true, but we're not in Jeznia," I point out, my voice soft, and his eyes snap to mine.

He looks at me like he has an argument at the ready, but he doesn't speak. He simply keeps his eyes glued to me. I take another step towards him as he remains frozen in place.

"You have my apology because you deserve one," I say. "What you decide to do with it is entirely up to you."

Silence fills the room and I stop my approach when I'm about five feet from him. We stare at each other, a strange tension filling the space between us. All the rage we've thrown at each other has emptied out while my apology lingers in the air. The pain, shame, and regret between us muddles any feelings of acceptance and forgiveness. Yet, he stares at me with such openness, willingness, and tenderness that more words he deserves to hear are pulled from me.

"Thank you," I practically whisper and his eyes flash a brief white.

"You do not owe me your gratitude," he replies, voice deep and firm.

"But I do. You took the time to put me in my place, to point out my hypocrisy. You didn't have to do that. Honestly, I hated every second of it, but I needed to hear it. I can't become a better person if no one ever challenges me or shows me my shortcomings. You showed me how much work I still have left to do."

"Once you take up residency in Jeznia, you'll see how pointless your world issues are," he tells me as an almost invisible smile touches his lips. "You'll see how pointless it *all* is. Be good or be evil. Do whatever you want while you're still living because you'll never get a second chance to do so once you're dead."

I laugh lightly and his smile widens an inch. "I'll take that advice to heart."

His grin turns soft as his shoulders finally release whatever tension he was holding in them. "Good. I don't offer my counsel to just anyone."

A giggle falls from my mouth before a comfortable quietness settles around us. Despite the emotional whirlwind I've just taken, I feel good. It feels good to clear the air between us. Maybe this moment had been building since the second we met and it finally came to a head.

All things considered it went pretty well. No one threatened anyone, though shamefully, the only reason why I didn't throw anything at him was because I didn't have anything near me. I'll need to work on that.

"I've got to return to Jeznia," Balthazar suddenly declares and my heart drops.

Stay. I want you to stay.

"Oh. Ok." I can't hide the disappointment in my voice.

"It'll only be for a couple of hours. Just enough to recharge," he says as he raises his hands and gives his fingers a wiggle.

"Oh my god," I gasp out as I realize he's referring to the cold. "Of course! Go, you should go now!"

He chuckles and it fills me with joy to see his smile reach his eyes. "I'll only be gone for a couple of hours."

"Take all the time you need," I reply almost instantly.

He arches an eyebrow, his smile turning into a playful smirk. "Sick of me already? Prefer I never return?"

My own playful grin slinks onto my face as I roll my eyes at him. "No, that's not what I mean. You *know* that's not what I mean."

"Do I? I may be able to speak telepathically with you, but I was unaware I could now read minds."

I blow out a large breath in playful irritation. "You can be real annoying at times."

He huffs out a soft laugh. "I try, Sloane. I really try."

A grin plasters itself onto my face as I say, "Get out of here. I'll see you in two hours."

His smirk turns tender as something unrecognizable flashes in his eyes.

"Two hours. Donec tunc, peccatum meum," he says as he bends at the waist to offer me a small bow.

My face scrunches into confusion as he blinks out of sight. That definitely wasn't English.

I stand there for a few minutes, contemplating if I have the motivation to scour the internet for a translation when I decide I don't. I've got two hours to kill. I'd rather spend that time taking a shower to wash off this horribly wretched day of sweat, almost being killed – twice, and being shoved face to face with my pitiful, disgusting selfishness.

XXI

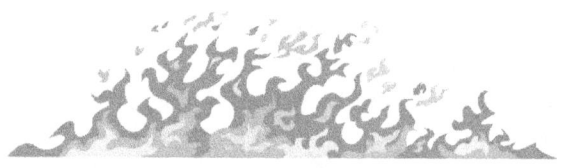

BALTHAZAR RETURNS TWO hours later at 6pm on the dot, a light thud the only indication of his arrival.

I'm sprawled out on the couch, a bowl of nearly finished popcorn beside me as I watch episodes of *New Girl*. It's one of my favorite comfort shows and, after the batshit crazy day I've had, the show is warranted.

Our conversation about sexism and my hypocrisy lingers in the back of my mind even as Jess and Nick's romance plays out on the screen. I have a long road ahead of me, but I want to do the work. I want to be a kinder, more compassionate person… at least to the people who deserve it. Maybe I will embrace Balthazar's *become evil* suggestion when it concerns the kind of people he accepts deals with. But everyone else… they deserve better from me; it's my responsibility to dismantle everything I've been taught and look at myself with a more critical eye.

The dirtied and stained Dolce & Gabbana suit has been replaced with a floral bodycon dress. Shamefully, I deliberated far too long on what to wear after my shower. Originally, I wanted to change into comfy clothes but decided if Balthazar was going to pay me a visit, I wanted to look good. For whose visual benefit? I'm embarrassed to admit the truth, even to myself.

"Back already," I ask from my spot on the couch, grabbing the remote to turn down the volume.

"You wound me," Balthazar feigns as he stands behind me. "Were you not eagerly anticipating my return?"

I roll my eyes as I throw a couple pieces of popcorn his way; he expertly swats them away. "Actually wait, yes I was."

"Oh?" he asks curiously as his hands settle on the back of the couch.

I tilt my head to look him fully in the face. "Yeah. It's about Sarah."

He clicks his tongue. "I see."

Is that disappointment? I hope it is.

"I was wondering how she knew how to summon you despite not being a bad person."

Balthazar has spent our entire time together drilling it into me that people who summon him are *bad* people. They're *friends* with *bad* people. Bad people stick together like super glue. Yet Sarah knew how to summon him but is destined for Odantha. It doesn't make sense. How can both be true?

Balthazar sighs heavily as his gaze shifts to Cece and Schmidt on the TV. "Some time ago, she was forced to watch a despicable swine summon me. Normally, I would have erased her memories, but when I looked into her eyes, I couldn't do it. I let her keep them, thinking that maybe one day she'd want to make a deal with me."

"She wanted to, but you said no," I tease. "That's not very devil of you."

Another sigh blows out his mouth as he places his elbows on the back of the couch and drops his face into his hands.

"No, it's not," he mumbles into his palms. "If the Lords of Jeznia were to ever find out–"

"You'd give them Hell," I finish the sentence as I shift around to sit on my knees and face him. He peers at me through the gaps of his fingers and I smile as I drag a finger lightly down his middle finger to the back of his hand. "You don't play by their rules. You never have and you never will."

He lifts his head from his hands as his eyes dart back and forth between mine. My heart beats fast inside my chest as butterflies swarm my stomach. I want to kiss him. I want to continue where we left off before we were interrupted by Sarah's summoning.

It'd be so easy to do. I only need to lean forward; he'd get the hint. Yet, I can't gather enough courage to do it. Some stupid small part of me wonders if he even wants to continue it. I behaved like a child earlier, throwing a hissy fit and saying things I can never take back. Not to mention that my seven days are up tomorrow. What if I finally make my wish and he disappears forever once it's granted?

Balthazar trails a finger down the side of my face, twirling a piece of my brown hair as he speaks.

"I didn't know Chad would be there."

My breath hitches, bottling up inside me with nowhere to go. I wasn't anticipating having this conversation with him. I figured after all that was said and done, we moved on from it. He already said if he wanted me dead he'd do it himself. What else needs to be discussed?

"I would never willingly put you in his path," he confesses and tears sting at my eyes from the guilt of all the mean things I said to him.

"I'm sorry I accus–"

"*Stop* apologizing," he growls in a low voice.

"It seemed too perfect to be a coincidence," I say as I explain to him why I accused him. "You snapped your fingers. You were gone and Chad was *right there*. I came up with the most logical solution. In my mind there was no way it was a coincidence."

"I'm a little disappointed I didn't think of such a scheme on my own. I could have saved myself from all these threats about wishing me dead," he states with a lopsided smirk.

I slap him on the shoulder as I try to bite back my own smile. "You're such an ass."

He laughs lightly before threading his fingers through my hair, his blunt fingernails gently scratching against my scalp. I lean into the heavenly touch, loving the thrum of excitement building inside me. If we continue down this path, we'll end up exactly where I want.

After a moment, his smile disappears and is replaced by a slight frown. "What did Chad do when you saw him?"

I release a deep sigh, my eyes glancing down and away from him as I answer.

"After the initial shock wore off, we fought. He wanted to kill me and I wanted to kill him," I answer as I pick at the leather of the couch. Balthazar does nothing to stop me.

"Fortunately, or maybe unfortunately, we were in the middle of the sidewalk so there were plenty of people to break up the fight. I think Matt heard me say something about Chad selling his soul, which is probably why he approached us in the first place. Once we saw Matt, Chad ran off like a

child, but that ultimately saved his life. If it weren't for you...
I'd be dead."

The tears are back and I try to blink them away but they
escape down my cheeks instead.

"I don't know why I'm crying," I say in embarrassment as
I dip my head to wipe the tears.

Balthazar grabs my face with both his hands and tilts my
head back to stare into my eyes. "I won't let anyone kill you."

"Yeah, I know," I say as I wipe the tears. Thankfully, they
aren't replaced by new ones.

"You do?" he asks in mild surprise, which is a little
strange.

"Obviously. Anyone who kills me kills you."

Anger crosses his features as his hands drop away from
my face and he stands to his full height. He towers over me
while I remain kneeling on the couch.

"Fuck, Sloane." His voice is dripping in irritation, like I
purposely did something to upset him.

"What?" I ask defensively. "What did I do this time?"

He moves fast as he yanks me up from the couch only to
sit me down on the back of it. The action startles me, drawing
a gasp from my mouth. My shock is quickly pushed to the
side when Balthazar shoves his way between my legs, his
hands gripping me firmly on my hips as the skirt of my
bodycon dress hikes up. He gazes down at me, his eyes full of
frustration, greed, and untampered hunger.

"I won't let anyone *kill* you because you're mine," he
declares in that sensually low voice, his face mere inches
from my own. "I won't let anyone *harm* you because you're
mine. I won't let anyone so much as look at you the wrong
way *because you're mine.* Have I made myself clear?"

The words send tingles shooting down my spine. My body becomes flush with desire as my heart pounds against my chest. I can't take my eyes off him; off the way he's staring at me like I'm the most precious thing in the world. I squirm in my seat, edging closer to Balthazar as my lips part.

"You're crystal clear," I say, tongue darting out to lick my lips. "Except, whoever said I gave myself for you to own?"

He growls loud and possessively, his eyes flaring white as his fingers dig into me. He pulls me against him, yet he physically fights himself to stay put. His muscles are taut as he dips towards my mouth, only to pull away when he realizes what he's doing. A knowing, satisfied smirk spreads across my lips as I trail a hand up his chest. He's waiting for my command. Good.

"Isn't it the other way around?" I ask in a low, seductive timbre as I tilt my head.

Pain blooms along my hips as his fingers sink into me. *That'll leave a bruise*, I think and it *delights* me. He's fighting so hard against his instincts to ravage me. All because he wants to please me, to submit to me. It's intoxicating to hold so much power in these feeble, human hands.

I lean towards his ear as my hand glides up his horn to the tip. It's sharp, dangerous, and only mine for the touching.

"If anyone owns anyone," I whisper into his ear, "isn't it that *I* own *you?*"

"Fuck," he moans as his head leans into mine, the only movement he allows himself to have.

I lick the outer shell of his ear, loving the way he tenses in my arms.

"It wasn't a rhetorical question, Lord Balthazar," I breathe out and he shivers so hard against me, I'm the one who moans.

"Yes," he answers, his hot breath caressing my neck.

"Yes what?"

A low growl reverberates inside his chest, rumbling against me. My underwear dampens as lust burns through me, uncontrolled and all consuming. He's contained his beast, but at what cost? When he finally lets go, I'll bear the brunt of it. The thought sends a thrill of excitement racing through me.

I take his earlobe in my mouth and give it a nibble. "I'm waiting, Lord Balthazar."

He inhales deeply, his entire body tensing, and it's in that moment I notice the space he's created between our hips. *Oh, that's cheating,* I think as I bring my hand down to ghost against his crotch. I'm only mildly surprised to discover that he's already rock hard. He hisses in reply, jutting his hips back despite his every carnal desire to move forward into my touch.

"Lord Balthazar, are you really going to make me ask again?" I ask as my finger and thumb pinch the tip of him still inside his pants. My punishment for moving away.

"You," he growls and immediately stops as I continue my punishment, sliding my finger firmly down the length of him. "Own..." he pauses again as my hand pulls away from him, his hips chasing after that feeling but my hand is already disappearing up his chest. "Me."

My fingers rake up his neck to his hair and I give it a light tug. "Good boy."

That's all the permission he needs before smashing his lips against mine. Our tongues immediately fight each other for dominance as he folds over me, enveloping me entirely in his warmth.

He finally allows himself to press up against me as he grinds into me. My underwear is fully soaked through, my body eager and excited for what's to come. I dig my fingers into his back as I drag my hand down to his butt. I squeeze it firmly, loving how taut it is before hooking my legs around him and pulling him harder against me. There are too many clothes involved.

He jumbles my thoughts as he pulls my bottom lip between his teeth, one hand cupping a breast. He rubs a firm thumb over the nipple, causing it to peak and harden as he expertly teases it. My body arches into him, seeking more of that intoxicating sensation.

He moves away from my mouth to attend to my neck, nipping and sucking down the column of my throat. His other hand ventures down to my underwear and he slips the fabric to the side. His cold fingers slide down my opening before he easily slips two fingers inside me.

"Fuck, Sloane," he growls as he works his palm against my clit, his fingers curling inward on their way out.

The sensation makes me gasp, my fingers clutching him tightly as my head falls back. I feel every inch of those cold fingers inside me. Incredible tingles shoot up my spine causing my toes to curl as he repeats his ministrations, firm yet smooth. Finger fucking has never felt this good before. I shift all my weight onto my ass on the couch, my arms clutching onto Balthazar so I don't fall over the edge.

"You're soaking wet," he says as he rubs his palm in a firm circular motion, building that sweet, delicious tension in me.

"More," I beg as I bury my face into his neck.

"As you wish," he breathes against me, ramming his fingers into me.

There's electricity in the air and I feel a cold sensation twirl and flick against my clit as I'm filled to the brim with his fingers. I moan in delight, arching as my hips against him. The cold magic continues its onslaught as he finger fucks me but the cold sensation breaks apart into two other sources.

Two cold tendrils of magic slink their way up to my chest before tweezing and pulling my nipples. Goosebumps arise along my skin and I sink into the sensations devouring me. I'm overloaded as it builds and builds and builds until I reach the crescendo, convulsing in Balthazar's arms as I clench around him. His fingers pump through my release and he only removes them when I've finally stopped moving.

He pulls away from me, firmly holding my gaze as he sucks his fingers dry.

"Delicious," he states as he laps at his knuckles, eyes never breaking away from mine.

My chest heaves as a light blush covers my face.

"You really think so?" I ask, working up the courage to speak my next words.

"I do," he hums out.

"Good. Get on your knees, Lord Balthazar."

His eyes flash wild and hungry as he slowly descends into a kneeling position. He's at the perfect height for me to hook my leg over his shoulder. I don't hesitate and I yank him close. He braces his hands against the back of the sofa, but doesn't shy away from me, instead placing a few kisses along my inner thigh.

Excitement swirls within me as I thread my fingers through his hair.

"Show me what a good, obedient devil you are," I purr and he eagerly bites my thigh. "Lick me dry, Lord Balthazar."

He snaps his fingers and my underwear disappears. He doesn't lunge for me the way I anticipate. No. He takes his time, savoring every delectable moment of it. He stares up at me from his kneeling position as he kisses his way up my thigh towards his target.

My chest heaves up and down as the excitement overwhelms me. I'm tempted to order him to speed up but I bite my lower lip to keep quiet. I need to let him go at his pace because I *know* he'll deliver.

He finally reaches his destination and latches his entire mouth over me. He drags his hot tongue up the length of me and I shudder a sigh. His cold fingers grip me tight as he swirls that expert tongue against my clit. My fingers dig into the back of the couch as my head falls back. God, how is he so good at this?

His tongue glides down me and twirls around my opening before lapping back up. He repeats the motion, his tongue a steady and firm drag against me. It's heavenly, better than I ever knew oral sex could be.

He works hard at building the tension, never once faltering, never once pausing. He keeps it steady even as my hips rock against him.

My breath quickens, my fingers stark white as they grip the couch. It feels so good it's tortuous. I'm close. It won't take him much longer. God, he's amazing at this.

"Moan for me Sloane," he says, the words rumbling against me.

"I'm close," I breathe out. "Don't stop."

He groans his approval before he sucks my clit, flicking his tongue against it in tandem. I shout, hunching over him as my legs squeeze tight around him. The orgasm hits me hard, shaking my body in quick bursts as I curl into him. Balthazar drinks me up while I ride out the sinful wave.

As I come down from the high, Balthazar languidly licks me from end to end. I glance down at him and my breath is stolen from me. Balthazar peers up at me with his nose and mouth still buried in me.

The *devil* is on his *knees* drinking what I offer him.

I tremble as a proud smirk splays across my face. "You're right where you belong, Lord Balthazar. On your knees, hard and throbbing, between my legs."

His eyes slide shut as he moans, plunging his tongue inside me. I gasp in delight but manage to grab him by the hair and pull him back. His eyes blink open, bleary and drunk.

"Do you want to fuck me, Lord Balthazar?"

"Yes," he whispers.

"Do you think you've earned it?"

"No."

My smirk pulls wider on my face as pure delirium pumps through me. He's mine. Completely, wholly, and irrevocably *mine.* He'll do anything I order; *anything* if it means it'll please me. That thought alone nearly makes me cum.

I continue to hold him by the hair in one hand and use the other hand to trail a finger down his jaw.

"No, you haven't. But I'm a generous owner, Lord Balthazar. I'll give you my permission–"

He moves fast as he comes up on his feet, arms wrapped around me, and yanks me off the couch. My hand lets go of his hair and I wrap my fingers around his horn. With all the strength I possess, I jerk the horn down towards the floor. There's resistance at first, but only for a second before he obeys. I pull him all the way down until his cheek is pressed against the floor. He snarls his dislike but I don't miss the way he ruts against the floor. He's getting off on his submission; it gives me the courage to continue.

"I'll give you my permission on one condition."

He goes still as he peers up at me. "Whatever it is, it's yours."

"You."

He doesn't react and I'm not sure he understands what I'm saying so I repeat myself.

"I want you. *That's* my condition."

"It's yours," he breathes out. "I'm forever at your service."

XXII

I RELEASE HIS HORN and he slowly rises to his knees. Wordlessly, I drop down in front of him, hands cupping his face as I drink in the sight of him. What a perfectly imperfect creature before me. So cunning and cruel, yet kind and *amenable*. Mine to mold. I wouldn't dare dream of passing him up.

"Take me to the bedroom, Lord Balthazar."

Effortlessly, he pulls me up with him as he stands before hooking an arm behind my knees and lifting me up. He carries me bridal style down the hallway to the bedroom, never once tearing his eyes from me.

I allow my hands to wander, to twirl and pull his hair, to grip and massage his chest. His steps are unhurried despite the raging erection in his pants. He carries me with the respect, dignity, and grace befitting of a goddess. It ignites the blood flowing through my veins. He'll worship me body and soul tonight.

When we reach the bedroom, he gently places me on the bed and nuzzles my neck. I lean into it only for a moment before bracing a hand against his chest and pushing him back. He huffs out his discontent but obeys.

"Strip," I order.

Balthazar raises up his hand to snap his fingers but stops when a disapproving *tsk* leaves my lips.

"I want a show, Lord Balthazar. Would you deprive me of that?"

"Never," he answers as he elegantly slips out of his suit jacket.

He's still in the same three piece suit he wore to visit Sarah. The jacket plops to the floor but I pay no attention to it as I watch his fingers deftly unbutton his vest. His eyes burn into me, watching every miniscule movement I make. The way my eyes trail his fingers, how I nibble my bottom lip in anticipation, how I squirm in my seat as I think about what's to come. He absorbs it all and lets it dictate his next moves.

The vest quickly follows the jacket on the floor. I inhale sharply as he tugs his dress shirt from his pants, flashing me a quick look at his torso hidden beneath the fabric. Painstakingly, he pops the buttons out one by one until the last button comes free.

He doesn't whip off the shirt and instead, lets it drape open, exposing only a column of his torso and chest for my eyes to see. It's a tease but I eagerly drink it in. My eyes roam over the smooth planes of his stomach, how the black tribal tattoo ripples and dips over his abs. My gaze travels upwards towards his toned chest and I'm only given a peak at it as his shirt still covers most of him. *I want to see more.*

Balthazar draws my attention back to his stomach as he drags a hand over it, the simple action pulling back some of his shirt and giving me exactly what I want.

"You own all of this," he reminds me, fingers pulling the shirt back until it drapes over his shoulder. "It's yours to command."

My eyes snap up to his and his face is full of euphoric lust, like he's moments away from cumming in his pants at the mere *thought* of me owning him.

"I know," I breathe out, our heated gazes locked onto each other, "and what a wonderful thing you are to own."

The shirt slowly falls down his arms and plops onto the floor. I don't hold myself back as my hands reach forward, sliding up the expanse of his abs and chests. His skin is soft to the touch, his nipples hardened and peaked as my palms roam over them.

He pops open his pants as my hands glide down his biceps. My eyes eagerly drop to the hem of his pants. His finger flicks the zipper, teasing me as he refuses to open it all the way. I dig my fingers into his forearms in aggravation at his slowness and he moans at the sensation.

"Show me what is mine," I order, nails leaving crescent shaped moons in his arms.

"As you wish."

His fingers drag down the zipper before he pushes his pants off his hips. He's still constrained in his boxer briefs, the cloth soaked through at the tip of him. Soaked through with need and desire *for me*. I clench for him, for his cock to be buried deep inside me.

"Show me *all* of it, Lord Balthazar," I demand as I sit back on the bed, showing my restraint by prettily resting my hands on my lap.

His thumbs hook through the waistband of his boxer briefs before he pulls them down. His cock springs free from its constraint, hard, throbbing, and reddened. The tip leaks with desire as he steps out of the boxer briefs.

I reach out, my hand encircling around him. He hisses as his body goes tight but I don't miss the subtle way his hips lean into my touch.

"Good boy, Lord Balthazar. You listen well," I say as I give him a slow, tight pump.

"Sloane," he whispers and I look up to his pleading, dual–colored eyes.

"You take what I give you. Nothing more."

His cock twitches in my hand, giving away just how much he loves the way I treat him. I pump him once more before I rise off the bed. He watches me, waiting for his next set of commands. I don't waste any time.

"Lay down on the bed, face up."

He listens well. I take a few moments for myself, soaking in the sight of him naked, laid out on the bed just because I told him to.

"Hands above your head," I order and he doesn't resist as he rests them behind his head.

I pull the body con dress up and over my head and toss it to the floor. I contemplate my next move as my eyes roam his body. He's leaked onto his hip, the sticky substance dangling from the tip and I honestly wonder if I could make him cum without touching him. *I'll leave that for another day.* Today, I'm just as eager as he is.

"You leave your hands there," I say as I climb onto the mattress and over towards him. "You don't have permission to touch me."

His eyes are exploring every inch of my body as I sit down on top of his hips. His cock is hot and firm beneath me and it takes all my restraint to stay put, to not insert him inside me. It's clear from the expression on his face that he's not listening. Irritated, I grab him roughly by the chin, a scowl on my face as I lean towards him.

"You don't have permission to touch me. Tell me you understand."

His pupils are slightly dilated and his cock pulses beneath me. It takes him a moment to answer, but the words come out clear. "I understand."

"Good. Remember," I huskily say as I lean down, pressing my cheek against his as I speak into his ear, "you've done nothing to earn this. It is my own generosity that's allowing you this opportunity. Don't get cocky. Don't get greedy. Take what I give you but nothing more."

"Absolutely," he moans out. "I'll do whatever you say."

I sit back, my hand releasing its tight grip on his face as I smirk. "Lord Balthazar of House Primis, I've broken you. *I* won, not you. Never forget you were the one who surrendered to *me*."

"I'd do it all over again if given the chance," he says, the answer taking me by surprise. "You're everything I dreamed of and then some. Take me however you want, Sloane. I'm yours."

There are no words I could possibly say. So instead, I lean down, capturing his lips with mine. He leans into the kiss but keeps his hands behind his head. I feel his arms twitch as he fights the urge to touch me and I smile into his lips, loving the power I have over him.

We kiss slowly, our tongues working together instead of fighting each other. It's deep, tantalizing, and addicting. I allow my hands to roam his body, fingers scraping down the sides of him as my hips grind against him. I delight in the frictional pleasure it brings me, my hips unhurried and rhythmic. He moans his approval, but I feel his hips flex beneath me as he desperately holds back from rutting against me.

My thoughts turn hazy as Balthazar kisses me like I'm a goddess bestowing him a gift he's undeserving of, yet eternally grateful for. I *drown* in it. In the sensations and emotions it brings forth. In the cosmic, spiritual connectedness of it. In the sensuality and passion of it. It's all consuming and I willingly let it devour me.

An eternity later, I pull away from the kiss, loving the way Balthazar trails after me before he remembers his place. I say nothing as I line him up, eagerly taking in his pulsing, hot length. It stretches and fills me to the brim, a gasp of approval tumbling out of my mouth. He hisses his delight, head slamming back into the mattress.

"Fuck, Sloane, you're tight."

"Oh? Is it too much for you? Do you want me to take you out?" I ask as I sink down onto him, knowing well enough he'll refuse.

"No," he growls the word heavy and deep, eyes flaring red and angry that I would ask such a question.

"But you were complaining I was too tight," I tease him, circling a finger around his nipple.

"You're not, you're perfect," he breathes out and I notice his fingers tightly gripping his hair as he pulls on it.

Staying put and not touching me is literally taking all of his willpower. It's intoxicating to watch how desperately he fights himself. Yet more so at how eager he is to listen to me, to *please* me, when he's dying to touch me. It's a beautiful thing, but I've had enough of this teasing. It's time to satisfy us both.

"My gift to you, Lord Balthazar," I say as I shift around on top of him.

I brace my hands on his chest, putting most of my weight on him as I begin rolling my hips. His cock is hot inside me, hitting the deepest parts of me with every grind of my hips. It's electrifying. His muscles tense and contract beneath me as his eyes fervently watch while I ride him. The way he looks at me lights a deep seated pleasure inside me that burns slow and steady. My entire body vibrates, sensitive to the touch as his eyes rove over me. I can't help that my hips get a little rougher with each roll causing the pleasure to build higher and higher.

Balthazar's hands fly out from behind his head. He reaches for me before he slams them back onto the mattress, growling out his frustration. He *needs* to touch me and I smirk down at him as I refuse to give him permission.

Instead, my head falls back as I quicken the pace. The friction between us rubs against my clit, increasing that familiar euphoric sensation. My fingernails dig into his chest as I ride him hard and steady.

His cock is perfect, filling me so completely in a way I didn't know was possible. I can't crave more of him to take because there's no more I can receive. I'm stretched out wide as I can to take him and it's ecstasy with every slide of his cock inside me.

"Balthazar," I moan his name as my weight dips forward, my hips rocking faster against him.

My breasts jiggle with my movements and Balthazar shreds the comforter in his tight grip at the torture of seeing but not touching me. It gets me off seeing that raw hunger caused by me. He's perfect. Absolutely perfect in every way, shape, and form.

My mouth drops open, breathy moans escaping me as I reach closer and closer to that sinful edge. Balthazar growls beneath me, knowing I'm nearing my time and unable to do anything about it. He can only watch.

"I'm close," I whisper, my hips slamming against him as I ride faster. "So close."

"Cum for me, Sloane."

The words send me over the edge as I hunch forward, a deep, undeniably satisfied moan leaving my mouth. My fingernails scratch against his chest as they curl inwards and my thighs clench him tight. He moves his hips beneath me to prolong my orgasm. A grunt of approval is pulled from me, my hand gripping his shoulder as my already sensitive body is overwhelmed with ecstasy.

"You're perfect," he declares, eyes drinking in every expression I make.

My chest heaves up and down as I come down from the high. Wordlessly, I lean forward, pressing my lips against his in a greedy kiss and he meets me halfway.

"Sloane," he moans against my mouth. "I need you."

"You already have me," I say, my breath a little labored from the work I've just done.

"No," he growls. "I need to take you. Let me take you."

I rest atop him, chest to chest, as my fingers thread through his hair. He's rock solid beneath me, body pulled so taut I worry he might pull a muscle. My body, on the other hand, is so sated I'm not sure if I'll be able to move. Judging from what he's said, I won't need to. He'll do all the work. Besides, he's done a good job listening. I should reward him.

My fingers reach up, grabbing him by the horn, and pulling his ear to my mouth.

"Show me how badly you need me," I order, placing a kiss just below his ear. "You have my permission to do as you please."

He moves fast, flipping us over so I'm on my back while he bears down on me. He's grabbed me by the left ankle, pushing it towards my head as he settles in between me.

"Your voice will be raw by the time I'm done with you," he declares and I smirk as butterflies swarm my stomach.

"Is that a promise?"

"A fact."

"Then let the games begin, Lord Balthazar."

Balthazar unleashes pent up desire so intense it could rival a thousand suns. He's relentless as he pounds into me with a force so jarring, it stutters my breath. He hammers away brutal yet perfectly steady as he grips my ankle so tight it'll leave a bruise colored anklet. My hands reach up to brace myself against the headboard as he thrusts powerfully into me over and over.

My sensitive body is in overdrive. Never mind my voice being raw. I won't be able to walk. It's *beyond* euphoric. I didn't know a state of being like this even existed. There are no English words to describe how *good* I feel as he releases his beast.

"You own me, Sloane," he grunts as he thrusts into me. I can't form words, my mouth hung open in a silent O as I do everything in my power to hold on for the ride. "This is what you own, peccatum meum. Every sinful, nasty, lewd desire of mine is your responsibility."

I can't – I don't think I can hold on anymore. It's too good, too much. I'm whimpering. I feel so good tears blot my eyes as he pounds me over and over. He pauses only long enough to hike me up farther onto his hips before slamming back into me.

"Balthazar," I moan, back arching as I lose my way. "Balthazar."

"I'm here, Sloane, I've got you."

My orgasm explodes in me like a kaleidoscope supernova. I ascend into the universe, intangible yet whole as feelings I never knew existed vibrate violently inside me. It's fireworks, misting rain, dew on a summer morning. Peaceful, quiet, beautiful.

"Sloane," a far off sound penetrates my ears. "Peccatum meum."

"Perfect," I whisper to the source. "It's perfect."

XXIII

I'M NOT SURE how much time passes before I wake. My body feels bruised and battered, but in the most sinful of ways. I've never felt more satisfied in my entire life. So whole, so complete.

I don't want to move, but the sensation of someone playing with my hair pulls me out of my daze. My head nuzzles the heat source beneath me as I curl into it. I refuse to open my eyes; they're too heavy and I'm too comfy.

"You're awake," a deep voice reverberates beneath my ear and freezing cold fingers ghost down my spine.

I hiss my annoyance, body tensing as goosebumps dart down my back. "Mm," I moan my answer.

"How are you feeling?"

"Mm."

"Words, Sloane. I need words."

"Good," I manage to utter as I snuggle deeper against him. He's so warm. I don't want him to ever leave.

"You?" I ask.

"Me what?"

My thoughts are foggy, not fully comprehensive as I slowly wake from my deep slumber.

"How are you feeling?" I finally ask.

"Indescribable."

"In a good way?"

"In the best way."

"That's good," I yawn as I stretch off him and finally venture to open my eyes.

The lights are low as Balthazar and I cuddle in bed. The comforter is puffy and soft as it bunches around us. It takes my eyes a few seconds to focus and when they do, they settle on Balthazar's serene, handsome face.

"Hello," he greets me, a tender smile capturing his lips.

"Hi," I smile back.

He's lying on his back, arm encircled around my waist as I cuddle against the side of him. We're naked under the covers, but he heats the space hot enough that clothes would be a hindrance.

"Did I... pass out in the middle of sex?" I timidly ask as the events replay over in my head.

His grin turns wicked. "You did."

"Oh my god," I bemoan, burying my face in his chest as it goes hot from embarrassment.

He chuckles, those icy cold fingers trailing up and down my spine. "It's a compliment, Sloane. You have nothing to be ashamed of."

"Says the guy who didn't pass out," I grumble and he laughs.

"You were perfect. Better than perfect," he says as he pulls me closer, hiking me up just far enough to place a kiss on my forehead.

"You mean it?"

"I would never lie about something like this."

"I only ask because I've never been… dominant over someone before."

"There's no way you're telling the truth." He sounds genuinely shocked.

"I am."

"Sloane, tell me you're lying," Balthazar says as he tilts my head back so he can look me in the eyes.

My blush deepens to a tomato red and I bite my lower lip as I shake my head before saying, "I've never… you're the first."

"Peccatum meum," he breathes out, "I will follow you to the ends of the universe."

I squint my eyes at him and can't hold back the light laugh. "Because I dominated you in the bedroom?"

"Because you're a natural, because you're destined to rule, because you'll never hesitate to take what's yours."

My heart flips inside my chest upon hearing his words and I glance away from him, too overwhelmed by it.

"Sloane–"

"Why do you like me?"

"What?" he asks, not at all hiding the surprise in his voice.

I keep my eyes trained on his tattooed chest, on the lazy path I drag my finger over his skin. "What about me made you like me?"

He's quiet for a few moments before inhaling deeply. "There are two things."

"What are they?"

"Are you insecure?" He asks bluntly, a bit too uncaring for how I might be feeling. *Still a jerk, I see.*

I smack him, *hard*, across the chest and he grunts but doesn't retaliate. "I'm trying to figure out why a Lord of Jeznia is pledging to follow a *human* across the universe, you asshole. That's why I'm asking, not because I'm insecure."

"Your quick–witted cleverness, for one," he answers without hesitation, "and your determination to fight me every step of the way even when you're terrified out of your mind."

With his ego, I would think being challenged by a human would make him murderous, not enamored. "Why do you like that I fight you so much?"

"A mere human with no powers does what so few Jeznians would dare to do. The question isn't why would I, Sloane, but why *wouldn't* I?"

I don't have a reply and instead, focus on the swirls of his tattoo, how my fingernail drags against his skin, how his chest rises and falls with each breath he takes.

"Are you going to divulge the reason for why you like me?" he inquires and I'm a little surprised he cares about that.

Is *he* the one feeling insecure? Or perhaps he's genuinely curious considering our beginning. Afterall, he was sent to kill me. How does someone fall in love with their potential murderer?

I take a few moments to ponder it over. There isn't one distinctive moment that stands out to me, but little moments over time. He may have been directly responsible for ruining my life, but he never ran away from it. He was always there, even when he didn't want to be.

He obeyed my ridiculous demands, taking me – a haughty, little human – to places I had *zero* rights going. He didn't have to show up when I summoned him on the day I found out I was dead. He had every right to ignore me, to show up seven days later for my wish and disappear forever again. But he didn't. Because even then he *cared*. He cared enough to take the time to weigh my soul. He cared enough to give me seven days to make a wish because I wasn't prepared for one. He cared enough to let me order him around and threaten his life.

He cared but I didn't see it until today.

"It was a slow realization. One that was clouded by hate for you." He chuckles as he rakes his fingers through my hair. "But the simple fact is that you were always there for me."

His fingers stop moving and I hold back the urge to look at his face. He probably doesn't want me watching him as he processes the information I give him.

"It's a weird juxtaposition; you being directly responsible for ruining my life but also being the only support I had. I think if any other devil took Chad's deal, they would've killed me. On the off chance a devil bought my soul, they would've left me high and dry. You stuck around. You gave me a place to live, food to eat, you took me with you on your deals, supplied me intel on Jeznia, protected me. When it's all said and done, you've been incredibly thoughtful and kind in your own messed up way... How could I not like you?"

He doesn't say anything, simply holds me tight as he presses his lips against my forehead. His actions speak louder than words.

"I need to head back to Jeznia," he says after a few more minutes of comfortable silence.

"You just went back," I point out.

"House business," he clarifies. "Would you like to accompany me?"

I think it over for a long moment before looking at the time. It's almost 10pm. I'd rather not go. I want to stay cuddled up in bed with no obligations to anyone or anything.

"I'll stay here," I reply.

"A wise choice," he says and I hear the smile in his voice. "I'm not sure how well I'd be able to concentrate with you sitting in front of me."

I laugh as I shake my head. "You're ridiculous."

"No. I merely know my limits. You're far more intriguing, enticing, and sensual than any House business ever could be."

"You're too good at smooth talking."

"Mm, I have to be. I buy souls from the undecided."

I pop up from my position and stare into Balthazar's eyes. He waits, watching me curiously to see what I'll do. I lean forward, pressing a kiss to his lips and he immediately cups my face.

"You should get going," I murmur against his lips just as the kiss starts to deepen. "Before we get sidetracked."

"I think I'll stay."

"Is it wise to miss a House meeting?" I ask as I trail kisses along his strong jaw.

He huffs out his frustration, hand gripping my hair only tight enough to pull me away from him. "No, it is not."

"Go. I'll be here when you get back."

I smile at him before placing a soft kiss to his nose. He hesitates, fingers caressing my scalp before all too suddenly, he disappears from my sight with a snap of his fingers.

He takes the heat with him and I instantly miss the warmth. In the end, I suppose it's a good thing as I'm in need of another shower. I take my time with it, enjoying the relaxation of it. As I lather myself down with soap, I don't miss the anklet Balthazar gifted me and I smile at its deep purple–yellow coloring on my skin. I like it better than I anticipated.

When I emerge from the bathroom, cleaned and dressed in pajama shorts and an oversized T, I head to the kitchen for some food. I cook a quick, simple meal before taking it back with me to the bedroom. My only desire right now is snuggling deep in bed and watching some movies.

I settle on a kids movie and enjoy my dinner in the emptiness of the bedroom. It's a little difficult to concentrate when my mind keeps wandering back to the sinfully delicious activities that were enacted on the bed. What a spectacular way to end my five month dry spell.

My mind drifts as the movie plays and I remember tomorrow's the seventh day. I'll have to make a wish or threaten to kill Balthazar if he doesn't agree to give me more time. The thought sickens me; I don't want him dead, but I need more time. He's taken me on every deal he's made and the vast majority of them were about money. None have inspired me for what I'd want to wish for and I certainly haven't figured out a way out of my contract.

My stomach flips in nervousness. I don't think Balthazar will voluntarily give me more time. It's a miracle he gave me seven days. How am I going to threaten him for more time when I know my words will be empty? Even *he* will know I won't mean it.

That's when a dreaded question penetrates my mind. What if this was all a part of his plan? He reaps all the benefits if I like him. Plus, he gets a fun little toy out of it until I drop dead and end up in the walls of Jeznia. But… could he really fake everything I've witnessed? He looked genuinely hurt when I unloaded all my disgust on him. Could he be that good of an actor?

There's so much I don't know about him. Seven days isn't a lot of time to accurately judge a character. He could be playing me like a fiddle and I wouldn't have a damn clue. Or worse. He could be using his magic on me.

I feel like I'm going to hurl everything I've just eaten. He used magic on me earlier when he was fingering me. I don't remember hearing him snap his fingers. That would mean the finger snap is for show. It would mean he could be using magic at any given moment and I wouldn't know. I've threatened him enough that he might have felt compelled to use magic on me. Make me fall in love with him so I'd think twice about killing him. It's a perfect con and I wouldn't even know.

Are my feelings even real?

"Damnit," I breathe out as I sink into the pillows, my hands vigorously rubbing my face.

How stupid can I be? I never once questioned the logistics of his magic or why he had to snap his fingers to use it. In hindsight, it sounds so stupid having to rely on a finger snap.

He fed me every little illusion, misdirecting me so I'd never question the truth. I ate every crumb he gave me when I should've thought how ludicrous the devil falling in love with a human was. It's right out of a romance novel. Shit like that doesn't happen in the real world.

"God, I'm so stupid," I mutter into the palms of my hands.

"Oh, I'm sure the Creator would agree."

XXIV

MY EYES SNAP up at the intruder's voice. Finthorn's
standing in the center of the bedroom wearing a fancy three–
piece suit with *both* arms. For a brief moment I wonder how
that's possible, but then remember he's a devil that has the
same job as Balthazar. He'd need magic to grant wishes. He
must have used magic to grow himself another arm.

"What are you doing here?" I demand to know as I sit up
in bed.

My palms have gone clammy as I clutch the bedsheet
within my grasp. I can't let him know how afraid I am to see
him here. How did he even know where to find me?

I have no leverage against him if he were to attack me. I
also don't know how Balthazar realizes I'm in danger. Maybe
he feels something when I'm on the brink of death, but that
might be too late in some cases and then *both* of us are dead.

"It took some time to track you down," Finthorn states,
ignoring my question. A sly smirk spreads across his lips.
"But it's nothing I can't handle."

"What do you want?" I ask as angrily as I can. Like I'm personally offended he'd show his lowly face to me and *not* acutely terrified out of my mind.

I have nothing to defend myself against him if he were to attack me. My best bet is to run for my life.

As subtly as I can, I shift around in the bed, attempting to keep my movements unnoticed. I can't have him anticipating I'll bolt out of the bed. I may not have a fighting chance against a devil like him, but that doesn't mean I'm going to make it easy for him.

"You're a smart girl, I'm sure you can figure it out."

There are a few moments of silence that consume the room. Neither one of us refuses to break eye contact. He's smiling a smug, shit–eating grin like he's confident no one knows he's stolen a rare diamond from the vault. He must know Balthazar is stuck in a House meeting, but I doubt Finthorn knows our lives are magically connected.

Maybe there's a way for me to get my life in danger *just enough* that it'll alert Balthazar to the trouble I'm in. That might give me a better chance at surviving this disaster. If I can make Finthorn angry enough to attack, but not so angry that he'll kill me, Balthazar will appear and deal with him.

My lips pull downward in a frown. Making a devil angry enough to attack but not angry enough to kill is a delicate line to be walking. *Still. I've got to try. I'm not ready to have my soul tortured for eternity.*

"You're seriously targeting me because you're too chicken shit to go after Balthazar?" I ask despite my pounding heart rate.

It thuds powerfully against my chest and if I weren't so busy clutching the blanket in my hands, they'd be trembling. My stomach clenches tight from the nerves and I force myself to take a slow, deep breath. It does nothing to calm me down, but it does keep me from vomiting. This is the *third* time my life has been put in danger today. I'm getting tired of how terrifying it is.

"I *am* going after Balthazar," Finthorn replies before pointing a finger at me. "By going after you."

"You think he cares that highly about someone he refers to as Ephirian swine?"

He stares at me for a short moment before allowing his eyes to roam around the bedroom. It reeks of money and luxury. Even I can see how strange it'd be for the devil to hook a human up with such a swanky apartment. Not unless there was a wish involved and everyone already knows what I supposedly wished for.

"I think he does," Finthorn says as his eyes slowly slide back to mine.

I can't think of a reply to debate what he's said. How can I logically explain a multi–million dollar condo? Being Balthazar's wife isn't enough of a reason. Especially when the cold enforces a time constraint for how long Balthazar can stay on Earth. He could have just as easily given me a dump of a place since he wouldn't be spending much time there.

"So what? You're going to kill me to get back at Balthazar?" I ask as I slink a leg off the bed. Finthorn doesn't seem to notice. "Isn't that a sure way to get yourself killed?"

"Oh, I won't be killing you," he says as his smile turns evil. "I'm just helping a wish get completed."

My eyes go wide upon hearing those words. Before I have time to do anything, he raises his hand and snaps his fingers.

My body is yanked through a vortex. Wind whips around me, wild and violent. It feels like I'm being pulled in every direction. It hurts. My limbs might actually be yanked off me from the sheer force of the wind. It lasts mere milliseconds but feels like a lifetime.

One moment I'm in bed. The next moment, I'm toppling over a fold up table and onto a cold, wet floor. A thick mildew and mold scent coats my tongue. Goosebumps rise along my arms. It's freezing wherever I am.

I awkwardly shuffle to my hands and knees, using the table as leverage while I glance around. The room is dimly lit; the only source of light coming from one fluorescent light bulb. It casts enough light to show I'm stuck in the corner of the room, but eventually the light fades and I can't see past it. Wherever I am, the room is large.

The floor is cold and unforgiving. Cement, maybe? It's painted dark green and the walls, from what I can tell, are yellow. The only furniture I can see is the fold up table, a foldable chair, and some filing cabinets. Based on that alone, I assume I'm still on Earth.

"Hah, he really delivered."

A cold chill runs down my spine as I turn towards the darkness. I can't see anything past the light but I know that voice intimately.

Chad.

"I thought he might have a hard time since that piece of shit seems pretty powerful," Chad says as he finally steps into the light.

My eyes immediately drop to the gun in his hand. He holds it out in the open, finger resting along the side of the barrel as he taps the gun against his thigh.

"But here you are."

I shift around to stand up, but Chad raises the gun at me.

"Uh–uh. Don't move."

"You're really going to kill me?" I ask and for once, there's no venom in my voice.

I have to assume the gun's loaded. I have to assume he has every intention of using that on me. One shot to the head and I'm dead with a one way ticket to Hell to be tortured for eternity. No Balthazar swooping in to save me. Not only that, but I assume Balthazar will die since my wish is still incomplete. If, by some miracle, he had planned on helping me out when I finally went to Hell, he can't do that if he's dead.

My bleak reality is staring me in the face. I can't provoke Chad the way I intended to do with Finthorn. Chad's a loose cannon. He proved that today when he attacked me in broad daylight. Who knows what would have happened if Matt hadn't shown up and scared him off?

"You're supposed to be dead," he says.

My body practically vibrates with rage. The *audacity* of this man–child. He truly believes he's been wronged all because I still breathe the same air as him.

My words waver from my fury as I speak. "Don't you get it? I *am* dead. You said so yourself. My family's already buried me. You've destroyed me. I have *nothing*. Isn't that worse than being dead?"

"It's not good enough."

"*How?*" I shriek. "How is that not good enough?

"Because. I want you to pay for what you did."

"*I have*," I scream, my voice cracking from the overwhelming emotions that consume me.

Rage. Fear. Disbelief. My vision blurs and when I blink, tears coat my cheeks. I want to scream at the top of my lungs. I want to beat him bloody until his face caves in. I want to torture him for the rest of eternity. He ruined my life and it's still *not good enough for him.*

He's getting rich and famous off *my* death, yet me being alive is still not good enough. I'm the one paying the price for *his* sins. He should be suffering the consequences, not getting rewarded for his misogynistic and sexist behavior.

"You're such a child," I yell, my anger hot and ferocious as it burns through all my other emotions. "You're getting everything you want and it's still not good enough! Did you ever stop to consider *why* I did what I did? Did you ever reflect on the things you said and did during our date?"

"I did nothing wrong," he grits out as fury crosses his features.

"Are you *joking?* You said women are inferior to men! You *threatened* me!"

"Don't act like you didn't deserve it. You needed to be reminded of your place."

"That! That is *exactly* why I poured my drink on you and why I made that profile! You can't go around threatening people and *not* expect to get checked! There are consequences to the things you say and do, you asshole."

He cocks the gun and my blood runs cold. He's going to kill me. He's actually going to kill me. All because of a fake profile I refused to take down. How do men like Chad exist? How is it that they go through life thinking they're always in the right and then gaslight people into believing they're wrong for calling them out? How is this happening to me?

I know I'm not perfect. I know there are things I need to work on. Like how easy I am to anger and that I jump to conclusions too quickly. But at least I don't go around threatening people and wishing them dead. Is what I did really so bad that it's worth killing over? All because I embarrassed him and made a fake profile?

"This isn't up for debate," Chad says as his finger shifts to rest on the trigger. "You're supposed to be dead so I'll make you dead."

BANG!

For a second I think he's missed, but then the pain floods in searing hot on the right side of my torso. I look down and see a very small hole in my white T–shirt. I yank it up to see what the damage is. There's a small hole in my stomach but so, so much blood. My brain is having trouble processing what's going on. I've been shot? I'm feeling lightheaded on top of all the pain. I keep trying to process the fact that I've been shot. Does this mean I'm going to die?

"You... shot me."

My voice is surprisingly airy and light as my gaze slides up to Chad. He's breathing heavily. Like he ran a marathon and barely crossed the finish line. His hand trembles as he keeps the gun pointed at me. Is he going to shoot me again?

I suddenly keel over, my hands gripping my side as I loudly groan. The pain is intense and hot, much worse than the initial pain I felt. My stomach churns and the room spins. It's too much. I want it to stop. Please, just make it stop.

My hands pull away from my side and I dare to look down at them. Blood coats my palms. *What is happening?* My vision warps as it fades in and out, threatening to make me unconscious, but I somehow hold on. There's so much blood. I can't stop it. It dawns on me that I'm going to bleed to death.

"You've done it," my voice is weak as I look up at Chad. "You've become a murderer. Have fun living with that."

"You were already dead," he snaps at me, his eyes wide and wild.

He's freaking out. His breathing doesn't calm down. His whole body trembles and he's drenched in sweat. He's either in the throes of a panic attack or close to it.

"I was and yet, I wasn't. You killed me, Chad. You're a murderer."

"Shut the fuck up! No, I'm not!"

"Yes. You are."

He pulls the trigger again.

BANG!

I don't feel the pain. In fact, I don't feel *any* pain. Is it because I'm in *too* much pain? Is it possible to stop feeling pain once you've hit a certain threshold? Or maybe it's because I've bled out too much and my brain is reprioritizing the emergency that's happening. Honestly, I'm just glad I don't hurt even more than I already do.

My gaze drops to my body in search of the newest bullet wound when I hear Chad's terrified voice fill the air.

"No."

"*Yes,*" the low, dangerous voice of Lord Balthazar enters the room.

XXV

M Y EYES SNAP over to Balthazar.

He stands off to my right side at the edge of the light, a bullet rolling between his thumb and index finger. His face is cold and angry, his black–red eyes dark and simmering. The fury radiates off him like a powerful, yet controlled fire. He glances at me for a brief moment, his eyes narrowing for a split second as his jaw clenches, before turning all that merciless wrath at Chad.

"You've made a grave mistake," Balthazar speaks, his voice eerily calm.

"I–I was just–the deal we made–she's supposed to be dead!"

Chad's weeping, tears streaming freely down his cheeks as the gun clatters against the floor. For someone as tall as Chad, he suddenly looks very small. He's not just trembling anymore. His whole body is shivering uncontrollably.

"She *is* dead," Balthazar states as he crushes the bullet in his fingers. "She's dead in every sense of the word except physically. *You* never specified the way in which she was to die."

"I did! I said she needed to be brutally murdered!"

"She was."

"But—"

Balthazar moves fast as he grabs Chad by the neck and slams him into the filing cabinets beside me. When he speaks, he sounds restrained, like he's holding back the rage of an entire world.

"I delivered on my wish and here you are sullying it. Are you not thankful for what I've done?"

Chad whimpers as he clutches at the hand around his throat. "It's not fair. I sold my soul so why does she get to live?"

"You made a deal with the devil, boy. How fair can it be?"

Balthazar releases Chad from his hold and turns his attention to me. His eyes drop to the puddle of blood beneath me. Too many emotions flit across his face that I can't grasp a single one. His fingers curl into fists as he finally meets my gaze.

"Do you regret it?"

His voice is surprisingly soft. There's a raw vulnerability emanating from him that touches my heart and soul. I let my eyes wander as they study the planes of his face, the furrowing of his brows, and the worry within his eyes. Worry, I realize, meant for *me*. That stark moment of clarity makes me understand what he's really asking me.

Do I regret *him*?

In that moment, all my fears about him tricking me, about him using his magic against me, about him misdirecting me, evaporate. The vulnerability he's showing me speaks volumes. Even if he started out with the intent of tricking me, the look on his face tells me he's changed his mind.

We may have met under horrific circumstances. We may have threatened to kill and harm each other. We might not be the healthiest or happiest pairing to ever exist, but we're better *together*. Despite everything horrific that's happened since meeting him, I'd do it all over again if given the chance.

So, no.

I don't regret him.

I hold his gaze confidently as I shake my head. "No. Not one bit, Balthazar."

A second later, his face shifts into a terrifying scowl, the horns on his head igniting in flames as his eyes glow red.

"Good," he growls before he turns his back to me and slits Chad's throat in one fell swoop.

It happens too fast for Chad to react. One moment he's cowering beside Balthazar, the next, blood is spraying from his neck. It coats Balthazar and some of it hisses against the flames of his horns. Chad reaches up, clutching his neck in a desperate attempt to stop the bleeding. His eyes are wide in fear and he drops to his knees. A hand reaches out to hold onto Balthazar's leg to steady himself. Balthazar lets him, but then Chad lets go, too weak to hold on, and topples over.

Chad lands on his back, his hand falling away from his neck as he gurgles on his blood. Balthazar stands over him as the flames on his horns flicker out and he calmly slides his hands into his pants pockets.

"You miscalculated," Balthazar states in a smooth, calm voice as he peers down at Chad dying. "You overestimated your worth and underestimated my obsession with her."

Balthazar nudges Chad with his foot. I can't see the expression Balthazar wears on his face as he stares down at

Chad, but I imagine it to be filled with utter disgust and anger.

"I am going to make your eternal afterlife unimaginably atrocious, Chad Dunner. It was unwise to try and steal from me."

Chad attempts to respond but all I can hear are chokes until finally, it stops. He's dead. He's out of my life. He can't hurt me anymore. The sudden influx of emotions has me overwhelmed. An unexpected sob escapes my mouth and Balthazar's kneeling beside me in a heartbeat.

"Sloane," he says my name the way only a lover would as he gently cups my face. "You have to wish for me to save you."

My eyebrows pinch together as I stare at him in confusion. "What?"

"You have to wish for me to save you. The rules of Jeznia and Odantha state I can't stop you from dying unless you wish it."

I open my mouth to speak the words but they don't come out. Do I really want to use my wish this way? Sure, Balthazar will save me, but in seven years, I'll end up as a tortured soul in Jeznia. But if I die now, I'll end up as a tortured soul in Jeznia. Both scenarios are the same. Being tortured in Jeznia is exactly what I'm trying to avoid. What do I do?

"Sloane," Balthazar begs as he grabs my hands in his. "You're wasting time you don't have. You need to make your wish now."

My eyes glance down at our entwined hands, at how desperately he clings to me. We've known each other for a few short days, yet it feels like a lifetime. Still, that's only how I feel. How does *he* feel about it all?

"Balthazar..."

He waits for me to continue, but I'm starting to fade out. Exhaustion and coldness have seeped in. I dip forward and he catches me, shifting me around to be cradled in his arms.

"Sloane, you have to make your wish before it's too late."

"Why do you want me to live?" I ask as I lean into his warm, comforting body.

"I need time."

"For what?"

"To figure this out."

My eyes beg to shut and I don't fight them. "To figure us out?"

"No, peccatum meum. There's nothing to figure out between us. I need time to figure out your deal."

"My deal?"

"Yes. Seven years is more than enough time for me to find a loophole. I refuse to let you rot in the walls of Jeznia."

I don't want that either. I want to be standing by his side. I want to be in that throne room full of Jeznian Lords who believe Balthazar is the one in power, but in reality, I'm the one who's holding his leash.

"*Sloane.*"

His voice is desperate and scared. I want to comfort him but I need to hear him say it. As long as he says it, I can give up getting out of the contract for him.

"Balthazar, I need to know. What is it you want from me?"

He turns my head and somehow I find the strength to open my eyes. He's staring at me with desperate eyes, worry etched onto that handsome face as he pushes hair out of mine.

"You, Sloane. I only want you."

"Even if I threaten to kill you?"

He chuckles despite the fear on his face. *"Especially* when you threaten to kill me."

"Ok."

I inhale deeply, my eyes sliding shut once more. I'm losing the strength to talk. All I need to do is utter the words. Balthazar and I will go from there. We'll figure it out. Together. Between the two of us, we'll find a solution. I know it.

"I wish..."

XXVI

"WE'VE BEEN OVER this a million times, Balthazar,"
I say as he paces the hallway before the throne room.

I've never seen him so agitated. The flames on his horns
dart down his spine and flicker out just above the hemline of
his pants. He's wearing his Lord Balthazar outfit; no shirt,
golden circlets around his biceps, dark harem pants, bare feet,
and tribal chest tattoo on full display. The muscles along his
back are corded in tension as he walks five feet down the
hallway, pivots, then walks five feet back.

"It's ironclad," I say as he approaches me.

His face is contorted into deep concentration, his eyes
glued to the floor as he paces. My words are bouncing off
him. He hasn't heard a single thing I've said.

Just as he reaches me, he pivots. My hand darts out,
grabbing hold of his wrist and snapping him out of his
thoughts. His eyes glance up as the look on his face shifts to
anger, but it quickly disappears when he sees me.

"You said it was ironclad," I remind him as I pull him close, my other hand reaching up to gently caress his face. "Stop your worrying."

"Every Lord in that room wants to see me burn," he states as his hand gently grabs mine and he leans his face into the palm of my hand. Despite his harsh words, the facial expression he wears is soft, gentle, and tender. "Even if it is ironclad, they can still vote against it."

"If they do that, we'll slaughter each and every one of them."

He smirks that devilish smile, his canine poking out from under his top lip as a sturdy arm wraps around my waist and yanks me flush against him.

"I like where your head's at," he purrs as he dips forward and captures my lips with his.

I giggle into his mouth as my hand slides up into the thick tresses of his hair. His hands drop down to my ass, gripping it firmly as he pulls me taut against him. Heat immediately flushes me, my stomach coiling in desire as our tongues clash. He kisses me like it's our last night alive, tongue memorizing my mouth while one hand sensually trails up my side to cup a breast. He circles his thumb against the nipple and a breathy moan leaves my mouth as I lean into him. I forget myself, forget where we are. The only thing I can concentrate on is Balthazar and where these actions will take us.

Suddenly, the large doors behind us creak open, but we take our time finishing the kiss. They've made us wait. It's only natural we make them wait. Balthazar deepens the kiss, lifting me off my feet so I can wrap my legs around his waist. I gladly do so, smiling into the kiss as my hands caress his face.

"The Lords are ready for you," someone states behind us.

"Mm," Balthazar hums as he slowly pulls away from me. "Who is ready?"

Such a wise ass. I laugh as I place a quick kiss on his lips. Balthazar gently puts me down before taking the lead and walking into the throne room. I follow close behind. Once we cross the threshold, my nerves get the better of me. I know Balthazar said it was ironclad, but like he said, if they want us dead, they'll find a way to achieve it.

Balthazar doesn't take his seat at his throne and instead comes to stand in the middle of the room. I stop beside him and cast a dirty look at Finthorn who stands mere feet from us. He's scowling just as deeply, but his attention is focused on Balthazar.

"My Lords," Balthazar says as he slowly turns about the room. "What an interesting way to spend my day." His expression darkens as his voice warps. "Be wise on how you choose to vote."

No one visibly reacts, but the air in the room shifts. I can see it in their frozen stances. They may have called this meeting to cast their judgment on Balthazar, but they're still afraid of him. *As they should be.*

"Now, let's hear what has to be said," he states as he turns his attention to Finthorn.

Balthazar is commanding the room the way he said he would. He's assured me countless times there's no case to be made against him and yet, now that we're here, I can't help but worry. This is a perfect opportunity to knock him off his pedestal. If *all* the Lords gang up against him, I'm not sure we have a chance. I only said we'd slaughter them because I knew it'd ease his worry. I don't know if we could actually do it. As it currently stands, all I can do is silently watch from the sidelines as Balthazar does his best to verbally eviscerate whatever Finthorn says.

"You killed your contract," Finthorn states simply. "The law dictates if you kill your contract for unjust causes, you must forfeit your life."

"Unjust cause you say," Balthazar says the words like he's humming them. "Tell me, Finthorn, why do you think I killed Chad?"

"I don't pretend to understand the minds of Lords."

"Oh, but you do," Balthazar growls angrily as he shifts his entire attention onto Finthorn. Finthorn noticeably shrinks but manages to hold his ground. "That is why you called us here today. You've urged your dearest Lord Taron to throw these claims against me in expectation that the rest of the Lords will vote me dead. You're counting on their hatred for me to overshadow how weak your case truly is."

"Why is his case weak?" Lord Carmilla asks from her bat throne.

"Chad Dunner, 1998, United States of America attempted to kill my wife," Balthazar answers without an ounce of emotion. "As you all know, not only am I allowed to do what I see fit to protect what is mine, Sloane Kensington, 1996, United States of America is also another contract of mine."

"But she isn't your wife," Lord Taron states. "That's a lie you constructed to hide the fact that you never granted her wish to begin with."

My stomach drops. How would he know that? Only Balthazar and I knew he hadn't granted my wish immediately upon extracting my soul. Was someone spying on us? Was Finthorn there after I had been shot and overheard me make my wish then?

"Oh?" Balthazar asks as he shifts his attention to Lord Taron, seemingly unaffected by the accusation. "What proof do you have of that?"

"Look at her," Lord Taron shouts as he angrily points at me. "There's all the proof we require."

All eyes shift to where I stand and my stomach flips. Not a single one of them looks at me without emotion. They all bear some form of resentment, hatred, or contempt. Considering the circumstances, it's rather tame. I can't say I blame them for how they feel. Balthazar assured me there's no law against what he did, but it wouldn't surprise me to hear that there's more of a general understanding that it *shouldn't* be done.

"She is rather stunning, isn't she?" Balthazar asks as a gentle smile grabs hold of his face while looking at me. "Just look at those magnificent horns."

I can't refrain from reaching up and touching one of the horns jutting out of my head. It's cold to the touch with a smooth surface. A little tingle darts down my spine as my finger glides up the horn towards the tip. There's minimal feeling in the horns. However, the base where the horns grow out feels strange when touched. I've never felt anything like it. My body is struggling to get used to the new additions, but I can't say I don't like them.

Unlike Balthazar's near pitch black horns, mine are black with gold marbling. The gold color streaks out like lightning, scattering in thin lines across the black surface. The horns are beautiful. I can't look away from them whenever I see my reflection.

"Still, that's no proof," Balthazar states. "She wished to be my wife. So, I made her *my wife*."

That's not true. I never wished to be his wife. I never wanted that title. I still have no idea what our relationship is or where it's going. But that's ok. I don't need to know that stuff right now.

When the time came for me to make my wish to save my life, I did the only thing that made sense. I found the loophole I needed.

"I wish to be a devil for all of eternity."

It's brilliant, really. Being a devil for eternity prevents me from having to live an eternal afterlife rotting inside the walls of Jeznia. Devils have magic. I have seven years to learn how to use my magic. So even if in seven years I end up within the walls of Jeznia, I'll break free.

Balthazar could have found some loophole when granting my wish like he had with Matt's immortality wish. He could have made me a weaker, lesser, feebler devil, but he hadn't. He created me as his equal.

I'm not as adept at using my powers the way he is, but the potential is there. It's why, despite the fact that Balthazar didn't do anything illegal, they might still vote against him to prevent him from becoming too powerful. It's one thing to find a wife the old fashioned way, but to make one perfectly equal to yourself has to be against their rules. Otherwise, *all* the Lords would do it.

"You had no right–" Taron starts to say but is cut off by Balthazar.

"Didn't I? She wished to be my wife. That's all the right I need. Are we really going to bend to the whim of such a low class devil?" he pointedly asks as his attention zeros in on Finthorn. "One who barely has enough merits to make it to the third circle."

"That's because you rule the eastern and western borders," Finthorn grinds out.

"Of the U.S."

It's not Balthazar who makes the clarification, but Lord Carmilla. Her expression is guarded, but I can see her calculating her next move very carefully.

"As Lord Balthazar previously stated, you have the rest of Ephiri to conduct your deals," she continues. "It is not his fault you're underperforming."

Finthorn's hands curl into tight fists as his eyes dart to the ground. I don't hide my smirk. That's the least he deserves.

"I've heard enough," she states as her eyes glance around the room. "I find Lord Balthazar in compliance with our current laws."

"Mother, you cannot be serious–"

"Quite so," she replies to her daughter.

"But he made a *human* a devil! He's sullied our species!"

"You will bite your tongue, Ivy, or I will remove it for you," Carmilla states in a threatening tone.

Ivy immediately keeps quiet. Carmilla pauses for a moment before directing her attention back to the Lords.

"We lacked the foresight to anticipate such a wish. We must honor it."

"You're too old fashioned, Lord Carmilla," the devil sitting at the centipede throne says. *Lord Ruulin,* Balthazar reminds me. "So what if we don't have a current law in place? He had no reason to grant her wish the way he did. We offer them the bare minimum, nothing more. He overstepped and should pay the price for it."

"I'm inclined to agree with Lord Ruulin," Taron states. "Simply because there is no law against it doesn't mean we should allow it to be recognized. I vote against him."

"Those in favor of Lord Ruulin and Lord Taron's judgment," Carmilla asks as her cold eyes scan the room.

My heart sinks as four out of six Lords raise their hands. The only two that don't raise their hands are Carmilla and Meik of House Anguis, the third House. Finthorn grins victoriously, unable to hide his joy as he turns to us. My breathing becomes shallow as anxiety rampages through me. Balthazar told me not to worry. He said he's done nothing wrong and they'd rule in his favor. Yet here we stand in the center of the room with all the Lords bearing their judgment down on us and only two voted *for* him.

"No witty remark to share?" Finthorn asks smugly, his hands in his pockets as his shoulders pull back.

He stands tall with his head held high. He's floating on cloud nine. Maybe even Finthorn thought he had no chance of winning and only went through with the case because of his pride. Now, though, he gloats happily, proudly, and unashamed.

My hand reaches out to Balthazar's and I squeeze it tight. He casts me a look out of the side of his eyes and gives me a quick wink before turning his attention back to the Lords.

"Lord Carmilla. Lord Meik. I won't forget your fair ruling."

Black smoke fills the center of the room and Taron shoots up from his throne.

"Stop him! He mustn't escape!"

"You're mistaken," Balthazar says as he holds up the hand that isn't squeezing mine. "I have no intention of fleeing."

The smoke billows and swirls. When it clears, a gasp falls from my mouth as the Records Keeper stands in the room. I'd forgotten how terrifying it looked with its head wrapped in barbed wire, the skin shredding under the metal prongs with every move it makes. How the blood dribbles down its face and the fleshy bits of its eye sockets stare out at the world. The hole that had been on the right cheek can no longer be considered a hole. Most of the flesh has fallen off, exposing the teeth and jaw. It looks painful, grotesque, and horrific.

The Records Keeper glances at Balthazar who nods his head in return. The Records Keeper moves stiffly as it procures a tennis ball sized red orb from its flimsy black shawl. I'm a bit surprised at how well the Records Keeper holds the soul in its boney frail hands.

"Sloane Kensington, 1996, United States of America. Her soul," the Records Keeper speaks in that grating voice and I wince at the sound.

"What?" Lord Taron balks.

"That can't be," Ivy says as her hand covers her mouth. "Even if he did turn her into a devil, her soul should still be white."

"It never was. It never will be," the Records Keeper states.

"What are you saying?" Carmilla asks and I can see a shred of satisfaction swimming in her otherwise cold eyes. She's pleased she voted in Balthazar's favor.

"The soul was never human to begin with," it states.

"You mean to say she would have become a devil upon her human death?" Meik asks from his snake throne. He looks equally as pleased as Carmilla.

"That I do not know," it answers. "Only the Creator or Death knows."

Meik, whose locs spill around his shoulders and cool umber skin glows in the firelight, entwines his fingers together as he rests his chin atop them. He gloats from his snake throne as his eyes glance around the throne room.

"Interesting turn of events, wouldn't you agree, my Lords?" he asks and is unable to hide his victorious smirk.

The room is silent. Finthorn's smug expression has vanished and he looks white as a ghost. Balthazar won't just rip his arm off this time. He'll kill him. *Not if I get to him first.*

"I see we acted too hastily," Ruulin states as he offers a smile, though there's no amusement in it. "I withdraw my vote."

One by one, all four Lords who voted against Balthazar withdraw their votes, leaving only Carmilla and Meik's votes in favor of Balthazar.

"It would appear you are found innocent of any wrongdoing, Lord Balthazar," Meik says.

"As I expected," Balthazar answers. He waves his hand dismissively and black smoke swirls around the Records Keeper. When the smoke is gone, so is the Records Keeper. "Now, how do you intend to deal with the swine standing across from me?"

For once, swine doesn't mean me. I stand directly beside Balthazar, our hands still entwined with each other's. Swine means Finthorn.

"Do you have a suggestion, Lord Balthazar?" Carmilla asks.

"If it pleases my Lords, I'd like to handle his punishment," Balthazar answers.

"I have no objections. Do the others?" she asks as her gaze sweeps the room.

No one says a thing. Finthorn says nothing as he hangs his head in defeat. He knew the risks of challenging Lord Balthazar, heir of House Primus, and took them anyway. The only one he has to blame is himself.

"Splendid," Balthazar replies as a smile spreads across his lips. "I trust our meeting has concluded?"

"Yes, I would think so," Meik answers.

"Lord Meik," Balthazar says as he dips his head slightly, then turns his attention to Carmilla and offers her the same slight bow. "Lord Carmilla."

He doesn't offer his good graces to anyone else and it speaks volumes in the room. It's as though he's extended a lifeline to the two Lords and let everyone else drown out at sea.

Seven Lords may rule Hell. They may even fight and argue over who holds the most influence within the realm, but it's clear who holds the true power. *Never cross a Primis*, I think to myself as I smugly stare at the four Lords who voted against him.

With no other words needed to be exchanged, Balthazar, Finthorn, and I disappear from the room.

XXVII

THE TRANSPORTATION DOESN'T hurt nearly as much as it did when I was human. There's less pressure pounding down on me on all sides. It feels like a tight hug instead of something that will crack my skull open.

We arrive in a room decked out for torture and torment. There are numerous places for someone to be tied down. In a chair. On a table. Hanging from a hook.

Various tools are strewn about the room. Some I recognize like a drill, pliers, and a handsaw. Others I don't know their name or their purpose, but it doesn't matter. I know they'll cause pain. Finthorn isn't going to have it easy before he dies. The thought delights me.

Finthorn deserves every bit of pain coming his way. He wrapped me up in a pretty little bow and hand delivered me to Chad. He sent me to *die*. I would have died, too, if I had already made my wish when Balthazar took my soul. I would have died if Chad had aimed for my head instead of my stomach. I would have died if Balthazar had been so tied up in whatever House business he was attending to that he couldn't get away. Finthorn essentially killed me. All because he can't stand the fact that Balthazar is a better devil than he is even without Zagon Primis's help.

Still, I wish it was Chad standing before me. Chad's the real person I want to torture. He destroyed my life, destroyed the lives of my friends and family. He took everything that mattered to me and burned it to a crisp.

Chad *deserved* to die. I'm glad Balthazar killed him, but he took my closure in doing so. I didn't get the opportunity to take back what Chad stole from me. I didn't get the satisfaction of seeing Chad's face when he realized *I* won in the end. So Finthorn will have to do.

"Any special requests?" Balthazar asks and Finthorn shakes his head.

"None."

"As expected from someone like you." Balthazar's voice is full of disdain.

Those words cause Finthorn to flinch and I wonder if they hurt more than the physical pain he's going to receive.

"Did you honestly think you stood a chance against us?" Balthazar asks as he plucks a tool from a nearby table.

He shifts it from hand to hand as he watches Finthorn's every move. Finthorn keeps his gaze on the floor, hands pressed to the sides of his thighs. Completely submissive. Perhaps he thinks he'll take all the fun from Balthazar if he's not fighting his fate. The thought pisses me off.

He *should* be fighting. He should be begging like I had to. He should be afraid the same way I was. He should be worried his life is going to end and that he'll be stuck in the walls of Jeznia to be tortured for eternity like I did.

My anger explodes white hot as I yank a long, thin pick from the table and furiously jam it into Finthorn's shoulder. He cries out but doesn't stop me or pull away.

"*Answer* him," I order as I push the object deeper into him.

Finthorn winces, his body naturally pulling away from the pain, but I go with him.

"Yes, I did," Finthorn mumbles.

"What led you to believe you had a chance?" Balthazar asks as he places his tool back on the table. He's trusting me with the torture and it leaves me feeling... odd.

"My own stupidity."

"No," I refute as I pull the pick out and jam it into him again.

He's *lying*. Finthorn's not that stupid. He would rather go behind Balthazar's back, hoping to never get caught, than to call a public trial with the Lords. Taron must have assured Finthorn he would be safe. Or maybe he demanded Finthorn call the trial after Taron saved his life. A debt repaid that screwed Finthorn over.

Finthorn winces but manages to bite back a groan.

"You're lying," I state in a low, irate tone. "Did Lord Taron set you up? Did he promise you you'd win or did he tell you to hold your head high when you die?"

He finally raises his eyes to mine and he's *livid*. He's boiling over in his hatred and it's taking everything in him not to lunge for me. He's *not* stupid. He knows the second he moves Balthazar will be on him like a shark on blood in water. Instead, he tries a different tactic as he shifts his attention to Balthazar.

"You let the Ephirian swine do all your dirty work, Lord Balthazar?"

"Yes, I do," he answers and I hear the smirk in his voice as he says, "She's better at it."

Finthorn spits in my face in response. Before Balthazar can move, I raise the hand holding the pick, motioning Balthazar to stop before he's even had the chance to move. Blood gushes out of Finthorn's wound. He doesn't appear to notice.

Instead, he's gone ghostly pale, fear capturing his face as he stares at the two of us, at how well Balthazar listens to my commands. Perhaps I should've been giving Balthazar orders right from the start if that's how Finthorn reacts to Balthazar listening.

I don't say anything as I methodically wipe the spit from my cheek. My rage has become so intense that it's gone quiet. My ears are muffled as the noise around me disappears. I flick the spit off my hand before wiping my hand dry on Finthorn's clothes.

"You're a pathetic excuse of a devil, you know that, Finthorn?" I ask him. "You blame Balthazar for your low merits when, in reality, you just don't work that hard. *Millions* of humans would love to sell their souls. You're the one screwing up. Not Balthazar. Not the other Contract Liaisons. *You.*

"It's maddening," I breathe out as I twirl the pick in my hand. "Maddening to think I was almost killed by someone as dumb as you."

My arm pulls back before swinging forward as I stab him again.

"I hate what you stole from me."

Stab.

"I hate that you almost won."

Stab.

"I hate that I'll never see my parents again."

Tears stream down my face.

Stab.

"I'll never see Ella again."

A sob erupts from me.

Stab.

"I lost my life! I'm not *human* anymore! I have to spend the rest of eternity in Jeznia–in *Hell!*"

Stab.

Stab.

Stab.

The pick clatters against the ground, my eyes blurry from the tears. They coat my cheeks as they descend to the floor. I inhale a shaky breath as it hits me all at once.

I died.

Twice.

On the day I met Balthazar and on the day Chad shot me. I'm not human anymore. Even if I could use my own magic to see my parents again, to see Ella again… I'm a monster. A devil. I'm *evil*. I can't go back. I can never go back.

A heart wrenching sob tears through me. I barely notice Finthorn dropping forward on his hands, choking on his blood.

"Sloane," Balthazar calls my name, his fingers curling around my elbow and I immediately jerk away from him.

"*Don't!*… Don't."

Finthorn gasps and it sounds wet. There's blood in his lungs. There's blood seeping out of him from multiple holes. Despite the situation he's in, he stares up at me defiantly. And then he smirks.

"I win," he declares and it shatters whatever last remnants of my humanity I have left.

A yell filled with all of my pain, all of my regret and anger, echoes through the room as magic pulses inside me. I feel it building, feel it circulating around us. The air tastes tart, like an apple that's been doused in smoke.

The magic pulsates as it swarms us. I feel it fill me to the brim. It's a terrifying sensation, like my body will split open from the amount of magic flowing inside it. Still, I trust in it, in whatever it is that I'm doing.

I place my palm on Finthorn's scalp and the magic inside my hand latches onto his head. My palm's temperature rises exponentially, the air becoming heavy with the sweet smell of smoked apples. It's so thick I think I might choke.

"Go to Hell," I state in a multi–layered voice as I stare into Finthorn's eyes. I watch as they go wide, as the last shred of his dignity is replaced by an unknown fear.

A crack echoes throughout the room before a shot of fire comes pouring out the back of Finthorn's head. It blazes hot and white before disappearing completely. Finthorn's dead body crumples to the ground with a thud, leaving only me and Balthazar in the room.

The scent of magic is gone. I'm completely and utterly drained as my knees give out. Balthazar catches me, wrapping his firm arms around me as he lifts me into his embrace and we disappear out of sight.

BALTHAZAR WASHES ME down head to toe, helps me dress into comfortable clothes, and tucks me into bed. It takes all of two minutes before I pass out from exhaustion.

When I wake up, I check the time on my phone. It's the next day, a little past 6am. I'm not tired enough to continue sleeping, but I don't want to leave the comfort of my bed. Balthazar is nowhere to be found. My assumption is he's back in Jeznia dealing with House business or somewhere in the States making a deal with some sorry sap.

I curl up against the pillows, pulling the comforter tighter against me. My thoughts drift as I stare at the empty spot next to me. I killed Finthorn. Not Balthazar. *Me*. For something he didn't even do. I used Finthorn as a lousy stand–in for Chad. I held no doubts or hesitation in my actions. I killed him coldly and full of anger. *I really am evil.*

I've spent the past week holding myself above all the people Balthazar made deals with when the ugly truth is I'm ten times worse than they'll ever be. I thought I was better than most people in general. I thought I was good because I cared about people, about basic human rights. But I'm not good. I'm evil. My red soul proves it. I've always been destined for Jeznia. I was fighting the current, trying so goddamn hard to be good when it was a lost cause.

I don't know how to feel about that. So much of my pride and identity has been wrapped up in how good I was. Now, it's gone. My entire perception of myself was wrong – *is* wrong. I don't know who I am anymore.

Suddenly, Balthazar appears in the room and he starts to quietly pull the comforter back before he realizes I'm awake.

"You're up," he says in surprise, eyebrows furrowing as he slinks into bed beside me.

"Yeah. I slept for a long time."

"You're sure you don't need more?" he asks as he pulls me over and I happily ditch the pillows to cuddle Balthazar.

"I'm good. I'm not ready to leave the bed, but I don't need more sleep."

"There are other things we could do in bed that don't involve sleeping."

I laugh as my arm sprawls across his stomach. "Later. Right now, I want to cuddle."

"I feel you need reminding that I am Lord Balthazar Primis, heir to House Primis, the most powerful House in Jeznia. *Cuddling* is not something I do."

"It is now. I own you and if you don't do what I want, then you don't get a reward."

I don't miss the sharp inhale he takes or how he holds me a smidgen tighter upon hearing my words. I smile as I snuggle deeper against him.

"That's what I thought," I mumble.

"A born natural," he mutters to himself and I imagine he's doing everything he can to keep this cuddling session tame.

"Where did you go?" I ask after a few moments of silence.

"I had some deals to make," he answers as he combs his fingers through my hair.

The action is so intimate yet natural. It feels as though we've been doing it for hundreds of years. I sink into that comfort and familiarity. Balthazar radiates the essence of home and I'm no longer afraid to get lost in it, in him. He picked up the broken pieces of my life, sheltered me, and let me put it all back together. He's my safe space now and I revel in that.

"You were sleeping rather peacefully," he says. "I didn't want to wake you."

"I appreciate that. Thank you."

He grunts a reply before a comfortable silence settles between us. I draw random patterns atop his chest as he combs my hair, his blunted fingernails gently scratching against my scalp. We sit in that silence for an undefined amount of time. Balthazar may not know it, but his presence grounds me. He helps clear my thoughts and doubts, helps me focus on the bigger picture instead of what could have been. For instance, I can't help but wonder why did the Lords let me go?

"Balthazar," I say quietly, my voice barely above a whisper. "Why did the Lords take back their votes when they saw my soul?"

"Because your soul is Jeznian, which means no one understands why you were turned into the devil you are."

My face scrunches up in confusion as Balthazar's finger gets stuck on a knot in my hair. He takes great care in getting the knot out.

"What do you mean?" I ask. "I literally *wished* to be turned into a devil–or your wife, according to them. Why would no one understand why I got turned into a devil?"

"Your horns," he states evenly as he releases a calm, deep exhale. "They indicate you're a high caliber devil."

"I don't understand what you're saying."

I really don't. I've never heard him use the term high caliber devil before. I assume it's self–explanatory but one can never be too sure.

Also, what do my horns have to do with anything? How are they related to being a high caliber devil? It's as if he's speaking a foreign language, except I understand the words he's saying, just not their meaning.

"You haven't seen enough devils to know, but the size of their horns is indicative of their power," he answers as he trails a finger down my neck. "Direct offspring of Lords typically have similarly sized horns. The further away you get from the direct lineage, the smaller the horns, the less powerful the devils are. A distant relative could become powerful enough that their horns grow in size, though that's not as common.

"In case you're still not understanding, your horns are the same size as mine. I didn't do that, Sloane. In truth, I barely granted your wish as I knew the backlash we would receive if I had fully granted it. I only intended to grant enough to ensure you wouldn't die and wouldn't be left to be tortured for eternity. That's it."

"Then how...?"

I can't even complete my question. I'm flabbergasted. What is he saying? That it was *me* who turned myself this way? None of this is making any sense.

"Remember the smell of the air when you killed Finthorn?" he asks.

"Yeah."

"That's old, deep magic, Sloane," he says, completely devoid of all emotions.

A cold chill darts down my spine. I can't recall a time I've heard him sound so distant. Like he's talking to me as if I'm a stranger to him.

"Balthazar," I say as I prop up to stare at him.

He shifts quickly, flipping me onto my back as he hovers over me. He firmly holds my wrists in his hands as he stares at me with cold, dark eyes. I swallow in apprehension, unsure of what he intends to do.

"Balthazar," I say his name again, hoping a flash of recognition will fill his gaze, but I see none.

"Every Lord in that room let you leave because only an idiot attacks a devil they know nothing about. It doesn't matter if they know they're stronger than you. Brute strength isn't the only way to kill someone. Finesses and stealth work equally well. They let you leave because they have no information on you."

I remain quiet as I stare up at him. Is he saying he's now uneasy around me? He clearly stated I'm more powerful than he intended. Does that mean he regrets it? Regrets me?

"I anticipate each Lord will do their best to figure you out for their own precautions. If they find out you use old, deep magic... it won't be safe for you. Not even Zagon Primis knows how to use old magic and he's the oldest amongst the Lords. If he gets wind that you use old magic..." His eyebrows pull together as a somewhat pained expression grabs hold of his face. "The decisions I make to protect you will make you hate me."

"Hey," I whisper as I break my hand free to cup his face.

I can see the fear in his eyes and it breaks my heart. He's not scared *of* me but *for* me. That's what all this distance is between us. He's *scared*. My heart twinges painfully in my chest.

"I won't let them find out, ok? You don't have to worry about me."

All I have to do is not to get found out... for the rest of eternity. Shouldn't be too hard, right?

"With your permission," he says, "I would like to teach you how to use normal magic. It'll be odd if the Lords find nothing on you."

"Ok, sure, if you think that's best," I answer, my thumb gently caressing his face and I offer him a small, reassuring smile. "Let's do that. And hey, I have the rest of eternity to get strong using normal magic. You won't always have to protect me, ok? I'm going to become your equal, Lord Balthazar."

He smirks large and wide as he leans forward to capture my lips with his.

"Spoken like a true queen," he murmurs against my lips.

"Damn right," I laugh as my arms come up to wrap around his shoulders.

He leans down, allowing the weight of him to rest atop me as his arms slide underneath me and nuzzles his face against my neck.

"To the reign of High Queen Sloane and Lord Balthazar," he murmurs against my throat.

My arms and legs wrap around him tight as my right hand settles on the back of his head. I'm going to do whatever it takes. I'll make myself his equal even if it kills me. Balthazar is my life now. I refuse to let someone else come along and rip that away from me again. I need to protect what's mine. *No one* will be able to screw with me ever again.

"We'll be unstoppable," I whisper.

I'll make sure of it.

Epilogue

I**T'S EXACTLY AS** I remember. A crooked mailbox, beige siding, dark brown door, and two cars parked on the driveway instead of inside the two car garage. I don't know what I was expecting, but *normal* wasn't on the list.

My stomach churns as my fingers twist and pull each other. All I have to do is ring the doorbell, yet I'm frozen in my spot. What if they turn me away? What if they cuss me out? I want to give them closure but instead I could reopen old wounds. What is the right thing to do?

I don't know how much time passes with me standing at the edge of the property, gazing at the house I once called home. Eventually, my mother dares to open the brown door, a slight scowl upon her face as she stares at me from behind the glass door.

She looks just as I remember except maybe a few more gray hairs upon her scalp. Same sloped nose, high cheekbones, and pointed chin.

"What do you want?" she asks as she props open the glass door.

There's no friendliness to her tone and my heart sinks. She used to be a warm ray of sunshine to anyone who crossed her path. I barely recognize the woman before me.

My heart hammers inside my chest as my mouth goes dry, but I force out the words.

"Your daughter had a charm bracelet. There was a whale, a soccer ball, a book, a cat, and the number three on it," I tell her from the street.

I had scoured the internet on mediums and how they gave away information. The ones who seemed legit always gave away vague, but detailed information. *I'm picking up on* or *I'm seeing* as their go to phrases. I studied and studied and studied before I finally pulled the trigger and took the trip out to my parents' house.

"How did you…" she trails off as she steps out onto the stoop.

"May I come up?" I ask and she nods her head.

I exhale a shaky breath as I walk up the familiar path to the front door of my childhood home. Balthazar promised me his magic would work until the end of the day so that I could stay with them for as long as I'd like. He changed every feature about me, turning my brown hair red, my hazel eyes blue, my tanned face pale and littered with freckles. He also made me shorter as well. Nothing about my appearance links me back to Sloane Kensington. Today, I'm Megan O'Conner, psychic and medium.

"Hello," I greet her breathily, unable to tame my swirling emotions. "I'm Megan. I know this is a bit unorthodox, but I'm a psychic. I speak to the dead. When I heard about your daughter on the news, I tried connecting with her and she responded back. If you want to tell me to fuck off, go to Hell, call the police on me, I'll turn around and never see you again. If you'd like to hear what I have to say, I'd love to have a chat with you and your husband."

She's staring at me in disbelief, in anger, and in suspicion. I can see the longing to speak to me, her daughter. She probably has a million questions for me. Probably wants to know what really happened. If I was alive before I got cut up into eight pieces. If I knew my life was in danger. If I'm ok.

But there's also hesitation in her gaze. Megan is a complete stranger to her. My case was sensationalized on national news. I'm sure my parents have had their fair share of interactions with psychopaths seeking any bit of information about me for their own amusement, not caring these are actual people suffering and grieving.

"I promise you I'm not here to ask you any questions about your daughter or dig into your lives. I just thought… if it were me, I'd want to hear what she has to say. I wanted to give you the option to say yes or no."

"What else did she have?" my mom asks, hand gripping the edge of the glass door as she continues to scowl at me, but I'm not blind to the unshed tears in her eyes.

"She keeps saying a name," I reply, purposely sounding slightly confused like all those other mediums did. "Does Kitty Cottontail mean anything to you?"

My mom drops to her knees upon hearing the name of my favorite stuffed animal, a stifled cry leaving her mouth. I immediately kneel beside her, comfortably placing a hand on her shoulder as I fight back my own tears. *Fuck, this is hard,* I think to myself as my emotions threaten to overwhelm me.

I knew it wouldn't be easy staring my parents grief directly in the face, but I hadn't anticipated how intensely it would affect me. My entire life I've never really seen my parents so vulnerable. They were great at shielding me from their hardships.

I swallow thickly around the lump forming in my throat. A moment later, my dad comes rushing out from the living room. He sees his wife crumpled on the stoop and fury ignites on his face. Livid, hazel eyes, the ones I inherited, glare at me as he stalks towards the door.

"Get the hell off my stoop," he bellows with practiced ease, like he's been forced to do this time and time again since I've died.

My heart shatters and I can't hold the tears back any longer.

"I'm sorry," I reply as I stand up and back away from them. "I didn't mean to cause any harm.

"Rick, no, stop," my mom begs as she grips his hand. "She's the real deal. She can speak to Sloane."

He face falls as if this isn't the first conversation they've had about me.

"Cheryl–"

"Tell him," my mom begs me. "Tell him what you told me."

I repeat what I told her. The charm bracelet and the name of the stuffed animal.

"Where did you get that information?" he demands to know. "It had to be posted somewhere."

"I didn't look for it," I answer him, my voice warped. "I promise you I have no ill intent. I just thought, if I could, I'd like to help you get closure."

My parents are *broken*. My death destroyed them and seeing it face to face is killing me. I want to tell them it's me, that *I'm* Sloane, but how would I explain everything? How can I tell them their baby girl is a *devil?* I can't do that to them. I've already caused them enough heartbreak.

"Rick, please," my mom begs still kneeling on the ground. "I want to hear what she has to say."

His jaw clenches rapidly as he keeps his hateful gaze on me but he nods his head. He puts my mother first like he always does. Quietly, he helps her to her feet and guides her inside the house. I hesitate only for a moment before following them inside. I almost beeline it to the dining room but remember I have to pretend I know nothing about this house. So instead, I stand awkwardly by the door, unsure if I should follow after them.

"Follow me," my dad's gruff voice orders and I follow him into the living room.

He helps my mother onto the couch while I take a seat on the loveseat. They exchange a few words between each other, my dad asking my mom if she'd like water or something to eat. He doesn't ask me.

When he disappears into the kitchen to retrieve my mom a glass of water, she turns her attention to me.

"You can talk to my girl?" she asks, hope filling her voice.

"Yes," I answer shortly, not wanting to divulge too much. "I'll answer any questions you have to the best of my capabilities."

My dad returns a short moment later and takes a seat beside my mom, protectively wrapping an arm around her shoulders. He's still glaring at me and I do my best to ignore it.

"Did she suspect Chad would attack her?" my mom asks.

I wait a few moments, pretending to listen to the spirits before I answer. "No. She didn't."

"Does she know why he attacked her?"

After a few moments of silence, I shake my head. "No."

There's no way I can answer yes. Too much of that answer involves Balthazar and Jeznia. It's better to lie.

"The police say she went on a date with him and that she made a fake profile about him, but that's just not my girl. Sloane would never do that."

"I keep getting this sense of unease around their date," I tell her. "I don't think the police were wrong about the profile. Something felt unsafe about her date with Chad. When I concentrate on the fake profile, I get this feeling of, like, a warning. As if she was trying to warn others about him."

"That sounds like Sloane."

It's my dad who speaks. He's finally lost the glare on his face and looks a little more at ease.

"She wanted to warn others about him but she didn't think he'd attack her?" he asks.

I shake my head. "The attack feels like a surprise to me. The warning she made doesn't match the attack. Does that make sense?

"I keep getting he's a big jerk, a jerk who can't keep his mouth shut, a jerk who is disrespectful, a jerk who calls people names. I don't think she left that date thinking he'd harm her."

"Was she... did she... suffer?" my dad asks and his voice breaks off as he hastily wipes his eyes.

"No. She died quickly. She's very grateful for that."

My mother openly sobs and my dad holds her tightly as he cries with her. My eyes go skyward as I try to prevent my tears from escaping. My lips press tightly together but I can't stop the trembling of my chin.

Minutes pass as the two of them cry and when they calm down, I decide to give information without being prompted.

"She loves you two very dearly. She loved the life you provided her. She's sorry she can't be here with you anymore, but she needs you to know that she's ok. She's in a good place and she'll always be with you."

My dad nods his head as my mother cries some more. We spend the next two hours conversing, reminiscing about my childhood as best I can without giving too much away. By the end of it, both my parents are hugging me tightly.

"Thank you," my dad says as he squeezes my shoulder.

"We can't thank you enough. What you've given us…" my mom trails off and I smile at her.

"I'm glad I could help. Thank you for giving me the opportunity to meet you two. I wish you the best on your healing journey."

We exchange one more goodbye before I leave. I get into the rental car and for a few moments, I sit there in silence. I gave my parents the closure they needed. Hopefully, they'll be able to move forward and enjoy the remaining years they have left on Earth.

But more importantly, I got the closure *I* needed. I got to say goodbye to my parents. I got to see them transform from grieving to healing a little bit. I got to say goodbye to the girl I used to be and to the woman I was becoming. I'm no longer Sloane Kensington, 1996, United States of America. She died. I'm now Sloane Kensington, devil, owner of Lord Balthazar, heir to House Primis.

Jeznia better be prepared.

Preview

Becoming the Devil – Book 2

I

"CHANGE THE COLOR of the pigeon," Balthazar instructs as he sits languidly on the bench in the Boston Common.

I stand roughly five feet from him as pigeons peck and waddle between us. Balthazar has both his hands draped along the back of the bench, his long legs spread out in such a classic man spread that it mildly irritates me despite how attractive he looks.

He's in casual clothes instead of the classic suit he wears when bargaining for souls. He picked the perfect outfit for the cooler weather. Grey cashmere sweater with fitted dark jeans and brown leather boots. I can't help but assume he's sweating underneath his layers, but then again, he's most likely using his magic to keep himself comfortable.

Balthazar left his black hair un–styled and instead has it pushed back with a thin black headband. It gives him a youthful look, like he's fresh out of college and not in his mid–thirties.

His olive skin is a little tanner than when we first met. I suspect that's due to the amount of time he's been hanging outside with me these past few days. He stares at me with black irises that are sprinkled with red specks. The sunlight that manages to penetrate through the tree canopy reflects off his glossy, black horns. Overall, the entire air surrounding him screams casual, relaxed, and perhaps maybe even the tiniest bit bored. I do my best to ignore that last part as I focus on the reason for why we're here.

"What color should I change it to?" I ask as I look at the group of pigeons.

Today is my first magic lesson. It was only three weeks ago that Chad shot me, nearly killing me. If it hadn't been for the fact that I still had a wish to make, I would be dead, rotting in the walls of Hell – Jeznia, according to the locals.

I used my wish to save my life while simultaneously finding a loophole preventing me from being tortured for my afterlife. I wished myself to become a devil for all eternity. Balthazar granted it without hesitation.

He later confessed he never intended on turning me into the powerful devil that I apparently became. That happened because of the old magic I possess. But old magic is a dangerous thing to have. If the Lords of Jeznia find out I have old, deep magic, they'll either kill me or do unspeakable things to get access to it. To prevent that from happening, Balthazar insisted he teach me normal magic; the kind of magic every devil uses. I agreed to his lessons because the other option wasn't really an option.

So here we are, our first lesson of teaching me how to use normal magic and Balthazar wants me to change the color of a pigeon.

"Any color you want," he answers without a care in the world.

I stare at the multi–colored bird and consider making it all one color is probably the easiest way to go about this. Although technically that means I'm changing 4+ colors at the same time. Maybe it would be easier trying to just change one color. Though that would mean focusing on a smaller area on the bird instead of the bird as a whole. If I really think about it, both scenarios are *equally* difficult because they require a different set of focus and intent.

"Sloane," Balthazar says my name, his voice laced with mirth, and my eyes snap up to him.

He's smiling a crooked grin, the right side of his lips pulling up as he stares at me in open amusement. How does he get more handsome the longer I know him? Shouldn't I become immune to it as time goes on?

"You're overanalyzing the task," he states and a heat floods my cheeks at his call out. I didn't realize I was so easily read.

"Do I change *all* the colors or just one?" I ask despite my embarrassment. "This is the first time I'm attempting something like this. I don't know which one is easier."

His eyes glance down at the birds as he studies them before he answers. "Make it all the same color."

I frown, not too pleased with his answer, but trusting him all the same. Afterall, he's the expert here. He should know what he's talking about.

"Ok. I'll change it to brown."

He nods his head and I stare at the bird closest to me. It's minding its own business as it pecks the ground for any leftover seeds. It's a chunky bird and I can't help but smile. The bird pecks mere inches from my feet, not at all alarmed or bothered anytime I move.

"Sloane, peccatum meum, as much as it pleases me to watch you, focus on the task at hand."

A glare settles on my face as my attention darts up to Balthazar. I'm not purposely stalling. I literally have no idea what to do. He said to change the color of the bird, but he didn't tell me *how* to do that. Does he expect me to know what to do without ever having done this before?

I don't hold back from letting him know my thoughts. "You're a shitty teacher, you know that? You haven't given me any advice on how to actually *use* magic."

His jaw juts back and forth, a displeased look crossing his features as he strums his fingers along the back of the bench. Looks like I've stumped him and a flash of satisfaction courses through me. I manage to suppress the smug smile that's begging to be let out. That smugness would only cause tension between us and get me nowhere with my first lesson in magic.

"You've got that clever brain inside your head, why don't you put it to use?" he challenges after a few moments in silence.

Irritation zings down my spine at his lack of accountability. Why did he even bother suggesting he'd teach me how to use magic if he's not going to do that? Seriously. I get teaching may not be intuitive for him since Jeznia is all about taking care of yourself and no one else, but it's infuriating that he offered to help if this is how he's going to teach.

"What is the point of having you as a teacher if you aren't even going to help?" I protest, my arms crossing over my chest as all my weight shifts to my right leg. I'm not going to let him off easy just because of his upbringing. But if I want his help, I need to offer him a little motivation. This question should do the trick. "Do you secretly want the Lords to find out about me?"

"Not in the slightest," he answers without hesitation. "I have faith in you, Sloane. You'll figure it out on your own."

Well that backfired real fast, I internally grumble to myself. His words are a double edged sword. It's incredible knowing he believes I'm intelligent enough to figure it out on my own and that he believes in me. But I don't want to be doing this on my own. I want help, I want his input and suggestions, I want us to figure this out *together*. That's how we did it with my wish and that's how I want to do this with my life.

"Friendly reminder that you supplied information to me about Jeznia," I tell him. "Your help and information is how I figured out how to word my wish. I didn't come up with it out of thin air."

"Fair point," he muses as he leans forward onto his knees. "Very well. Draw your magic forward."

A couple of seconds pass by as I wait for him to offer more feedback, but he remains mute. I flail my arms out in annoyance. "What does that even mean?"

"Exactly how it sounds," he states in mild exasperation. "Draw it forward. Pull it forward. Reach out to it. It's about intent—"

"That! Saying it's about intent is way more informative than 'draw it forward," I use a mocking tone when I say *draw it forward* to emphasize my point.

"Sloane, I'm begging you, do not test my patience," he says as he pinches the bridge of his nose.

"Oh yeah?" I ask, hand resting on my hip. I can't resist the natural urge to do the opposite of what he's asked. "What are you going to do about it?"

His eyes flash white, his jaw clenching and unclenching. He's so predictable that sometimes it's laughable. Any time I challenge him, no matter the time or place, it drives him crazy, but the *good* kind of crazy. He loves it. The back and forth, the threats, he even enjoys degradation. It makes him putty and, over these past three weeks, I've learned how to use that to my amusement and entertainment.

"You wanted this lesson," he reminds me as he sits back against the bench. It's irritating how calm he appears when just seconds ago, I was pretty sure he was ready to lunge at me for a kiss. "*I* wanted to bury myself deep inside you over and over again, but you requested this lesson instead."

Mortified, I quickly glance around our area, my face flushed as I worry someone walking by might have overheard what he said. It's my own stupidity for playing with fire in such a public space.

Thankfully, no one meets my gaze so I hope that means no one heard him. Feeling a little reassured no one is paying attention to what we're talking about, I turn my attention back to Balthazar. He's smirking, more than pleased with himself.

"I'm going to get you back for that," I promise him and his smirk deepens.

"I look forward to it. Truly."

My heart skips a beat at the lust I see swimming within his eyes. We're too compatible for our own good. How are we going to get anything done? Right now, I'm kind of regretting asking for this lesson instead of doing what Balthazar had suggested. We could be in the throes of passion instead of arguing over how to change the color of a pigeon's feathers.

Balthazar must sense my waning attention because he pulls our focus back to the issue at hand. "Draw your magic forward with the intent to use it. Change the pigeon to brown."

I stare at him for a few moments, too drawn in by how handsome he is. My eyes soak in his plump lips, his toned body, his menacing presence. Memories of him pounding into me from all kinds of angles has a slow heat coiling in my stomach.

A sly smile spreads across his lips as if he knows *exactly* what I'm thinking. *Cocky bastard*, I think and hate the fact that he has every right to be. Rolling my eyes, I use all my willpower to turn my attention to the pigeon standing roughly a foot from me.

It's now or never. My arms shake out as my weight teeters back and forth on my feet. For good measure, I take a couple deep inhales. Hopefully that'll help center and focus me.

It's time to use some magic. My heart pounds against my chest and I try to quell the nauseating nervousness that eats away at me. I don't want to hurt the pigeon or even cause it distress, but how else can I learn magic? *Oh god, if I kill it, I won't be able to use magic ever again,* I think. The anxiety barrels into me, bile sitting in the back of my throat at the thought of accidentally ending the pigeon's life.

"Sloane," Balthazar urges me as he stands up from the bench.

"Let me go at my own pace," I order, shaking out my arms one last time before I close my eyes.

Draw the magic forward with intent, Sloane. Nothing to be afraid of. Just let normal magic come forward nice and gently. The hair on my body stands on end as electricity thrums in the air. At the same time, I can literally *feel* magic flowing through me, starting at my feet and working its way up. It's different from the last time. This magic is lighter.

It's also slipping through my fingers every time I try to grasp it. The old magic was heavier, thicker, and it did whatever I told it as soon as I thought it. This normal magic is like smoke, swirling away every time I reach for it.

"You'll need to open your eyes to try the magic out," Balthazar's voice cuts through my concentration.

"I can't grab it," I tell him, eyes still shut as my hands grab at the empty air.

"That's because it's outside of you," he says.

Upon hearing those words, my eyes fly open. Lightning the color of rich, shimmering gold streaks across the space surrounding me. Despite the sunny and bright day, I can see a thin layer of lavender smoke swirling around me where the lightning resides. My hand reaches out, the purple smoke billowing around my fingers before a lightning streak zaps my hand. It stings worse than a static shock, but less than a paper cut.

"Is this… normal?" I ask, completely captivated by the small lightning flashing through the purple smoke.

"I have never seen magic work this way," Balthazar answers.

Panic darts through me upon hearing his statement and the words fly out of my mouth, "Won't the Lords be suspicious when they see my magic working like this?"

"Sloane," he breathes my name like an ode. "You're a human who was born with a Jeznian soul that has now become a devil. They won't expect normal from you because there's nothing normal *about* you."

I can't tell whether he means that as an insult or a compliment but it eases my panic all the same. My lips press into a thin line as I refocus my attention on the magic swirling around me. Being normal isn't something that exists, but I imagine being too different in Jeznia will certainly have its drawbacks. Everyone in Jeznia already hate me for being a pathetic miserable human, for being Balthazar's wife, and for bending the rules I had no right bending. Having special magic isn't going to go over well with the Houses. Not that I *want* their approval, but I can't deny how much easier it will be to have things go as smoothly as possible instead of running into a roadblock at every turn.

"Try turning the pigeon brown," Balthazar calmly repeats, snapping me from my thoughts.

I nod my head as I turn my attention to the pigeon. It's now walking around the leg of the bench, pecking at the ground for any leftover seeds. I concentrate on using my magic to change the pigeon from gray to brown. As my thoughts intensify, the lightning increases, crackling like a firecracker as it darts around the air in rapid succession.

The more I focus on holding on to the magic, the wilder it feels. Desperate not to lose it, I act impulsively. I mentally reach out to the pigeon, a booming *BROWN* echoing within my mind, and the lightning streaks out at the bird. There's a brief shriek from the pigeon as it's zapped by the magic before it flutters its wings to escape. Balthazar stops it, using his own magic to keep the bird in place, and we watch as the bird transforms. Not gray to brown but into a white duck.

Balthazar clicks his tongue as the duck quacks, stumbling on its feet as it gets used to its new body.

"Interesting choice, Sloane."

"I didn't do that on purpose," I argue as I watch the duck flop down before scurrying to its feet. "I just… It felt like I was losing the magic."

"So, you hastily reacted before you lost control."

"Yeah," I answer shamefully, my attention dropping to the pavement and I wince as the duck quacks again.

"Truth be told, I'm impressed you were able to use magic on the first try," Balthazar states before snapping his fingers. The duck changes back into the pigeon in an instant.

My eyebrows pinch together as I turn towards him. "You are?"

"It took me a year before I could use my magic on purpose," Balthazar confesses, his eyes lingering on the pigeon as it stands motionless. Like the poor bird is going through a midlife crisis after being changed twice.

My heart drops at hearing Balthazar's words as worry burrows its way into my heart at the implications of what his confession means. I can't hold back my question as anxiety drives the word forward out of my mouth in a meek voice. "Really?"

"Yes," he answers simply. He continues on, talking as though he's discussing the weather and not revealing important information about himself. "My mother started teaching me about magic when I was two years old. It wasn't until I was five that I finally felt it, six when I finally used it with intent, and ten when I took on my first job."

"Wait, you didn't feel your magic until you were five years old?" I ask in genuine surprise.

"Correct."

I nibble on my lower lip as I watch Balthazar. His hands are in his pockets as he watches the pigeons peck around us and the expression on his face doesn't give away what he might be feeling inside. Is he jealous I can use my magic right away? He said he's impressed, but is that just to mask his envy? The urge to tell him that our circumstances are different overwhelms me. He was a boy when he started practicing magic. Maybe the fact that I'm older gives me a better advantage.

"Maybe magic doesn't manifest until you're five years old," I suggest, hoping that it'll ease any of his resentment he might be feeling.

He glances up at me, his expression indifferent as he says, "I wouldn't know. I've never met any devil children."

Something about that statement cuts me deep, his words a visceral reminder of how lonely his life has been. How cruel and unforgiving life has been from the moment he was born. I take a step towards him, my hand reaching out to grab his arm. I can feel the coldness seeping through the fabric of his clothes. The cold has crept up to his elbow. He's spent too much time on Earth. He should head back soon to recharge before the cold sets in even more but I can't let him go home without clearing the air.

"Are we… ok?" I ask and his eyebrows furrow together as he tilts his head.

"Why are you asking that?"

"Just that…" I trail off as I think of the best way to say what I want to say. "Does it bother you how quickly I've used my magic in comparison to yourself?"

He chuckles as his hands slide out from his pockets and he grabs me possessively around the waist. "Not in the slightest, peccatum meum."

Concern morphs onto my face as I stare up at him, my hand resting against his chest. He says that, but is he being honest? Most men would feel inferior, incompetent even, if the woman they were dating easily excelled at something that took them years to accomplish. Doesn't he feel the same way?

"Are you sure?" I ask. "Because I would totally understand if you felt that way."

He dips his head forward to rest his forehead against my own. "I assure you, Sloane, I have no feelings of envy or jealousy towards you. If anything, I'm relieved. You'll learn magic much quicker and will become a formidable opponent much faster than I anticipated."

"Promise me you'll tell me if your feelings ever change?"

He pulls his head away from mine, a frown marring his face as his hand on my waist slips beneath my shirt. I hiss and shrink away from him, goosebumps flaring along my skin, but I quickly adapt to his freezing hand and settle back in place.

"Why is this a concern for you?" he asks as his fingers continually squeeze and release my waist.

"Because," I breathe out as my eyes look anywhere but his. "I know you're not human, but most guys have a hard time when the woman has more power in a relationship. You're a Lord of Jeznia, heir to the most powerful House, but then comes along little ole me who learns magic like it's nothing. Most people would feel resentment."

Balthazar's ice cold fingers dive into my hair, gripping it hard enough to force my head backwards so I'm forced to look him in the eyes.

"Rid yourself of these foolish thoughts," he orders as he firmly holds my gaze. "I expect my owner to exceed me, to exceed the strength and power of Lord Balthazar of House Primis, heir to High King Zagon Primis. I will not settle for less."

"But isn't that just for, like, sex? You don't really mean that, right?" I ask.

We've never really talked much about how we view our relationship. For the past three weeks, we've been coasting along and doing what feels natural to us, but we've never defined the relationship. I have no idea whether we're on the same page or not, but I've been ok with the way things have been going. I haven't felt the need to have "The Talk" with him, but right now it seems like we should. It'll be good for both of us to know what the other expects.

He arches up an eyebrow, his fingers still holding my hair as he stares down at me. "You wish to partially own me?"

My mouth opens and closes as I stare up at him, not entirely sure what my answer is. Do I want to own him? In a way, yes. I want him to be mine and only mine. But I don't want to strip him of his freedom or will. I want us to be as equal as we can be. I enjoy dominating him in the bedroom, commanding him and watching him fight against himself to obey me, but he isn't a *thing* for me to keep. He's his own person. I don't ever want him to feel less than me or objectified by me.

"No one owns you, Balthazar," I answer. "You're strong enough to be your own person. I want us to be equals. I want us making decisions together, communicating with each other about our wants and needs. Do you... not want that?"

He squints his eyes at me, his lips puckering to the side of his face, and I can't refrain from smiling at the face he's making. He looks confused and perhaps a little put off by what I've said. Like I just told him that in order to grow up big and strong he has to eat the vegetables he doesn't like.

"Sloane," he says my name with utter seriousness that it causes my stomach to drop.

He's going to reject me, isn't it? Of course he is. I'm learning magic easier than he did. I'm a threat to his status in Jeznia. It would be dumb of him to keep me around. The Lords will think of him as a joke if he stays with me. Never mind what his father, the High King, will think.

"You were born a human with a Jeznian soul," he says as he affectionately pushes hair behind my ear. "When I used magic to turn you into a devil, the magic *inside* you took over and made you what you are now. Your innate magic is more powerful than you understand. The magic the Lords collectively possess, me included, is child's play compared to your own."

He pauses for a moment, his eyes darting back and forth between mine before he offers a gentle, almost invisible smile. "I'm under no illusions of who is the more powerful one between the two of us. I don't care about that. *You* own me, Sloane, through and through. It is not just a 'sex thing'."

Something clicks into place after hearing his words. Like I've been waiting for him to give me permission to truly grow and embrace this powerful magic inside of me. He's given me the freedom to become whatever I need to be, regardless of the power disparity that might grow between us. I can go forward now without fear, without anxiety, and without hesitation. Balthazar will support me through it all because he embodies the ideology that a success for me is a success for him. I could not have met a more perfect equal than him.

My hand reaches up to his horn as I personify the role of master he has graciously given me and I tug the horn down so we're eye to eye. He doesn't resist, the hand playing with my hair dropping away as the hand gripping my waist holds me tighter in excitement.

"Ok," I breathe out as we lock gazes. "I own you, Balthazar, so you better not break my heart."

He smirks wide and eagerly. "I wouldn't dream of it, peccatum meum."

End

Acknowledgments

The best way to start anything is to simply dive right in, so here I go!

My beta/sensitivity readers – Kelsea R., Alexia, and Lwazi. The three of you helped shaped this manuscript into what it became. Your feedback was incredible and your enjoyment of the story was what made me realize I had something special here. You three gave me the confidence I was genuinely lacking. I can never thank you enough.

Merci Réne – I know we barely know each other, but you are so incredibly kind. You were the first person to truly welcome me into the bookish community on TikTok and not only did you volunteer to read my manuscript, but you've also been a cheerleader of mine despite knowing so little about me. That truly left such an enormous impression on me and I'm grateful to have made your acquaintance.

Kimberly Maciejczyk – it *all* started with you, girlie. You're literally the reason why I write. I don't know if I would've dipped my toes into it if you never turned me on to fanfiction when I was fifteen years old. You have single–handedly turned me into this. You've read all of the craziest shit I've ever dared to write and supported it to the high hells and back. Your critical feedback on the first draft of Bargain with the Devil shaped this manuscript into what it is today. I love you every second for it. Your words, never minced but never hurtful, are what every writer needs. You see the plot in a way that highlights all my blind spots, poking holes in places that should be fortified. I will always rely heavily on your input to make my writing the best that it can be. You deserve the world and more, my friend. I love you, my sister from another mister.

Mackenzie Newman – your support has always been a blessing. The way you have encouraged me, daily, to chase after my dreams and how authentically, as well as vocally, you believe in me makes me cry. Thank you for always being an outlet for my every doubt, my every fear, and the rare days I think I'm killing it. Your love for Bargain with the Devil gives me the biggest ego boost ever. The first time you read BWTD and how quickly you flew through it was life changing for me. Literally. That started the whole journey of wanting to publish this manuscript. You are the reason why this book is in the hands of strangers now. So, everyone who enjoyed the story, thank Mackenzie Newman for that! I love you, girl. I'm grateful every day for the friendship we have and I look forward to what our future brings.

Zoë Mahoney – you, my friend and dear cousin, are a rock star. I live for your hype–girl responses. Truly. They keep me motivated and excited for every project I'm working on. Your eagerness and readiness to respond to all my texts, to read every little excerpt I send your way, your critical feedback on my cover design, on my concept and stories, is beyond appreciated. I literally cannot put into words how much you have helped me develop as a writer but also just as someone who enjoys creating. I am so grateful to have you as a part of my life and for you to be intimately involved in something so incredibly important to me… it has me tearing up every time I talk about it. I love you, girl. You made this happen in a way you'll never understand.

Brianna Johnson – I'm going to start crying just thinking about what an amazing older sister you are. I've only recently embarked on letting you in on what I write, but you have always been a huge supporter of me becoming a writer even without having read a single word. I will never forget the day you told me "I picture our future of us living together, you writing your books and me owning a dog and taking it on hikes." The fact that you perceived me at a desk typing away, writing stories altered my brain that day. It was the first time I became aware that others in my life saw me as a writer and not just me hoping one day I would be one. And this was before you even had the chance to read any of my stuff. It floored me and changed me, for the better. I also can't even begin to thank you for all the support you've given me over the years that has nothing to do with writing but everything to do with being your little sister. I am so grateful to you and everything you do. I love you, sis.

My parents, Lisa and Russell Johnson – I am so incredibly grateful for the life you provided me. Dad, your genuine interest in my writing empowered me to continue to reach for the stars. You have always read everything I have ever shared with you (to this day you still ask about old stories I've completely forgotten about) and your interest in learning about my passion fueled my confidence to continue down an unconventional path. I am still genuinely shocked at your open sincerity in hearing about my writing. Thank you. It means the world to me.

Mom, you helped shaped me into who I am today. Your sacrifices gave me opportunities I didn't truly appreciate until time had come to pass. You may not have always understood my passion for writing, but you've always had my best interests at heart. Thank you. I love you.

Last but certainly not least, my husband, Tuan Vu – if it weren't for your advice, I would not be self–publishing right now. Thank you for always encouraging me to move forward and for bringing rationality to my fears. Your support has been a steady rock for me to lean on. You've listened to me ramble on about characters you know nothing about, you've helped me flesh out plot holes that made absolutely no sense, and you've encouraged me to go 'make millions' no matter how ridiculously small my chances are. "You will always lose 100% of the shots you never take." Thank you for always giving me a lending ear, for nurturing my passion instead of trying to kill it, and for supporting me endlessly as I figure out what it is I want to do with my career. I love you. Thank you for everything.

Meet the Author

Alessandra Vu is a stay-at-home parent of two. She started writing reader insert fanfiction when she was 16 years old and gradually shifted over into original stories. Her favorite genres to read and write are fantasy romance (romantasy), paranormal romance, and urban fantasy romance. Her favorite book series is *The Hidden Legacy* by Ilona Andrews and her favorite comfort series is *The Lunar Chronicles* by Marissa Meyer.

alessandra03330

Want to learn more? Use the QR code to view Alessandra's website, socials, and more!

www.ingramcontent.com/pod-product-compliance
Lightning Source LLC
Chambersburg PA
CBHW072341020726
47506CB00004B/952